DUTY AND HONOR

Because of a Woman

Book 10

Home on the Range Series

Rosie Bosse lives and writes on a ranch in Northeast Kansas with her best friend and husband of many years. Her books intertwine history with fiction as she creates stories of the Old West. May you meet some new "friends" and revisit old ones in this tenth novel in her Home on the Range series.

DUTY AND HONOR

Because of a Woman

Rosie Bosse

Cover illustrated by Cynthia Martin

Duty and Honor

ISBN: Soft Cover – 978-1-958227-31-2
ISBN: eBook – 978-1-958227-32-9

Post Rock Publishing
17055 Day Rd.
Onaga, KS 66521

www.rosiebosse.com

This book is dedicated to the memory of Paul Pumphrey.
Enjoy reading the rest of my books in Heaven, Pauly.

Do You Laugh When You Sleep?

"Do you laugh when you sleep?" he once asked of me,
That weathered old man as he struggled to breathe.

Alone much his life, a hard one he lived,
His pleasures were few yet he still had a grin.

We became friends some years ago,
When I stopped in to talk as he played dominos.

He didn't share thoughts until close to the end,
And then he asked me if I was his friend.

He didn't know faith like how I was raised,
But God came to stay on his final day.

He wasn't alone for Jesus was there,
To hold both his hands and show him He cared.

I wonder sometimes, now that your life is complete,
Tell me, my friend, do you laugh when you sleep?

Rosie Bosse

Prologue

Duty and Honor, Because of a Woman, is the tenth novel in my Home on the Range series. It is set in 1880, and the story travels from Cheyenne in the Wyoming Territory, across Kansas, and back to Cheyenne.

While most of my characters are fictional, in this novel, you will be introduced to a special woman by the name of Betty Fairchild. I want to thank this pistol-packing horsewoman for allowing me to use her full name *and* exaggerate her story. Aunt Betty, as she is known to her friends, will turn 100 this year. Aunt Betty, may you enjoy being part of this story!

Kansas City–Two Cities, Divided By a River

Kansas City, Missouri, began as a trading post for the many traders who frequented or lived in the area. The first trading post was established in 1821 by Francois Chouteau, the son of a French family from St. Louis.

The Kansas side of the city formed in 1838. It was first called City of Kansas but that was soon shortened to Kansas City. A trail connecting the river landing in the town of Westport to the Santa Fe Trail was established first. Within several years, commercial buildings and businesses began to appear along the river bluffs.

The years leading up to the Civil War were bloody ones for Kansas City since the Missouri River separated the slave state of Missouri from the free state of Kansas. After the Civil War ended in 1865, the city's population blossomed. Railways were built and the first bridge across the Missouri River was completed.

The wealthy built their mansions on Quality Hill on the Missouri side while the West Bottoms on the Kansas side became the center of the booming cattle industry. Stockyards, warehouses, and packing houses filled the area.

Kansas City on both sides of the river was a mecca of activity.

The Pacific House Hotel

The Pacific House Hotel was built in 1861 at 401 Delaware Street in Kansas City, Missouri. It was rebuilt in 1869 following a devastating fire the year before and was updated several times after that. It was considered the finest hotel in Kansas City for nearly 15 years, earning the nickname, "Palatial Pacific."

The elegant Victorian hotel offered 24 guest rooms. The parlor at the top of the curving stairs opened to a large outdoor veranda that overlooked the front of the hotel. The hotel also held a ballroom, a dining hall, a men's billiard hall, and a magnificent bar. It was owned for a time by an uncle of Jesse and Frank James.

Water Closets and Outhouses

By 2000 B.C., indoor plumbing for bathing as well as sanitation was being used in parts of the world. Remnants of toilets and sewers have been found in the ruins of ancient cities in Pakistan as well as in Rome.

The first flushing toilet was invented in 1596. Unfortunately, it did not flush after every use, and nothing kept the fumes from rising in the room. As a result, it never gained popularity.

In 1775, a Scotsman named Alexander Cummings invented the S-trap in the plumbing for flushing toilets. It allowed water to be trapped, keeping the stench from escaping. In a tribute to its design, the S-trap is still used today.

When a flush toilet was added to a home, it was placed wherever it would fit in the house, often in a small space by itself. That was usually under the stairs or in a closet. From that came the name, water closet.

While flush toilets quickly caught on, ridding cities of waste materials was now an even bigger problem. The cities stunk. In addition, the raw sewage led to outbreaks of diseases including cholera and typhoid. Still, London's first sewer system as not begun until 1859. In America, the first sewage treatment plant was built in 1890 in Worcester, Massachusetts.

Of course, as flushing toilets became more popular, the narrow pipes that removed the water required something more dissolvable than wads of newspaper or corncobs.

In 1857, Joseph Gayetty of New York invented the first "toilet paper." His paper product was designed specifically for wiping. However, it was too expensive and did not catch on.

Clarence and Irvin Scott designed a perforated roll of toilet paper in 1890. Hotels and other distributors bought their products under various names. The Scott brothers were embarrassed by the association of their family name with the paper and did not add their name to their invention until 1903.

Outhouses were a mainstay for most people in rural America for many years. A large hole was dug in the ground, and a small shack called the outhouse was placed over it. The shack was made of available materials, hopefully with a hinged door. The seats on the inside were usually made of wood. While some outhouses contained one hole (one open base to sit on), others had several. Toilet paper, once invented, was a luxury and often not available. Corn cobs and newspapers were a common part of the cleanup process.

When the opening beneath the outhouse filled to about two thirds full, a new hole was dug, and the outhouse was moved to the new location. The old opening was filled with dirt.

If one was lucky enough to find a public outhouse while traveling, the likelihood of anything to "clean" with would have been rare. Users were expected to bring their own materials. In fact, according to some stories, that is where the term "wrong hand" came from. Folks ate with one hand and wiped with the other. Since most people were righthanded, the left hand became associated with the "wrong hand."

Indoor plumbing in the United States was not common until the 1930s. It was even later than that for some of the rural areas.

Jesse James

Jesse Woodson James was born September 5, 1847, near Kearney in Clay County, Missouri. This area of the state was primarily settled by emigrants from Kentucky and Tennessee. It soon became known as "Little Dixie." Alexander Franklin James or Frank was Jesse's older brother. Jesse also had a younger sister, Susan Lavenia James.

Jesse James died in St. Joseph, Missouri, on April 3, 1882. He was shot in the back by Bob Ford, an eager, new recruit to Jesse's gang. Ford was fascinated by Jesse, but he also wanted the bounty money he was allegedly promised by Missouri governor, Thomas T. Crittenden, reward money offered by the railroad and express corporations.

Remembered as an outlaw, Jesse James is known to have robbed numerous banks and trains although some he has been credited with probably were not his doing. Some say he was a Robin Hood-like outlaw. Others say he was only for himself. Regardless of what he did, Jesse James was certainly a product of his time and place in the violent history of the Kansas and Missouri border.

The Pinkertons

A barrel maker by trade, Allan Pinkerton immigrated to the Chicago area in 1842. Five years later, while searching for lumber along the Fox River, he came across a band of counterfeiters. He surveilled the gang and helped the police to make arrests.

He was soon offered the position of deputy sheriff of Cook County, Illinois. Shortly after that, he became Chicago's first detective and an agent for the United States Postal Service. In 1850, he opened his own private investigation firm, Pinkerton National Detective Agency. In 1856, Pinkerton hired the first-ever female detective, 23-year-old widow, Kate Warne, whom Pinkerton said was one of the best investigators he ever employed. The agency was also the first to create a criminal database and was a precursor to the Secret Service.

By the late 1850s, Pinkerton's men, or "Pinks," were well-known for hunting down outlaws, especially train robbers, and offering private security for the railroads. The company's logo was a large, unblinking eye with the slogan, "We Never Sleep." That slogan gave rise to the term, "private eye."

The Kansas Towns of Victoria and Herzog

Victoria, Kansas, is in Ellis County on the south side of Interstate 70 about 11 miles east of Hays. In 1880, two towns were located there. While Victoria was a British colony, Herzog, to the north, was begun by Volga Germans.

George Grant arrived in America in 1872 in search of a location to build his country estate where he planned to retire. He was a successful silk merchant so proximity to the railroad was important to him. After arriving in Ellis County, Kansas, in the fall of 1872, Grant purchased nearly 100,000 acres of land from the Kansas Pacific Railroad. With his land purchased and his community planned, he returned to England to recruit families of nobility.

Thirty-eight Scottish and English immigrants were the first inhabitants of the new town of Victoria, named after Queen Victoria of England. Grant was very specific in his requirements of the type of cattle, sheep, and crops that were to be produced in his new community as well as the types of houses that were to be built.

While the original inhabitants of the new town of Victoria were families, many of those who followed became known as "remittance men." These young men were provided money by their families in England. Although the money was sent to purchase land and businesses, the young noblemen were more interested in entertainment. Soon, Victoria was home to the Victoria Hunt Club, a racetrack, and a cricket club. Dances and other social activities were common, and money was spent freely.

Some parents began to reduce their sons' allowances when they realized the money was not being used as they expected. As the funds dried up, more and more of the young playboys returned to England. Other settlers found the land and the wind unwelcoming, and they followed.

While Victoria struggled to survive, in 1876, a large group of Volga Germans (German Russians) settled on the north side of the railroad tracks about one-half mile north of Victoria. They named their new town Herzog.

Herzog grew quickly. Because it had so many inhabitants, it soon became the most important of the many German colonies in Ellis County.

By the turn of the century, Herzog and Victoria were essentially merged. Their official merger took place in 1913, and the combined towns became Victoria.

Angus Cattle

When Grant returned to Ellis County with his first recruited settlers on May 17, 1873, he also brought four black Aberdeen Angus bulls to cross with his Texas longhorns. These were the first Angus cattle introduced in the United States. Ten years after the first bulls were imported, the American Aberdeen Angus Breeders Association was formed.

The Angus breed was considered freakish by some and unusual by all because the cattle were polled—that is, they had no horns. Also, they were the only breed that was all black. However, they soon caught on. The angus bulls crossed well with the longhorns and produced calves that handled the harsh winters as well as the hot summers. In addition, the Angus-cross cattle gained weight more efficiently than the longhorn breed.

Bierocks

Bierocks are a culinary delight readily found in many parts of Kansas, and especially where there is a high population of Volga German descendants. They consist of a sweet, leavened dough filled with cooked ground beef, chopped onion, and shredded cabbage or sometimes sauerkraut (fermented cabbage). They are oven-baked until they are golden brown.

The bierock originated in Russia and was brought to Ellis County, Kansas, by the Volga Germans in the 1870s. In their home country, this delicious meat pocket was called a pirogi. Those hard-working Germans also brought with them Turkey Red seed wheat (a nutrient-dense, hard red winter wheat) and peony bulbs.

Ellinwood, Kansas, and Its Underground Town

Located on Highway 56 about ten miles east of Great Bend, Kansas, the little town of Ellinwood is rich in history. Although it was not settled by German immigrants, the original founders gave many of the town's streets German names to appeal to German settlers.

The Santa Fe Trail met the north bank of the Arkansas River on the west edge of present-day Ellinwood and was active from about 1821 to 1880. This location was also a popular camping spot for wagon trains as well as for soldiers and traders because of the easy access to water. In addition, Ellinwood was a cowtown for a time.

The town was begun in 1871 when the Atchison, Topeka & Santa Fe Railroad chose that area as part of their route. When the post office opened February 1, 1872, the name of Ellinwood was chosen in honor of Colonel John R. Ellinwood, a civil engineer who worked for the Santa Fe railroad.

When Abilene, Kansas, told Texas cattlemen that their herds were no longer welcome, a number of residents from the new town of Ellsworth, Kansas, traveled south and invited drovers to bring their herds there.

Large herds of cattle were driven up the Cox Cattle Trail, an offshoot of the Chisholm Trail, to Ellsworth from the mid-1860s until 1873. Even though the Ellinwood businesses wanted their money, efforts were made by the local farmers to stop the drives from coming through Barton County. This was due not only to the amount of grass and crops they consumed but because of tick fever as well. Kansas lawmakers listened and new laws pushed the herds farther to the west.

The rapid growth of Ellinwood in the 1870s and 1880s caused many new businesses to go underground. Before long, tunnels and passageways connecting the underground businesses filled the two-block-long main street on both sides of the street. Many of those businesses catered to men. Around eleven saloons were known to operate under the streets as well as a harness shop, a barber shop, a laundry and bath area, several brothels, a merchandise sample room, and even a meat storage area.

The tunnels were divided by a rock wall with a narrower tunnel on the street side where the coal dropped from the sidewalk above was stored. The wider tunnel to the inside was the width of a man's arms stretched outward—supposedly so he could hold himself upright as he traveled between the many places of interest after imbibing too much of the local brew or whiskey.

Not all the tunnels are currently traversable as the city filled some of them in when the sidewalks began to sag. The rest were filled in the 1980s. However, parts have been restored and tours are available. The thick, brick and rock walls still stand in the tunnels that have been uncovered. Some of the businesses are also intact. They include a saloon, the stocked harness shop, a bath area, and the barber shop. The sample shop and a small book exchange are also visible.

Ellinwood was not the only Kansas town or city to build tunnels beneath their streets. Tunnels were quite common, and their reasons were varied although most began for utilitarian purposes. Caldwell, Ellsworth, Lincoln, Leavenworth, Douglass, and Fort Scott also have tunnels beneath some of their streets. However, only Ellinwood has actively promoted this piece of history as a tourist attraction—so far, anyway.

The Wolf Hotel

The Wolf Hotel was built in 1894 in Ellinwood by John Wolf for around $10,000. It was built as an addition to the Delmonico Hotel which once stood just north of the still-standing Wolf Hotel. The Wolf addition boasted fifteen rooms, a new lobby, underground stores, and the Bank of Ellinwood. The combined hotels were called the National Hotel. The large hotel was a sought-after place to stay on the plains of Kansas.

I refer to the Wolf Hotel in this novel even though it was built later than the timeline of this story. However, I thought the history of the old hotel needed to be included.

The First Barbed Wire

The first wire fences consisted of one strand of wire and no barbs. Cattle constantly pushed through or broke the single wires. In November of 1868, Michael Kelly patented his improvement to wire fencing by twisting two wires together allowing them to hold barbs. His invention became known as the "thorny fence," and was much more effective. The two-strand, twisted design made it stronger, and the barbs demanded the cattle's respect since the barbs had sharp points.

In 1874, Joseph Glidden, a farmer from DeKalb, Illinois, designed a method to lock the barbs in place on the double-strand wire. He also invented machinery capable of mass-producing his creation. Glidden's United States patent was issued on November 24, 1874, six years after the invention of the barbed fence. His patent survived court challenges from multiple inventors. He prevailed not only in the court but also in the marketplace. Mass production of the wire made it more affordable, and by 1880, around a million miles of barbed wire fencing were being added each year in the West.

Barbed wire drastically changed how cattle were handled in America, especially in the West, though not everyone appreciated the new invention. It limited the movement of people and cattle. The long lines of fence often had few gates, and maintenance involved riding the fences to look for loose or broken wires. Many cowboys detested fences of any kind, and "riding fences" was not a favored job.

Barbed Wire and Telephone Lines

Alexander Graham Bell patented his telephone in 1876, and early phone companies focused on the urban areas. Wires and poles were expensive, and there were not enough people in the far-flung rural areas to justify the cost.

However, the rural areas had barbed wire. For a $25 investment that included a phone and batteries, a farmer or rancher could build his own phone system using his barbed wire fencing. Fence posts were built with whatever material was available, and the necessary insulators to run the telephone wires were designed with the same ingenuity. To turn the metal fence wire into a telephone line, it just had to be connected to the telephone with a piece of smooth wire.

Typically, the top wire of the three-wire fence was used as the phone line. Any material available was used to separate the wire from the post to prevent grounding, including leather scraps and corncobs. However, the most accessible were the necks of glass bottles.

Glass was used to store many liquid items, especially alcohol. Once emptied, it became trash and was discarded. Alcohol bottles and saloons gave innovative men a ready supply of insulators.

The glass bottle necks were broken off and wooden pegs were whittled to fit into the bottle opening. Holes were drilled in the pegs to allow for attachment to the fence, and the barbed wire was run across the outside groove of the attached bottle neck.

With no switchboard, all phones on the system rang at the same time so specific rings were created for each family—a long and a short ring, two longs, etc. Most systems also had one ring meant for everyone. This was how they participated as a group whether in an emergency, to share good news, or for community music on a Sunday night. The system only allowed calls within the network. Long-distance calling was not available.

Up to 20 phones could be connected through one system. However, the more phones and the longer the wire, the poorer the connection. Still, it was better than nothing.

The "party line" also offered the opportunity to "listen in" on calls other than your own, and many chose to do that. However, when more people picked up their phones to listen, the poorer the connection became.

Rural ingenuity connected the inventions of barbed wire and the telephone in ways no one likely foresaw. This rural phone system was commonly used through the 1910s and in some locations, even later. However, the party line system remained long after that, with some still in use in the rural areas of America in the 1980s.

The Great Cat Heist

Cats are not native to America. However, once they were introduced, they reproduced rapidly. For many residents of the early West, cats were appreciated. Rodents such as mice and rats were an ongoing problem.

Seth Bullock was sheriff of Deadwood, South Dakota Territory, in the late 1800s. In some of his notations about his work, he wrote about a wagonload of cats that was hauled to Deadwood in 1876. The story below combines his account with other sources.

Dora DuFran, a notorious madam at the time, contracted a local teamster, Phatty Thompson, to deliver cats to her brothel, the Green Front Hotel in Deadwood. Not only were the rodents dirty and destructive, but the male patrons often tried to shoot them, endangering residents and causing even more damage.

Phatty often made runs of freight between the town of Cheyenne in the Wyoming Territory, and Deadwood in the South Dakota Territory. Being a businessman, he decided to fill his wagon with cats.

When he arrived in Cheyenne, he offered some local boys $.25 for each healthy cat they caught. Of course, domestic cats were easier to catch so many pets were part of the 80 cats that disappeared from Cheyenne that night. Included in that haul was a pet Maltese.

It took about three weeks to haul a load of anything between Deadwood and Cheyenne, and the cats were no different—although their noise level was much higher. They did escape once when Phatty's wagon overturned, either at Lightening Creek or Spring Creek depending on the quoted source. They were tempted with food and "herded" back into the large cage.

When Phatty arrived in Deadwood, he allegedly sold his cats for $10 each. A Maltese cat brought $25. There is no record of him making a second run of cats anywhere although his profit would have been high on that load.

Whether all the cats were sold or how many escaped is somewhat disputed. However, by 1877, the cat population in Deadwood had exploded. It was also around that time when brothels were first called "cat houses." Coincidence? Perhaps...

Camels in the West

In 1855, Congress approved funding for "the purchase and importation of camels and dromedaries to be employed for military purposes." By 1857, the United States Army owned 75 camels. They were placed at Camp Verde in Texas and were used to haul supplies to San Antonio. In June of that year, the herd was split and around 24 were sent to California.

There was some success in the experiment. Records show a California camel train making a successful summer drive 1,200-plus miles through semi-arid land and mountains. The camels traveled 30 to 40 miles per day and carried over 1,000 pounds each. In addition, they could travel for six to ten days with no water.

Unfortunately, the promoters of this scheme focused only on the camels' assets. None of their vices were discussed, nor did anyone consider the language the camels were used to. The camels were trained in Arabic and were talked to softly. In addition, their native drivers were "born" into the business, bringing with them over 1,000 years of experience.

The muleskinners could not give commands in a language the camels could understand nor were the camels used to shouting and cursing. In addition, the camels were not as agile as mules and often collided with each other on narrow trails. They were despised by the teamsters who were expected to trail them.

The camels' ability to escape during the night and travel 16 miles an hour to locations unknown was another aggravation. They would leave if turned loose to graze, and an evening stroll of 25-30 miles was common. The teamsters preferred to shoot them rather than return them to camp.

Horses and mules shared the teamsters' dislike of camels. A camel's unfamiliar call and smell as well as his size terrified most domestic animals. The frightened horses broke loose and stampeded across the plains, followed by the mules. Every effort to organize a camel caravan resulted in chaos.

While the introduction of the camels was initially pushed as a solution to chasing marauding Indians through their barren homelands, there is no record of that ever happening. However, the Indians of the Southwest *did* acquire a taste for the huge, ungainly animals, and they hunted them for meat.

When the Civil War began, many camels were turned loose to fend for themselves. Others were sold at auction. The camels that roamed freely continued to terrorize the mule trains. They appeared suddenly and spooked the mules, scattering freight and drivers. The great "ships of the desert" had become "the terrors of the plains." Even when not in use, camels were despised.

Camels were actively used for less than ten years by the United States Army. For many troopers and teamsters, that was ten years too long.

I hope you enjoy this novel as much or more than the first nine in this series. May it be another book that is hard to put down! My books are all available on my website listed below or ask for them at your favorite library or bookstore. Digital and paperback copies are also available through most online booksellers. Thank you for choosing to read my Home on the Range series.

Rosie Bosse, Author
Living and Writing on a Ranch in the Middle of Nowhere
rosiebosse.com

April 1, 1880
Cheyenne, Wyoming Territory

CHAPTER 1

Because of a Woman

MIGUEL STEPPED OUT OF THE LIVERY AND STARED UP the street. The letter falling out of his vest pocket caught his eye, and he cursed under his breath as he shoved it back in.

"Nettie, I guess you did just what you said you were going to do. You went and married another fellow because you were too afraid to love me.

"Well, Ned's a good man and he will treat you right." Miguel laughed wryly as he stared down the street toward the Tin House. "Guess these last six months of trying to reform went out the window. I'll just go back to my old ways. It's easier on my heart even if it's harder on my body."

Miguel sauntered down the street. His face usually had a smile hiding just under the surface, and while he didn't smile as much as his brother, Angel, he did laugh easily. Black, curly hair showed from under his hat and the bushy mustache on his upper lip needed trimming.

Women called to him from their windows as he strolled by the dance halls and saloons. Miguel waved at them as he grinned, but he shook his head.

"Not today, ladies. These two days were for remembering and thinking. Perhaps another day. I must get back home, or Angel will think I returned to Texas." He tipped his hat and winked at them as he laughed.

As he passed the express office, Elmer Tinley waved him in.

"I have a couple of letters here for you. The envelope on one was destroyed. The address was gone except for Cheyenne, Wyoming Territory." Elmer's face blushed a little as he added, "Sorry, Miguel. I had to read it to know who to give it to."

Miguel looked at Tinley in surprise as he took the letter. He unfolded it and frowned as he read the date. "Why this is dated November 10, 1879. It's already April 1 of 1880. It sure didn't take any five months to get up here. I could have walked it here quicker."

"There were a couple of derailments last winter. I guess some mail was caught up in it." Tinley handed Miguel a second letter.

"This one just came in yesterday." He grinned at the young man in front of him. "I decided to hang onto these instead of trying to track you down. That post you picked up two days ago sent you on quite a drunk, and I didn't want to be responsible for any more difficulties."

Tinley's voice was sincere as he pointed at the letters. "Sure hope these contain better news." He patted the younger man on the back and hurried back to his desk.

As Miguel turned around slowly, Tinley commented softly, "East mail goes out on the train tonight if you want to send something back."

Miguel didn't answer. He was halfway through the letter and was smiling by the time he finished.

"Well, Kansas City isn't as far as Texas anyhow. Maybe I'll take a trip south. I have been gone for two days, but I'll talk to Angel and Gabe. They might need some bulls brought north from Kansas. Then I can make part of this a working trip." He opened the second letter and the smile on his face slowly faded. He read it again and cursed as he wadded it up. He started to throw it down on the street, but paused and shoved it back into his pocket.

"Heck of a thing to invite a fellow to come visit and then four months later, change your mind." His frown slowly changed to a grin.

"Of course, the mail is unreliable. Perhaps I will go anyway. Since it took five months for the first letter to arrive, perhaps the second didn't make it at all." His walk was a little jauntier and a full smile was on his face when he arrived at the Tin House.

A table of men in the back called to him and Miguel slid through the full tables to join them.

"Good morning, señors! And what will señor Lance say when half of his crew is so late getting home?" He dropped into an open chair and grinned at the men seated around the table.

Jonesy chuckled and reached over to slap Miguel on the back.

"Aw, we have the mornin' off. Besides, the way ya was drinkin' last night, we thought we might have to fish ya outta jail." His eyes were more serious as he added, "You shouldn't go on the prod like that when ya been drinkin', Miguel. You coulda killed that hombre if we hadn't hauled him outta there. An' he was jist a drunk cowboy passin' through. Didn't do a thing to ya."

Miguel stared at Jonesy before he shrugged his shoulders. "Perhaps the same should be said of this cowboy. I would thank you, but I don't remember this fight. Now come, let us speak of more pleasant things such as the weather. I think this winter is almost over."

The men ate hurriedly when the food arrived, and Miguel stood. He put his hat over his chest and bowed to his friends.

"Señors, it has been a pleasure, but I have a busy day." His grin became bigger as he added, "Until we are all drunk again."

Miguel dropped some money on the table. As he pulled the money out of his pocket, a letter fell to the floor. Miguel didn't notice it as he strolled out of the eating house. The rest of the cowboys didn't see it either.

Jonesy spotted the letter when he stood. He picked it up. Miguel was nowhere in sight. Jonesy shrugged as he shoved the letter into his own pocket. "Guess I'll git this to him another day. Or maybe I'll just give it to Angel. I see him more often." He grinned at his friends as he bobbed his head toward the west.

"I'm headed to church. A feller was through here last week an' told me that was a good way to meet women. Ain't meetin' none drinkin' like we been doin' so we jist as well try church. There's a prayer meetin' today an' food after. I think I'll mosey on down there."

The rest of the men stared at Jonesy a moment. A tall cowboy with red hair that poked out in all directions was the first to follow. "Jist as well. Don't have to be back to the Rockin' R till this afternoon." The riders mounted their horses and followed the stream of buggies through the streets toward the little church on the outskirts of town. They stared as women, young and old, began to arrive.

Red spit on his hand and tried to smooth his hair down. "We shoulda tried this a long time ago. Come on, fellers. Let's find us a good seat."

CHAPTER 2

A Talk With His Sister

MIGUEL SAT DOWN AT THE KITCHEN TABLE. HE WAS quiet as Merina filled his plate. She muttered in Spanish as she slapped the plate down in front of him.

"I think you have been drinking for two days. And for what? What has it gained you?"

Miguel moved his fork around for a moment before he looked up at his sister.

"Nettie wrote me. She married one of the fellows who helped her brother and me get her out of Hole in the Wall."

Merina's eyes were wide as she stared at Miguel. She dropped into the chair across from him and put her hand over his. Miguel shrugged.

"Ned's a good man. Nettie said she won't have to worry about him coming home at night or where he spends his time when he goes to town.

"So, sí, I have been drinking. For six months, I have been trying to change. And for what? To have my heart broken? It is easier not to fall in love." He pulled Flory's first letter from his pocket as he laughed.

"Now this one—she does not expect me to behave. No, señorita Flory is a flirt, and she likes to play.

"I think I will go to see her. Gabe wants me to ride the train south to pick up those bulls in Kansas. I think I will go just a little farther east and visit señorita Flory for a day. Maybe even two before I chase the bulls."

Merina's face changed to a scowl. She shoved the plate toward Miguel and stood to glare down at him.

"Shame on you, Miguel. Señorita Flory is Anna's sister and that makes her our family. And if Anna is upset, Angel will be angry with you.

"You do not toy with señorita Flory. You leave her alone."

Miguel grinned up at his sister and Merina turned away from him. She slammed the breakfast dishes around before she faced him again with her hands on her hips.

"It is time for me to leave. We are meeting with the priest today. Nate is going to be baptized. You should go too. You can ask God for forgiveness and go to confession. Father Cummiskey has been asking about you. And perhaps when you can show you are responsible, some woman other than those in the saloons and dance halls will turn your head."

Gabe walked into the house just as Merina slammed the bedroom door. He looked from Miguel toward the closed door before he picked up the pans that had fallen on the floor.

"Your sister is a little emotional right now. That baby she is carrying is due soon. I think it would be good if you didn't make her angry." His voice was soft as he added, "And I don't like it when she cries."

Miguel threw his fork down and stood.

"I am headed south today. If you will give me your ticket and payment for those bulls, I will pick them up." He pulled his hat on and paused by the door. "I will be going to Kansas City first. I will get the bulls in Victoria on my way back."

Gabe stared at Miguel for a moment and slowly nodded. "I will wire George Grant's niece. Grant just passed away. She inherited and her new husband is handling the business there." He paused before he asked Miguel, "So you are thinking you will be there in what, five days?"

Miguel thought a moment and slowly nodded. "That should work. It will take me about a day to get to Kansas City and another ten hours to get back to Victoria. I was planning to spend two days in Kansas City so that will give me an extra day if something doesn't go as planned."

Gabe handed his brother-in-law a ticket and some money. He looked hard at him as he spoke.

"I'll wire Grant the payment for the bulls but here's some traveling money. And that is for the business part of this trip. I won't be funding your womanizing side trip." Gabe's face softened and he gripped Miguel's shoulder.

"Be safe, Brother. You know whiskey makes you reckless, and there won't be anyone there to back you up."

Miguel's face broke into a grin, and he winked at Gabe.

"You should not worry, señor—I know people everywhere. Always, I find friends who want to join me at the card tables and in the saloons." Miguel touched his hat and sauntered out to where his horse was tied. He was whistling as he led it to the barn. He was still whistling when he rode by the house on his favorite horse with a blanket roll tied behind his saddle.

Merina jerked open the bedroom door and watched Miguel silently from the kitchen window. She turned to face Gabe.

"Miguel is going to get in trouble. I can feel it. Perhaps you should send someone with him."

Gabe hugged his wife and kissed her large belly. "I don't have any spare men. Besides, Miguel always gets his job done. He just goofs off more than the rest of his family." He grinned down at his wife.

"Now, my wife, why there is no wasting around in her at all. Shoot, she was pregnant within a day or two of marriage. Yep, she is just my kind of woman."

Merina glared up at Gabe but finally laughed.

"This is true and perhaps you should bring the buggy around in case Doc Williams needs to check me today. My stomach has been cramping."

Gabe's eyes opened wide, and he rushed to hitch the buggy. Emilia and Rollie had spent the night with Anna and Angel. Merina and he were picking up the little ones when they finished in town.

"I reckon a buggy would be best with five- and six-year-olds anyway."

Gabe was smiling when he swung the buggy up by the house. He quickly tied his team and was back out with Merina. When he pretended to strain as he lifted her up, Merina rolled her eyes.

"Perhaps if I had married a strong man, he would be able to lift a small woman. I think my husband does not work hard enough."

Gabe chuckled and flexed his arm when Merina took hold of it. "I think maybe my wife needs to see more of my muscles. Perhaps when we get home—"

Merina hit him with her elbow, and they were both laughing when the buggy pulled out of the yard.

CHAPTER 3

Flory's Surprise

MIGUEL CLIMBED DOWN FROM THE TRAIN CAR AND stretched. He had been riding for nearly twenty-four hours and he was stiff. He looked around and slowly walked toward the livestock cars. He grabbed his saddle and was soon riding toward the bath area.

"As soon as I am cleaned up, I believe I will go see señorita Flory. Perhaps she will tell me why she did not want me to come." His dark eyes sparkled, and he chuckled as he added, "Or perhaps she will be so pleased to see me that she will forget about the second letter."

Miguel polished the silver conchos that adorned Demonio's saddle and bridle. He adjusted his guns before he mounted and rode east. It was nearly noon when he knocked on Oliver Maynard's door.

The maid glared at him and spoke stiffly, "One moment, please." She shut the door, but Miguel could hear her talking.

The door was quickly pulled open. Tillie stood there looking at Miguel in surprise.

"Miguel! I didn't know you were in Kansas City! Please come in. We just sat down to eat, and you are welcome to join us."

Miguel's smile was large as he followed Tillie inside. It faded a little when he realized Flory was not there. However, it was large again when Tillie introduced him to her husband.

"Ollie, this is Miguel Montero. His brother married Anna."

Tillie's smile faded as she looked from one man to the other.

"Flory is gone for the rest of the day, and we don't expect her back until late tonight. One of her best clients needed to be fitted for a special dress. She wanted Flory to go shopping with her for accessories. Afterwards, they were going to the theater for the evening performance." Tillie cocked her head and frowned as she studied Miguel's face.

"What brings you to Kansas City?"

Miguel studied Tillie's face for a moment before he answered. He couldn't tell if she was angry or curious.

"I came to see señorita Flory. I have two days here before I must head west to pick up some bulls."

Tillie's frown became bigger. However, when the three of them sat down to eat, the conversation was lively. Miguel enjoyed himself. He did notice though that Tillie barely spoke of Flory. Ollie didn't mention her at all.

When dinner was over, Ollie invited Miguel to share a brandy and a cigar with him. The older man took a deep puff on the cigar and his eyes bored into Miguel.

"Did Florence invite you to come and see her?"

Miguel squirmed in his seat and nodded.

"She did but the letter just arrived. Most of the envelope was gone. She sent it soon after her visit to Cheyenne."

"And that was the only letter you received?"

Miguel's body went still. His eyes were cool when he looked up at Ollie.

"No, señor. Señorita Flory sent a second letter and told me not to come. The two letters arrived a day apart. She did not say why so I came. I decided to pretend the second letter did not arrive. Whatever the reason was for her to ask me to stay home, she can tell me face-to-face."

Ollie's eyes sparkled with what could have been humor for a moment as he continued to study the young man in front of him. He drew deeply on his cigar and turned away. When he faced Miguel again, his eyes were cold.

"If you came here to trifle with Florence, I will horsewhip you and run you out of Kansas City. And that will be to keep Tillie from shooting you herself.

"Florence has become like a daughter to Tillie and me. I won't have young men playing her for a fool and running away when they are done. If that is your intention, you may leave town now."

The young vaquero's cockiness was gone as he studied the glowering man in front of him. Oliver Maynard had seemed so quiet and unassuming during dinner. The man was angry now though.

Miguel hadn't accepted a dressing down from anyone in a long time, but he sat quietly as Ollie spoke. He finally raised his head to look Ollie in the eyes.

"I assure you, señor Maynard, I have done nothing with señorita Flory that my sainted mother would not have approved of. I came by to see her because we had fun together in Cheyenne. While my intentions are not for a permanent relationship, one never knows. Perhaps there is more." Miguel lifted one shoulder in a shrug before he continued.

"Never have I ridden this far to see a woman." Miguel's dark eyes sparkled for a moment before they became serious again. "I promise you I will be a gentleman. The small señorita's virtue is safe with me." Miguel's voice was soft as he spoke.

Ollie pulled the cigar from his mouth and stared at it for a moment. He shoved it into the glass tray on his desk and sighed deeply before he sat down.

"Florence is with child. She won't talk to us about it. It must have happened about the time she went to Cheyenne because she is beginning to show." Ollie's gray eyes drilled into Miguel.

"Tillie and I thought perhaps the two of you—"

Miguel stared at Ollie as he absorbed the information he had been given. His dark eyes were hard as he watched the older man.

"Sí, of course you would think that." Miguel spoke sarcastically as he watched Ollie. Then he frowned. When he spoke again, his voice was softer. "Perhaps señorita Flory has fallen in love with someone."

Ollie shook his head.

"No, she has cut off all her suitors. She hardly goes anywhere. When she is here, she spends most of her time in her room." Ollie looked away and cursed under his breath. "And she cries a lot.

"Now you show up. That is why we thought perhaps you and Flory—maybe you—"

Miguel stood up. His dark eyes were furious as he stared at Ollie.

"Señor Maynard, I have not always been a man whom fathers would like to have around their daughters, but never have I forced myself on a woman. And not once did señorita Flory encourage any advances from me. We danced together only at the dance and then I took her to Badger's house. She did not invite me in, and I did not ask her to do so." Miguel's hand shook a little as he pushed it through his hair.

"I will go now to find this man. And I will be back tomorrow to see señorita Flory."

Ollie didn't respond until Miguel was almost out of the room. His voice was quiet when he spoke.

"Try the Crystal Palace."

"You know this man?"

"I have my suspicions but nothing I have been able to confirm. Now if you find him—"

Miguel's smile was cold as he nodded at Ollie.

"Until tomorrow, señor. Thank you for your hospitality and for your care of señorita Flory."

Miguel was quiet as he walked down the long walk to the street. He could see Tillie through the kitchen window, and he doffed his hat to her before he rode away. Then he cursed.

"I will kill this man. I will kill him slowly." Miguel's hands were shaking, and he took a deep breath. A coldness slowly settled over him and he smiled. His hands were once again still, and he urged his horse to a trot.

CHAPTER 4

To Cheat a Cheater

MIGUEL TOOK HIS HORSE TO THE CLOSEST LIVERY. HE rubbed Demonio down, gave him some hay, and dropped down in the stall beside him.

"Let us take a nap, Demonio. It could be a long night." It was nearly six that evening when Miguel awoke. He saddled Demonio and held him to a walk.

Miguel stopped short of the Crystal Palace and studied the street. He rode slowly past the saloon and walked Demonio partway down the surrounding alleys as well as completely around the saloon before he dismounted.

He tied his horse in a slipknot to the rail in front and adjusted his guns. He glanced up and down the street before he started toward the saloon. He loosened the knife inside his shirt as he walked and slowly climbed the steps to the boardwalk. A cold smile was on his face as he pushed through the swinging doors of the saloon.

A cowboy drinking at the long bar looked up and nodded. Miguel sauntered toward him and ordered a whiskey. Then he turned around to face the room with his elbows on the bar.

"This seems to be a busy place. Perhaps because it is a Friday, yes?"

The cowboy swirled his beer and shrugged. "Wouldn't know. It's my first time here. I helped my boss drive some cattle up here and then he let me go. Tried to short me some of my pay too but a knife in his throat made him a little more agreeable."

Miguel stared at the man and nodded somberly.

"Perhaps you should come up to Cheyenne with me. My brother is hiring riders." Miguel's face broke into a friendly grin, and he put out his hand. "I will not tell you my name just yet, señor, but my brother and I, we appreciate a man who isn't afraid to use his knife."

The cowboy stared at Miguel for a moment before he gripped the newcomer's hand. "Roscoe Reed but my friends call me Reed." He turned around to face the room with his beer in his hand and nodded toward a table where some loud young men were playing cards.

"Those fancy fellers been playin' cards for most a two hours. An' see the feller in the little round hat? He's been a cheatin' the whole time. His buddies are too drunk to notice. He buys lots a drinks, but he don't drink much his own self."

Miguel stared at the table a moment before he glanced at Reed. His face was still but his dark eyes sparkled.

"That is very perceptive for a man who appears to be drinking."

Reed grinned and shrugged.

"Don't think much of a man who cheats—an' even less of a man who cheats his drunk friends. He's a bragger too an' that ain't impressive neither."

Miguel studied the card players for a time. He slowly straightened.

"I think I will deal myself into that game. I could use a little road money."

Reed stared at Miguel and snorted.

"Yore funeral but if ya want to play, I'll come on over in a bit an' watch yore back."

Miguel strolled over to the table where the men were playing and watched for a moment. Reed was right. The man in the bowler hat *was* cheating and cheating poorly.

One man looked back at Miguel and nodded toward his cards.

"This is my last hand and then I'm done. Cletus took all my money, and my pop won't be so happy with me when I ask him for more."

When the man stood, Miguel looked around the table as he leaned on the back of the empty chair.

"Perhaps I may join you gentlemen? I am just a lonely cowpuncher who likes to play cards, perhaps a little too much." His smile was large as he looked around the table. Cletus looked him over, trying to size him up. He nodded and the rest of the men shrugged.

Miguel sat down. He threw a handful of money on the table and sat back in his chair with a smile.

One of the players slapped the deck down in front of Miguel.

"Poker is our game. It was James' turn to shuffle, so you are up." He put out his hand. "John is my name. What shall we call you?"

"Delgado is what most call me, but my sainted mother called me Gordo. Now shall we play?" The rest of the players called out their names. Only Cletus did not say who he was.

Reed grinned to himself and shook his head. *Obviously, no one at that table speaks Spanish since gordo means fat and delgado means slim.*

Miguel fumbled with the deck and dropped a few cards before he finally was able to shuffle them. Cletus watched him carefully. Reed strolled up and stared from the fumbling Miguel to Cletus. He sighed and shook his head. He ordered another beer and leaned against the wall to watch. Miguel finally had the cards shuffled and awkwardly tossed them across the table to the players. He looked at his hand and smiled excitedly.

Cletus's eyes glinted with excitement and the game began. Miguel didn't win on the first hand, but he didn't lose much either. Cletus lost the most and the quietest man took the pot. Slowly the other players peeled off until just Miguel and Cletus were at the table. Reed brought over two fingers of whiskey for each man. Miguel drank his quickly and rubbed his hands together. He steered the conversation toward women and Cletus was soon bragging about his conquests.

"That last gal I took out was quite the looker. She couldn't hold her liquor though. Got plowed-under drunk." He winked at Miguel lewdly and added, "'Course I made sure to slip a little somethin' in her drink to help her relax, an' it sure did. She was a slippin' an' a fallin' all over the place. An' then her clothes fell off."

Reed watched Miguel closely. He saw the cowboy's hands tighten on the cards. When Miguel looked up, his smile was cold and his eyes were hard. Reed swore under his breath as he straightened up. He didn't know where his new friend was going with this game, but he knew it wasn't for fun.

"Perhaps, señor, you should introduce me to this señorita. If she is so friendly, I might want to call on her myself."

Cletus swigged his drink down and stared at Miguel through bleary eyes. He slowly shook his head.

"Can't do it. Ollie Maynard is like an ol' bulldog an' his wife is even meaner. They didn't like me before, an' now, they are just downright nasty.

"Maynard thinks he's a big man in this town, an' he pulled all his business out of Pop's store. 'Course Pop don't know why, an' I sure ain't tellin'.

"Don't matter though. That gal is just some orphan Tillie took in. Don't have no folks an' no money. Nobody would believe her if she tried to point a finger at me, what with Pop's money an' his standin' in this community.

"'Sides, that gal ain't even takin' callers anymore." He laughed and hiccupped once before he continued. "Word is she don't remember nothin'. She don't even remember goin' to the Thanksgivin' Dance with me." He frowned as he studied his cards.

"Tillie does though. She caught me after church last week an' threatened to horsewhip me in public if I ever showed up at her house again. She means it too. She's a violent woman, an' I don't understand what ol' Ollie sees in her." Cletus shoved back his chair and pulled out his pocket watch. He moved it back and forth as he tried to focus on the time. Finally, he cursed and shoved it back into his pocket.

"I'd better head for home. I don't know what time it is but I'm guessin' it's late." He started to pull the pile of money toward him when Miguel leaned forward.

"Perhaps, señor, we should play one more hand before we quit. Five Card Draw, yes? Let's go for all or nothing. Everything in front of you for my horse and saddle." Miguel whistled and his horse came rushing through the saloon doors. The silver conchos on the saddle and bridle gleamed in the light. When a man tried to grab the reins, the horse reared and pawed the air, shaking its long black mane as it spun.

Cletus looked dully from the horse to Miguel and licked his lips. His eyes narrowed down, and he frowned as he stared hard at Miguel.

"How do I know you won't cheat?"

Miguel's smile didn't reach his eyes. "But gentlemen don't cheat, do they, señor? And we are friends, yes? Surely you would not cheat your friends. To make it fair, we can even call for a new deck."

Miguel signaled to the bartender for a new deck. He pointed toward a cowboy standing at the bar.

"Perhaps, señor, you could check the deck and make sure it is not marked?"

The bartender had started to pick up a deck behind him but at Miguel's comment, his hand paused. He grabbed a deck from under the bar and handed it to the cowboy.

The cowboy shuffled and cut the cards, feeling the edges and corners. He grinned at the bartender and strolled across the floor to hand them to Miguel.

"Yore cards, mister. Fresh deck an' she feels fine."

Miguel set them in front of Cletus.

"And to show you that this is a game for gentlemen, I will let you shuffle them."

Cletus stared from Miguel to the cards. He awkwardly shuffled marking three of them in the process. He set them in the middle of the table. Miguel smiled as he cut the deck three times.

"Winner takes all, señor. Perhaps you will deal me a royal flush." He stared at his horse and frowned as he shrugged. "Or perhaps not."

Cletus smiled and shuffled the cards. Confusion registered on his face as he felt multiple knicks on the sides of the cards. His hands were shaking when he dealt, and they trembled as he laid five cards in front of each of them.

Miguel picked up his cards. His face didn't change as he stared at them.

Cletus's face slowly broke into a grin. He discarded one card and laid down two pairs, queens, and fours.

Miguel turned his cards over. His hand was a straight flush—five, six, seven, eight, nine, and ten of spades.

Cletus stared at the cards for a moment before he jerked himself upright.

He pointed at Miguel. "You cheated!" he shouted. "You had to cheat. I—I—that hand was impossible. I—that couldn't happen!"

Miguel's face never changed as he pulled the money toward him. He pushed it into his hat and dumped it in his saddle bags.

Cletus's face was red, and he was breathing heavily. He shouted as the cowboy led his horse toward the door. Miguel finally turned around and stared at Cletus.

"Perhaps we were not so much the friends after all, yes? Maybe someone would like to check that deck of cards. He will find some marks on it that were not there before, I think."

Reed stepped forward. He spread the deck out on the table. Multiple cards were marked including all the cards in front of Cletus. None of the cards in front of Miguel were marked.

Miguel's cold eyes cut into the angry man. "I think if you are going to cheat, you should not drink so much whiskey. It makes you careless, even when you play with your friends."

He winked at the cowboy at the bar and chuckled as he walked out.

CHAPTER 5

Harsh Punishment

MIGUEL WAS HEADED DOWN THE STREET WHEN REED caught up with him.

"Cletus is going to lay for you. You should have shot him for calling you a cheater."

"Sí, but he was not armed. Perhaps we will wait for him, yes?"

Reed studied Miguel and shook his head.

"You took quite a chance in there. I'm not sure how you managed to get the cards you did. That deal could have ended up a whole lot different than it did."

Miguel grinned and shrugged. "Perhaps señor Cletus was not the only one who was cheating...Still, even if I had lost, Demonio would have come back to me, so what would I have lost? I had little but my horse when I started."

Reed stared at Miguel and laughed.

"Mighty reckless. You talk like a man who has little to lose. I like that and I like you."

The cowboy who was at the bar pushed through the doors. He spotted Miguel and Reed. He slowly walked toward them. The three men walked around the corner where Miguel stopped. His face was serious as he looked at the two men beside him.

"Señors, what I must do next is very dangerous. The señorita whom Cletus spoke of is special to me. I must make him pay for what he did to her. I do not ask you to help me. I just ask that you lead my horse up the street." He handed Reed his hat and took the other man's hat from his head. "Get Cletus to follow you. If you hear noise behind you, let my horse take care of what he can. Only turn around if you hear feet running close behind you."

The second cowboy grinned at Miguel and pushed out his hand. "Temple Winters. I know Reed here but who are you? 'Cause I know ya ain't Gordo or Delgado!"

Miguel grinned and nodded as he shook the man's hand.

"Sí, I am Miguel. Miguel Montero. Go to the Pacific House Hotel and check in under Gordo Delgado. Tie my horse with a slip knot when you arrive there. He will let no one ride him but me. I will join you when I am finished with my business." He grinned at them and handed Reed some money as he added, "Tonight we will sleep well since señor Cletus was so generous with his friends' money."

Miguel faded into the shadows while Reed and Temple turned up the street toward the Pacific House, leading the black horse. Reed pulled Miguel's black hat down over his face. The silver conchos woven through the hat band glistened when the light caught them. He slowed his walk to a stroll and the two men sauntered up the street.

Cletus stumbled through the saloon doors. Two men were with him. Each carried a club. Cletus pointed toward the two cowboys walking north up the street.

"There he goes. My money is in those saddle bags. Put those two cowboys out of commission for good and bring my money back to me. I'll be waiting for you down by the cattle pens."

The two men tried to run silently up the street. Their version of quiet made Miguel chuckle. *Let them try to sneak up on Demonio. He likes no one to walk behind him, especially not a stranger who is running.*

Miguel watched for a moment. Demonio kicked the first thug, pitching him backwards. The man's cry was cut off as he hit the brick street, headfirst. The second thug barely dodged a kick himself. However, he ran into the butt end of a six gun. Demonio galloped away while Temple and Reed continued up the street as if nothing had happened. They left the two men lying where they fell.

Cletus was already hurrying south down the street. He didn't turn around when he heard the scuffle behind him. Miguel followed him silently.

When they were nearly to the cattle pens, Miguel grabbed Cletus and dragged him into an alley. He shoved him to the ground and put his knife against the terrified man's neck. The alley was dark and even though Cletus could see a shadow of the man in front of him, he couldn't see the man's face behind the bandana.

"This is for all the ladies you have done wrong, especially the last one. I don't think you will be behaving that way again after tonight."

Miguel shoved Cletus' neckerchief into his mouth and quickly bound his hands and feet. Then he pulled a wet piggin' string from his pocket and dangled it in front of Cletus.

"I think I will tie what you are so eager to share. Perhaps they will fall off before someone finds you." Miguel shrugged. "I do not know."

Cletus' eyes opened wide. He tried to scream, but Miguel's hands were quick and efficient. Cletus was still screaming behind the neckerchief when he passed out.

Miguel dragged Cletus' limp body farther into the alley and threw some trash over the still man. A horse snuffled and Miguel whistled softly. Demonio walked toward him.

"Come. We must be quiet, my friend. No one must see us here tonight."

Miguel rode quietly down the dark streets, staying on dirt as much as possible. It was nearly one in the morning when he arrived at the hotel, having wound almost in a circle to come up to the hotel from the north. He loosened the saddle girth and whispered to his horse, "I'm sorry, my friend. Tonight, you must stay tied here. Tomorrow, I will take you to the livery and you will have a fine meal." He tied Demonio at the end of the rail in the shadows and slipped quietly into the hotel. He pulled the ledger across the desk and lit a match to read the names and room numbers. When he found Gordo Delgado, he chuckled softly and went silently up the stairs.

He tapped lightly on the door. Reed pulled it open with a gun in his hand and Miguel slipped inside. Reed pointed toward the window.

"Temple went down to the livery. He is going to sleep in the loft. He figures someone will be here at first light looking for two men, and he wanted to make sure he wasn't one of them." The cowboy grinned and added, "He said you owed him a fine meal though. He sure hated to miss a good night's sleep in such a swanky hotel as this one."

Reed waited a moment to see if Miguel was going to share any details. When Miguel said nothing, he nodded toward the floor.

"I put my bedroll on the floor, so the bed is yours. This here carpet is soft as a bed anyhow. Besides, you are the one payin' the bill on this deal." He grinned at Miguel and rolled up in his blankets.

Both men were soon asleep with their guns beside them.

CHAPTER 6

You Cowboys Are Trouble

TEMPLE WAS RIGHT. SOMEONE WAS BEATING ON THEIR door before daylight. Miguel rolled out of the bed and jerked the door open with a gun in his hand. He was in his britches and socks, but his hat was on.

"Something we can help you with this morning, Sheriff?"

"We are looking for Cletus Littleton. You know where he might be?"

Miguel stared at the sheriff for a moment before he pushed his hat up and scratched his head.

"I played cards with a man last night. He didn't introduce himself, but some of the other young men at the table called him by that name. I did not hear his last name though."

"Well, he is missing. I am taking you in as a suspect."

Miguel's eyes were hard as he stared into the lawman's face.

"I think, señor, if you talk to the hotel clerk, you will see that I checked into this hotel shortly after I left the Crystal Palace. And señor Cletus was still inside the saloon when I left." He paused and added, "I know this because he called me a card cheat when the marked cards were all in front of him." Miguel smiled at the sheriff.

"I won, Sheriff. Why would I attack a man when I had all his money *and* my horse? He was the one who was angry. He lost. Perhaps he went someplace else to drink. Maybe he is passed out somewhere, nursing a bad headache."

"Those two bodies we found in the street say otherwise."

"Bodies?"

"Two men were found on the street after you left. One had been clubbed and the other looked like he had been kicked in the head by a horse or a mule. He had a hoofprint in the middle of his forehead and he is dead. The one who was clubbed might make it. He's in bad shape though."

Miguel nodded somberly.

"Sí, some horses and mules, they have no tolerance for foolish men. Perhaps these men were chasing someone, yes? And this señor Cletus—he knew these men in the street?"

The sheriff glared at Miguel. *This cowboy acts innocent but I'm betting he had something to do with this deal. And I'd bet my last dollar he has something to do with Cletus missing too.* The sheriff's brows furrowed as he stared at Miguel. *I just can't figure out why.*

"Let me see your guns. If one of them has blood on the butt, you are coming with me."

Miguel stepped back to let the door open all the way. He handed the sheriff one gun at a time. He had no intention of giving the man both his guns at once.

The sheriff cursed as he handed the second gun back to Miguel. When he spied Reed leaning on an elbow on the floor, he pointed at him.

"Let me see your gun."

Miguel took the gun from Reed and handed it to the sheriff. Once again it was checked but no blood was found. The sheriff handed it back with a scowl as he continued to glare at Miguel.

"Sheriff, I just arrived in your town, and I knew no men at that card table in the Crystal Palace. I also do not know these injured men of whom you speak. Now I have my money and my horse, so they did not rob me. And neither my compadre nor I hit them so it must have been someone else they were chasing.

"Perhaps you should ask some of señor Cletus's friends. He was cheating them all night. Maybe they were involved in that altercation."

The sheriff stared at Miguel a moment longer. He cursed again and turned away.

"I want you out of this town today. The next train west leaves this evening and you had better be on it." He swung his eyes over to Reed. "And you too. You cowboys are nothing but trouble."

"Sí, I think your town is not so friendly. Maybe your women are not either. I do not know as we have not seen any.

"Adios, Sheriff. And be sure to ask señor Cletus's friends about his cheating." He shut the door and turned around with a grin.

Reed stared up at him as he chuckled softly.

"You are trouble, Miguel. You sure are. Now let's go get some breakfast. Temple was going to wait at the livery until we came down. And maybe we should leave town before this evening. We can always catch the train we need in another town."

Temple was cleaning the butt of his gun when they arrived at the livery. Miguel looked at him and laughed.

"I think, señor Temple, I might owe you more than breakfast."

Temple grinned and nodded. "Reed here said you knew of someone hirin' riders. I'll ride along with ya if that's true. I've weared out my welcome in Kansas, an' Texas ain't callin' my name neither."

"Sí, my brother and my sister's husband are hiring. I think they will be pleased to have two such fine hombres working for them." He waved his hands to the west as he spoke.

"I am to pick up some bulls west of here in Victoria. We will ship them home to Cheyenne.

"The Kansas Pacific is the train we must catch. It leaves town at seven tomorrow morning. We could catch it today but that is very soon." He paused and added, "I must go see a certain señorita. If she wants to spend time with me—" Miguel shrugged. "Yes, I think I will be on the train tomorrow morning."

Reed stared at Miguel and frowned. "I think we need to leave today. I'm not sure what you did to Cletus but when he is found, all Hell will break loose. I'd like to be gone before that happens." He looked over at Temple.

"I know a fellow out west of town who has a little ranch. How about we head on out there this morning? We can meet Miguel in Lawrence tomorrow morning. I'll check the times to be sure nothing has changed, but the Kansas Pacific should go through there around eight-thirty." He looked hard at Miguel and shook his head again.

"I ain't met a woman yet who was worth a rope necktie—and that's what they'll try to do if they can hang any of that deal on us."

Miguel grinned at his friends as he nodded.

"Sí. That is what they will do. Perhaps I will try to blend in, yes?"

Reed looked from Miguel's hat to his horse. He snorted.

"Blend in? You stand out like a black bull in a pen of red heifers! Yore jist askin' for trouble."

Miguel chuckled. He opened his saddle bags. He spread his bandana on the ground and dumped the money he won onto it. He split it into three parts and gave each of his friends a third.

"Now you have enough to buy your tickets, and I will not be so tempted to play cards again before I get home. Come. Let us eat breakfast before you leave."

CHAPTER 7

Miguel's Proposal

MIGUEL RUBBED DEMONIO DOWN BEFORE HE saddled him. He rode toward Tillie's house with a smile on his face. He spotted some flowers close to a fence and stopped to pick the yellow daffodils that were pushing through the brown grass. Daffodils were a sign of spring, and yellow had always been one of his favorite colors.

Ollie was gone when Miguel arrived, but Tillie opened the door.

"So, you *are* back. I suppose you want to see Flory." She studied the smiling vaquero and asked, "Are those flowers for her?"

"Señora, I wish to see señorita Flory, but the flowers, they are for you. For you because you threatened to horsewhip a bad hombre who pretends to be a man." His smile became larger as he added softly, "But I don't think he will pretend to be a man again for a very long time. Perhaps never."

Tillie accepted the flowers as she listened closely to Miguel. When he finished, she smiled.

"I wasn't sure I was going to let you see Flory, but now I believe I will. Ollie told me he liked you, and I believe I do too.

"Flory hasn't been down for breakfast. She doesn't come out of her room much except for meals, and she misses many of those."

Miguel nodded and walked to the base of the stairs.

"Señorita Flory!" he called. "I have come many miles to see you. If you do not come down, I will come up. And I think that would not be so good for a proper young lady."

There was a rush of feet and a door opened. Flory's blonde curls were bobbing all over her head as she stared down the stairs.

"Miguel! Why are you here? I told you not to come!"

"No, señorita. I have a letter in my hand. You invited me to come see you and here I am. Now am I to come up or are you coming down?"

Flory's eyes were wide as she stared at Miguel. She shook her head.

"I will come down." She started to shut the door but opened it again before she added, "And don't you dare come up here."

"Five minutes, señorita Flory. Five minutes and then I am coming up."

Flory gasped and closed the door. Miguel grinned as he listened to the scurrying above him. In just a few minutes, the door opened, and Flory hurried toward the stairway.

Miguel almost caught his breath. Flory's growing stomach was visible to him even though the dress she wore was designed to disguise it. Her face was pale, but he didn't think he had ever seen her look prettier. When she reached the bottom of the stairs, Miguel bowed and took her arm.

"Come. Tillie said that breakfast was ready. She has some eggs and—"

Flory covered her mouth and rushed into the room that Tillie called her water closet. Miguel heard Flory gag and choke. He heard water splashing. Soon, Flory was beside him.

Miguel looked at her with concern. "You are all right? Are you sick?"

"Let's go to the sitting room." Flory smiled at Tillie.

"I think I will just have some tea this morning if you don't mind, Tillie. I'm not very hungry." She glanced sideways at Miguel and blushed as she pulled him toward the sitting area.

When they were seated, Flory took a deep breath. Her hands were shaking, and tears sparkled in the corners of her eyes.

Miguel smiled as he watched her. Finally, he took her hands. He kissed one of them and continued to smile at her.

"Don't cry, Flory. I already know of the bambino inside you. I have been to see the man who is responsible, and he is sorry for what he did. In fact, he will be sorry for the rest of his life." Miguel frowned briefly and shrugged his shoulders before he added, "Whether it is a long life or a very short one, I do not know."

Flory's blue eyes were wide as she stared up at Miguel. Her breath caught and she began to cry.

"But I don't remember. I don't even know his name. I don't remember anything."

"That is because he drugged you. He is sorry for that as well. But let us not talk of that man. Let us talk of you and me.

"Your child needs a father, yes? Perhaps you should marry me. I will be a father to your child and a husband to you. Everyone will suspect the child is mine because...well, because I have not always been such a good vaquero. They will run the dates through their minds, and soon the talk will be that it is my child.

"So let us make it my child. We can marry today. I must move some bulls to Cheyenne in two days, but you can come this week or next. You tell me when and I will be at the train to meet you." He dropped down on one knee and put his hat over his heart.

"Marry me, Flory. Marry me and may we have many happy years of dancing, and laughing, and making more babies."

Flory's face turned pale as she stared at Miguel. She shook her head.

"No, I can't. I have never been faithful to one man in my life. I can't promise you a lifetime."

"And neither have I ever loved just one woman. It will be a new thing for us, but together, we can do it. Marry me today and come west to live with me."

Flory stared at Miguel. She waffled back and forth between laughing and crying.

"This is foolish. You are being impetuous, and I am being silly for listening. A lifetime decision like this should be given much thought."

"And I am sure you have been doing lots of thinking since you found you were with child, yes? And what solutions did you come up with?

"I have been thinking of this since yesterday. I have been asking myself many questions.

"Never have I ridden this far to see a woman, and especially one whom I knew only for a few days.

"Only one other woman did I think I wanted to marry. Yet when I had the opportunity to ask her, I ran away…twice. She was a wise woman and never gave me a third chance.

"Now, there is you and here I am. I do not want to run away. I want to be here with you today, and tomorrow, and as many days after that as we will have together.

"I think we will argue some. Maybe we will even fight, but we will love as well. And we will laugh much. I think if a man and a woman can laugh together, perhaps they can live many years in happiness."

Flory's eyes filled with tears as she listened to Miguel. When he finished, she began to cry in earnest.

"That was beautiful, Miguel."

As he pulled her close, Flory whispered, "You have a very kind heart, but you hide it behind jokes and teasing." She smiled up at Miguel and nodded.

"I will marry you, but I don't want to come later to Cheyenne. I want to go with you now."

Miguel laughed and pulled Flory to her feet. Then he lifted her up and spun her around. When he sat down, she was on his lap. He kissed her and slid her back on the seat beside him.

"Let us go now. We will talk to the padre. And if he doesn't want to marry us, I'll tell him that we are going to be traveling together for many miles…and who knows what might happen."

Flory blushed and Miguel laughed.

Tillie stood just outside the door and listened to Miguel's proposal. She frowned. "Miguel is known for his lack of responsibility. What if he runs off?" When she heard the two young people moving toward the door, she moved away and busied herself at the wash area.

Flory's sparkle was back, and she was breathless when she rushed into the kitchen.

"Miguel asked me to marry, and I said yes! We are going to talk to the priest today if we can catch him. We hope to get married this evening. Miguel's train leaves at seven tomorrow morning and I am going with him!" Flory was almost running as she left the kitchen and Miguel's smile was large.

Tillie followed them as they rushed toward Miguel's horse. She called out before they reached the street.

"Miguel, you hitch my buggy. I don't want you riding with Flory on your lap until you are married."

Miguel paused as he looked from Tillie to Flory. He finally grinned and nodded.

"Sí, señora Tillie. I will put my horse in your stable if you don't mind. Last night was very long and I think he is tired. He is a fine caballo, and he would appreciate a clean stall."

Flory followed Miguel to the stable, and Tillie could hear their happy voices from the house. She shook her head as she smiled.

"They are like two kids going off on a picnic. They have no idea how hard marriage will be, especially with a little one coming so soon. And they haven't even thought about a place to live!" She sighed but smiled again. "Still, it won't be impossible. Miguel has a wonderful family and Anna will be close by. I am sure they won't be homeless. Flory is not much of a cook though.

"Perhaps I'm overly concerned because she has become like a daughter to me. My, how I am going to miss her. And Anna too. I guess I will be making more trips to Cheyenne."

CHAPTER 8

A Visit from the Sheriff

TILLIE HAD JUST FINISHED WIPING OFF HER TABLE when she heard horses. She frowned as she looked out the window. "What is Charlie Bassett doing with that tinhorn sheriff?" She jerked the kitchen door open and stepped into the doorway.

"Good morning, Charlie. I see you are keeping poor company today."

Charlie hid a grin and Sheriff Longfellow glared at her.

"Mrs. Maynard, is your husband at home?"

"Oliver isn't here but whatever business you have with him may be discussed with me. We have no secrets."

The sheriff fidgeted in his saddle. His face turned red before he finally responded.

"Mrs. Maynard, it is my understanding that your husband threatened to horsewhip young Cletus Littleton. He is said to have promised to run him out of Kansas City for wanting to keep company with an orphan girl in your care."

Tillie stepped out of her house and glared at Sheriff Longfellow. She slowly walked toward him until she was directly in front of his horse. The man was doing all he could to keep from backing his horse when Tillie grabbed the reins.

"Sheriff, Ollie didn't threaten to do that. *I* did. Cletus Littleton is an overblown shell of a hustler who thinks he can do as he pleases because his father has money. And Miss Whitman is not just an orphan—she is my niece.

"Neither Ollie nor I will tolerate any man drugging a woman and forcing himself on her, let alone one as young and innocent as our Florence.

"I filed a report in your office last November, and you refused to investigate it. You didn't even talk to anyone. You said you didn't have enough evidence. Now here you are trying to accuse Ollie of something you heard on the street? You are a sham of a lawman." Tillie turned her wrath on Charlie.

"Charlie, you were known as a tough lawman in Dodge City. Why don't you pull that badge off this tinhorn and pin it on yourself? Maybe some of these crimes would be investigated based on the gravity of the charge and not on who *supposedly* was involved."

She glared from man to man before she addressed the sheriff again.

"And where is young Cletus? Maybe I will use my horsewhip on him yet."

The sheriff's face turned a mottled red and Charlie cleared his throat before he spoke.

"I don't think that will be necessary, Mrs. Maynard. Someone waylaid Cletus last night. Dragged him off in an alley down by the stockyards. His hands and feet were tied, and his bandana was stuffed in his mouth. And they—well they—they incapacitated his manhood with a piece of wet rawhide. He is in the hospital now."

Tillie stared at Charlie in shock while he continued talking.

"He swears it was the cowboy he was playing cards with last night, but he couldn't see his face. The man wore a bandana.

"Cletus said the man didn't talk much. He threatened him with a large knife and then tied him up. Cletus passed out before the man—before he finished. He wasn't found until an hour ago. Unfortunately, the rawhide had dried and tightened even more. Cletus is—well, he is maimed for life."

Tillie looked from one man to the other and laughed.

"Good. He deserved that and more. And if you find the man who did it, please thank him for me.

"Now is that all?"

The sheriff cleared his throat.

"I was hoping to speak with Miss Whitman."

Tillie jerked her arm up to point at the sheriff and his horse shied, almost dumping him on the ground.

"You will do no such thing. You didn't bother to talk to her last November when I tried to file a complaint, and you certainly are not going to talk to her now.

"Maybe you should check with his so-called friends. Ollie has watched him cheat at cards. He is a poor card player and an even worse cheat. If his companions weren't so inebriated, they might have noticed that too.

"And just maybe one did.

"Now if you have nothing else to discuss with me, you may leave. And don't come back unless you want to start investigating crimes committed by some of your upper-crust playboys." Tillie turned and began to stomp away. She had only gone a few steps when she stopped and spun around to point at the sheriff once again. Her face was pale, and her breath was coming quickly.

"You want to solve a crime committed by some no-name cowboy whom no one saw, no one can describe, and no one knows? And just because the accused man tied rawhide around the balls of that sorry excuse of a playboy! No real man would have to drug a woman to have his way with her."

Tillie snorted and she was nearly shouting when she added, "Get off my property, Sheriff! I may run against you in the next election just to get rid of you!"

Charlie Bassett was almost laughing. He tipped his hat to the angry woman.

"Tillie, if you file, I will serve as your deputy." He was still chuckling when he followed the sheriff down the street.

Sheriff Longfellow glared at Charlie.

"I know that woman is involved in this somehow."

Charlie studied the man beside him and shook his head.

"No, Frank, she is not. She was as surprised as we were when I told her what happened.

"And this could have been avoided if you had investigated that crime last winter. You have even less to go on now than you did then. You chose to drop that case because of who was involved—Harold Littleton's son.

"Before you kick this pile of fresh dung, you had better investigate that rape claim.

"And another thing, what were those two thugs we found on the street doing with clubs? Who do you think hired them? Both of those fellows are on Harold Littleton's payroll. Are you willing to investigate him too?

"Cletus didn't give you enough to go on and you are in over your head. Old Harold is just furious because his precious son won't be siring any children. Between you and me, I say that's a good thing.

"You have a talk with Harold, and you tell him exactly what Tillie told you. You offer to dig in that pile of excrement. And you be sure to tell him that the stink will get worse, and more boots will get dirty the deeper you go. Let's see how far he wants to push this.

"I'm guessing Littleton will squawk for a time and then he'll walk away. He knows what his son did. This likely wasn't the first time. And he sure doesn't want any of that to go public.

"Or you can just resign now and head east. Maybe you can find some tame little town to settle down in." Charlie looked hard at Frank and added quietly, "You are done here regardless of what you do. You might even want to catch the first train that direction today."

Charlie rode west shaking his head.

"This is what a town gets when the city fathers try to hire the cheapest man they can find. Too bad Masterson isn't around. He'd clean this town up.

"I could too but my lawing days are over. Running a saloon is easier—and safer for sure." He grinned as he pushed his horse to a trot. "Besides, the money's better." He was still chuckling about Tillie's threat to run for sheriff when he arrived at the livery.

CHAPTER 9

A Quick Wedding

MIGUEL WAITED NERVOUSLY FOR FLORY AT THE ALTAR. Tillie insisted he go to the church alone that evening and wait for them. She told him Ollie and she would bring Flory themselves.

He fingered the small ring in his vest pocket. Finally, he took it out and stared at it a moment. He polished it for the fifth time with his bandana and dropped it back into his pocket. His eyes crinkled at the corners as he hid a grin.

"See, Mamá, something good did come of all my gambling! I won my bride a ring and a nice one at that." Miguel grinned as he thought of the card game where he had won the ring.

I guess all three of us will be pleased that I won. Demonio and I like flashy things, and I think Flory will like her ring.

A side door opened at the front of the church and the priest stepped out. He was smiling and Miguel forced himself to relax.

"Miss Whitman will be out in just a moment." He patted Miguel on the back and smiled at him. "Your bride is even more nervous than you are."

Miguel continued to fidget until Flory stepped out of the side door followed by Oliver and Tillie. She was carrying a bouquet of daffodils, and she wore a yellow dress. Miguel could see the tears sparkling in the corners of her eyes and he walked to the side door to meet her. He tucked her arm in his and kissed her cheek before he led her to the front of the church. Oliver and Tillie followed him. Tillie was dabbing at her eyes while Oliver patted her other hand.

The priest was brief, and the ceremony was a quick one. When the pastor held out his hand, Miguel gave him the small ring. The priest blessed it and gave it to Miguel to place on Flory's hand. The single ruby was surrounded by small diamonds. The gold band was wide. It was too large for Flory's ring finger, so Miguel placed it on her middle finger. Flory stared at it for a moment and looked up at him in surprise. He winked at her as he squeezed her hand, and the priest pronounced them husband and wife. Miguel picked Flory up and kissed her as he spun her around. When the priest cleared his throat, Miguel laughed and set her back down. He started to lead her out of the church, but the priest stopped them.

"Just a moment, young man. You have some papers to sign. Even though this ceremony was a fast one, this marriage is legal and binding. You are both going to sign this marriage certificate. Mr. and Mrs. Maynard, as witnesses, you need to sign as well. Only then, Miguel, may you take your bride to wherever you are going."

It was nearly dark when they walked out of the church. Oliver cleared his throat and nodded toward the carriage.

"Miguel, you take the carriage. Our driver will pick us up in a few minutes." He wiped his hand across his face.

"I took the liberty of making a reservation for you at the Pacific House." He smiled slightly and handed Miguel a key.

"The dining room is open until nine tonight if you are hungry. You just give them your name and a table will be waiting for you."

Oliver looked from one to the other and his face crumpled as he reached for Flory. As he hugged her, he whispered, "One of the doormen will drive you to the train station and they will bring our buggy back here. Miguel may tie his horse behind. And, Florence, you come back to visit us. We are going to miss your bright smile and happy laughter."

Tillie sobbed when Flory hugged her.

"Oh, Flory. I just might have to move to Cheyenne. I am going to miss you so. Now you write." She turned to Miguel.

"And you, young man, you make sure our Florence has a home. Once you are settled, you keep an extra bed for when I visit." She hugged Flory as she whispered, "You wire me when that baby arrives too. You know I will be coming to stay. I want to help for a time after that little one is born. That is what grandmothers do, you know."

Flory nodded tearfully as she returned Tillie's hug.

Miguel listened quietly but his body went still as he thought about what Tillie had said. *Where will we live? I didn't think that far ahead.* He grinned slightly as he considered Aunt Betty's house. *I have stayed with her many times when I had difficulty riding upright in the saddle after too much drinking.*

Miguel almost laughed as he thought of Aunt Betty Fairchild. The old woman was a fixture around Cheyenne. She lived east of town in a shack on some of the land the Monteros owned. She wore a beat-up cowboy hat, old boots, and carried a pistol as well as a big knife whether in overalls or an old dress—and she preferred overalls. In the short time Miguel had known Aunt Betty, she had told him many stories of her younger days when Wyoming was not yet a territory and certainly wasn't as settled as now.

Aunt Betty would let us move in with her for a time until I find something. She often tells me I am welcome to stay when I bring her coal.

Miguel grinned as he thought about how Aunt Betty had convinced the Indians she was crazy.

"I saw a war party ridin' in from the east. That's been nigh on thirty years ago. I be almost a hundred now so I reckon I was in my seventies then. Those Injuns was all painted up, black 'round their eyes, an' scalps a hangin' from their hosses.

"I stripped down to my red longhandles quick-like an' pulled on my favorite hat—that old one with all the bullet holes in it. I grabbed a kettle off the stove an' my rolling pin. I jumped on my smallest hoss an' ran him toward those wild Injuns as fast as I could ride. My legs was almost a draggin' on the ground. I liked that little hoss though. He had sand.

"I sang 'Shall We Gather at the River,' as loud as I could while I raced toward them Injuns. When I forgot a few words, I jist added some cuss words fer effect. I beat on that pot an' rolled my eyes. I had jist put my chaw in an' I shore warn't goin' to waste it, so I spit ever' oncet in a while as I sang an' jerked 'round on that hoss.

"Those Injuns was a jabberin' an' rollin' their eyes when I rode right into 'em. I let a little a that toabaccy juice fly when I got in the midst of 'em. It hit one a their hosses, an' that Appaloosa jist went crazy. Reared so high it plumb went over backwards. The brave what was ridin' it bailed off an' jumped up behind one a his friends. That downed hoss must a hit his head or somethin' 'cause he jerked 'round some an' then stiffened all up. Looked like he died right there.

"One a those Injuns made like he was a gonna put a spear right through me, but the brave in charge knocked his hand away. That's 'cause Injuns, they be afeared of crazy folks, an' they shore thought I was crazy. Their hosses was a millin' all over an' those Injuns' eyes was mighty fearful. I tried to smack one of 'em with my rollin' pin since he was close-like an' that was jist too much.

"They took off outta there like all Hades was on their tails." Aunt Betty grinned and winked at Miguel as she added, "That's when I realized I had plumb fergot to button up the back-end a them red, holey longhandles. My ol' white backside was a shinin' out the hind end, and I'm a guessin' it looked like I was a carryin' a couple a big ol' lamps back there.

"I sure hated that hoss dyin' though. He was a fine-lookin' animal. 'Course, I was always short on meat. I figgered since he was dead, I jist as well eat 'im. I took out my big knife an' dropped down beside 'im.

'Bout that time, he come to. He was a tryin' to get up, so I climbed on his back. We went for one heck of a ride. That Appy horse, he wanted to get back with his friends, so we took in after those Injuns. I reckon those braves thought I was a chasin' 'em on a dead hoss!

"When that hoss finally slowed down, I turned him 'round an' rode 'im back home. He wouldn't go nowhere near my pot an' rollin' pin though, so I jist left 'em out there a couple a days."

The old woman's eyes twinkled and she chuckled.

"About ever' two weeks or so after that, Crazy Woman—that's what I called that hoss—we would take us a night ride. I did that regular for 'bout a year to keep the fear in those Injuns. After that, I rode that way whenever I felt like it.

"I plumb loved that hoss, an' Crazy Woman, he learned to like me too. Oh, I knowed he was a stud, but that name put more fear in those Injuns. They come back to watch from time to time, ya know. We'd ride fast an' wild. Me in my longhandles an' Crazy Woman painted up with red faces all over 'im. I'd sing to 'im an' call 'im by name.

"Crazy Woman learned to enjoy those rides. 'Course, when I rode 'im to town, I called 'im Patches. He was pertineer civilized on those trips. It was like he knew how I wanted him to act.

"I had that hoss nigh on thirty years 'fore he passed. Took me two days to dig a hole big enough to bury 'im." Aunt Betty's old hand shook just a little as she wiped her eyes roughly.

"Never had to worry 'bout huntin' again though. Meat jist showed up to my place. A haunch a venison, an antelope—even a buffalo heart now an' again. Those Injuns left me some nice hides over the years too.

"Never had me no trouble after that with Injuns. No siree. Not a bit. No trouble, fresh meat, an' nice hides now an' then. Yep, that there deal worked out jist fine." Her grin became bigger when she added, "That brave what smacked the spear—he was Broken Knife's pop. Broken Knife avoids me, but he sends one of his young men up here once a month with some meat." Her laugh was more of a cackle as she winked at Miguel and added, "And some a that meat still has a brand on it!"

Miguel chuckled softly when he thought of Aunt Betty sharing her house with Flory. The wizened old woman drank whiskey, smoked a pipe, and chewed tobacco. She kept a spittoon beside the table, but her eyes were bad, and she often missed. She also brought her chickens in the house at night to keep the coyotes and foxes from getting them.

No, I had better wire Badger and see if he has something we can rent or buy in Cheyenne. Flory might like that since she will probably want to work with Sadie at Martha's dress shop.

Flory looked at Miguel in question when he chuckled again, but he shook his head.

"Memories, señora Montero. Just remembering this fine day."

Miguel helped Flory into the carriage and turned it north toward the downtown area.

Flory was quiet for a moment as she turned the ring on her finger. She finally took it off and looked inside. She was quiet as she read the inscription.

"Where did you get my ring? I'm sure you didn't have time to buy it here." She paused a moment and asked softly, "Did you buy it for the woman who turned you down?"

Miguel looked at Flory in surprise before he shook his head.

"No, I won it in a poker game this afternoon. I looked for a game where a woman with small hands was playing. Once I found one, I looked over her jewelry. If she had a ring I thought would work, I sat in for a time. It took me four saloons and half of my winnings from last night, but I finally won. I had to put up Demonio's bridle, and he wasn't very happy with me.

"I told him that he didn't need it. I can guide him with my feet. Still, he was pleased to have it back." Miguel grinned at Flory and whispered, "It is much prettier on you. Her fingers were fat, and it barely fit her pinky."

Flory stared at Miguel as she giggled.

"Miguel, I'm not sure we are starting this marriage the right way at all. My wedding ring probably belonged to an old whore, and who knows where she got it."

"Ah, but the first person to wear it wore it with love. See? It says, 'With my love. Forever, for Always.' I think it is the perfect ring. Besides, that padre blessed it and now it is ours."

He hugged Flory and she snuggled up next to him.

"Thank you," she whispered. "It is perfect."

When they arrived at the Pacific House Hotel, Miguel jumped down and lifted Flory out of the buggy. The doorman was there quickly to take the buggy.

"You must be the Monteros. This way, please. Mr. Maynard asked that we give you our best table."

CHAPTER 10

Frank and Jesse James

MIGUEL HELD ONTO FLORY'S ARM AS THEY WERE LED across the large restaurant. He glanced at the men playing billiards in the adjoining room and chuckled. When Flory looked up at him, he nodded toward the men.

"Jesse and Frank James are playing billiards in there as cool as can be. You'd never know they were wanted by the law in half a dozen states. Of course, their uncle owns the billiard hall so why not."

Flory stared at the men for a moment. She was quiet until they were seated. She studied Miguel's face and cautiously asked, "You know them, or do you just know who they are?"

Miguel squeezed Flory's hand.

"I know them. I rode with them on a couple of jobs when I was younger." He winked at her and added, "Before I met a good woman and found a reason to come home every night." When he saw the look of fear on Flory's face, he patted her hand.

"Don't worry. I was a nobody. No one cared if I stayed or left. I left. I have seen them only a few times since then." Miguel leaned back in his seat as he spoke quietly to Flory.

"I never liked robbing folks. I was poor all my life. I wasn't proud of myself for taking from such people as I grew up with. Some say the James brothers are generous and care about the poor, but I disagree. They are for themselves.

"They are polite fellows though. If they stop by the table, smile your pretty smile, and say hello. I won't tell them we just married. I will introduce you as my wife and say I am buying cattle. Both of those things are true, so we won't have to lie."

The waiter came by and handed them menus.

"Mr. Maynard said to put your meal on his tab so choose what you want. The steak is quite tasty if you want a suggestion. We are using Angus-cross cattle now, and the meat is tender."

Flory looked around the busy restaurant and her face lost some of its color.

"I see some of the women in here whom I sew for, and not all of them know I am expecting."

"Ah, but señora, we are leaving tomorrow. What they think does not matter so much. Let them be confused. Just be polite if they come to say hello. Perhaps they will think I am a wealthy cattleman who swept you off your feet. They will be confused but they will ask no questions."

Flory looked across at Miguel and laughed. "I know you are a cowboy. Will we even have money to eat once the baby comes? I might not be able to work for some time after that."

"Señora Montero, my family owns a ranch. Even though I haven't been around much to help, it is still partly mine. And I promise you I will spend more time chasing cows in the future and less time in the saloons.

"Now come. Let us order some of this fine food since your husband does not have to pay today."

Miguel looked up. His body went still as two tall men walked toward him, weaving through the tables. He stood up.

"Hello, to my friends. Frank, Jesse, may I introduce you to my wife? Florence, these gentlemen are Frank and Jesse James. Their home is not far from here." He pointed toward two open chairs.

"Please. Sit down. We were just ordering."

Frank shook Miguel's hand and Jesse did the same. They both bowed to Flory before they turned their eyes back to Miguel.

"We can't stay but we saw you and thought we would say hello. What brings you back this way? You moved West, didn't you?"

Miguel nodded. "Sí, to Cheyenne. I am buying cattle. I ranch with my brother and my brother-in-law. We are introducing black cattle. We plan to cross them with our longhorns." He pointed at the steak that was being set in front of a gentleman at the table beside them. "I hear that combination makes a superior steak."

Jesse studied Flory for a moment and nodded. He finally smiled and put on his hat. He tipped it to her and bowed once again.

"Mrs. Montero, I didn't think I would ever meet the woman who would settle this cowboy down. Best wishes on your trip back home.

"And Miguel, if you ever need a job, be sure to look me up."

Miguel chuckled and shook his head.

"I think, señors, I like my wife. I prefer to go home to her every night. No, I think I will stick with ranching."

The two men turned away and Miguel sat down. He watched the two brothers as they casually walked out of the eating house. He shook his head.

"They are bold. See the man across the room with the heavy gold chain across his chest? Older man. A younger man is across the table from him.

"They are Pinkertons. And still, those brothers stroll through here like they own the place."

Flory saw lots of men in the room with heavy gold chains across their chests, so she wasn't sure who Miguel saw.

"Over there. The third table from the bar." Miguel nodded his head in the direction he was looking again.

"As lawmen, Pinkertons are not limited to a certain jurisdiction. They may arrest men wherever they are found. Bad men to have on your trail. They must not be after the James brothers yet, but they will be. I guess Jesse and Frank just haven't killed the right man yet." Miguel winked at Flory.

"No more talk of bad men. I am reformed. Tonight, I want to enjoy my wife. Do you want to eat quickly so we can play longer, or would you like to make this a long meal?"

Flory blushed a deep red.

"Miguel! Don't talk like that here. Someone might hear you!"

"But señora, we are married. We can talk however we want, yes?"

Flory dropped her eyes and Miguel laughed. He sighed loudly and nodded.

"I think perhaps you want to eat slowly. For you, I will do that. After all, the night is young." He was still smiling when he signaled to the waiter.

CHAPTER 11

A Gentleman

AS THEY WALKED OUT OF THE RESTAURANT, MIGUEL pointed upstairs.

"Perhaps you would like to take a bath? I can ask that a tub be drawn for you. They might even have water in the rooms already."

Flory nodded excitedly. Her smile slowly faded as she looked up at Miguel.

He grinned at her. "I need to take care of my horse and that will take me about fifteen minutes. Thirty if I take a bath myself before I come up.

"Let's get you to our room and I will arrange for a bath." His eyes sparkled with orneriness as he added, "Perhaps the tub will be large enough for both of us."

Flory blushed and didn't respond. When Miguel opened the door, she gasped.

"Look at this room, Miguel. It is so big! And the floor is so soft I just want to take my shoes off." She unlaced her shoes and kicked them off, falling backwards on the bed.

"The bed is so soft. Oh, I can't wait to take a bath."

Miguel's dark eyes were unreadable as he watched his new wife. He cleared his throat and backed out the door.

"I'll see to that water." He slapped his hat against his leg as he walked down the hall.

"Perhaps I should take a cold bath. I'm not sure Flory is ready for all that comes with marrying. It could be a long night."

Miguel was gone for nearly an hour when he finally tapped softly on Flory's door. She didn't answer, so he unlocked it quietly and slid through.

Flory was asleep. Her blonde curls spilled over the pillow, and she was curled in a small ball in the middle of the bed. Miguel gently picked up a lock of her hair and let it slide through his fingers.

"Sí, it is going to be a difficult night." He undressed but paused when he was about to drop his britches.

"I left my longhandles up north, so I'd best leave my pantalones on."

He lifted the covers and slid in next to Flory. She smiled in her sleep and snuggled against him. Miguel looked down at her in surprise as he put his arms around her.

"Maybe this won't be such a bad night after all."

It was nearly midnight when Flory awoke. She realized the person she was lying against was not her sister and she gasped. Miguel's arm was over her chest, and she gently pushed it down. He stirred in his sleep and moved it back to where it was. She lay there quietly for a moment. Finally, she tried to get up, but Miguel's arm was heavy around her.

I can stay here where it is warm and sleep the rest of the night or I can get up. Or I can wake Miguel and make him move over.

She looked over her shoulder at his face and whispered, "Are you awake?" Miguel didn't respond.

Flory scooted down in the bed and slid under his arm. She sat up as she spoke, "Miguel, I know you are awake. I saw you smile."

The moon was shining in the window and Miguel opened one eye. He grinned at her and rolled over on his back with his arms under his head. He was laughing as he watched her.

"I am now. What do you have in mind?"

"I—well I—I don't have anything in mind. You were just very close to me."

"Sí, that is the way married people sleep, or so I have been told. Now come back to bed. This bed is much warmer with you in it. Besides, I can see you shivering."

Flory's eyes were large as she watched him.

"I have never slept with a man before and you make me nervous."

Miguel lifted the blankets. "Come back to bed, Flory. I won't ever force you to do anything with me you don't want to do. Now come. Come and cuddle with me so we can enjoy this nice bed. I think it will not be so comfortable on the train."

Flory stared at Miguel a moment before she slid under the covers. She was shivering and Miguel pulled her close to him.

"Kiss me, Flory. Kiss me just once on our wedding night."

Flory turned her head to look at him and Miguel kissed her gently. She stared up at him and whispered, "Kiss me again, Miguel. I like it when you kiss me."

The room became quiet, and the large moon slipped behind a cloud.

Miguel's voice was soft when he spoke. "Señora Montero, I think I am going to enjoy this married life."

CHAPTER 12

A New Friend

REED AND TEMPLE WERE WAITING AT THE STATION when the train pulled into Lawrence. They both stared from Flory to Miguel.

Miguel grinned at them and pulled Flory up next to him.

"Señors, please say hello to my wife. Flory, these fellows are Reed and Temple. They are going north with us. We need hands and they need a job. I think Angel and Gabe will be pleased."

Flory smiled and her dimples were large. She shook hands with both men. Miguel quickly pointed toward their horses.

"Let's get the horses loaded. This stop is a short one."

While the men were loading the horses, Flory hurried to the small privy. The stench was almost unbearable, and she held her breath as long as she could. A young mother with two small children was waiting just outside the door when she opened it. Men were beginning to congregate, and Flory whispered, "I'll watch the door for you, but hurry. I don't want to miss my train."

The young woman was out quickly and the two of them rushed to the horse tank to wash their hands.

Flory's face was friendly when she asked, "So are you going West? Perhaps we will be on the same train."

"Just to this side of Hays City. My husband is meeting me in a small town called Victoria. We married in Iowa and settled there on a small farm. He came out here to homestead nearly six months ago. He promised to send for me when he had our cabin built. It's not quite done but it is finished enough to live in.

"I have missed him terribly." She smiled at Flory as they sat down. "My name is Esther. And you are?"

"Flory. Flory Whitman but Montero now."

"Is your husband traveling with you?"

Flory nodded excitedly and pointed toward Miguel. He was talking to Demonio as he led him toward the train.

"Yes, we are going to pick up some bulls and then we are headed home to Cheyenne. Miguel just hired some new hands so they will be helping him." She laughed and rolled her eyes. "I'm afraid I won't be much help on a ranch. I have never worked outside, and I can barely cook."

The young woman was quiet as she turned to look at Miguel. The ornery vaquero caught Flory looking in his direction. He swept off his hat and held it over his chest as he blew her a kiss. Flory giggled.

The young woman beside Flory stared from Miguel to Flory and laughed dryly. "Well, isn't he a romantic fellow!"

Flory blushed and nodded. "We haven't been married long. Neither of us expected to fall in love but here we are." She sighed as she sat back in her seat. "And Miguel is so handsome. Sometimes I can barely breathe."

The young woman studied Flory's face from the side and looked down at her growing stomach. She asked carefully, "How long have you been married?"

Miguel slid into the seat on the other side of Flory.

"Ah, time is of so little importance when one is in love, yes? It seems it was only yesterday that Flory became my bride." He patted her stomach and added with a wink, "But of course, it had to be much longer.

"What about you, señora? You take the train to Victoria?" When Esther nodded, Miguel continued, "That is where we go as well. We are buying some black bulls to take north with us. We will cross them with our longhorn cows." He smiled at her and chucked the oldest boy under the chin.

"And you, chico, do you want to be a cowboy someday? Perhaps a vaquero like me. You can ride a fine horse and smile at the ladies." He winked at Flory as he added, "And perhaps someday, you will marry a woman as beautiful as the two who share this seat."

The boy appeared to be around seven and he nodded excitedly.

"I want to be a cowboy, but Pa says I need to be a farmer. He said cowboys don't make any money."

Miguel nodded somberly. "Alas, that is sometimes true, but then it can be said of all endeavors, yes? If one does not work and get just a little lucky, if the cards don't fall the right way from time to time, things can go badly. Life, it can be very difficult." He grinned at the serious young man and winked at him as he whispered, "But if you have a fine caballo—that is a beautiful horse—the women will all look at you. And maybe someday, you will be as lucky in love as your father and me."

The young woman laughed out loud as she shook her head.

"My, you are just full of charm and wind, aren't you!" She put out her hand. "Your wife said your name is Miguel. I am Esther and these are our boys, Noah and Adam. Joe is their father. He will be meeting us in Victoria.

"I haven't seen our homestead yet. Joe said it isn't as green around Victoria as it was in Iowa. However, he was able to buy more land than the original one hundred sixty acres he homesteaded. We are going to milk cows and try to grow wheat." She smiled at Flory as she added, "Joe says everyone needs to eat.

Miguel pulled his hat over his eyes as the two women began to visit. He smiled as he listened to Flory's excited voice. He had dozed off by the time the conversation moved to sewing.

"Oh yes, I did make this dress. I am a seamstress. I hope to work with a woman in Cheyenne whose work is well known, even as far as Kansas City.

"I have worked out of a dress shop in Kansas City for nearly a year. It was a wonderful experience. I am so looking forward to sewing and designing with Mrs. Parker in Cheyenne."

Esther smiled softly as she touched the faded cotton dress she wore.

"I can't remember the last time I had a new dress. Joe works hard but we were just never able to get ahead. I love to sew too. I made both the boys the shirts they are wearing, and I make most of Joe's as well." She smiled at Flory and laughed softly. "I have never made anything so beautiful as your dress though."

Flory paused a moment. She picked up her travel bag and took a package out of it. She held out the package to Esther.

"Take this. One of my clients gave the fabric to me and I don't wear dark colors." She tore a corner of the package open. "You can see the fabric is beautiful. I was going to make a dress for my sister. She is married to Miguel's brother and lives just outside Cheyenne. She doesn't like anything fancy though so I would have to argue with her." She placed the package in Esther's hands. "You take this. Make yourself something pretty and surprise Joe."

Esther's rough hands touched the shiny fabric, but she shook her head.

"I can't. It is much too costly, and we barely know each other."

Flory pushed the package back toward Esther. She wrapped the woman's hands around it as she smiled at her.

"Keep it, Esther. Let me do something nice. I don't have many skills to share with other women so let me give you a gift.

"Besides, the woman I was staying with in Kansas City let me remake as many of her dresses as I wanted." She pointed at the large trunk sitting against the back of the train car. "That is completely full. I am supposed to share them with my sister's friends in Cheyenne." Flory giggled as she whispered, "Maybe one of them will teach me to cook!"

Esther looked startled but she laughed. She took a piece of cake out of her bag and handed it to Flory. She quickly wrote on a piece of paper and gave that to her new friend as well.

"There. I just gave you your first recipe, and I put my address on it. I am an excellent cook so if you ever need more help with cooking, just write to me. I can send you some more of my favorites."

CHAPTER 13

Flory's Confession

ESTHER'S CHILDREN FINALLY FELL ASLEEP, AND THE young mother slept as well. Flory watched them for time. Finally, she turned to Miguel.

"Miguel. Are you awake?" She waited a moment before she poked him. "Miguel!"

Miguel opened one eye as he grinned at her.

"Sí, señora Montero. I am much awake now. What is so important that you must wake me from a beautiful dream about my wedding night?"

Flory stared at him as she slowly blushed.

"Shush, Miguel! Someone will hear you! These seats are close together."

Miguel chuckled. "And what was so important that you needed to ask me now?"

"I have something I must tell you."

Miguel took off his hat and scratched his head while he watched his wife.

Flory twisted her hands together and her face grew paler as she started to speak.

"I'm—I don't know how to cook. Anna did all the cooking before we moved West, and Tillie had a cook who prepared most of their meals. The ones she prepared on her own, she made for Ollie. Those were their special times together, and I stayed out of the kitchen.

"I'm afraid I know little about cooking, and I only have one recipe to follow—for cake."

Miguel sat up in his seat and stared at Flory seriously.

"I think if I had known this yesterday, perhaps I would not have asked you to marry me. Food is quite important to me."

Flory's eyes grew wide as she listened. She sucked in her breath and her face became pale.

Miguel chuckled and winked as he leaned over to Flory. He whispered, "Perhaps we will need to find other things to do that will make up for how hungry I will be every day." Miguel's dark eyes were sparkling. Flory's cheeks turned pink, and she covered her mouth as she tried not to laugh.

"You are very bold, Miguel. I am serious though. I know little of cooking and since I have become pregnant, I can hardly stand the smell of most food."

Miguel studied her serious face and shrugged his shoulders.

"Then perhaps I will cook. I can show you some simple foods that my mother made. Besides, we will see much of Anna and Angel. Gabe and Merina too. They will teach you. Martha as well.

"Of course, if I beg my sister and complain about how hungry I am, she will feed us. I do not think we will be so hungry."

Flory slowly shook her head.

"Where will we live? I can't stay in the bunkhouse with a bunch of men."

"I sent Badger a wire. I told him I was bringing a wife home. I asked him to find us a little house in Cheyenne, one that is not so far from Martha's dress shop. That way, you can walk there if you want.

"Angel and Anna live on the ranch we own with them. It will not be so far for me to ride out to work there every day or even ride to Gabe's if I need to." He patted Flory's hand and kissed her cheek.

"Relax, señora Montero. There is little to worry about except how to make your husband happy. And that you can do.

"Now come. Cuddle up next to me and let us take a nap. I have much work to do when we reach Victoria."

CHAPTER 14

Victoria, Kansas

FLORY POINTED OUT THE WINDOW OF THE TRAIN excitedly.

"There are two towns here, Miguel. One to the north and one to the south. Which one is Victoria?"

Miguel pointed to the south. "That is Victoria and the one to the north and east is Herzog. I am thinking they will be one town someday since they are only a half mile apart." Miguel laughed and gestured with his hands.

"There were originally lots of remittance men in Victoria." When Flory, Temple, and Reed all looked at Miguel in confusion, he added, "They are young men who receive money from their families, mostly in England and Scotland. They don't work. They just play all day. They're about as useful as a four-card flush.

"This town has a hunt club and even a racetrack, all built with their money." He grinned as he added, "Unfortunately for them, when their parents learned that the family money was not being used to buy farms and build businesses, they cut off the funds. Many of the playboys went back home.

"Some of the early settlers followed as well when they realized not all the ground was suitable for farming. Some of the ground is good for farming but there is much grass here as well." Miguel pointed to the north.

"The town of Herzog was founded by people who call themselves Volga Germans. I don't know what that means but they are hard workers." Miguel stared at the pens where ten black bulls were standing.

"Look there, amigos! Our bulls are already here. Let's get them watered and maybe we can be back on this train today."

The three men rushed off the train and Flory watched them from the open door. The ticket master hurried by, cursing under his breath. When he saw Flory, he stopped and his rough face turned a dark red.

"My apologies, ma'am. The track is damaged west of here and we are going to be delayed for at least two hours, maybe longer while it is repaired." He pointed south with his thumb.

"You might want to get some food while you have time." He paused and added, "I know your tickets were to go on into Cheyenne tomorrow, but we can change them if you can get those bulls loaded today."

Flory smiled prettily at him before she rushed down the steps. She ran toward the cattle pens and climbed up on the fence. Reed saw her and hollered at Miguel.

Miguel rode his horse toward her with concern on his face.

"The train is delayed for two or three hours. Now you can for sure get the bulls back on the train today!" Flory's face showed her excitement. Miguel listened and nodded as a smile crossed his face.

"Reed! You and Temple get those bulls fed and watered. I am going to try to track Grant's niece down and see if I can get a bill of sale. Since the bulls are here, she should already have payment."

Miguel rode back to where Flory stood on the fence. He handed her $3. "See if you can find us something to eat. If we are lucky, we will be in Cheyenne by morning!" He turned Demonio south and rode at a trot toward the livery. Flory could see him talking to a man. Miguel nodded and turned his horse south out of town at a lope.

Flory jumped off the fence and turned just in time to see a man swing Esther around before he set her in his wagon. Esther was laughing and she pulled on her husband's arm when she saw Flory.

"Joe, this is Flory Montero. We met on the train. Flory and her husband are buying some black bulls to take north with them."

Joe smiled as he looked toward Flory and nodded. "They do well here, and since they are from Scotland, I am guessing they will do well up north too.

"George Grant passed away just recently. He left his land to a niece. Her husband is running things now." He pointed his thumb south.

"They just live south of town about five miles and back east a mile or so. Grant put together a nice chunk of land. His niece wants to hang onto it."

Flory listened closely to Joe as he talked. She smiled at Esther and the children.

"Is your farm south of town as well?"

"No, I settled north of here. We're surrounded by a bunch of Germans, and I have to work hard to keep up with them. Those boys know how to farm. Good people too." Joe waved his whip as he added, "We need to get home. We have six cows to milk. They will be lined up and waiting on me." He smiled at Esther. "It will sure be nice to have some help outside.

"It was good to meet you, Mrs. Montero. Best of wishes on the rest of your trip." Joe clucked to his team and wheeled them around to head north. A child was seated on either side of him, and the little family looked happy.

Flory's brow puckered slightly as she watched them. "Six cows!" she murmured. "I have never even milked one cow let alone six." She hurried down the street toward a shop where people were eating fresh bread with some kind of meat filling inside. The sign in front said "Bierocks."

CHAPTER 15

A Good Trade

FLORY SLOWED AND STOPPED AS SHE STARED IN THE window. The shop was busy, and the smell of fresh bread was appealing. She could smell beef and something else that she didn't recognize. She paused before she hurried in.

The clerk's smile was large and even though her English was broken, Flory caught enough to understand that bierocks were fresh bread filled with ground beef, cooked cabbage, and onions. She bought two for each of the men and one for herself.

"These smell wonderful. They should be filling too. And looking at the number you are selling, they must be quite popular here." Flory smiled as she placed $2 in the woman's hand. "Are they hard to make? I think my husband will like them."

The old woman smiled at her and nodded. She called someone in the back and a young girl rushed out with a piece of paper in her hands. The old woman handed it to Flory.

"For you. Make them for your man. They make him strong and help him to work hard."

Flory looked from the woman's smiling face to the piece of paper. When she realized the woman had given her a recipe for the bierocks, Flory's breath caught in her throat.

"Thank you so much!" She pulled a dainty handkerchief from her pocket and handed it to the woman. "You take this as my way of saying thank you. That is tatting around the edges, and I embroidered the letter "W" in the center." She pointed at herself. "Florence Whitman."

The old woman took the handkerchief with shaky hands. She stared at it before she pointed at herself.

"I am Wiesner, Liliosa Wiesner. Thank you." She gripped Flory's hand with hers. "Go with God."

Flory's smile was large as she backed away from the counter. She waved again from the door and rushed back toward the train.

"My second recipe! And they smell delicious. And I am not even heaving." She slowed to a walk and stopped to sit on a bench beside the town well. She bit into the bierock and closed her eyes as she chewed.

"So delicious. I can't wait to share these with Miguel." Flory sat on the bench for nearly an hour as she watched the people hurry by.

She heard someone call and looked up to see Miguel riding toward her. He was smiling when he stopped.

"I see you are eating our supper without me. Come. Ride with me back to the train." His dark eyes twinkled as he reached down his hand. "We are married now so you can ride on my lap."

Flory stood and looked around. She started to shake her head, but Miguel grabbed her and lifted her up in front of him.

"Now give me a bite of what you are eating so I can see if I like it."

They rode back to the train station. Flory was talking excitedly. Miguel was smiling as he listened to his wife. He chewed contentedly.

"Sí, I have eaten these before. Once when I went through Ellis with a herd of cattle. You can make these?"

"Yes, the woman who sold them to me gave me her recipe. Then I gave her my handkerchief and her last name started with 'W.' She was so nice." Flory chattered on and Miguel pulled her closer with a smile.

Flory didn't notice the older woman who frowned at the young couple, nor did she hear what the woman said.

"Just look at that young woman riding on that cowboy's lap. I declare. *I* certainly would never do that." She clucked and muttered to herself as she hurried on down the street. The old man walking beside her said nothing, but he grinned and winked at Miguel.

Miguel slid Flory down onto the train platform. Reed and Temple had the bulls loaded and the train whistled. Temple grabbed Miguel's horse and led Demonio quickly onto the train. He was back shortly and the four settled into their seats.

Reed took the bierocks tentatively and handed one to Temple. The quiet cowboy took a bite and nodded his head.

"My ma made these some 'fore she passed away." He pointed to the west. "I grew up south of Ellis. Pop was from Texas, but Ma grew up here." He chewed contentedly as he looked out the window. "Ma didn't want to leave after they married so Pa ran a few cattle an' farmed some. I didn't want to farm so I left. I only had one sister an' her husband runs things now."

Flory looked away from the window and smiled at Temple.

"Do you want to stop and visit them? We will be passing right through Ellis, and we are a day early."

Temple shook his head and chuckled.

"Naw, the folks are gone an' my sis' husband thinks I'm after the farm. He'd probably sic his hired hands on me. He's a big man in the community now. Started an elevator an' bought more land. My sis likes her standin' in the community, an' they made it clear they didn't need no problem brother messin' up their lives." He grinned and added, "I ain't always been so tame as I am now." Temple took another bite and laughed softly.

"I reckon I'll go on north with you. I ain't been farther up than Nebraska. I liked those Sandhills, but I never stay put in one place. My feet get to itchin' an' I move on." He grinned at Miguel as he added, "So don't expect no long-term employment from me. I doubt I'll be around come next spring."

Miguel laughed and his eyes sparkled as he looked over at Flory.

"And that, my amigo, is why you need to find a good woman. If señora Flory hadn't married me, I would be in Mexico by now, probably in jail. Sí, a good woman is what you need."

Flory laughed and the four visited for a time. She finally fell asleep with her head on Miguel's shoulder.

Reed was quiet for a time. He finally looked at Miguel seriously.

"I think you should be careful. Old Harold Littleton is a mean man. He puts on a nice face in public but in private, he's a whole 'nother deal. Beats on his wife an' cheats anyone he can without gettin' caught.

"I don't know what you did to his son but if you maimed him bad, his pop will be lookin' for revenge. He dotes on Cletus an' he'll be comin' for you. 'Course, it won't be him. He'll hire whoever he thinks he needs to for a fast, clean job." Reed added softly, "And not just you. He'll be after your little wife too. He'll try to wipe out anyone who can shed a bad light on him or his son."

Miguel was still as he listened. When Reed finished, Miguel's smile was cold.

"Then we will be ready for him, yes? Or perhaps, I should go back to Kansas City. Maybe I should make this man—poof. He could just disappear."

Reed shook his head. "Not you. They'll be lookin' for you. Maybe I should go. Temple too. We would blend in with the other cowboys who show up there after drives."

Miguel stared at his friends for a moment but shook his head.

"Let's wait. If he sends someone for Flory or for me, then you can go. Perhaps they will think that Cheyenne is too far away."

Reed frowned and shook his head. "You watch out. He'll send a man, maybe several. An' whoever he sends, they'll be finishers. Don't expect 'em to brace you face on neither. They'll probably try to shoot you from cover."

Miguel's face was hard as he listened. He finally shrugged. "It has been tried, and still, I am here. Let us sleep now. Cheyenne is over fourteen hours away so those bulls will need to be watered somewhere. I think it will be a long ride for all of us."

CHAPTER 16

Home to Cheyenne

THE TRAIN STATION IN CHEYENNE WAS CROWDED. Since the train was nearly three hours late, those who had been waiting to board were anxious to get on. The ticket master rushed by, his florid face even redder than normal.

"Get those horses and bulls offloaded. We need to pull out in ten minutes, and we are already late!"

Miguel and his men rushed to open pens. The bulls were soon off the train. Temple led the horses off while Reed grabbed their tack. Flory was trying to drag her heavy case when Miguel appeared. He grabbed one end while another cowboy grabbed the other. They hoisted it off the train and onto the platform. Miguel was breathing heavily. He grinned at Flory.

"I think, Mrs. Montero, you must learn to travel lighter. Your trunk is more than this strong vaquero can carry by himself. Besides, these hands were meant for caressing beautiful women, not for lifting heavy trunks."

Flory blushed prettily and Miguel laughed as he lifted her out of the train.

"Come, let's find a buggy. Perhaps Rooster will drive you to Anna's—unless you want to ride with us to Gabe's ranch."

Badger appeared in the crowd. He winked at Miguel and bowed to Flory.

"Miss Flory, I have my Martha's buggy here. Would you'ins like a ride ta yer new home? It is jist down the street a piece. Annie Small an' her husband, Tiny, live right next door." He winked at Miguel and added, "I figgered a young woman such as yerself might like womenfolk next door since this durn cowboy won't never be ta home."

Flory rushed toward Badger and hugged him.

"Badger, it is so good to see you. And thank you for finding a house for us. Miguel told me he wired you, but I didn't know if you could find one on such short notice."

Badger's bright blue eyes twinkled and he nodded.

"Oh, it were a chore all right, but I got 'er done.

"Now ya lazy cowhands, grab that there trunk. I ain't a young feller no more an' if Miss Flory travels like her sis does, I know it's too durn heavy fer me ta drag." He nodded toward the tired bulls.

"I had Rooster bring some hay up fer them there bulls. Be sure ta pay 'im 'fore you'ins head out ta Gabe's. Miss Anna is teachin' today but I reckon she'll be by oncet school's out." He hugged Flory again before he lifted her up. His voice cracked as he added, "Good ta have you'ins here, Miss Flory. Yur sis missed you'ins, an' the rest of us did too." He grinned as he looked over at Miguel.

"'Sides, Miguel here's been a lookin' fer a good woman in all the wrong places. 'Bout time he found one worth keepin'.

"Now ya fellers come on with me. My Martha's been a workin' over ta the Monteros' new house. She's been a fussin' over breakfast since early mornin'. Ya jist as well eat a bit an' let them there bulls rest some 'fore ya trail out ta Gabe's." He reached out his hand to the two smiling cowboys.

"Badger McCune's the name. Welcome ta Cheyenne, fellers. We's a little short on women here, but the crowd you'ins 'ill be hangin' 'round have some mighty good cookers.

"Now fork some hay ta them there bulls. You'ins cin foller us over ta the Montero's. Don't take too long though 'cause I ain't a waitin' on ya ta eat."

Badger wheeled the team around while the three men rushed to fork some hay. Temple opened a gate so the bulls had access to water. The three men mounted their horses and loped to catch Badger. They could hear the animated little man talking long before they caught up with him.

CHAPTER 17

Flory's Welcome

MARTHA LOOKED UP WITH A SMILE WHEN SHE HEARD Badger's voice. Her breath caught when she saw Flory's growing stomach and then her smile reappeared. She rushed to the doorway and waved at the young people.

"You all come on in here and eat. And, Flory, you give me a hug. Sadie was so excited when I told her you were moving out here. We are both hoping you will want to help her in my shop. She just can't keep up." Martha hugged Flory and was still talking as she dragged the younger woman through the door.

Martha pointed at a bedroom just beyond the kitchen.

"You fellows haul that trunk in there. This house has two bedrooms but that one is the biggest. And Flory, that quilt is for you and Miguel. Some of the women here in town get together to quilt once a month. We rushed to finish this one when we heard you and Miguel married. That is called a double wedding ring design." Martha ushered Flory to a chair. She kissed her cheek and whispered, "I am so pleased you married Miguel. He is a good man."

Martha rushed to the stove.

"Now you men sit down. Badger ate early this morning, but I'm guessing he is hungry by now. Just make yourselves comfortable, and I will have a plate in front of each of you shortly."

Temple and Reed were quiet as they started to eat. However, Badger made up for their lack of conversation. Martha mostly smiled although she stepped in if the conversation slowed. The men relaxed as they ate and by the time the meal was finished, the conversation was brisk.

Martha looked over at Miguel.

"Now, Miguel, you bring Flory over this evening. All the kids are coming in and we are going to have a little post-wedding party. And Flory, you don't have to bring anything, so you just rest this afternoon."

Flory smiled at Martha. When she finished, she hurried to help clear the table.

Miguel kissed Flory's cheek and motioned to the door.

"I'll bring some water in so you can take a bath. I'll plan to be home by five." He rushed out the door and was soon back with two buckets of water. Martha pulled a tub out from under the cabinet and Miguel dumped one bucket in the tub. He set the other on the floor and hurried to catch up with his men.

Badger nodded toward the door. "I'm a goin' ta head on down to the mercantile and pick up that order of provisions. We'uns 'ill be back shortly." He was gone in a rush.

Flory hurried to heat some water to wash the dishes. She smiled at Martha.

"Thank you so much for finding this house for us. I know we didn't give you much notice." Flory's bottom lip trembled as she spoke, and she turned away quickly as she wiped her eyes.

Martha turned the young woman around and placed her hands on her shoulders. She spoke softly as she smiled at Flory.

"Flory, you and I both know that baby growing inside of you is a gift from God regardless of the story surrounding it. And that is how it will always be treated. You don't have to explain anything to me. Now you have your cry, but just know your baby won't be loved any less than the rest of our grandchildren."

A sob caught in Flory's throat, and she sank down in a chair as she looked at Martha.

"Miguel is not the father. I don't even know who is, but somehow Miguel found out. I'm not sure what he did to the man. He didn't tell me. He just said he made sure that man wouldn't be treating any other women the way he treated me." Flory laughed through her tears as she added, "Miguel asked me to marry him the next day. I knew I was being impetuous, but I said yes. We were married in Kansas City. And Martha, we are so happy! It is like I found a part of me that was missing. He is kind and gentle, wild and funny, and so loving all wrapped up in one." She smiled as she whispered, "I've never loved a man before. I've never even been faithful to one man. But—but—Miguel is different. I love him, Martha."

Martha smiled at Flory and kissed her cheek.

"And that is all that counts. That baby is Miguel's now and that is how we will leave it. Now you let me wash these dishes." Martha hurried to the sink as she continued to talk.

"We bought this house from a couple who wanted to move to California. The wife didn't like all the snow we have here. She said she was leaving with or without her husband. She was in a hurry, so we bought everything—lock, stock, and barrel. They left nearly all they owned right here and took the train west with just one trunk between them.

"Badger was able to get it for a bargain price so you can rent from us, or you can buy it. Either is fine with us. You stay here as long as you want." She smiled at Flory again.

"I do hope you will come to work in my shop. I'm sure you have a little time before that baby is due to arrive. The ladies I quilt with are hoping you will join our quilting group too." Martha chuckled as she added, "Although I think it is maybe because they want to pepper you with questions about Kansas City and all the fashion news—maybe even more than having another set of stitching fingers."

By the time Badger arrived, Martha and Flory had the little kitchen cleaned and shining. Flory hugged Martha. She hesitated a moment before she asked, "Do you think you can teach me to cook, Martha? I know little about cooking or anything in the kitchen to be truthful. I want to learn though. I want to be able to make meals for my family."

Martha beamed and nodded. "Let's start Saturday afternoon after we close the shop. Do you have something you want to try?"

Flory rushed to her traveling bag and pulled out the bierock recipe.

"A woman in Kansas gave this recipe to me. Both Miguel and I liked them. Lots of foods make me sick, but these didn't. They were delicious too." She showed Martha a second small sheet of paper.

"I'd like to make this cake too. I met a friendly young woman on the train, and she gave me this recipe for the cake she shared." Flory blushed as she added, "I am embarrassed I know so little about cooking, but I have never cared before. Anna did most of the cooking when we lived together, and Tillie had a full-time cook. Besides, I don't really care what I eat. Sometimes I go all day without eating. Food just isn't that important to me.

"Miguel works hard though. He says he isn't concerned about my lack of experience in the kitchen, but I want to learn to cook for him."

Martha smiled and hugged Flory again.

"We'll have you cooking in no time." Martha laughed as she whispered, "You know, I can't darn to save my soul. I pay a woman to darn Badger's socks. I have never told him I can't darn, and he never comments even though I am sure he knows. I trade that woman fresh bread, and we are all happy.

"Now you rest up so you can visit this evening. I know how tiring traveling can be, especially when you are carrying a little one," and Martha hurried out the door.

CHAPTER 18

Sisters and Brothers

FLORY HAD FINISHED HER BATH AND WAS BUTTONING her dress when she heard Anna's voice. She rushed outside to meet her sister.

Anna hugged Flory and then looked at her stomach in surprise. She frowned but before she could speak, Angel took each sister by the arm. He led them toward the house as he smiled at them.

"Señora Flory, I think it is good you have decided to move to Cheyenne. My wife has missed her sister. I was afraid she would make me move to Kansas City and then what? I don't know what a handsome vaquero such as myself would do there. I would have to get a job entertaining the ladies and I don't think my Anna would like that so much."

Anna looked at her husband in surprise and he shook his head slightly as he smiled at her. He called behind him to the children who were racing around the yard.

"Zach and Amanda—come and tell your auntie hello. Auntie Flory married your Uncle Miguel, and she is going live here in this house."

A young boy and small girl came running into the house. Flory dropped down onto the floor to hug them.

Amanda stared at Flory's stomach and then looked up at her face.

"Auntie Flory, your tummy is much bigger than it was when I saw you last."

Anna frowned and whispered to her, "Shush, Amanda. That is not polite."

Flory laughed and put Amanda's hand on her stomach.

"That is because there is a baby in there. See, you can feel it kick and move around."

Amanda's eyes became large as she felt the baby move beneath her hand. She looked back at Anna.

"Momma! Feel Auntie Flory's stomach. That baby is running around inside of her." She frowned a little and then asked, "How do babies get inside mommy's tummies? I have always wanted to know that. And how do they get out?"

Her eyes were large as she asked Anna, "Do you have a baby in your tummy, Momma?"

Angel chuckled as he lifted Amanda up and swung her around.

"God puts them in there and he decides when they should come out. Now why don't you two get those cookies your mother made. I think we should all have one."

Angel smiled down at Anna as he pulled her closer to him. He winked at Flory before he spoke.

"Your sister does have a bambino in her stomach, but she has not told anyone yet. I think it will come in the summer, probably while I am very busy. My wife, she doesn't worry about making my life so hard. I think—" Angel laughed when Anna bumped him with her elbow.

"Angel wanted to tell everyone immediately. I wanted to wait until I started to show, but he said he is going to tell everyone tonight. I think this little one should arrive in August or September. Our little school may be looking for a teacher again this fall."

Anna took Flory's arm and pulled her into the bedroom. She looked at Flory closely as she asked, "When are you due, Flory? And why didn't you tell me you were expecting? I'm your sister. You could have told me."

Flory's eyes filled with tears.

"I didn't tell you because I wasn't planning to keep the baby. Tillie and Oliver were going to find a family to adopt it. Miguel didn't even know I was pregnant until he came to see me. I—he—the baby is not Miguel's." Flory's voice cracked as she whispered, "Even I don't know who the father is."

Anna's eyes opened wide as she listened to her sister. She frowned at her.

"What do you mean you don't know who the father is? Good grief, Flory!"

Flory began to cry, and Anna's face crumbled. She hugged her sister.

"Oh, Flory. I should have followed my heart and gone to Kansas City. Angel was right. I have been so worried about you. I just knew something was wrong. I did tell him I was going to see you as soon as school was out to make sure you were not in trouble. I wanted to leave right away, but I could not leave with school in session. Then Miguel told us he was going to Kansas City. I felt a little better because I knew he would tell me if you were sick. I never dreamed you were carrying a child." Tears filled Anna's eyes as she hugged her little sister.

Flory pulled away and looked up at her sister. "I didn't tell you because you would have come, and how would that have helped me or you? A man did me wrong, Anna. Miguel said he drugged me and that's why I can't remember who it was or anything about what happened.

"Miguel found out though. He did something to the man who was responsible. Miguel won't talk about it though, so I don't know what happened.

"When he arrived, I tried to tell him I was pregnant, but he already knew. When he came back the next morning, he asked me to marry him. I knew I shouldn't, but I said yes. It just felt right, Anna."

Anna hugged her sister. "Flory," she whispered, I am so glad you are here.

"Miguel's wire to Angel said, 'Bulls coming Tuesday. Bringing two hired hands and a wife.' Angel and I were shocked." Anna kissed Flory's cheek and whispered, "And I am so pleased you married Miguel. Not only have I missed you, but I can see your contentment. That makes me so happy."

Anna stepped back and looked into her sister's face. She held Flory's shoulders and asked softly, "Did you tell Sampson?"

Tears leaked from Flory's eyes as she nodded.

"I tried to tell him. We spent quite a bit of time together. Not exclusively but we always had fun. He was good friend—at least I thought he was.

"He picked me up from work one evening shortly after I found out I was with child. He kissed me for the first time before he lifted me into the buggy. I think he was going to ask me to marry him—at least that is what the look in his eyes told me.

"When I tried to tell him, he wouldn't let me finish. I'm not sure what I said because I was crying. He just held up his hand as he stared at me. His face showed so many emotions—shock, hurt, anger—no not anger—total fury.

"He lifted me into the buggy and took me to Tillie's without talking. When I tried to talk to him, he wouldn't look at me. He just looked straight ahead and said, 'We have nothing more to discuss.'

"When we arrived at Tillie's, he walked me to the door and said, 'Please tell Anna I will be selling the mine. I will mail her the paperwork when the sale is completed." He looked me in the eyes and added, "There is no reason for you or me to ever speak again.'

"That was the last I heard of him. Tillie told me he left the next morning. I stopped going anywhere but work after that. I wasn't going to tell anyone else. Of course, that wasn't going to work for long because I started to show.

"And then Miguel came to see me. I—he—his reaction was not what I expected.

"Oh, Anna, I know Miguel and I were foolish and silly for marrying so quickly, but I am so happy. I found my true love, Anna!"

Both sisters were laughing and wiping tears away as they walked into the kitchen. Angel smiled. *Yes, it is good Flory and Miguel married. These sisters have missed each other.*

CHAPTER 19

SETTLING IN

FLORY WAS SOON WORKING WITH SADIE IN MARTHA'S shop. It was everything she had hoped it would be. After two weeks, she was much more comfortable and was enjoying her work.

She had just finished measuring a woman for a dress when Nate appeared. He was in a hurry and rushed by her, barely speaking.

"Martha, Gabe sent me to town to pick up Doc. He thinks Merina's baby will come today. Merina refused to come in and see the doctor. She said she is not yet in labor, and it would be a wasted trip. She said she is not ready yet. She has more work to do before this baby arrives.

"He was hoping you would come out and watch the little ones for a couple of days just in case he is right."

Flory had followed Nate back into the shop. She stepped forward with a smile on her face.

"Let me go, Nate. I am finished with my appointments for the day. I can go with you now. I'll grab my coat." She paused and blushed slightly as she looked at Martha, "If that's all right with you."

Martha nodded and laughed. "That is fine. I'll come out on Friday night so you can go home. I'll see you on April 23."

She was laughing as Flory rushed out the door. She turned toward Sadie with a smile.

"My what a flood of babies we are going to have around here. Flory and now Anna too. Why we will have three little cousins all the same age."

Sadie looked up with a smile on her face. "Add Annie to that list. She and Tiny are expecting as well. I'm not sure how far along she is but she is getting quite big. Of course, she is a small woman and Tiny is huge. Who knows how big her baby will be.

"We are going to need more quilts and quite soon. It's a good thing we started our monthly quilting bees."

Both women watched as Nate helped Flory into the buggy. The two were laughing and talking as Nate wheeled the buggy around and hurried his team toward Doc's house.

Sadie smiled and laughed softly.

"Nate is such a sweet boy. I hope he marries a woman who appreciates his heart when that time comes."

Martha nodded as she smiled.

"Flory too. She's a little sweetheart. And what a pair she and Miguel are. They were so cute together at Anna and Angel's wedding dance. Still, I never dreamed they would marry. Both were such free spirits.

"That little Flory is a worker too. She can get more done in a day than most women in two. And she's so excited to learn how to cook.

"Yes, I think she and Miguel bring the best out in each other, and I can't wait to meet this new little one."

Sadie laughed and the two women visited quietly as they turned back to their work.

CHAPTER 20

Strangers on the Road

FLORY WAITED IN THE BUGGY WHILE NATE RUSHED inside Doc's little office to talk to the young doctor. He was back quickly. He grabbed the lines and turned the team south toward Gabe's ranch.

"Doc is coming?"

Nate nodded. "He wanted to bring his own rig. He was with a patient. Josie said she would help him finish so he could hurry along." Nate frowned slightly as he looked over at Flory.

"I saw several strangers in town. They looked like rough characters. You didn't see any new faces in Martha's shop, did you?"

Flory stared at Nate for a moment and slowly nodded.

"There was a man in this morning. He was only there for about five minutes. He said he was interested in a shirt but when Sadie offered to measure him in the outside room, he changed his mind and left.

"He was a large man, quite rough. I was glad Sadie didn't have to measure him. His clothes were filthy, and he didn't look like he had bathed in some time."

Nate grinned and then his face became more serious.

"You didn't recognize him, did you? Miguel wants to know whenever we see any strangers, especially if they go to Martha's shop."

Flory stared at Nate again. She could feel her stomach contract with fear. She took a shaky breath, but she forced herself to smile.

"I will describe him to Miguel. I had never seen him before." She smiled and took Nate's arm.

"Now tell me why Gabe thinks Merina might be in labor. I need to take lessons."

Nate laughed and the two of them visited for the next three miles.

They were about five miles south of Cheyenne when three riders rode up behind them.

Nate frowned when the riders slowed their horses and began to follow the buggy. He placed his rifle between his legs and handed Flory a six gun.

"Slide this under your skirt. I am going to slow the team down so those men pass us. I don't like it when men follow me. And if we take off fast, you drop down on the floor. I don't want you to catch a stray bullet."

Nate pulled back on the lines to bring the team to a slow trot. As the men came alongside the buggy, he nodded at them.

"Morning, fellows. Thought you might be in more of a hurry than me, so I decided to let you pass."

Nate's voice was friendly, but his blue eyes watched the riders carefully. Two of the riders went on by, but the third one slowed his horse down even more to keep pace with the buggy.

"Howdy, ma'am. You wouldn't be Miguel Montero's wife, would you?"

Flory stared at the man a moment. She nodded just as Nate bumped her side. She glanced at him. Nate's eyes were hard, and he was moving the rifle slowly across his lap. Flory felt fear rise in her chest like bile. It was so great that she almost gasped for air. She pushed her fear down and took a shaky breath as she smiled at the man.

"Yes, Miguel should be meeting us on the road. He was coming to town to pick me up. When Nate came by the shop, I decided to ride out with him." She smiled again before she added, "We are meeting Miguel's brother and our brother-in-law. We are selling cattle tomorrow, so the local ranches pulled extra hands in to get ready to gather."

Nate listened and kept his face still. He knew Flory had just told a lie. He had guessed the rough man riding beside them was the same man who had been in the shop earlier. Now he knew it was true and the two of them were in danger.

The two riders in front turned their horses sharply in front of the buggy. The team stopped suddenly. They reared and tried to turn when the riders pushed their mounts closer. One man reached for the lines and Nate whipped the team. He shoved Flory to the floor as he raced his team between the two riders.

The man riding beside them cursed and grabbed for his rifle.

"Stop them! Littleton said to kill the Montero gal, and we can take care of that right here!" he roared as he spurred his horse.

Flory gasped and Nate leaned over the seat as he raced the team down the rough road.

He grabbed the six gun beside Flory and fired it behind him three times.

"Flory, you be ready to jump. We are taking this road way too fast. If we hit a rock, this buggy could flip. But don't you be afraid. Anybody who hears those three shots will know we need help. Now you be ready. And hang on until I tell you to jump!"

The horses were running full speed. Between the men chasing them and the gunfire, the team was spooked. The buggy's right front wheel hit a large rock and the buggy careened to the left. The back wheel hit the same rock and the buggy started to flip.

Nate grabbed Flory's hand and jerked her up.

"Jump and hang onto me!" Nate gripped the rifle in one hand and wrapped his other arm around Flory as they dove out of the buggy. They jumped just as the buggy flipped on its side. The frightened horses kept running and the buggy was dragged sideways for nearly fifty yards before the tongue broke and the buggy splintered.

Nate tried to land with Flory on top of him to protect her. The fall nearly knocked the wind out of him, and he almost lost his rifle. The riders were charging their horses down on the two people when Nate began firing his rifle. He shot the closest man and winged the second. The third rider turned his horse straight for them. Nate threw his body over Flory's just before the man ran his horse over them. Then all three men were gone.

Pain filled Nate's body. He hurt everywhere and his head was pounding. He couldn't see and he rubbed his eyes as he felt for his rifle. Something wet was running down his face. He rolled off Flory and tried to stand. His leg collapsed under him and he fell. His heart was pounding, and terror filled him when he saw the remaining two riders turn their horses again. They raced back toward the two people on the ground. This time, Nate aimed his rifle for the closest horse. The animal broke stride and reared as it went over backwards. The second rider turned his horse and raced north toward Cheyenne.

Nate struggled to his feet. He used the rifle as a cane and stumbled toward the downed horse. The rider was dead, and Nate fell as he tried to turn around. He pulled on his rifle as he tried to get up, but his leg wouldn't hold his weight. He dragged himself back to where Flory lay on the ground.

Flory wasn't moving. Her right leg was bent at an unnatural angle and her face had no color. When he put his hand under her body, he could feel the wetness of blood.

"Flory! Flory! You wake up now. The boys will be coming and Doc too." Nate tried to lift Flory's head, but he passed out and fell to the ground beside her.

CHAPTER 21

TROUBLE!

GABE'S HANDS LOOKED UP WHEN THEY HEARD THE three gunshots. They rushed as a body for their horses and followed Miguel up the road. Two men caught the frightened team and tried to stop them. A third rider joined them, and they finally slowed the team enough for a rider to jump astride one horse. He gathered the loose lines and sawed on them to bring the horse to a stop. The rest of the riders raced on up the road.

They arrived at the gory scene just as Doc appeared from the other direction. He pulled his buggy around and was off before it even stopped.

"Don't touch them! Let me check them over before you move them!"

Gabe slid off his horse and dropped down beside Nate. The young man stirred and struggled to stand. Gabe shook his head. He pointed at the dead outlaw in front of them.

"Were there more than two?"

Nate nodded. He rubbed his eyes roughly as he tried again to stand up.

"Flory? Is she going to be all right? It's my fault. I flipped the buggy."

Doc was quiet as he checked the young mother. His eyes were grim when he looked up.

"Bring me that board with bands on it from the back of my buggy. It's under the seat. I don't want Flory moving around if possible. We'll slide her in the back of my buggy. Miguel, you ride back there with her. If she comes to, you keep her still.

"Nate, you come with me too. I want to look you over as well."

Gabe looked around for Angel. Jonesy caught his eye.

"Angel is gone. He took off as soon as Nate said there were three men. I don't know who all rode with him, but Temple and Reed were with him for sure."

Gabe nodded. His blue eyes were like pieces of glass in his face.

"Nate, I've got to get back to Merina. As soon as the baby comes, I'll be in to check on you." He looked over at Jonesy and then back at Nate. "Any idea who these fellows are?"

Nate shook his head and then winced.

"Flory said a stranger came in Martha's shop this morning. She lied when one of them started asking her questions so I'm guessing that was him.

"They rode up behind us. I wasn't sure what to do. I thought they might be trouble, so I slowed down to let them go by.

"Two of them grabbed for the horses and that's when I whipped the team and ran it between them. The horses were running full out when the buggy flipped." His face was angry when he added, "They rode down on us. I got the first one and winged the second one. The third one rode his horse right over top of us. Him and the one I winged were fixing to do it again, but I managed to shoot one of the horses. It landed on top of its rider and killed him. That's when the third fellow took off out of here."

Gabe's face was hard as he listened to his little brother.

"They mention any names?"

"Yeah, one yelled that Littleton wanted Flory dead. I didn't know who that was, but Flory seemed to know. She was even more scared then."

Gabe looked over toward Miguel. The slim rider was leaning over Flory talking to her. He looked up when Nate spoke.

"I will be making a trip to Kansas City. This stops today." Miguel's voice was soft, but Gabe heard the deadly undertone in it.

He walked over to Miguel and squeezed his shoulder. "Angel will find him, brother. You won't have to make that trip."

Miguel shook his head. "No, I go for the head of the snake. The head must be removed before the snake stops biting."

Gabe didn't respond. He squeezed Miguel's shoulder again and turned toward the short rider waiting beside him.

"Jonesy, you get over to your bosses' ranch and find Molly. I don't care if you have to ride clear to Laramie. Find her and bring her to my place. I don't want to deliver that baby alone."

Only Tobe remained with Gabe, and they turned their horses toward home. They both watched as Jonesy raced his horse toward Lance's house. Six more riders were headed north toward Cheyenne to make sure Angel had all the help he needed. Doc turned his buggy around slowly and followed them.

Gabe and Tobe pushed their horses to a lope and were soon in the ranch yard. The house was quiet. Gabe dropped his reins and rushed inside.

CHAPTER 22

THE FIRST BIRTH ON THE DIAMOND H

Merina was kneeling on the floor of the bedroom when Gabe rushed into the house.

"It's coming. The baby. It's coming," she panted. She pointed at his hands. "Boil some water—and wash your hands."

Merina sucked her breath in sharply and sank back on her haunches.

Emilia was staring at her sister with big eyes and Gabe grabbed her. He led her to the door.

"You go with Tobe and take care of Watie. He needs to be rubbed down and you can help him."

Tobe was headed to the barn but when he heard Gabe, he stopped. He led the horses back to the house with a smile on his face.

"Come on, Emilia. You help me rub your Pa's horse down. Then you and I can take Barleycorn for a ride. I know where there are some chokecherries. They aren't ripe yet, but I'll show you where they are. We can smell the flowers now and you can pick the berries when they turn purple."

Emilia looked up at Gabe and then ran outside. Tobe lifted her up and she talked excitedly to him as he led the horses across the yard.

Gabe rushed into the kitchen. He poured some hot water in the wash basin and washed quickly. He dumped more hot water in a bucket and grabbed some rags before he hurried back to the bedroom.

He knelt on the floor beside Merina. She gripped his arm and groaned as another contraction hit her.

"There is only you to help me. You must do as I say now. Soon, I will not be able to tell you what to do." Merina's face was taut, but her voice was calm as she spoke.

Gabe's hands shook as he touched her face. Merina smiled at him.

"I have helped many times. Maybe it won't be so difficult." She grunted loudly again and almost bent over. "My contractions are close together and strong. I think this labor will not take so long."

"Help me to squat. You catch the baby. It is coming now. Make sure the cord—" Merina gasped and added, "Make sure the cord is not around the baby's neck. Tell—tell me if it is."

Gabe caught the baby as it slid out. He almost dropped it as it wiggled and began to scream. He looked up at Merina with a big smile as he grabbed for a rag.

"It's a girl and she's fine." He frowned and pointed at the baby's stomach. "That cord is still attached though, and the other end is inside you. You want me to cut it?"

Merina shook her head and reached out her hands. She cried softly as she held the baby against her chest. She wrapped the baby and then held it up to nurse as she smiled up at Gabe.

"Let's call her Grace. Your Grace gave me you. I think this child should have her name."

Gabe stared at his wife for a moment and a tear slid from his eye. He wiped at it roughly.

"Tarnation, Merina. I don't cry and look at me now."

Merina laughed softly and kissed Grace. "Grace Gabriella. You are beautiful."

And she was. The tiny girl had a wealth of black hair. She was round and plump. Gabe had never seen a newborn baby before, but he was quite sure Grace was the most beautiful one ever. He touched her cheek and then kissed Merina. They were both smiling when Molly rushed into the room.

Her face slowly relaxed as she hurried to Merina. She touched the baby's soft hair and smiled.

"Well, you didn't need me at all." She felt Merina's stomach and handed Gabe the baby. "You take this little one for a moment. We'll be finished here in no time and then I'll fix the two of you something to eat. I doubt Merina has eaten all day."

CHAPTER 23

An Angry Husband

MIGUEL RODE IN THE BACK OF THE BUGGY BESIDE Flory. Doc had her strapped to the board she was on. He wanted Miguel to hold the board steady and talk to Flory if she came to.

Flory's eyes opened just as the buggy arrived in Cheyenne. Her eyes dilated and she struggled to get free.

"Shh, Flory. You are tied to this board. Doc wants to make sure you don't move so much. Now lie still. We are almost to his office. Once he checks you over, he will let you move."

Flory stared at him and the fear in her eyes made Miguel even more angry.

"Don't be afraid, Flory. The men are dead. Nate shot two of them and Angel went after the third man. I do not think that man will live."

Doc was out of the buggy quickly. Nate climbed out slowly and followed him.

"Help me carry Flory inside, Miguel. I will check her over and then I will call you." Doc smiled at Miguel. "I would appreciate it if you would take care of my horse. I was hard on him today and he could use a good rubdown."

Miguel helped carry Flory into Doc's office. He stood in the doorway as he watched Doc rushing around. Flory was crying and Miguel tried to go back inside.

"No, Miguel. I will be able to work faster and more carefully if you are not here. Now go. I will call you." He gently pushed Miguel out the door and closed it. He poked his head back out and pointed at Nate.

"And Nate, I want you to sit down and wait on me. I don't want you up any more than necessary. Miguel can take care of the horses by himself." Doc shut the door and his voice was soft as he spoke to Flory.

Miguel stared at the closed door before he walked slowly outside. He led Doc's horse and his own back to Doc's small stable. He gave each of them some grain and rubbed them down as he talked.

"I will leave on the train today. I will go to Kansas City and find this man. Never will he be able to hurt like this again. Perhaps Angel will go with me." Miguel's anger made him numb, and he could feel the coldness pour through his body." He cursed under his breath. He threw the brush in the tub where he found it and strode out of the stable. His footsteps slowed when he saw Father Cummiskey.

The priest was just dismounting from his mule. He smiled at the angry man.

"I heard about the accident and thought I would check on the patients. Come, Miguel. Walk with me a moment." As he studied the younger man's face, he added, "What happened was wrong, but you must not seek revenge."

Miguel didn't answer and the priest continued.

"Let the law handle this, Miguel. Sheriff Boswell has been informed. He rode out after Angel and the rest of your riders. He will get the information he needs." Father Cummiskey smiled. "He always does, you know."

Miguel stopped. His voice was soft as he looked at the priest.

"Sheriff Boswell has no authority in Kansas. The man who ordered this is powerful. He will not stop until Flory is dead and me as well." His eyes were hard as he stared at the priest.

"His son is the reason Flory is with child. She did not agree to his advances. I met this man when I played cards there. He bragged about what he did.

"I followed him. I made sure he would never hurt another woman. I did not kill him although it mattered little to me if he lived or died. Now the father seeks revenge.

"No, I think this man must be destroyed. He must be killed.

"You would kill a wolf that kept destroying your sheep, yes? Every night, he would destroy more of them, and he would not stop until all the sheep were dead." Miguel shook his head. "No, Padre. I must do this."

"Let the law in Kansas City take care of this man."

Miguel smiled at the priest, but his smile was cold and deadly.

"I will go to Kansas City. I will see what that sheriff there has done. If he has done nothing, then I will take care of this man. As long as he lives, Flory's life is in danger."

The priest listened. He knew what Miguel said was true, but what he had told the angry husband was correct as well.

Miguel suddenly grinned at the priest.

"Perhaps I will take Badger's mule with me. I will need a pack mule on such a long trip."

Father Cummiskey frowned at Miguel and shook his head. His face was somber as he held open the door.

"I think if mules had souls, I would be very concerned about the future of that one."

Miguel finally laughed and the two men went inside. Nate was with Doc, and they sat down to wait.

CHAPTER 24

A Young Hero

ANGEL APPEARED IN THE DOOR. HE SLIPPED THROUGH and sat down by Miguel. He said nothing for a moment as he looked over at the priest.

"Good afternoon, Padre. I think there is a man in the jail who has much need of confession. He confessed some to me, but I have no such calling as you to be able to forgive him his sins." Angel's eyes were twinkling as he added, "His list of sins was very long, and even though he was sorry, I believe his suffering will be long and difficult."

Father Cummiskey stared at Angel and sighed.

"You Monteros make my calling difficult. You are good men, but you always take justice in your own hands."

"As you do, Padre. I saw those men who tried to assault you. They received the beating they deserved. I think I would like to have you on my side in a fight." Angel's voice was bland, but his eyes were twinkling. The priest laughed.

"You have me there. Yes, I will stop to see that man. I think confession is always good for the soul and the spirit too."

Doc followed Nate out of his examination room.

"You keep those ribs bound now. They are going to be painful for some time. That bruise on your back is a large one too. Your knee was twisted so keep that brace on it for at least a week. Have Gabe rub some horse liniment on you tonight. Do that once a day and maybe you won't be so stiff. And no roping until you can raise your arm without wincing.

"You were a lucky fellow today." He paused and added seriously, "Flory lived because you threw your body over hers, but no more heroic acts until you are healed." He smiled when Nate grinned at him.

"I'm going to head on home, Doc. Merina might have had her baby by now and I want to save Gabe a trip to Cheyenne. I'll get a horse at the livery."

Miguel followed Nate out the door.

"Take my horse, Nate. If Demonio is not back by the time I am ready to leave, Angel can give me a ride to the livery." He grinned at the young man and added, "Just loop Demonio's reins around the saddle horn and turn him loose when you get home. If I'm not there, he will come back to town to find me. Demonio is not always such a nice horse, but he likes me."

Nate laughed and then winced. "Probably because you are a matched set." His eyes became serious when he spoke again.

"It was bad today and I'm real sorry Miss Flory was hurt. I hope she'll be all right. Those fellers were determined to kill her."

Miguel was quiet a moment before he turned Nate to face him. He squeezed the young man's shoulders as he spoke.

"Flory lived today because you saved her. I owe you for that, my brother. I will not forget. Thank you."

Nate turned a little red and he shook his head.

"I didn't do anything special. Any man would have done the same. Maybe better. I wish I hadn't flipped that buggy."

"No other man was there. Only you were the one to help.

"Now tell my sister nothing until after the baby comes. Then only tell her part of it. We don't want her angry too." Miguel's eyes were laughing as he turned away.

Nate laughed as he headed outside. Demonio laid back his ears and Nate spoke to him softly.

"Now you be nice. Miguel said to ride you home. Then you can come on back here and find your boss."

Demonio snorted but he didn't try to bite when Nate tightened the girth. The young man's movements were awkward as he favored his left side. He was soon headed south. Demonio wanted to run but Nate held him to a gallop.

"You are quite the horse, Demonio. I see why Miguel likes you so much."

Demonio snorted again and Nate laughed. He winced again and held his hand over his ribs as he rode.

CHAPTER 25

News Good and Bad

DOC WAS TALKING TO ANGEL AND FATHER CUMMISKEY when Miguel walked back inside. He hurried to join them.

"Florence was hurt badly. Her right leg is broken in several places. I splinted it but the top break is a bad one. It is going to take some work on her part to get full movement back. Even then, she will be on crutches for a time." He added softly, "There is also a good chance she will lose her baby. She is having contractions and I have no way to stop them.

"I would like you to stay with her tonight, Miguel. She is frightened already and the fear of losing a child is always difficult. She is bleeding some and I want her to lie still.

"She is also quite bruised." Doc shook his head. "Thank Heavens Nate threw himself over her. One of those horses ran right over the top of him. There are even a couple of hoofprints on Nate's back. They were both exceptionally lucky." He handed Miguel a can.

"This is a cream Badger uses. He gave me the list of ingredients and I made it myself. It smells much better than horse liniment and I want you to use it on Florence. She is going to be sore and stiff for some time. This will help." He frowned and shook his head. "I never dreamed as a doctor I would ever be taking medical advice or learning how to make medicine from someone such as Badger."

Angel laughed but Miguel was staring toward the examination room.

"I think I will go see my wife now. Thank you, Doc." Miguel left quietly, and Angel watched him go.

When the door closed, Angel asked softly, "Señora Flory, she will be all right, yes?"

Doc nodded slowly. "She was hurt badly, and she is frightened. She may have some internal injuries as well. I can't tell because of how the baby is positioned."

He looked directly at Angel.

"Florence is a little fragile right now. And if she loses this baby, she will be even more so. Besides, she is not used to the rough ways of the West yet. She is going to need care to come out of this."

Angel listened closely and slowly nodded.

"When she is better, perhaps we will take her out to stay with Merina. My sister will be in the house more for a time. I think riding a horse would be good for señora Flory too. It will help her to stretch and get strength in her muscles. Merina can take her riding.

"Miguel will be close to her as well...unless he decides to go after the man who did this." Angel was quiet a moment before he added, "And I think that is what he will do."

Doc frowned at Angel and shook his head.

"Miguel needs to stay close for at least a week, maybe longer. Florence's condition, both mental and physical, is critical. Her husband needs to be close until she stabilizes. After that, I can't tell him what to do." Doc smiled as he added, "Now wish Florence well and then go home. She needs to get some rest."

Angel nodded. He tapped lightly on Flory's door and then stepped inside. Flory was crying and Miguel was talking softly to her. Angel waited a moment before he slipped back out.

"I am going to get my Anna. She should be with her sister."

CHAPTER 26

A Sister's Love

ANNA LOOKED UP WITH A SMILE WHEN SHE SAW ANGEL appear on the playground. School was out and the children gathered around "Mr. Teacher" as they called Angel. When Mr. Teacher came to the school, he usually brought treats for all the students. Today, they were rewarded with hard candy. They all had smiles on their faces as they rushed in separate directions for home.

Angel strolled up to the school and grabbed Anna. He swung her around before he kissed her. She was laughing when he let her down.

"I think, señora Montero, that bebé inside you is growing. Your bump is growing larger." Angel touched her stomach where the child inside her was beginning to show. Anna laughed again and nodded her head.

"He is. Let me finish here and then I will start on supper." She paused when she saw the buggy.

"We are going for a ride?"

Angel nodded as he followed her into the school. His voice was serious as he spoke.

"Señora Flory was in an accident. The buggy Nate was driving hit a rock and flipped over. She is at Doc's. I knew you would want to go see her."

Anna's breath caught as she listened closely to Angel. She grabbed her cloak and rushed toward the door. She paused and looked back at Angel. Her eyes were large as she studied his face.

"It is not like Nate to be reckless."

Angel was quiet as he searched for the words to say to his wife. He took her by the shoulders and spoke quietly.

"They were being chased and had to jump. Nate rolled to protect Flory. I believe they were both quite lucky.

"Perhaps if Molly is around, she will let the children stay with her for the night. You should take some clean clothes for them. It may be late when you get back tonight."

Anna was running when Angel finished talking. She was back quickly with clean clothes. Angel had wiped the slate boards and stacked them neatly on Anna's desk. He followed her out of the school and lifted her into the buggy. He whistled sharply and the children came running. He winked at them.

"Your mother and I need to make a fast trip to Cheyenne. I think we will let you spend the night with the Rankins if Molly is around. It might be late when we get back. That will be fun, yes?"

Zach and Amanda both nodded excitedly. Zach was in first grade and Amanda was four years old. Even though she was young, she went to school every morning. In the afternoons, she took a nap and then played at Molly's house. Anna had special work for her to do and Amanda loved school. Spending the night with her friends was always exciting though.

Molly was hanging clothes on the line when Angel drove the buggy into her yard. She asked no questions when Angel asked if she would keep the children. She squeezed Anna's hand and nodded. The children tumbled out of the buggy and rushed off to find their friends.

"Why don't we just call off school tomorrow? I will send Paul over to Beth's. He can make a few stops along the way and pass the word. I'm sure the children will enjoy a longer weekend, and their parents won't mind some help at home." Molly smiled up at Anna and whispered, "We are praying for Flory. You go and see your sister. I'll keep the children as long as you need me to."

Anna's mouth trembled as she nodded.

"Thank you, Molly. Since I don't have to pick the children up, I may stay with Flory tonight. Angel will keep you updated."

Anna was quiet as Angel turned the buggy toward Cheyenne. She finally looked over at him.

"I think you are more concerned about Flory than you are showing. Please tell me what Doc said."

Angel fiddled with the lines to the horses before he looked at his wife. His face was agitated when he spoke.

"Doc is worried about Flory, both her body and her mental state. He is afraid she will lose the baby. He said she is fragile right now, and he wants Miguel to stay close for a week or so. Miguel is angry though and I'm not sure he will.

"They were attacked by three men. Nate didn't know who they were, but Flory was afraid when she heard one of them speak the name of the man who sent them. Miguel knew the man for sure.

"Fury and fear have overtaken Miguel. He wants to find the man who ordered their attack. I am afraid he will leave. If Flory seems to be getting better, he will leave to seek revenge. He will travel east to find this man." Angel added quietly, "And if Flory becomes worse, he will lose control. Miguel is very...what do you say...volatile. He will go crazy with anger. He won't care if he lives or if he dies.

"This is a very bad time for them."

Anna was quiet for a moment. She gripped Angel's arm and a sob caught in her throat before she spoke.

"Did you know the child Flory carries is not Miguel's?"

Angel fidgeted in his seat before he replied. "Miguel has not spoken of his trip to Kansas City, and neither have Reed or Temple." Angel tapped the lines on the backs of the horses and added, "I think a man there did señora Flory wrong."

"Yes, but Flory remembers nothing. She tried to tell Miguel when he arrived in Kansas City, but he already knew. He found out who the man was too." Anna was trying to keep from crying when she looked over at Miguel.

"Your brother surprised me. I never dreamed Miguel would marry let alone raise a child that was not his." Anna wiped a tear from her face and took a deep breath.

"They have been so happy. It is like they have both found their soulmates. I was so worried in the beginning because they are both so—so—irresponsible. Somehow though, they have brought out the best in each other."

Angel was quiet as he listened to Anna. He hugged her as he whispered, "I think señora Flory is not as strong of a woman as my wife. Or as brave. My wife, I am afraid of her myself."

Anna stared at Angel a moment before she laughed.

"You know just how to calm me. Now let's go faster. I want to see my sister."

CHAPTER 27

A Husband's Fury

ANNA JUMPED OUT OF THE BUGGY BEFORE ANGEL could help her down and rushed into Doc's office. Josie, Doc's wife, hurried toward her.

"Come this way, Anna. Flory is in this first room."

Josie knocked softly and then opened the door. Miguel stood when Anna entered. She hugged him and hurried to Flory's side. Her sister's face was almost white, and Flory's eyes were closed. She didn't respond when Anna touched her. Her skin was cool. In fact, it was almost cold.

"Flory lost the child. She has bled much. Doc said she was hemorrhaging. He finally got the bleeding stopped but she has lost much blood." Miguel's hand shook as he rubbed it across his eyes.

"Angel is here?"

Anna hugged Miguel again. "Yes, he brought me in the buggy." Her voice shook as she added, "Thank you, Miguel. Thank you for loving Flory. You are good for her."

Miguel didn't answer. He leaned over to kiss Flory's cheek.

"Flory. Mi Amor," he whispered and then left the room quietly.

Angel was just walking into Doc's waiting room when Miguel appeared. The brothers met and Angel followed Miguel outside. Miguel's hands were shaking, and his face was cold when he looked at Angel.

"Flory lost much blood. Doc does not know if she will live. He said it is up to her. If she has the will to get better, she may pull through. Otherwise, she will not last the night."

Angel listened quietly as his brother spoke. "He does not want to attempt a transfusion? I have heard of this being done."

"Doc said it was too risky. He does not have the correct equipment, and he is afraid to use what he has. Right now, her chances are not so good, and many things can go wrong with a transfusion. He is afraid it will kill her.

"Also, Anna's blood would be best since they are related, and Anna is with child. An infection would put everyone at risk." Miguel's voice broke as he added, "I believe Flory is dying and I cannot watch the life drain from my wife. I am leaving."

Angel turned his brother around to face him.

"No, Miguel. Flory needs you here. Let me get Father Cummiskey. You stay here until he arrives."

Miguel shook his head. "You get the padre, but I will not stay."

"Then I should go with you. I am your brother and—"

"No, Angel. I do not care if I live or if I die. I do not believe I will be back. You cannot come. You have a wife and children to care for. No one can come with me."

Miguel turned away. He stumbled as he walked to where his horse stood waiting. He mounted Demonio without looking back and was soon headed south out of town.

Angel watched him go and then rushed to the buggy. He arrived quickly at the little house where Father Cummiskey lived. He raced up to the door, but the priest answered before he could knock.

"I just heard Mrs. Montero lost her child. I will go with you now."

The priest was quiet as Angel raced the team up the street. He finally looked at Angel as he spoke softly, "Miguel has gone?"

"Sí. My brother said he could not watch as the life leaves his wife." Angel's voice was quiet as he spoke. "He is mucho angry, Padre. He goes to kill the man who is responsible, and he does not care if he lives."

"Then we will pray for both Miguel and the men he meets. We will ask that the Good Lord guides his heart, and we will pray that señora Flory lives. We cannot control your brother's actions, but we can ask that he listens to God.

"Now come. I will administer last rites to Mrs. Montero. We will ask the Good Lord to heal her heart and her body."

Father Cummiskey hurried into the doctor's office. He smiled as he reached for Anna's hands.

"Anna, it is good to see you. Pray with me. We will ask for help from above today."

CHAPTER 28

MIGUEL

MIGUEL STOPPED AT GABE'S RANCH. HE LED DEMONIO into the barn. When he returned, he led a large mule. He had a packsaddle on the mule and a leather halter around his head with no lead rope attached. Demonio's mane had been cropped short and his long tail was roughly trimmed.

Merina watched Miguel from the kitchen for a moment. When he led his mounts toward the house, she hurried to pack some of the food Molly had made. She waited for him to speak. When he said nothing, she handed him the pack.

"You go to Kansas City? That is where the man lives who you believe ordered the attack?"

Miguel said nothing and Merina hugged him.

"Come back to us, Miguel. Your family loves you. I know you believe you must do this but be careful. If he is as evil as you believe, he will have spies watching for you."

Miguel laughed harshly. "That is why I changed rigs. They expect a dashing vaquero but instead, they will see a lonely cowboy and a cantankerous mule. I even shaved my mustache." He tossed his black hat onto the table and pointed at it.

"Tell Nate he can wear my fancy hat. I found an old one in the barn." He pointed his thumb over his shoulder. "That mule of yours is a thief, I think. I found an old hat in his stall along with a blue shawl. The shawl looks like one you used to wear."

Merina's dark eyes sparkled. "Mule asked me nicely for the shawl and I gave it to him. And I do not think he will appreciate you dragging him all over. He may not even want to go with you."

A flash of humor passed through Miguel's eyes. "That is why he has no rope. We agreed that he will only go where and when he wants.

"When I finish in Kansas City, I will put him on the train and send him home. We had a discussion and Mule agreed to help me get this man. He did not agree to help me after that or travel any farther though."

Merina hugged Miguel tighter. She looked up at him and whispered, "And Flory? She will be alright, yes?"

Miguel turned away and brushed his hand roughly across his face. His eyes were hard when he looked down at his sister.

"She lost the baby, and she lost much blood. Doc is very worried about her. I think she will not live, and I do not want to watch the life drain from my wife."

"How will we get hold of you?" Merina followed her brother outside. She was sucking her breath in to keep from crying.

Miguel shook his head before he mounted. He spoke softly.

"I do not think I will be back. I care not if I live or if I die."

CHAPTER 29

A Long Night

ANNA STAYED BY FLORY'S BED ALL NIGHT. SHE alternated between crying, praying, and scolding her sister.

"Flory, you don't need to die. You *will* yourself to get better. Now you wake up. You decide to live."

Anna talked about their childhood. She talked about Miguel and how much he loved Flory. She even talked about the children that Flory and Miguel would have together.

Flory never answered but sometimes, a tear would slide out of her eye. Anna finally fell asleep in the early morning. Josie came in and laid a quilt over her, but Anna didn't wake up until nearly seven the next morning.

She felt her sister's shoulder. Flory was still pale, but her skin was warmer.

Anna shook her sister gently and Flory frowned.

"Don't you frown at me, Florence Whitman Montero. You open your eyes now and talk to me. You have slept long enough. You must eat something, and you need to talk to me. Only then may you go back to sleep."

Flory opened her eyes. They were bleary as she stared at her sister.

"You *are* here. I dreamed you were scolding me, and I tried to run away. You kept following me though." Flory's eyes filled with tears. "I lost my baby, didn't I?"

Anna nodded as she struggled not to cry.

"You nearly died as well. By God's grace, you survived."

Tears ran down Flory's face. She turned her head to look out the window for a time before she looked back at Anna. Her voice was quiet when she spoke.

"When I found out I was with child, I was upset. I didn't want this baby. I was angry first and then sad. Then Miguel came to see me. He said we would raise it as our own—he said everyone would think it was his and we would love it that way as well. And I did love it, Anna. I did." Flory sobbed as she turned her head away from Anna.

"Flory, please don't cry. There was nothing you could do to keep the little life inside you. No one could stop your baby from dying but just know that he is very loved. He is loved by all of us and now he is loved by everyone in Heaven as well." Tears leaked from Anna's eyes as she added, "You know Mother and Father will care for him."

"He was a boy, wasn't he? Miguel always said he was a boy. He called him his son."

Anna nodded again as she hugged her sister, and they both sobbed.

The two sisters talked and cried for nearly an hour before Flory fell asleep again. Anna fell asleep as well. When Angel checked on them at noon, both sisters were still asleep. Anna's head rested on Flory's pillow and their faces were next to each other.

"Sí, my Anna's love will heal her sister." He leaned over to kiss Anna's cheek and quietly left the room.

When he came back that evening, both sisters were awake. Flory was still pale, but she was drinking warm broth. Martha had come by and brought food. Badger had sent some of his potion as well.

"Badger said he didn't think you would need this, but he sent it anyway. He said to leave it with Doc Williams if you didn't use it."

Martha's eyes sparkled with merriment, and she kissed both sisters as she rushed around the room, folding blankets, and tidying things.

"Badger and I will plan to take Flory home with us until she is able to be up and around. Angel said she is going to stay with Merina and Gabe after that."

Flory looked from Anna to Martha and shook her head.

"No, I need to go to my own house. Miguel will be there. Besides, I must get back to work. Sadie needs me to help her with her sewing business."

Anna's breath caught in her throat, but Martha just smiled.

"No, Flory. You broke your leg, and the break is quite severe. You are going to be struggling to get around for a time, and we want to make sure you have the help you need.

"You can stay with me for a few days. Once you can manage your crutches, Merina wants to work with you on horseback. She is convinced horseback riding will help you strengthen your muscles. She said it will help your leg to heal as well."

No one there mentioned Miguel, and Flory didn't ask any more questions. She was soon asleep, and Martha led Anna out of the room.

"Angel, you take this girl over to our house. She needs to sleep in a bed, or you are going to have two sick women instead of one."

CHAPTER 30

A Long Ride and a Little Advice

It took Miguel four days on horseback to reach Ogallala, Nebraska. He slept in the livery with his horse. The next morning, he put Mule and Demonio in train cars by themselves. His eyes were cold as he settled back in his seat, and no one attempted to talk to him. His ticket gave him passage to Leavenworth, but he left the train just outside Lawrence. It was late in the evening on Tuesday, April 27, when he arrived in Kansas City.

Miguel rode his horse slowly through the quiet side streets, and Mule followed. He could hear saloons going several blocks away, but there were no lights on in the residential section he passed through. He looked around as he watered his horse in front of the first livery he came to. He dismounted stiffly and went to find the hostler. No one was around so he fed both animals some grain and forked some hay.

"You fellows stay here until I come for you. I need to find where this man lives. Then we will pay him a visit."

Miguel followed a group of rowdy cowboys into a saloon. They had brought a herd of cattle up from southern Kansas and were going to have a night on the town before they headed back home the next day. A friendly cowboy with red hair and bowed legs pushed in beside Miguel. He called for a beer and leaned on the bar. The rider watched Miguel nurse his whiskey while he drank his beer.

"This saloon is quiet tonight but come Friday, she'll be a hoppin'."

Miguel shrugged. "I wouldn't know. I plan to be long gone by Friday."

"You come in with a herd?"

"Naw, I been playin' nursemaid to a bunch of cows west of Ogallala. I'm tired of cold weather though. I think I'll head on south. I hear it's warmer down there. I'm tired of snow."

"My boss is hirin'. We are takin' a herd north into the Montana Territory. The boss thinks he'll get better money up there." The cowboy turned his beer before he looked over at Miguel again.

"Ever been up that way?"

Miguel nodded.

"I followed a herd up there last year. It was a long drive and we crossed lots of rivers. I hope you have a good trail boss."

"Not sure. The boss just hired him. I think he is more gunfighter than cowman. The boss thought we might need to shoot our way through a couple of places."

Miguel looked up from the whiskey he was swirling in his glass. His eyes were cold, and the cowboy almost backed up.

"If I didn't know the trail boss, I wouldn't go. Too many things can go wrong. And a gunhand might look for trouble he could walk around. You need an experienced trail boss to trail cattle that far." He grinned at the man as he added, "Unless you don't care if you live. Then go ahead and trail with whoever you want."

The cowboy stared as Miguel talked. He drained the rest of his beer and backed away from the bar. He had a frown on his face and the beer didn't even taste good. He cursed and walked over to the table where his partner was playing cards.

"Sully, we need to talk."

"Not now, Roscoe. Let me finish this hand. And bring me another beer."

Roscoe frowned. "You finish that hand but I ain't buyin' another beer. We need to talk."

The man to Sully's left laid down three aces. The cowpuncher cursed as he threw down his cards. "Three ladies and she didn't even let me win. I'm all in, boys. Roscoe wants to call it a night. You fellows have most of my money anyhow."

He pushed back his chair and Roscoe pulled him toward the door.

"Maybe we should rethink this drive. I was talkin' to a tough-lookin' hombre there at the bar. He asked if we knew our trail boss. Shoot, I never met 'im. Never even heard of 'im.

"That feller said he trailed a herd up north last summer. He said it was a long one. Now I kinda like my sorry life. I ain't a plannin' to end it sudden-like just 'cause we want to see some new country. Maybe we should take a ridin' job up farther north. We can work our way up there or sign on with that feller you know up in Nebraska."

Miguel pulled away from the bar and strolled outside. He nodded at Roscoe and paused before he spoke.

"If you want a riding job up north, talk to John Kirkham in Ogallala. He has a big spread north of there and seems to hire quite a few hands. He knows folks too, so he'd know who was hiring. Last I heard, he was talking about trailing another herd north.

"Kirkham's a careful man. Might be a good one to trail with." Miguel stepped into the shadows and strolled on down the street. He didn't look back.

The two riders watched him until he disappeared. Sully looked over at Roscoe.

"That the feller you just talked to?"

"Yeah. Met 'im at the bar. He didn't tell me his name."

"I met that fellow down to Texas several years ago. He was a reckless man. Just didn't seem to care who he braced. If he said that drive could be bad, I reckon he's right.

"Let's go see the boss an' draw our time. We still have half our wages comin'. That will be enough to ride north a spell. Maybe we can pick up a job here an' there to get a little eatin' money." He slapped Roscoe on the back.

"Good listenin', pard. I reckon that's why I like to ride with you."

CHAPTER 31

A Friendly Bartender

MIGUEL CONTINUED DOWN THE STREET UNTIL HE reached a fancy hotel. He strolled in and found a place at the bar. Once again, he ordered a whiskey and nursed it as he listened. There were lots of young men drinking at the bar and one was talking loudly to his friends.

"How's Cletus? I haven't heard a thing about him since he got out of the hospital."

"Quiet down, Jasper. Now drink your beer and let's go. We need to meet Harold's man in fifteen minutes." The man's voice was quiet as he spoke. The rest of the young men said nothing.

"What do I need to be quiet for? Everyone knows that Cletus lost his manhood. Nobody knows how but I have some ideas of my own. I'm guessing that the father or a brother of one of those gals he messed with showed up and—"

The first man slammed his beer down on the bar.

"Jasper, I said to shut up. Now no more talking." He looked around at the three young men beside him who were drinking quietly.

"Come on, fellows. Let's go. And, Jasper, if you open your mouth one more time, I'll have Ox there light you up hard enough that you won't see daylight for a couple of days."

A large bruiser grinned at Jasper as he cracked his knuckles. The five men sauntered out of the bar. Jasper looked at his half empty glass, took a quick drink and followed them.

Miguel dropped some money on the bar and had just stepped away when Jasper cursed.

"What are we headed north for? Harold lives south just a couple of blocks. Where are we meeting him anyhow?"

Ox dropped Jasper with one punch. The rest of the men kept on walking, leaving the young man where he had fallen.

Miguel stepped out of the bar and fell into step behind the five men. He kept to the shadows and looked in the windows of the saloons as he strolled along.

The men were talking quietly, and Miguel couldn't hear what they were saying. Finally, one of the young men stopped. The rest of the group paused as he looked around at his friends in frustration.

"What are we doing anyhow? I know Harold wants us to watch the trains coming in from the west but what are we supposed to do if we see this fellow he wants so bad? And how do we know who he is? I know a little Spanish but not enough to understand a conversation." He frowned and shook his head. "I don't like this deal at all."

The man who had spoken in the saloon chuckled.

"We'll find out soon enough. Old Harold has a mad on. Besides, the pay is good…and we have Ox here." He grinned as he slapped Ox on the back.

Miguel leaned up against a support post and lit a cigarette. He watched the men continue up the street. When they turned in at the Pacific House, he ground out his cigarette, pulled his hat down lower, and headed for the hotel.

He pushed through the swinging doors of the Pacific House Saloon and continued to the bar. He took a position where he could watch the men in the mirror.

The five men continued to a table in the back. Two of them took a seat across from a pompous man in a derby hat. The other three lounged against the wall.

Miguel tossed some money on the bar when the bartender came by.

"Whiskey. And make it your good stuff."

The man glanced at Miguel and nodded. He pulled a bottle from under the bar and poured two fingers in a glass. He set it in front of Miguel. He paused as he indicated the bottle in his hand.

"You want me to leave the bottle here?"

Miguel grinned and shook his head.

"Naw. One shot will be enough. I just got paid out an' I figgered I'd have me one good drink before I have to go back to that rotgut stuff they call whiskey down the street." He turned around and leaned his elbows on the bar.

"Quiet tonight."

"Well, it's a Tuesday. Come Friday, she all changes. You just passing through then?"

"Yep, headed back south to catch another herd. Maybe one of these days I'll save enough money to bring one up myself." He stared into the glass in his hand and grinned over his shoulder at the bartender. "Probably not though. I like my whiskey."

The bartender laughed.

"You cowboys are all alike. You work hard all month. Then you come to town and drop all that hard-earned money in one night. Just doesn't make sense to me."

Miguel chuckled and nodded.

"We are a misunderstood group of gentlemen, that's for sure."

He visited with the bartender until Harold stood. He drained his glass and grinned across the bar.

"Barkeep, that was fine whiskey. I'll remember you the next time I come through here."

The bartender laughed again as he nodded toward the back of the room.

"The next time you might want to take a bath first. If the boss wasn't so preoccupied tonight, he'd tell me to refuse you service and have one of his bouncers toss you out."

Miguel chuckled and strolled toward the door. He walked south toward the awning of a closed shop. Its overhang threw a dark shadow on the sidewalk. He ducked back into the darkness and waited.

CHAPTER 32

A Ride to the River

HAROLD LITTLETON STRODE OUT OF THE PACIFIC House Saloon. The five young men headed north while Harold turned south. Miguel followed him, staying in the shadows. When Harold walked up the steps to a large house on a corner lot, Miguel turned around. He slipped through side streets until he reached the livery.

The hostler was sleeping in a small office inside the livery. Miguel saddled Demonio and dropped the pack saddle on Mule. The old man didn't wake, and Miguel left $2 beside him. The old hostler's eyes opened as Miguel mounted his horse. He watched as the cowboy rode quietly out of the barn.

"The only time a feller leaves in the middle of the night is when there's trouble. Trouble behind him or trouble comin'. It ain't my trouble though an' I saw nothin'." The hostler shoved the money in his pocket and rolled over. He was soon snoring again.

Once again, Miguel took the side streets to Harold Littleton's house. This time, he went a block farther into the residential section of town before he turned back east. A lamp was on in the living room and Miguel could see Harold sitting behind a large desk. He had papers spread out in front of him, and he was muttering under his breath as he studied them. Miguel studied the house and the area around it. All was quiet so he slid the pack off Mule.

"This is what you came for, Mule. One way or another, this ends tonight," Miguel whispered. "And if I don't make it out of this deal alive, you and Demonio head home.

"The tricky part will be getting Littleton to go with me to the river. Maybe I can get him to ride Demonio and I will ride you. Now you two cooperate and work with each other." Mule snorted and Demonio tossed his head.

Miguel tiptoed up to the porch and tapped on the door.

"Mr. Littleton? We found that man you are looking for." Miguel's voice was soft, but it carried through the door.

Harold looked up quickly and hurried to the door. He jerked it open and stared at the stranger standing there in surprise.

"I was told to wake you. Those fellows found your man."

"I told those boys not to come here, and that meant nobody."

"Yes, but he is camped down by the river. He is packed light, so they don't think he intends to stay long."

Littleton squinted up at Miguel.

"Who are you? You aren't one of the boys I hired."

Miguel shrugged. "Just a broke cowboy. Those boys needed a runner, and I was handy.

"I can give you directions if you want." When Littleton stared at him, he added, "Or you can go over to one of the liveries. You can pick up a horse there."

"Why don't I ride your horse and you ride that big, ugly mule. We can move faster if I don't go to the livery. Besides, I want this done quiet."

Miguel shrugged. He walked over to Mule.

"Now, Mule, you stand still. It might take me a little to get on you." He placed a hand on Mule's back and prepared to jump when Mule dropped down on his knees. Miguel laughed.

"You never can tell about a mule. Sometimes they cooperate and sometimes they don't."

Littleton stared at the mule. "You don't even have a bridle on that mule."

"Don't need one. He's a pack mule. He gets balky if I try to lead him, but he follows along just fine—if he wants to go where I am going. Mules are notional."

Littleton rode in silence for a moment and then he looked over at Miguel.

"Where are you from? I can't place your accent."

"Born on the back of horse and I've ridden it all over. I don't stay in one place too long."

"You wanted by the law?"

Miguel was quiet for a time. When he looked over at Littleton, his voice was hard.

"That's not a question you ask a man, Littleton. Especially when you are riding out to kill a man you don't even know."

Littleton sucked in his breath sharply. "I didn't say we were going to kill him."

"Didn't you? Listening to those fellows talk, that sounds like the only way you'll stop him. And just so you know, I won't be part of that killing. Once I get you to the river, my part in this deal is done."

Harold Littleton's florid face was hard in the moonlight. "You're done when I say you're done, cowboy. Now how much farther? I'm not used to riding a horse."

Miguel pointed at the river below them. A fire was winking below them. It was set back from the water a short distance. Littleton turned Demonio toward the fire, but Miguel stopped him.

"That is a signal fire. We don't want to get too close to it. We are headed for that dark cove between those trees."

When they arrived at the river, Miguel slid off Mule. He looked up at Littleton. His voice was soft as he spoke, "Your cheating days are over,

Littleton. Take a good look at this face. I'm the one you were looking for." He slapped Demonio on the back and whispered, "Now!"

Demonio charged into the water. He reared and pitched until Littleton nearly lost his grip. Littleton cried out but his cries were lost in the sound of the splashing water. Mule followed the bucking horse into the river. Soon the water was deep enough that both animals had to swim.

Littleton fell under Demonio's flailing hooves as the horse spun. Mule grabbed the struggling man. He dragged him farther into the river and dropped him when a floating tree hit both of them. Miguel couldn't tell if the kicks that Mule gave the downed man were a result of the mule trying to break free of the tree branches or if they were done for another purpose. Demonio was trembling slightly as he clambered up on the bank. Mule followed. He snorted and turned toward town.

"Now, Mule, you hold up. I need to get that pack saddle and then we are going to find a livery."

Miguel rode quietly toward Littleton's house. He grabbed his gear from the alley across the street and quickly put the halter and packsaddle back on Mule. He tied what was left of the supplies to the back of Demonio's saddle. He rode quietly in a wide loop and came up to the business district from the back side. There was a livery on nearly every corner, and Miguel chose one that looked old and shabby.

He walked his horse quietly into the barn. A voice from the back spoke up. "Just pick ya an empty stall. There's feed an' hay in each of 'em already. It's two bits for both a your hosses if ya leave 'fore I get up of the mornin'."

Miguel muttered a thank you. He pulled the wet saddle off Demonio and tossed it up on the side of the stall. He brushed the horse as he talked softly to him. When he turned toward Mule with the currycomb in his hand, the animal snorted at him. Miguel chuckled.

"You're all right, Mule. Perhaps you and I will be friends someday." The mule stared at him, and Miguel laughed again. "Or maybe not."

He dropped down in the hay beside his horse and was soon asleep.

Miguel had Demonio saddled early the next morning and was at the train station ten minutes later. He filled out Mule's shipping ticket with delivery to Badger McCune, Cheyenne, Wyoming. The name signed as the shipper at the bottom of the ticket read Jinglebob Jones.

"Now don't put any other livestock in that car. The mule is plumb cantankerous. Badger sold him to me and I'm sendin' him back. I'll toss some hay in there before I go, but don't you go in. Open the door for him to water when you are about halfway to Cheyenne. Leave it open. He'll get back in if he wants. If he doesn't, don't try to catch him. Just let him go. He knows his way home."

The ticket agent frowned as he looked from Miguel to Mule. He finally shrugged.

"That's fine but you'll have to pay for a full car then."

Miguel nodded. He opened the door to the livestock car and Mule climbed in. He tossed a good amount of hay inside. He paused before the sliding door.

"You did a fine job this trip, Mule. Perhaps I'll see you again sometime." Miguel grinned when the mule ignored him. He slammed the door and dropped the bar in place.

As Miguel rode past the ticket agent, he pointed back toward Mule's car.

"You might want to put a sign on that door. That mule can act friendly, but he is not an animal to be trusted."

CHAPTER 33

OPEN RANGE

AS HE PAID THE TICKET AGENT, MIGUEL THOUGHT about riding through Council Grove. He didn't want to talk to Flory's aunt though. Instead, he opted for the more open lands of southwest Kansas.

"Maybe I'll head to Dodge City. I can tie one on there."

Miguel rode past the bustling towns of Baldwin City and Ottawa without stopping. He stopped several times to rest for a few hours but didn't make camp until Thursday evening. He stopped in a little grove of trees just outside Cottonwood Falls. The grass was plentiful so both horse and rider rested until midmorning before they traveled farther. Miguel had just saddled Demonio when two men rode toward his camp.

One rode in while the second stayed farther back.

"You're on private property, friend. We are here to escort you off." The man's voice was gruff, and he pushed his horse close to Demonio.

Miguel stared at the two men and chuckled softly.

"If you are asking me to leave, that must mean we are not truly friends, yes?" The smile on Miguel's face didn't reach his eyes and the first rider sat a little straighter on his horse.

"Don't you get smart with me, cowboy. I'll rope you and drag you out of this country if I have to."

A gun appeared in Miguel's hand.

"Perhaps. Or perhaps I will let my horse chase you and your companion back to the hole you crawled out of. Or maybe I will drag you while my horse runs quickly through these thickets and trees."

Miguel was still smiling, and the man backed up.

"Look, we are only taking orders. Our boss doesn't like strangers on his land."

"Then perhaps your boss should post a sign or put up a fence. The last time I rode through here, this was all open range. Perhaps your boss is claiming land that does not belong to him.

"You and your friend drop your guns. Your rifles too. And don't make any sudden moves or I will turn my horse loose. He loves to chase other horses. If one of you should fall off…well, he would probably run over the top of you just for fun."

The two men sullenly dropped their guns.

"And now your boots. If you talk nicely, I will leave them close to your horses. If you do not, I will scatter them over the prairie while I ride away."

The closest man started to argue and Demonio lunged for his horse with his mouth open. The gelding screamed as it twisted to get away. The rider was dumped on the ground. He lunged to his feet with a curse and Miguel cocked his gun.

"Right now, señor, you have your britches. I think you will not look so dashing if you must walk back to your ranch missing both your boots and your pants.

"Now stand over by that tree. Perhaps I will leave your horses at the next fence I see…or maybe I will just turn them loose."

Miguel grinned at the men as he dropped their long guns back into their rifle boots. He shoved their guns and high heeled cowboy boots into their saddle bags.

"Adios, amigos. Enjoy your morning walk."

Miguel was still smiling when he turned the horses loose about two miles away. He had just pointed his horse to the west again when he heard hoofbeats racing up behind him.

He pulled his horse to a stop and waited as the rider rode towards him. He frowned when he saw it was a woman. She was carrying a rifle, and it was pointed at him.

"Those were Bar S horses you were leading. Where are the riders?"

Miguel pushed his hat back as he grinned at her.

"I am thinking they are about two miles behind you, but they won't make such good time in their socks."

The woman's face twisted in anger.

"You drop your guns. I am taking you back to headquarters. My father will deal with you."

Miguel placed one hand on the pommel of his saddle and the other on his leg. His eyes were cold as he stared at the woman.

"I don't think so. I am just riding through. Now if you say this land is yours, you should have it posted. Otherwise, I must assume it to be open range, and that means I may cross it unbothered.

"So go ahead and shoot me if you think you must—but you had better make sure you kill me with the first shot because you won't get a second chance."

The woman stared at him, and her eyes opened wide.

"You wouldn't dare shoot a woman."

"A lady, no. A woman who has threatened to kill me, yes. Now put down that gun. You may take those horses back to your riders and I will be on my way.

"Or go ahead and shoot. One of us will not leave this place today."

Fury flickered through the woman's eyes. For a moment, Miguel thought she was going to shoot him. He had never shot a woman before, and he wasn't excited to do so now. Still…

The woman's hands wavered, and she dropped the barrel of the gun until it was pointed at Miguel's horse.

"Maybe I will just shoot your horse."

"Señorita, I assure you my horse's life is more important to me than my own. If you hurt my horse, I will take your life for certain.

"You are young, and I do not think you want to stop living today. Me? I don't care whether I live or whether I die, so shoot me or not. It is your choice."

Miguel's smile was gone, and his face was hard as he stared at the woman.

The woman finally shrugged and put her rifle back in its boot. She pointed straight west.

"Keep going that way and you will see a gate. Close it behind you and you will be on open range again." She watched him carefully as she added, "Or turn left and you will reach our ranch headquarters. We could use another hand if you are looking for a job. Come up to the house for supper tonight and we can talk about it."

Miguel returned her gaze and shook his head.

"No, I think I will continue on to Dodge where the women are friendly and don't threaten to shoot me." He touched the brim of his hat and rode west at a slow trot.

The woman watched him ride away before she gathered the horses. She started back to the east, looking over her shoulder several times at Miguel's parting back. She frowned and muttered under her breath. Her long, red braid shone in the sun. Her riding outfit was modest, but it did nothing to disguise the curves it covered. Ann Gleason was not used to being backed down. And most men would have jumped at an invitation from her to come up to the ranch house.

She dropped the reins in front of the walking men and glared at them.

"You boys have one job and that is to keep trespassers off this land. Next time, keep your guns and use them."

One of the riders said nothing but the man who had spoken to Miguel jerked his gun out of his saddle bag and dropped it in his holster. He sat down on the ground to pull on his boots. He sat there for a moment as he glared up at her.

"Miss Gleason, I am tired of you lording it over us. If you wanted him dead so bad, why didn't you shoot him yourself? I am guessing you had him dead to rights.

"And I know why. Because you knew he would shoot you and you didn't want to die. And you know what? I am going to follow him. I think I'd rather ride with a fellow like that than work for you and your mean old man.

"You are a good-lookin' woman, but you are plumb mean inside. And if you don't put that bitterness inside you to rest, soon you will be old *and* mean."

Ann stared at the rider in shock and then grabbed for her rifle. A rope dropped over her shoulders and the second cowboy took up the slack. Ann was jerked out of the saddle and dropped unceremoniously on the ground.

The second cowboy's grin was large as he looked down at her.

"You don't know how many times I have wanted to do that. Now you just sit there, Miss Ann. You can flip that rope off, nice like, or I will tie you up with your own piggin' string.

Ann jerked the rope off her shoulders and the cowboy slowly rewound it as he rode toward her horse. He looped the reins over her gelding's neck and smacked it with the coiled rope. The horse squealed and raced off toward the south.

The man looked down at his friend still sitting on the ground.

"Reckon we'd better cut out of here. We sure don't have a job here no more. When Old Man Gleason finds out we roped his precious daughter and set her afoot, he'll be after us."

He grinned at the furious Ann again.

"Ma'am, we have worked for your pa nigh on a year and not once have you even tried to learn our names. I don't reckon we'll be missed none.

"Come on, Poe. Let's hightail it out of here."

As the two men raced their horses to the west, the first rider grinned at the man beside him.

"Now you know Poe ain't goin' to be so pleased that you used his name."

The second rider laughed and nodded.

"Sure won't, but he would have done the same. Now keep an eye out for that feller that took our boots. I don't want to get shot."

CHAPTER 34

No Longer Enemies

THE TWO COWBOYS SLOWED THEIR HORSES AND RODE toward Miguel at a walk. He was standing in front of the gate and his gun was drawn. His face was hard, but he slid the gun back in his holster when he saw the two men were grinning.

"You fellows get fired for not killing me?" He opened the gate and led Demonio through as he spoke.

"Somethin' like that. That gal is mean and her pa is worse. We decided we would rather ride with you than take another dressin' down." The man who was speaking grinned larger as he added, "Besides, when Tay here roped her, I knew we were dead if we stayed."

He led his horse through the open gate and put out his hand.

"I'm Chancy Logan and Tay there is my twin brother. We hail from Missouri way.

"We were ridin' west when Old Man Gleason offered us a job. That was pertineer a year ago. He tried to short us wages every month for most of that time. We finally got paid for last month just yesterday and he paid us for April too." He grinned as Miguel shook his hand.

"If you don't mind, we'll ride along with you."

Tay shut the gate and offered his hand to Miguel as well. His grin was exactly like his brother's.

Miguel looked from one to the other and chuckled.

"I'd say you fellows are like double trouble, yes? You are welcome to ride with me but I'm not sure where I'm going after Dodge. Maybe north, maybe south."

Tay shrugged.

"Don't make us no never mind. We can find a ridin' job wherever we land." His face was curious as he looked at Miguel.

"Miss Ann offer you a job? I don't know that any man has ever backed her down. Sure you don't want to stay? Shoot, if you played your cards right, you could maybe own this spread someday."

Miguel's face was serious, but his eyes glinted as he shook his head.

"I don't think I would like to be married to a woman who threatened to shoot me the first time we met. She might do it if we had a fight... and I'm thinking if I hitched up with a woman like that, we certainly would fight. No, I like my women sweet.

"Besides, I like saloons and the whiskey that pours there freely." He waved his hand across the land in front of them.

"Perhaps you gentlemen will be so kind as to show me the fastest way around these fences...and a way that does not cross the path of any other angry women."

Tay grinned and Chancy led south at a gallop.

"Let's put some distance between that fence and us. That old man is just mean enough to come after us, and who knows what Miss Ann will tell him we did."

Miguel slowed his horse down. He pointed his finger to the west.

"Then perhaps we should ride west for a time. I believe the town of Cottonwood Falls is not too far away. Perhaps we should get supplies there. I don't have much grub left and with three of us, we will run out quickly." He grinned at the two men. "In case señorita Gleason chases after us."

Tay looked at Miguel and then shook his head. "We can buy supplies, but I don't think we should spend the night there. Gleason might put the word out that we hurt his daughter." His grin returned as he added, "'Course, Miss Ann doesn't care to know any of the riders. Poe is the one she will be looking for.

"Let me ride in. If the word is out, I'll pretend I'm part of the search party.

"You can bet she paid attention to what you looked like. Besides, you are a stranger in these parts and folks might notice."

Miguel slowly nodded.

"Let's make camp then. Maybe lead Chancy's horse and put the supplies on it. We'll plan to head out as soon as you get back. Let's put some miles between that ranch and us."

Tay was gone quickly and Chancy built a fire.

Miguel pulled Demonio's saddle off and rubbed his horse down. Then he resaddled him. He leaned back against the tree. He pulled a piece of jerky from his saddlebag and offered one to Chancy. The cowboy accepted it as he looked at Miguel curiously.

"You hail from down south? You remind me of a fellow I knew from Texas some time ago."

Miguel paused his chewing and nodded.

"I grew up down on the Brazos River, but I've been all over since I was sixteen." He stared at the jerky before he took another bite but said no more.

"You know a fellow by the name of Angel Montero? You remind me some of him." Chancy's eyes twinkled as he added, "He was more of a dandy though. I never saw him dirty even when he'd been in the saddle for five or ten days. Don't know how he did it." Chancy chewed for a time then added quietly, "He carried a gun, but it was his knife that he loved. Talked to it like a woman."

Miguel looked at Chancy. His face showed no expression, but his eyes glittered as he spoke.

"Heard of him. How do you know him?"

"We rode for the same spread for a time. The last I saw of him, he said he was headed north with a herd.

"There was a little gal by the name of Laurel in Denison. She worked down on Skiddy Street. Her husband hired her out there as a dance partner. Angel kind of looked after her for a time.

"There were four or five of us in that dance hall the night Angel left. We all rode for a spread not far from there. He asked us to make sure no men got too friendly with her.

"Laurel was a nice gal. She shouldn't have been dancing in that place for sure.

"I drank too much one night not long after that, and I begged her for a kiss. She let me take her outside and then she whacked me a good one. When I woke up, she was gone."

"Perhaps you did not do such a good job of protecting her. I don't think that is what this Angel meant for you to do."

Chancy's face turned red and he shook his head.

"I was drunk. I couldn't believe it when she agreed to go outside with me. Why, I was almost nervous! You're right though. Angel wouldn't have been happy with me. I never saw him after that though. Laurel either.

"Her boss was fit to be tied because Laurel just up and disappeared.

"Duke Dugan was her husband's name. He was a lousy husband and a mean man. He was killed not long before that. He tried to cheat at cards and got caught." Chancy threw a twig into the small fire.

"I say good riddance.

"Never could figure what that little gal saw in him. Women are just confusin'. What would make a nice gal marry up with a scoundrel like that when there are so many men to choose from?"

Miguel was quiet as he listened. He chuckled softly.

"I think my brother would not be so angry with you."

Chancy looked up at Miguel in surprise. He grinned and nodded.

"I just knew you were related. Well, I'm glad to hear that. Angel is a good man but he's deadly too. You must be Miguel. You didn't tell us your name out by the gate, and I wasn't going to ask."

Miguel tossed another twig into the fire. He chuckled again before he spoke.

"Laurel, she left with a herd shortly after that. She pretended to be a boy. The trail boss, he took her along and then she fell in love with one of his riders.

"They are now married and live up by Cheyenne. They have two little ones. Twins. A boy and a girl, and they both have red hair like her husband." Miguel's smile became bigger. "Rusty is a good man, and they are happy. That trail boss married my sister last year and now all my family lives around Cheyenne."

Chancy grinned at Miguel.

"I believe I'll hang around you a little more, Miguel, and if you head home, I'll go along. I haven't seen that north country. I think I'd enjoy it up there."

Miguel's smile faded and he didn't answer.

Chancy frowned to himself. *Something must have happened, maybe to Angel. I don't think I'll ask Miguel any more questions about his family.*

CHAPTER 35

TIME TO MOVE

TAY WAS BACK IN A COUPLE OF HOURS. "WORD'S OUT. We need to move now."

Miguel repacked the supplies and tied them behind his saddle while Tay and Chancy tried to hide the campsite. They poured water over the embers and made sure the site blended in with the grass around it. The three men were quickly mounted and headed southwest.

Chancy looked over at his brother.

"Sheriff stop you?"

Tay grinned and nodded.

"Sure did. He asked if I had seen Poe. I told him I hadn't. I said I was in to pick up supplies. Said we might be out for some time. I never said we were *lookin'* for Poe. I just let that sheriff think it!" His grin became bigger and he added, "Poe is sure goin' to be sore about this deal."

Chancy frowned. "I hope they don't shoot him without talkin' to him first."

"Naw. He's way down to the south end of the spread. The boss sent him down this mornin' to start gatherin', him and two other fellers. They were to gather some first-calf heifers and bring 'em closer to headquarters. The boss has a man comin' out tomorrow who might want to buy 'em.

"I'll bet the boss blowed clean up when Miss Ann come a squallin' home. The old man thinks the sun rises on that gal, but she's more like a hailstorm with thunder and nasty lightnin'." Tay frowned and shook his head. "And who knows what she told her pa."

"So how did that sheriff know to ask about Poe?"

"A couple of the boys found Miss Ann close to where we left her. They were supposed to relieve Chancy and me since we'd been out since last night.

"She sent Red a hightailin' it to Cottonwood Falls to look for us. She took the other feller's horse and left him afoot.

"'Course, Red, he knew he should be lookin' for Chancy an' me but Miss Ann said to put the word out about Poe. An' that's just what he did.

"In fact, Red saw me ridin' into town. He waited for me when I left an' we talked some. I told him what had happened. He said he figured it was somethin' like that.

"Miss Ann's madder than a wet cat in a flour sack though. She wants all three of us dead." He looked over at Miguel and added quietly, "She told Red you tried to get fresh with her. Then she claimed Chancy an' me just stood there an' did nothin'. 'Course, she didn't know our names except that one of us was Poe. She knew what we looked like though.

"I think it would be best to move fast."

Miguel frowned. "Stories like that can get a man killed. I think we will skip the towns and ride southwest. Ellinwood should be two- or three-days ride from here if we don't hit any more fences.

"I need a good bath and a shave, and there's a barber there who is one of the best. Besides, all the places we will want to visit are under the town." He grinned at his companions. "Saloons, bathhouse, laundry, and cat houses all under the streets where the good folks above don't have to deal with them or us cowboys either. And this time, I'm taking a bath in first water."

When Chancy looked at him in confusion, Miguel grinned. "They use that bath water three times and you pay accordingly. I'd think long on that though. That third water is a little thick." His dark eyes twinkled as he added, "Maybe if I win enough gambling, we can sleep in the Wolf Hotel." He shrugged and added, "Or if my luck is not so good, we will sleep with our horses. Either way, we can get a bath and drink a few beers." His dark eyes were laughing when he added, "But I do not share my bed with other men even if they are my amigos!"

Chancy and Tay laughed, and the three men pushed their horses to a lope. The three riders tried to cover their tracks. Even with all their backtracking, they still reached Ellinwood four days later.

CHAPTER 36

A Town Beneath the Streets

IT WAS MAY 4, AND THE TOWN WAS SHUTTING DOWN for the day. However, the party beneath the streets was just getting started.

The three men left their horses in the livery and headed down the steps at the end of the block to the town beneath the streets. Miguel led the way to the barbershop. He ordered first water while Chancy and Tay tossed a coin to see who won first water and who would use the second.

The bath area was quiet when they arrived. However, all seven tubs were soon full. Within an hour, the small area was crowded with men who lounged and smoked as they waited to take baths.

The steam from the laundry hissed. The damp, hot air didn't encourage soaking for too long, and the men were moved in and out of the long tubs quickly. The tubs were dragged toward the back of the room and dumped in a sort of ditch that ran along the wall. They were barely rinsed before they were refilled.

Chancy shook his head. *Miguel was right. That water is downright murky when one feller gets finished. It will be thick when the second gets out.*

They had sent Tay to pick up clean clothes while he waited on Chancy's water. Chancy didn't care much what he wore but Miguel had specific orders as to what Tay brought back.

Miguel and Chancy walked next door to the barber shop while Tay finished. A short cowboy grinned as he climbed into Tay's dirty tub to use his allotted third water.

The man who was running the laundry pointed at their dirty clothes.

"If you want those washed, just pile them together over there. I'm behind now but I'll be caught up by morning. You can pick them up before you leave town. We are open all night and most all day too down here. I do close for a few hours over breakfast though."

Tay nodded and then jabbed his thumb behind him.

"How many saloons are down here? I've never seen a town under the streets before."

"Oh, there are at least eleven saloons, a couple of brothels, a harness shop and even a library. Looking at your new duds, I see you found our mercantile. We have about everything down here a man could want. This part of town is two blocks long, and businesses are on both sides of the street.

"An eating house just opened on the other side. They call it Granny Fay's First-Rate Food, and it fills a man up." The man laughed before he added, "Fay used to own one of the brothels, but she got tired of the men calling her Granny. She finally decided to make her living another way. 'Course, she has a good following.

"Now if you fellows have any reading material on you, the library is always looking for new books. They'll swap you but I doubt they'll pay. No money in libraries, you know."

The friendly man grabbed a load of clothes and started back toward his washtubs. He turned around and hollered after Tay, "A word of advice—if you want to stay at the Wolf House, you had better make reservations right away. It will be full in an hour or so, maybe even by now. 'Course, they don't let no dirty bodies sleep in their beds and that's why she fills up so fast."

Tay nodded and waved to the man. He was smiling when he entered the barbershop.

The barber had just finished with Miguel and was starting on Chancy. Tay took his place on the bench to wait. He pointed out the window.

"That man in the laundry recommended we eat at a place called Granny Fay's. Said the food was good."

Miguel looked startled. He laughed as he nodded.

"I'm sure it will be. I'll have a beer while I'm waiting on you boys. Then we can head on over there."

CHAPTER 37

Granny Fay

GRANNY FAY'S WAS BUSY. A PRETTY WOMAN WITH SOME hardness around her eyes was greeting customers.

Chancy thought she might be around fifty. She didn't look much like a grandma though, not by how she was shaped or by the way she dressed. The woman paused and looked up when Miguel walked through the door. A smile spread across her face.

"Miguel, you little sawed-off troublemaker! Get over here and give me a hug!"

Miguel strolled toward the smiling woman with a grin on his face.

"Hello, Fay. I didn't expect to see you in this business."

"And that would be thanks to you, you slippery sidewinder. You called me Granny when I invited you upstairs five years ago and that name stuck. I was furious too. It's a good thing you ran out when you did or you'd be dead." She glared at Miguel before she laughed.

"It took me about an hour to get over it though. Business picked up after that for a time." She shrugged. "That life is for a younger woman though. A man offered to buy my place several months ago and I just decided to sell while I could. I figured if I ever needed to move this business upstairs, I could do it where the old one needed to stay down here." She grinned and added, "And he paid me a premium besides.

"Now I can capitalize on my name and still be respectable. Of course, I had to sign an agreement with the buyer to not offer any of my previous job perks to my customers here." Fay winked at Chancy and he turned red. Tay laughed.

Tay tipped his hat as he continued to grin.

"Ma'am, I'm Tay and that shy feller there is my brother Chancy. We heard you had some of the best food around and decided to see for ourselves. 'Course Miguel here didn't tell us that he already knew you."

Fay stared from Tay to Chancy. She winked at Chancy again.

"There would have been a time I'd have offered to take both of you boys upstairs at the same time." Her blue eyes were twinkling. Tay didn't know if she was joking or not but Chancy turned even redder. He mumbled and started to turn around.

Fay grabbed Chancy's arm.

"I'm just funnin' you. Now come on. Since you are friends of Miguel's, I'll give you my best table." She looped her other arm through Miguel's and led them to the back of the room.

"Tell me about that brother of yours, Miguel. Is he still single? I always enjoyed his stories. And Spur? I think you boys knew him down in Texas. What's he doing now?"

Miguel laughed as he sat down. He grinned as he looked up at Fay.

"You didn't move fast enough, Fay. They both married last year. Spur married a widow with three kids and one on the way. Her husband had died while she was pregnant.

"Angel married a schoolteacher from back east. They have a little one coming this summer plus they took in a couple of little orphans."

Fay stared at Miguel a moment before she stuttered, "No way did Spur marry let alone a woman with kids!"

"He did. I haven't seen him since he married but the word is he's plumb happy. He settled right into family life. Seems to like being a dad."

"And how about you, Miguel? You didn't go and get married too, did you? I've had about all the shocks I can stand today already."

Miguel's face lost its smile. He looked down for a moment. When he looked up, Fay could see his smile was forced.

"What are you offering today, Fay? Give us three of your best meals and then tell me where I should go to gamble. I need to play a little poker to win enough money for a hotel room tonight."

Chancy frowned slightly. *There's that sadness again. Maybe Miguel got himself married and it went bad. Or maybe he was to marry and she ran off. I'm not asking though. If he won't talk of it to an old friend like Fay, he doesn't intend to talk about it at all.*

Fay hurried off and Tay leaned back in his chair. He grinned at the two men in front of him.

"Chancy and me have a little over $110 between us. Now my brother won't let me carry any money because I'm not as responsible as him, so just what are we going to do while you gamble?"

Miguel grinned at the two brothers.

"You are going to quietly sip your beers without drinking enough to get drunk. I want you to keep an eye on the game, and that means I want you sober. One can stay at the bar and one can wander over to my table. I don't want anyone to know we are together though. Just keep an eye out for trouble and watch my back.

"We'll split what I win. Of course, I might lose. Then, we will be sleeping in the stable and I will be borrowing money from you." He winked at the brothers.

Tay laughed but Chancy was quiet. Their new companion hid his thoughts under jokes and smiles. It was something to keep in mind.

The men quit talking when their food arrived. All three would have agreed that Fay had found a second calling that she did well.

CHAPTER 38

Old Friends

FAY SAT DOWN TO VISIT WHEN THEY WERE NEARLY finished. The little eating house was still full but there was no longer a line at the door. Tay nodded toward the door.

"Business slow down about this time most evenings?"

"A little. It will pick up again around nine tonight. We stay open until two in the morning if business is good. If we're not busy, I might close early." She grinned at the men.

"I do what I darn well please down here. I know the hours we should be busy, and I know when things are going to slow down.

"My cook used to be my bouncer, so he is used to long hours. Besides, I pay him well. He has done me right for lots of years."

Chancy looked back in the kitchen where a large man with a bald head was cooking. The man's biceps bulged through his shirtsleeves and his partially-open shirt was stretched tightly across his hairy chest. The man glanced at their table more than once while Fay talked and Chancy could feel the goosebumps come up on his back.

Fay caught Chancy staring back in the kitchen and she laughed.

"That's Babe. He can be as mean as he looks but he's as gentle as a kitten most of the time. We don't get many complaints about his food though." She laughed again as she looked back at Babe and he grinned.

Fay's face changed as she looked at Miguel. She pulled a worn envelope out of her pocket and laid it on the table in front of him.

"That came about two weeks ago. A rider dropped it off with Babe. He gave it to me when he saw you come in tonight. The rider who left it said it was urgent that you get it.

"Babe told the man we hadn't seen you in three years. The man insisted Babe take it. He said Angel was certain you would show up here. That rider was to give it to Babe or me, and to no one else."

Miguel looked at the envelope a moment before he quietly shoved it inside his vest. He said nothing.

Chancy stood. "Come on, Tay. Let's wander down the way and grab a beer. I've got a terrible thirst coming on."

The two men left, and Fay put her hand over Miguel's.

"Maybe it is good news, Miguel."

"I don't think so." Miguel glanced across the busy eating house. When he looked back, Fay was surprised by the pain in his eyes.

"I did marry." Miguel paused, and when he looked at Fay again, she could see the rage in his eyes. "A man from my wife's past paid to have her killed." he picked at the tablecloth before he continued.

"She was hurt badly after the buggy she was in rolled. The doc said he didn't give her very good odds to live. She was pregnant and almost bled to death when she lost the baby." Miguel wiped a shaky hand across his face.

"She was dying when I left Cheyenne. I just couldn't stay and watch the life leak out of her. I went to Kansas City to find the man who had ordered her death."

"And you found him?"

Miguel nodded. "I did." A hint of the old Miguel showed in his eyes as he added, "I guess the old man didn't appreciate me tying off his precious son's manhood. Now the son will no longer be a young bull who hurts women, and the old bull is dead." The smile left his face and he shrugged.

"I didn't have to kill the father. My horse and my sister's mule did it for me.

"I headed west after that. I met Chancy and Tay when they tried to shoot me for crossing their boss' land. The boss' daughter wasn't happy that I lived." Miguel grinned at Fay.

"They decided to ride with me instead of being strung up." He looked away and was quiet.

Fay waited for him to finish before she asked quietly, "And now what?"

Miguel shrugged. "I don't know. There is nothing for me anywhere now." His dark eyes were bleak as he spoke. "Perhaps I will pick a fight tonight that I can't win."

Fay frowned at him.

"That could kill Chancy and Tay too, you know. They consider you their partner and they would fight to the death for you. I think that would be a selfish thing to do. And I doubt very much your wife would be happy with you." Fay smiled at Miguel as she squeezed his hand.

"She must have been a special woman to trip you up. You haven't even hit the brothels yet tonight, and that would have been your first stop five years ago."

"She was sunshine and light. When we were together, we laughed all the time." Miguel shook his head and grinned at Fay. "We were both irresponsible and married on a whim. And still—she was the one, Fay. She was the part of me that was missing. The part I was looking for and didn't know it."

Fay put out her hand.

"Give me the envelope, Miguel. I will read it. If it is more bad news, I will give it back to you or I will throw it away. But maybe it will be good news. Let me read the letter. Maybe your wife lived."

Miguel shook his head. Fay rolled her eyes and deftly lifted the envelope out of Miguel's pocket. She laughed softly when he glared at her.

"Never have a conversation about unrequited love with an experienced pickpocket, Miguel." She waved at Babe.

"Bring us a bottle of my good stuff."

Fay waited until Babe returned to the kitchen. Then she poured each of them a drink and lifted her glass.

"To old friends, old memories, and happy endings." Fay tapped Miguel's glass and drained hers. She waited until he finished his drink before she opened the envelope. She read it quickly, frowned and read it again. She was smiling when she looked up.

"Flory lived, Miguel! Your wife is alive and recuperating at your sister's ranch. Angel said you need to come home quickly. The young men are all convinced she is a widow. He said he is tired of running them off!"

Miguel stared at Fay. His face became pale, and he took the letter with shaking hands. He read it quickly and dropped it to the table as he stared at her.

Fay was laughing and Miguel stood. He grabbed her and swung her around as he laughed.

He picked up the letter and shoved it into his pocket. The smile on his face was huge.

"Now I have to gamble because I don't have enough money to get home." He kissed Fay's cheek as he whispered softly, "Thank you, my friend. Thank you for stealing my letter. I wouldn't have read it, and I might have never gone home." He turned and strolled out of the room. He paused by the door and tipped his hat to Fay. The sparkle was back in his dark eyes when he spoke.

"Granny, if you ever get tired of this place, Cheyenne has much need of older women. We have many old men who are just wishing for wives." He ducked the glass Fay threw at him and was laughing as he sauntered down the tunnel towards the first saloon.

CHAPTER 39

A Reckless Man

CHANCY AND TAY LOOKED UP WHEN MIGUEL STROLLED into the saloon. He looked around the room and then eased his way to their table.

"Hello, my amigos. I see you have been drinking without me. So did you find me a card game with some unlucky men so I can take their money?"

Chancy frowned. "I don't think you should play this game. I can feel the tension here. Let's try another saloon."

Miguel looked at him in surprise and slowly nodded.

"Sí. There are ten other saloons to choose from."

He led the way out of the dark saloon just as a man stood and yelled, "I'll shoot all of ya!"

The three men dove for the door and slid around the corner. They put the rock wall between them and the men shooting inside the saloon.

Miguel stood and grinned at Chancy as he pulled him up.

"I think I will listen more often to you, señor. I think perhaps your instinct to survive is better than mine." The three crossed under the street and strolled along, looking in saloons as they passed. They finally stopped at one called The Three Ds.

The men pushed up to the bar and Tay pointed at the sign.

"What are the three Ds? Drunk Devils Die?"

"Nope, but maybe it should be." The bartender wiped the bar with the towel he kept tucked inside his belt and grinned at them. "Drink an' Dance Downunder. We been open nigh on three years now, an' that's longer than most of these places last.

"What'll ya fellers have? The beer's cold an' the whiskey's hot."

Miguel turned around with his beer in his hand. He watched one of the card games in progress for a time. He glanced over his shoulder at the bartender.

"Who are the fellows playing at that table over there?"

"Cobb is the big fellow. He ranches south of here. Big outfit. The other men are from out of town. Don't know them." He looked at Miguel closely. "They play for high stakes though, and Cobb rarely loses."

"He plays a little loose with his cards."

The bartender looked hard at Miguel and began to carefully wipe his bar again. His voice was soft when he spoke.

"I wouldn't say that too loud. Cobb tries to run this town. He even owns this bar and that means I work for him. He thinks he's a king and I reckon he kinda is."

Cobb looked up just then. Miguel grinned at him as he touched the brim of his hat and lifted his beer. His voice was loud as he directed his voice to Cobb.

"To cows, to money, and to cards. May you have more than you need of all three, señor."

Cobb stared at Miguel and almost rose to his feet. Instead, he settled back in his seat.

"Maybe you'd like to join this game, unless of course you are just another loud-mouthed cowhand who talks more than he works."

Miguel laughed easily and nodded.

"It is true that I like to use many words. But then I can ride anything with hair, and I have loved many women as well. Perhaps one of your daughters, yes?"

Cobb lunged to his feet and jerked for his gun.

Miguel drew his easily and had it pointed at the angry man. He looked around the saloon. Nearly a fourth of the men there had their guns drawn as well and they were all pointed at him.

He laughed and slid his gun back into his holster. He shrugged.

"Perhaps we should play some cards, señor. Then we will see which of us talks more." He started for the table and Chancy set his beer down. He nodded at Tay and the two men separated as they moved to opposite sides of the room. Lots of men were moving to get a better view of the upcoming game, and no one seemed to notice the two brothers.

The cowboy who had been drinking beside Tay was the only man in the room who showed no interest at the possibility of gunplay. He never turned around and just continued to nurse his beer. Only when Miguel called for a new deck did he look up. He put his hand out to the bartender.

"I'll take that deck. And make sure it's a new one. I'd hate to think you give a man marked cards." His voice was soft, but his eyes were hard as he stared at the bartender.

The bartender cursed under his breath and muttered, "I knew those three fellows were trouble. Now that big mirror behind my bar is going to get shot out again, and it will be another six months before I can get another one in. And the boss will dock my pay for every week it takes."

The cowboy grinned at him and nodded.

"Could be. Maybe you should look for a new boss." His grin became bigger, and he pointed his finger toward the end of the bar. "I'll take that shotgun you have under the bar too."

The bartender cussed again as he handed the stocky cowboy his shotgun. He pulled off his apron and threw it down as he walked around the bar.

"I quit. The money here isn't bad but I am tired of nearly dying every night." The door swung behind him as he stomped out.

The cowboy turned around. He pointed the shotgun at the table where Cobb sat.

"Cobb, this is going to be a fair game or I'm going to split you in half. You know I don't care if I live or die, so I just hope you try something." He tossed the cards toward Cobb and a cowboy caught them. The man placed the deck carefully on the table and backed away. The cowboy holding the shotgun looked around the room.

"Now back up, boys. I want a clean shot at King Cobb if he pulls something."

Miguel looked back at the cowboy. He pushed his hat up as he scratched his head.

"I think, señor, if you shoot this man that I will be shot as well. Now dying unnecessarily by a shotgun with two barrels is not how I planned to leave this world. Perhaps we should discuss this."

The cowboy grinned at Miguel. "Guess you'd better be quick then. Now start playing."

Tay listened as the cowboy talked. He nudged the man beside him and asked quietly, "Who's the feller holdin' the shotgun. He seems to be on the prod."

"Yeah, he is. His name is Frieder. He has a little ranch next to Cobb's. He has good water and Cobb wants it. He worked that place with his sister after she lost her husband. That was nigh on two years ago.

"His sister broke her leg three days ago, and Frieder rode to town to get the doc. While he was gone, Cobb had some of his men run a herd of cattle through their place. Ran them right over top of his sister's two little ones. They were playing in the barn and tried to get to the house. The momma rushed outside to get them. Some of the riders tried to turn the cattle but it was too late. They was all three run over. Then Cobb blocked the road to keep the doc from getting' through.

"Frieder fought to get back home, but it was too late.

"Yep, he's got reason all right. I reckon Cobb didn't see him in here or he would have had him killed. Heck, I didn't even notice him until he turned around.

"Frieder's not a gunman but he's tough as boot leather. It will take more than one bullet to bring him down if it's not a kill shot, and he'll take a pile of men with him." He nodded toward Miguel.

"I hope your friend is a card sharp. Cobb will figure a way to cheat and then he'll have your friend killed. You and anybody else who rides with him will be lucky to make it back up to the streets tonight."

Tay listened closely. He grinned and stepped away from the man who had been talking.

"Well, you'd best not talk to me then. Folks might think we are friends." He moved to the outer edge of the crowd and leaned up against the stone wall at the back of the saloon. He slipped the thong off his gun and loosened it in its holster.

Chancy was on the other side of the room. The two brothers barely looked at each other but each was sure he knew what his twin was thinking.

CHAPTER 40

No Friendly Game

COBB THREW A PILE OF BILLS DOWN ON THE TABLE. Miguel stared at the money and chuckled. He looked around the room.

"Señors, you do not know me, but I came here to win. If you would all like to add a little to my pot, I will do my best to make us all some money." He grinned at them and added, "If I lose, I will not be able to repay you, but if I win? Then we will all be richer and with this man's money too." Miguel winked at Cobb as he grinned.

Cobb looked around the room. His hard eyes were cold.

"Any man who lays money on this table had better have a fast horse. There won't be room for him in this county when this game is finished."

Frieder stepped forward. The stocky cowboy had wide shoulders and a big smile. He stared at Cobb as he laid down $200.

"I sold some cattle last week. I'll be the first to start this pot." His eyes were hard as he looked around the room. When they came back to Cobb, he added, "And no man tells me what to do, Cobb. For sure not a back-shooting killer who targets women and babies." He stared hard at Cobb and then spit on the floor. He backed up, keeping his shotgun pointed at the man.

Cobb's face turned pale, and his eyes narrowed down. He despised Frieder. Not only did the man refuse to move, but neither was he intimidated by Cobb's threats.

"Keep talking, Frieder. I'll have you buried by daylight."

Frieder cocked both barrels and laughed.

"If I go, you go—and I'm purty sure you want to live more than I do."

Miguel stepped between the two men. He pushed the gun barrel up and slid the money toward Tay.

"You keep an accounting. If you don't know a man's name, ask him."

The pile of money on the table grew quickly and Cobb's face became redder with each addition. Chancy glanced at the total written on Tay's tally sheet. When everything was added, Miguel's kitty was nearly $3000.

Miguel smiled at Cobb. "Let us begin. I must win much money from you to repay my amigos. And since you are at a disadvantage, I will even let you deal first. Proceed, señor."

Chancy stared and shook his head. Cobb was furious and Miguel continued to bait him. *I'm not sure what that letter said but it didn't seem to whoa Miguel back on being reckless. I hope the three of us make it out of here alive.*

The game began. Cobb won a little the first three hands. His cruel face showed his pleasure, but Miguel remained unconcerned.

As he began to deal the sixth hand, he smiled at Cobb. His hands were quick as he shuffled the cards.

"I believe I will have to work a little harder, señor. You are quite skilled with the cards, I think. Quite lucky too."

Cobb's lips tightened and Miguel laughed. He looked around at the gathered crowd.

"Do not worry, my amigos. This game is going to move faster. I do not think we will be here all night."

Miguel looked at his cards. His face showed nothing, but Cobb's breath came a little quicker and he laid down $300. He smirked at Miguel.

"Raise me or fold."

Miguel frowned as he looked at his cards. He raised $400. Cobb looked at his cards again and then laughed triumphantly.

"I'm going to use you to wipe down that bar, cowboy...and then I'm going to kill you."

Miguel shrugged as he looked at Cobb.

"Perhaps, but you will need to beat me first." He dropped the last of his money in the center of the table to top the amount Cobb had bet. Then he reached inside his vest and laid his wallet on the table.

"Call or raise. I am growing tired of this game."

Cobb stared at Miguel and looked again at his cards.

"I call." He laid his cards down in front of him. It was a straight flush of six through ten. Cobb tapped the cards and laughed. He started to scoop the pile of money toward him when Miguel laid his cards down.

Miguel's hand was a royal flush. Cobb stared. Five cards were fanned out on the table, face up. The red diamonds showed clearly against the darkness of the table. A ten, a jack, a queen, a king, and an ace. King Cobb was beaten.

Cobb jerked to his feet.

"Impossible! That was an impossible hand! You cheated!"

The room became quiet as the men listening understood what he had just said. Frieder stepped forward.

"Take off your coat, Cobb. Let's look in your sleeves."

Cobb's face was purple with rage. He jerked his left hand up and a small gun slid into his hand. He shot Frieder and the man pulled both triggers of his shotgun. Miguel dived away from the table as the force of both barrels lifted Cobb and threw him against the wall.

Frieder lurched sideways. He looked down at his chest and staggered. He held onto the shotgun though. Several men tried to help him, but he shook them off as he staggered back to lean against the bar. Chancy and Tay stepped forward. One pushed the money into a hat and the other covered the room with his gun. Miguel's gun was also drawn, and no one had seen that happen.

"Now you boys hold tight. Tay here will count this and give you back what you put into the pot. Then we'll split the rest." Miguel's voice was cool as he looked around the room.

One man pointed at Cobb's body. The shotgun blast had nearly torn his body in two. The lapels of his coat were riddled and frayed. A bloody wallet had slipped out of his pocket and was laying on the floor.

"What about Cobb's wallet? He always carries a pile of cash."

Tay stepped forward and pointed at the wallet. "That money should go to Frieder. It's not much compensation for losing his family but it's a start."

Miguel nodded.

"Somebody get a doctor. Get Babe too. He should be able to slow this bleeding until the doc gets here."

Frieder looked down at his chest. He staggered as he slipped to the floor.

"Ain't gonna make it. Too much blood."

Miguel chuckled and shook his head.

"Surely you do not intend to die from such a small gun. You were nearly six feet away and a small gun like that is not accurate that far.

"Let's let the doc check that wound. Perhaps you have many more tough years left in you."

Frieder stared at Miguel a moment.

"I cain't stand the sight of blood." He coughed as he looked down at his chest. His face turned white and he shuddered before he looked at Miguel again.

"How about you? Get any buckshot in you?"

"I think it is good that I am a very quick vaquero. You were quite sudden, and you did not give me much time to dive to the floor." Miguel laughed softly. "Besides, there is now enough dinero for you to double what you laid down." His face became serious and he added, "Plus you are going to receive all that Cobb had in his pockets."

Frieder closed his eyes and tears leaked out of them. "It don't matter. I don't care about the money or my little spread. Cobb destroyed it all when he took my sis and those little girls."

Miguel spoke softly. "Sí, I understand. Still, it is not good to spend your life in sorrow. Perhaps you would like a change, yes? Come north with me. Sometimes distance can heal a heart."

Frieder looked away. "Maybe. Don't rightly care. It would be easier to die right here."

Babe arrived and he pushed Miguel aside. He stopped and pointed at Miguel's back before he leaned over Frieder.

"When I am done here, we need to get that buckshot out of your back."

Miguel looked at Babe in surprise. He touched his back where he felt stinging. When his hand came away bloody, he stared at it and frowned.

"I think I did not move as quickly as I planned."

A man lifted Cobb's arm and was laying him down on the floor. An ace and a king of diamonds fell out of his sleeve. He held them up to show the men who were picking up their money and a murmur went through the crowd.

Miguel winked at them and grinned.

"It seems that new deck had a few more cards than it should have or else one of us was a cheater. Perhaps both of us." He shrugged and added, "I guess we will never know." He climbed to his feet and pointed at one of the swinging doors leading into the saloon.

"Come. Help me to take this door off so we can move this man over to Doc's office."

The men soon had Frieder carried to the doctor's office. They gathered in the room until the crotchety old man threw most of them out. He snorted after he examined Frieder.

"Shoot, that bullet glanced off his chest and tore through a little muscle on his side. He'll be stiff for a time, but he'll be back in a saddle in a few days." He shook his head and laughed softly.

"Frieder nearly passes out anytime somebody bleeds. Cows or horses he can handle but not people.

"Not sure how he handled it when the kids got hurt. He told me that he could work on livestock, but people were a whole nother deal." He jabbed his finger toward Miguel.

"Now you lay down on this table and let me look you over. Babe told me you have some buckshot in your back, and I want to take that out."

Doc prodded in Miguel's back for about five minutes. Then he applied some salve and wrapped a rag around him.

"Keep that on there until you get home. Then take a good bath and leave it off. That shot wasn't too deep so you should be fine." He glared at Miguel and added, "But you had better leave that wrap on there for the next few days!"

Miguel nodded somberly but his dark eyes sparkled.

"Tell me what I owe for me and for my amigo too. I'll take care of his bill since he did all of us a favor." He looked toward the railroad as he pulled some money out of his vest pocket.

"The train still come through here around four every afternoon?"

Doc nodded. "It does and don't be late. She don't wait on a man or livestock either. There are no cattle going out on this one so the stop will be a short one."

Miguel nodded and yawned.

"We just as well get some sleep, boys. We can get up late tomorrow and laze around a little before we catch that train." He pointed at Frieder.

"Tell this man we'll be at the boarding house if he wants to stay in town." Miguel thanked the doctor again and strolled down the street to the boarding house.

CHAPTER 41

A Bad Accident

THE MEN WERE UP BY SIX THE NEXT MORNING. THEY had just finished their breakfast and were crossing the street to the train station when a stagecoach came careening down the street. The driver was slumped over the seat sideways. The men started to jump back when they heard a woman scream.

"Katie! Paula! Get out of the street!" A mother was running into the street to grab her children. They were trying to run toward their mother, but the runaway horses were bearing down on them.

Miguel didn't hesitate as he raced toward the runaway team. He grabbed the traces of the closest lead horse and held on as he was dragged down the street.

"Whoa, boys. Whoa down." He swung his leg up over the lead horse's back and sawed on the lines. The horses slowed slightly. Miguel swung the team to the far side of the street, away from the frightened children. The stage bounced from side to side, nearly tipping over. He was finally able to get the horses stopped and he dropped to the ground. The frightened horses were shaking and trembling, and Miguel held tightly to the lines. He talked to the team softly as he tried to calm them down.

Chancy and Tay jerked the doors to the stage open. A woman and man nearly fell out. The brothers grabbed the two passengers and dragged them away from the stage.

Tay ran back for the driver. He caught the dead man's arm and pulled him off the seat. Just then, a rider raced his horse into town. He was hollering loudly for the sheriff as he spurred his horse down the main street. He sawed on the reins, but it was too late. His horse struck one of the stage horses as the rider tried to swerve around the crowd that was beginning to gather.

The frightened team lunged and surged toward Miguel. The lead horse closest to Miguel reared, pawing the air. His hoof hit Miguel in the chest. Miguel staggered back, still holding the lines when the frightened horses in the rear began to lunge. They surged in their harnesses and reared as they charged him. Miguel tried to leap out of the way, but the swing horse knocked him down. The six-horse team once again raced down the street, running over Miguel, and bouncing the stage along behind them. It careened to the left and rocked back to the right, this time flipping over.

The horses didn't slow. They dragged the grating and grinding stage behind them until the tongue broke off. The horses ran on into the early morning, the tongue bouncing behind them. It hit and cut the back horses as the broken wood smashed into the ground and flipped back up in the air. Finally, the horses were out of sight. All was quiet for a moment on the dusty street.

The town quickly came alive as people rushed to help. The woman who had screamed rushed toward Miguel.

She was crying as she leaned over the battered cowboy.

"I'm so sorry, Miguel," she whispered. "You saved my children. I owe you everything."

Miguel stared up at her for a moment as he tried to smile.

"Señora Pumphrey? You tell Polly I did it for him." Miguel tried to laugh but it was more of a groan. He smiled as he squeezed her hand.

"My old amigo traded in a pard for a wife and some kids." He tried to smile again and then clenched his teeth as he whispered. "I think it was a good trade."

Chancy and Tay were soon beside Miguel. Chancy leaned over him and then stood. He hollered, "Get the Doc. We need him *fast*!"

He dropped back down beside Miguel. The vaquero pulled him down closer. His voice was barely a whisper when he spoke.

"Take care of my wife. You tell her I love her. You tell her I was coming home. I—I—tell her I'm sorry. Tell my Flory..." Miguel's hand relaxed on Chancy's shirt and slowly slid away.

Chancy's hand shook as he gripped Miguel's. He slowly sat up. His chest was tight. Tay looked away when Chancy looked toward him. The two men said nothing.

Doc was already running toward them. He leaned down quickly to check Miguel and then slowly rocked back on his heels. His voice was soft when he spoke.

"This man is dead. Do you fellows want to bury him here or take him back home?"

Chancy didn't answer but Tay gestured toward the west.

"We'll take him home. Do you have an undertaker? Otherwise, if you can tell us where to find some wood, we can build a coffin ourselves."

Frieder pushed through the crowd. He stared down at Miguel. His voice was trembling when he spoke to the cowboy beside him.

"Tell Johnson over at the barbershop that we need a coffin and we need it fast. This fellow needs to be on that four o'clock train today."

Chancy and Tay lifted Miguel's body. They followed Frieder to the barbershop and laid their friend on a table inside the door.

The barber looked up from the man seated in his chair. He dropped his razor and wiped his hands as he walked toward the men. He tossed a towel to the man who was still seated and looked down at Miguel.

"I can have a coffin ready for you in a couple of hours." He paused and asked softly, "You want the top nailed shut?"

Chancy and Tay were quiet, but Frieder nodded. "Nail it on. We can pull it off when we get there if we need to."

Mrs. Pumphrey had followed them, and she stepped forward.

"Would you like some women to prepare him?" She looked over at his three friends and gave them a shaky smile. "Miguel was a partner to my husband for a time before we married." Her voice caught in her throat as she continued. "My husband never let just anyone call him Polly, but he liked Miguel." Her smile became wider as she added, "He called Miguel 'Bandy' because he always referred to him as 'that little Mexican bandit.' In fact, they both refused to use each other's given names.

"They rode together for several years though and remained the best of friends." She touched Chancy's arm. Her voice caught as she tried to smile at him.

"We can clean him up a little. Maybe put a fresh shirt on him?"

The three friends stared from Miguel to the women. Chancy nodded.

Mrs. Pumphrey pointed behind her at two of her children.

"Andrew, you, and Katie go home and get your father. Ask him to come to town at once." She looked back at the three men standing in front of her.

"If you can tell me where Miguel's warbag is, I will send one of the children for it. He probably has a clean shirt in there." She smiled again and put out her hand.

"My name is June. Let me take over now. We will have Miguel ready for you men to take home in plenty of time."

CHAPTER 42

A Sad Pard

APOLLO PUMPHREY HAD TEARS IN HIS EYES AS HE helped carry Miguel's coffin onto the train. Polly was a small man in stature, but his size was misleading. He was fearless and as tough as nails. He shook hands with the men who were traveling with Miguel.

"You give Angel my regards. Those Monteros are a fine family." He shook his head as he looked at the coffin and laughed softly.

"Bandy was wild and reckless. He should have died lots of times in the nearly three years we rode together. Crazy thing that something so simple as a runaway team would take his life." He rubbed a hard hand across his eyes and looked out across the rolling plains. "You just never know."

He jumped out of the train just as a black horse charged for the open door. People screamed as Demonio jumped into the passenger car.

He reared when Chancy put out his hand.

"Come on, boy. We'll put Miguel in your car. You can keep an eye on him." Once again, the men lifted the coffin. They carried it out of the passenger car and walked back to where a door was open on a livestock car. Demonio followed beside them with his nose nearly on Miguel's coffin. The men set the coffin down gently.

Apollo laughed softly. "Old Demon. He has been with Bandy for as long as I have known him. I guess he intends to keep watch over him now too." He dropped down from the car and walked over to stand beside his wife. The little family waved. June dabbed her eyes as they watched the train pull away.

Chancy was quiet for a time. He finally looked over at Frieder.

"That cowboy who was hollering for the sheriff had run off some bandits who held up the stage. They shot up the driver, but old Johnson still managed to get the stage away. He was shot bad enough that he died though. He had the team moving mighty fast and when he died, there was no one to control them. They had been running out of control for nearly a mile when they hit town. Those bandits were chasing the stage and didn't give up until right outside town.

"That fellow who spooked the horses was sure sorry. He almost cried when he found out Miguel died."

Frieder and Tay were quiet as they listened. Chancy nodded his head toward Frieder.

"I wasn't sure what you would do. You didn't have to make this trip. I don't think the end of it will be so easy."

Frieder shrugged.

"Not much in my life has been easy. Ang lost her husband two years ago. I stopped to see her between riding jobs and stayed to help. Nothing for me here now. Besides, I figure I owe Miguel and his family for making Cobb pay." He was quiet as he looked through the slats of the livestock car.

"I never was much of a farmer, but Ang loved black dirt. Her and the kids helped put the crops in the ground. They helped take care of them too.

"Our spread butts up to the Pumphreys so I asked Apollo to work the land. He'll hold onto my share of the crops for me and keep an eye on my few head of cows.

"If I see something up north I like, maybe I'll sell out down here and make a new start with cattle." He shrugged and added, "If I don't find anything that calls my name, I might take a riding job and bounce around for a time. Either way is alright with me.

"The extra land will help the Pumphreys too. June's pa is wealthy but Apollo refuses to take any help from him. He's a proud man. Shoot, I might even let him work my land until he owns it. They all work hard and have been good neighbors too.

"Apollo even offered to help me go after Cobb the night Ang died. I knew we'd both die in the process though, and I didn't want to do that to June." He pushed his hat back and cursed softly.

"Hard thing to lose a loved one. I feel sorry for Miguel's wife. I sure don't want to be the one to tell her."

Chancy was quiet as he listened. He nodded toward his brother.

"Tay sent Angel a wire. Told him we'd be in Cheyenne tomorrow. He said we were bringing Miguel home, and that Angel should come alone.

"We figured it might be easier for Miguel's wife if she found out amongst family and not in the middle of town."

Frieder nodded. None of the men felt like talking. The car was quiet when Frieder suddenly chuckled.

"Did Miguel tell you his story about Apollo and the snakes?"

Chancy shook his head. Tay turned around to listen too.

"Apollo is deathly afraid of snakes. He hates all of them an' shoots every single one he can find.

"Miguel knew that an' messed with Apollo all the time.

"One time, Miguel found a nest of baby black snakes. He put 'em in a sack an' carried 'em back to the bunkhouse.

"He came in early that night. Made some excuse about bein' sick. Even skipped supper to make sure he was there when the fun started. He turned 'em loose in Apollo's bed. He went so far as to put a hot stone under the blankets to make sure those snakes had somethin' warm in there to make 'em stay.

"Miguel waited until he heard the boys coming to bed. Then he pulled that stone out of Apollo's bed and settled in to wait.

"It had been a long day and Apollo was tired. You saw how small of a fellow he was. Well, he was always cold. He dragged his bed closer to the fire that night, threw on some extra blankets, and crawled in.

"He had barely hit the mattress when he exploded out of there. He grabbed his six shooters and started firin' at that bed. The other fellows were all bustin' out of their beds, tryin' to get away.

"Not Miguel though. He knew what Apollo would do. He had pushed his cot as far away as he could move it, plumb on the other end of the bunkhouse. 'Course, he was laughin' so hard he fell out of his bunk.

"Apollo emptied two pistols an' was reachin' for his rifle when one of the riders stopped him. It took three men to hold onto 'im while the rest of the fellers pulled back the blankets.

"That bed was shot to hell but in all that firin', he only hit one of those little bitty snakes. The rest of 'em made a break for it when the boys pulled the blankets back. Those fellers spent most of an hour tryin' to catch the rest of those snakes.

"Apollo was madder than a wet hen. He wanted to shoot Miguel, but his six guns were out of bullets.

"When things finally quieted down and everybody headed for bed, Apollo pertineer killed Miguel a second time.

"His bed was shot all to pieces an' it plumb broke apart when he climbed in. He had shot that bed so many times that the bottom fell clean out of it. The mattress an' the blankets were full a holes too. He grabbed for his guns, but the other riders had hid his extra bullets. They wouldn't give him back his rifle neither.

"The boss showed up about that time. He asked what all the ruckus was about. Apollo pointed at the bed an' yelled, "This durn ranch is full a snakes an' now we've got 'em in the bunkhouse! I plumb ruined a good bed an' all my blankets too just tryin' to kill 'em. I figger the least you owe me is a new quilt!"

Frieder grinned as he looked at the two other men.

"'Course, Apollo didn't stay mad long. That boss was June's pa. She had been away at school an' when she came home, she took a likin' to that sawed-off little cowpoke. She made him a real nice quilt. Invited him on a picnic too. And that there was the end of Apollo's free and easy life.

"He never did leave Kansas. They settled on a little spread south of Ellinwood a ways, right next to Ang and her first husband. They ran a few cows and then decided to get into the hog business.

"Pork is in high demand now. Makes sense too. Who doesn't like a little bacon with his eggs?

"They settled down on that little spread. Now they have five kids, and those durn hogs are what pay the bills."

Frieder's smile slowly left his face as he stared toward the coffin.

"Miguel was reckless, but he was a good man. None of us knew him well, but I'm guessing he would have stopped those horses even if he had known he would die doing it. I'm guessing his only regret was making his wife a widow."

CHAPTER 43

SAD NEWS

THE TRAIN PULLED INTO THE CHEYENNE STATION fifteen hours later. The town was alive at seven in the morning, and the train depot was busy when Chancy pulled open the door of the livestock car. He saw Angel sitting in a wagon by himself. He dropped to the ground and slowly walked toward his friend.

Angel jumped out of the wagon and moved toward Chancy with a smile on his face.

"Hola, my amigo. It has been too many years."

Chancy could see the sadness around his friend's eyes even through his smile.

He gripped Angel's hand and shook his head.

"I am sorry to bring you sad news, Angel. Miguel was a fine man."

Angel said nothing as the two men walked toward the train car. Frieder had gone to get the horses and Tay was waiting beside Miguel's coffin.

"You remember my brother, Tay."

Angel nodded and the two men shook hands. The three of them lifted the coffin from the train and carried it to Angel's wagon.

Frieder watered the horses and joined them. Once introductions were made, Angel looked around at the three men.

"Come, my amigos. Ride out to my brother-in-law's ranch with me. Flory is staying there with my sister." He frowned and shook his head.

"Flory, she has been very sad for several days. I think perhaps she knows Miguel is not coming home. Her heart will be broken, but I do not think she will be surprised."

Angel was usually talkative, but he was quiet on the ride to the ranch. Chancy finally cleared his throat.

"Do we need to pick your wife up somewhere? Miguel said you were married."

Angel nodded his head. "Sí, my Anna is Flory's sister. She is the teacher at our little school.

"When I received your wire yesterday, I rode to the school. I told the children there would be no school for the rest of the week. I said their teacher needed a vacation." Angel's dark eyes flashed with humor. "The children call me Mr. Teacher, and they know my rules are never as strict as Miss Anna's. When I come to the school, they know I often bring candy. Sometimes, they get out of school early—often, it is both."

Angel's face became somber as he added, "Anna stays at the school during the week, and we will pick her up there. She wants to be with her sister today and tomorrow too." Angel was quiet for a time before he spoke again.

"Did Miguel get the message that Flory lived before he died?"

Chancy slowly nodded.

"He received a letter while we were in Ellinwood. He never said what was in it, but he was in a hurry to get home once it came." Chancy chuckled as he added, "Of course, he had to gamble to get some money. None of us had enough to get up here." His smile disappeared and he was quiet.

"How did my brother die?"

"He rushed into the street to stop a runaway team of horses. The stage driver had been shot, and the team was out of control when they came racing into town. They would have run right over some kids. Miguel was able to stop the horses, but they spooked a second time, and he was trampled.

"He found out before he died that those kids belonged to an old friend of yours by the name of Apollo Pumphrey."

Angel's eyes opened wide, and he laughed softly.

"Polly. He is quite the man."

He was serious once again when he added, "Yes, I think Miguel would have been happy to save the lives of those children—any children in fact. My brother was wild and reckless, but he had a kind heart."

Angel turned the wagon up a rough road toward a little schoolhouse and the men followed him. He looked around at them.

"Perhaps you will give our children a ride on your fine caballos. The ranch we ride to is only another five miles, and I do not want them to ride in the back of the wagon."

CHAPTER 44

HELPFUL NEIGHBORS

THE MEN WAITED UNCOMFORTABLY WHILE ANGEL went inside to collect his family. He was soon back with a pretty pregnant woman and two small children.

Tay grinned down at them.

"One of you kids can ride with me and the other can ride with Frieder there. My brother, Chancy, he's a little grumpy. I wouldn't recommend riding with him."

Chancy glared at him but he was just a little relieved. He didn't know how to talk to kids and Tay knew it.

The small girl ran towards Frieder. She stopped and looked up at him with a smile.

"Do you have any kids, Mister? I'll ride with you if you like little girls."

Frieder smiled down at her. He leaned over and grabbed her arm to swing her up in front of him as he chuckled.

"I sure have given lots of rides to little girls. And what is your name?"

"My name is Mandie and my brother's name is Zach. He's bigger than me but I can run almost as fast as he can."

Zach glared at her. "No, you can't, Mandie. The only time you almost beat me was when I tripped over that old tree. And even then, I still beat you.

Frieder smiled at Mandie. His eyes were watering and he looked away before he spoke.

"Well, you hang on tight now and you tell me all about your day."

Anna looked around at the men with a smile.

"My name is Anna. Please tell me your names."

The men introduced themselves and the little party returned to the road. They were soon headed south again.

Mandie chattered constantly. Anna looked over at Angel and whispered, "Maybe I should have her sit on my lap. She is going to drive that poor man crazy."

Chancy rode close beside them and commented softly, "Let her talk, ma'am. Frieder lost his sister and her two little girls about four days ago. That little girl's chatter is like medicine for him. You just let her talk away."

Anna's face was pale as she looked up at Chancy, but she nodded. *What a difficult journey this has been for these men. One is grieving while they all bring home the body of a friend.*

Angel slowed when a buggy appeared. Lots of little heads bobbed around and happy voices carried up the road. A tall man rode beside the blonde woman who was driving the buggy. Angel pulled his horses to a stop.

"Lance. Molly. It's a nice morning to take all those kids for a ride. Little cold for a picnic though," He added with a grin.

Emilia poked her head out.

"Angel, Granny Martha is coming out today and we are going to make bear balls. Granny loves bear balls and so do we!"

Molly's face blushed. She refused to look at the men while Lance laughed.

"Bear *sign*, Emilia. We are making bear sign, or doughnuts as some folks say." She smiled at Mandie.

"Would you like to come to our house and play today, Mandie? You too, Zach. You can help us make bear sign if you want. When we finish, you kids can all play outside."

The little boy frowned. "I'm not stayin' in the house with a bunch of women. I'll stay in the barn all day before I get stuck in that house."

Lance chuckled and reached out a hand toward Zach.

"I'm not sticking around for the making, Zach, but I sure intend to come home for the eating. You want to ride over to Rowdy's place with Rollie and me? The rest of the boys are over there already. He is going to try to shoot a wolf that has been bothering his horses."

Both kids quickly slid off the horses. Mandie ran toward the buggy and Zach grabbed Lance's hand to swing up in front of him. Molly continued home with her happy passengers.

Lance's face was tight, and he nodded at Angel.

"Sure sorry to hear about Miguel, Angel. We'll keep the kids as long as you need us to. Let us know what else you need help with."

Angel nodded.

"I'll see what Flory wants to do but I think we should bury him this evening. Probably around six or so."

Lance nodded and turned his horse toward Rowdy's ranch.

Zach was quiet as they rode. He finally commented, "I heard Angel tell Ma last night that Uncle Miguel died. I don't know how he found out though. I asked Ma but she didn't want to talk about it. She said we would talk today.

"Do you know what happened?"

Lance shook his head. "Nope, I don't reckon I do." He paused and shifted in his saddle. "Folks leave this world for all kinds of reasons, Zach. Most of the time, we just don't understand why. I reckon the Good Lord decided it was time for your Uncle Miguel to go.

"I sent one of the riders in last night to tell Father Cummiskey. I'm guessing he will be out today, so we'll all go over to your Uncle Gabe's this evening." Lance's voice was soft when he added, "I don't like funerals, but I go to them for the family.

"See, Miguel, he has already had his meeting with the Maker. This funeral isn't for him. Nope, it's for the folks who loved him.

"We have funerals to comfort the family and to remember the ones we love." Lance looked down at the reins in his hand and cursed under his breath. "Miguel will be missed."

Zach was quiet for a time before he asked softly, "You think my first ma and pa met with the Maker too? My new ma says they are together in Heaven, but I just don't know how they get there."

Lance squirmed in the saddle before he answered.

"I reckon your ma is right. I think those would be some fine questions to ask that padre though. He knows a lot more about the hereafter than I do.

"Now you two boys hang on. We need to pick up the pace if we are going to get to Rowdy's in time to eat before we leave." He grinned at the two serious little boys. "You never want to hunt a wolf on an empty stomach.

"My brother loves to eat so I'm guessing he will be having a second breakfast about the time we get there."

CHAPTER 45

Miguel's Family

MERINA WAS STANDING IN THE DOORWAY OF THE house when Angel swung the wagon around. He stopped in front of her. She had Grace in her arms, and she buried her face in Grace's blanket.

Gabe rubbed his hands on his britches as he walked out of the barn. His steps faltered as he walked toward the wagon. When Angel stepped down, he wrapped the smaller man up in a bear hug. Neither man said anything as they stepped back.

Angel lifted Anna down. She hurried toward the house and Merina walked out to meet her. The two women disappeared inside while the men milled around outside uncomfortably.

"How is Flory?"

Gabe shrugged his shoulders. "Good as can be, I guess. She was crying two days ago. She said Miguel was going to die and there was nothing she could do to stop it." He shook his head. "I'm not sure how she knew but she did.

"After you left last night, she went into her room and stayed there. When we got up this morning, she was gone. Merina found her at that little spot down by the creek where the boys fish. There's a big, flat rock down there just perfect for sitting.

"I guess she spent most of the night there. She won't talk to us, and she hasn't cried since we told her." He frowned. "That kind of silence isn't good. Flory is the kind of woman who needs to talk, but we just don't know how to help her."

Angel looked toward the house and nodded.

"Father Cummiskey will be out before long. Lance sent a rider in last night. We'll let him handle it. That priest has more experience than you and I do when it comes to human emotions, especially grief." His voice was soft as he questioned Gabe, "And my sister?"

"Merina is broken-hearted. She is convinced that Miguel died because he no longer cared to live, that he died without knowing Flory was still alive."

Angel nodded. "I will go talk to her. I think she will be proud of our brother when she hears of his death."

Gabe took the lines to the team. He glanced over his shoulder.

"You men can put your horses in the corral. Throw your bedrolls in the bunkhouse. There should be three extra bunks." Gabe put out his hand.

"I'm Gabe. My wife is Merina. She is Angel and Miguel's sister. Little Emilia is the youngest. She was in Molly's buggy. I'm guessing you met them on the road.

"Come on into the barn. You can tell me who you are and how you all knew Miguel."

The men visited quietly as they rubbed down their horses. Before long, they were back in the yard. Gabe led them to a picnic table set off to the side.

"You boys take a seat, and we'll have us some cold root beer. I'm guessing this yard will be full of folks before too long. Neighbors out here have a way of finding out when there is a death. They show up with all kinds of food. They stay to visit for a bit before they go back home."

Gabe set a jug of root beer on the table and handed each man a tin cup. He gestured around him.

"Merina and her family came up the trail with us from Dodge City last summer. I bought this place shortly after we arrived from a fellow by the name of Badger McCune. You will meet him and Martha today. They are the adopted grandparents of this whole clan—and trust me, it's a big one." He grinned at them and added, "Merina finally married me. Now we have a baby girl. Emilia lives with us as well."

Some riders appeared in the pasture and Gabe waved at them.

When they were closer, he called, "You boys come on up here and meet some of Miguel's friends.

"Nate, Tobe, Bart, Dink—these fellows are from down in Kansas." He looked at the three men and grinned. "I guess I just assumed that is where you all hail from."

Chancy chuckled and nodded.

"I'm Chancy Logan and Tay there is my brother. That serious hulk of a fellow across the table is John Frieder." Chancy grinned and added, "I don't know why we bother to give his first name. Everybody just calls him Frieder."

He nodded at a large, black horse with a chopped mane and tail that seemed to be standing guard by the wagon. "That's Miguel's horse. We haven't been able to get close to him since Miguel died. We couldn't even put a halter on him. We put Miguel's coffin in a livestock car and that horse rode with him all the way up here. We stayed on one end of that car, and he kept watch on the other end.

"I hope one of you can handle him."

"I'll get Merina. She will be able to lead him." Gabe headed for the house and was out quickly with Merina. She handed him the baby and walked slowly toward Demonio. She spoke in Spanish and only Gabe understood what she said.

"Hola, Demonio. You miss Miguel too, yes? Come. Let me get you some water and some grain. I will even bring some hay back here so you can stay by my brother." She buried her face in his neck and sobbed. "Sí, we both miss him." She pulled away and put her arm around the horse's neck. He followed her quietly.

The three men stared and Gabe grinned.

"Yeah, she kind of leads me around that way too." He kissed the baby girl in his arms and laughed. "I'm guessing this one will too. I've become an old softie." He strolled over to the well and talked to Merina for a moment. She took the baby, and Gabe continued to the barn.

Merina walked toward the men with a smile on her face.

"Thank you for bringing Miguel home. That was a difficult thing to do."

The men all pulled their hats off. They mumbled and Tay spoke as he nodded toward Demonio.

"That is a heck of a horse. Will he let you ride him?"

Merina laughed and lights sparkled in her eyes.

"Sí. Even Emilia can ride him. He was Miguel's horse, but we all raised him." She looked over at Demonio and he knickered softly.

"He doesn't love any of us like he loved Miguel though. Perhaps someday. I do not know."

They all watched as a young man walked toward Demonio. The horse nuzzled his arm before it put its head back over the side of the wagon.

Merina smiled.

"Nate is Gabe's brother. Demonio sees his kind heart. I think perhaps he will become Nate's horse someday." She looked around at the men.

"Please come to the house and join us for breakfast. Angel told us you had not yet eaten."

CHAPTER 46

Frieder's Story

FRIEDER SLIPPED OUT OF THE HOUSE AS SOON AS HE was done eating. His emotions were raw, and he didn't want to talk to anyone. He glanced back as he followed a little path toward the creek.

"Maybe I will find that rock myself. I could use a little quiet time without a lot of noise around me."

He had been down there nearly an hour when he heard a quick step behind him. He stood quickly and turned around.

A young woman with lots of blonde curls and large blue eyes stared at him.

Frieder pulled off his hat.

"Beggin' your pardon, ma'am. I'm not much for big crowds or high emotion. I came down here to do a little thinkin'." He twisted his hat in his hand as the woman stared at him. He stepped away from the rock and waited for her to pass. When she didn't, he nodded his head and turned to walk away.

"Wait." When Frieder turned around, the young woman asked, "Are you Mr. Frieder?"

Frieder nodded slowly and the young woman put out her hand.

"I'm Flory." Her eyes filled with tears as she looked up at him. "Your friends said you lost your family just a few days ago."

Frieder nodded uncomfortably and looked down.

Flory touched his arm and smiled up at him sadly.

"Please sit with me, Mr. Frieder. Tell me about your family. I feel so lost. I don't know who I am right now." She walked to the rock and sat down as she stared out at the large fishing hole.

"Miguel and I had no children. Oh, I know Anna married into the Montero family too, but somehow, it's different."

Frieder followed Flory to the rock reluctantly and dropped down beside her. He stared at the rippling water for a time before he leaned back against the tree behind them.

"Ang was my little sister. She married Mort when she was fifteen and came north to Kansas to farm with him." Frieder laughed. "Ang always liked to play in the dirt. She was delighted when she found out the cowboy she fell in love with was a farmer at heart.

"They were married a couple of months later, and it should have been a long marriage. It wasn't though. Mort was killed five years later clearing some trees. A tree broke the wrong way and came down on him.

"When our folks received word that Mort had died, they asked me to come up and see if Ang needed help. That was over two years ago."

"How many children did they have?"

"Two little girls. Mary Beth was born after I came. She was going to be two next month. Ang called her Sissy. Nellie was almost four." Frieder broke the stick he was twisting in his hands and cursed softly before he tossed it into the water.

"I don't even like farming. Somehow working beside Ang though, it wasn't so bad. Now that's not to say I liked it better than running cattle, but with Ang and the girls, it was fine.

"Ang was a hard worker. She'd tackle any job head on. And those little girls—I just loved them. They were like my own." His voice was soft when he added, "I would have stayed forever if I'd had a choice. I kind of liked filling in as their dad."

Frieder frowned as he looked over the water.

"Those cowboys who ran the cattle over Ang didn't plan to kill anyone. They were just following orders. King Cobb, he wanted my sister dead. He was a big cattleman and greedy to the bone. He wanted Ang's land and her water.

"He knew his men would refuse to hurt anyone. He said he wanted them to scare her a little so she'd take down her fence around her water. He said to just run those cows through the yard, and nobody would get hurt.

"Those cowboys weren't in favor of it, but they agreed. 'Course, they didn't know Ang had broken her leg or that the little girls were playin' in the barn.

"When those little ones heard the noise from all those horns crashin' an' the cattle bawlin', they ran for the house. Nellie was carryin' Sissy. Those cowboys said she didn't drop her until—until—" Frieder cursed and shook his head.

"The riders tried to turn that herd, but they couldn't get it done. Those cows ran over the top of Sissy and Nellie. Ang too when she tried to get to them.

"Cobb didn't care though. He was a mean man, mean all the way through. He had already pushed out or killed several other small ranchers next to him to get their land.

"Ang was next. She had a creek and a nice spring that fed her pond… and he wanted all of it."

"You weren't there when it happened?"

"No, I'd gone to town to get the doc. I tried to set Ang's leg, but it didn't look right. I didn't want her to be crippled, so I wanted the doc to look at it.

"He was gone when I reached Ellinwood, so I left a message for 'im to come out when he could. I headed back home.

"King Cobb an' some a his killers blocked the road to my house while I was gone, an' I couldn't get through. His gunmen threatened to kill me if I tried. We had a standoff for nearly five hours.

"I finally broke through 'bout two in the mornin'. I took three of those gunmen with me too. They were all lounging 'round their campfire without a care in the world.

"When I rode into the yard, I found Ang an' the little girls." Frieder wiped his eyes and pushed back a sob.

"Those riders had graves dug. They figgered I'd kill all of 'em an' they weren't goin' to fight me.

"I thought about it too. I thought hard. I knew it wouldn't bring Ang back though. I could hear her tellin' me to forgive 'em.

"That's the kinda woman Ang was. Me, I ain't quite so good a man, but I let 'em live for her." Frieder cursed again and threw a rock into the water.

"There was hardly enough of 'em left to bury. We buried 'em though. Right there under a big tree.

"Those riders left that day. They picked up their bedrolls an' rode out. Two of 'em was cryin' an' the third man threw up twice while we was buryin' 'em.

Frieder put his head in his hands. He was crying as he whispered, "Ang an' those little girls died alone. I wasn't even there."

Flory stared at Frieder in horror. Then she put her arms around him. She pulled the cowboy's head against her and held him as he cried.

Frieder wiped his face and sat up. He muttered under his breath and cursed softly as he looked at Flory.

"I'm sorry, Mrs. Montero. I didn't mean to cry, an' for sure not all over a new widow." He started to stand. A sob slipped out of Flory, and Frieder sank back down.

CHAPTER 47

Two Lost Hearts

FLORY WIPED HER EYES AND SMILED BRIEFLY. HER voice was soft when she spoke.

"Miguel and I married less than five weeks ago. I was carrying a man's child I didn't even know. Miguel found out somehow. He offered to marry me to give my child a name."

"We met last fall at Anna and Angel's wedding. We had so much fun together. We were both so young, so carefree.

"That all changed when I went back home to Kansas City.

"I was terrified when I found I was with child. The people I was staying with offered to help me find a home for my baby. I was going to give it to someone else to raise.

"I had invited Miguel to visit before—before—anything had happened. I wrote him after and told him to stay home.

"He came anyway. He pretended he had not received the second letter." Flory looked over at Frieder and laughed.

"Miguel was very dashing. He was so gallant and very much the gentleman. He was quite a trickster too.

"Somehow, he found out who the man was. I'm not sure what Miguel did to him. He never told me and neither did his friends. He just told me the man who hurt me would never bother any more women.

"We were married in Kansas City and left for Cheyenne the next day." Flory smiled as she looked across the water.

"I had never been in love before. Oh, I had many suitors. I loved to flirt, and I broke many hearts. With Miguel though, it was different. It was like part of me was searching for something. Somehow, he filled that part.

"We were barely married two weeks when the wagon Nate and I were riding in was attacked. The father of the man who hurt me had offered a bounty for both Miguel and me.

"Nate saved my life, but I was badly injured. I lost the baby and nearly died." She held out her leg. A large brace showed from under her skirt. "That's when I broke my leg."

"When I awoke, Miguel was gone. Angel told me he had returned to Kansas City to get the man who was responsible for my accident.

"He said Miguel thought I was going to die, and he didn't want to watch my life seep out of me." Flory's voice was soft when she spoke. She looked over at Frieder and smiled.

"I was scared but I knew Miguel would come back. He had too.

"Besides, he led a charmed life. He was always defying death, and yet he made it out alive." Flory's breath caught in her chest, and she clenched her fists as she tried to breathe.

Frieder put his arm around Flory and patted her back awkwardly.

"Two days ago, that all changed. When I awoke, I just knew something was going to happen to Miguel. I could feel it in my soul. I panicked. I knew he had died. I didn't know how or why. I just knew he was gone." She took a shaky breath and added quietly, "I was right. Angel came out last night and told us Miguel had died on a street in Kansas.

"I was done crying though. By that time, I was just numb.

"And I'm still numb. I feel lost. I don't know who I am or what my purpose is anymore. It's like I am in a bubble, and all the people around me are on the outside moving around in slow motion. I can see them laugh and talk, but I can't feel anything."

Frieder didn't know what to say so he was quiet.

Finally, he leaned back against the rock and commented quietly, "We are a couple of sad sacks. My pop used to tell me that when I cried. I didn't really understand what he meant, but I think that description fits us.

"So now what? Do we keep mopin' around, cryin' 'bout what we had? Or do we stand up, brush ourselves off, an' get back on that big horse of life?"

Flory stared at Frieder and shook her head.

"I can't. I don't know where to go."

"Who said you have to go anywhere? Sometimes when I'm sad, I just let my horse do the decidin'. Maybe that's what we need to do. Quit worryin' 'bout what's to come an' have a little faith.

"I'm not what you'd call a church-goin' man, but I believe the Good Lord is out there somewhere. I reckon He cares about us some, or we never would have been created.

"See that sparrow up there? I'll bet he nearly died thirty or forty times this past winter. He don't remember that though. He just knows he needs food for today. Not tomorrow. Just today. An' he believes he will find it." He smiled at Flory and patted her hand.

"Maybe you an' me should be sparrows today." He grinned at her as he held out his hand. He paused a moment. A frown filled his face and he muttered, "Now if we can just keep those durn kids from shootin' us with their slingshots. Why I can't begin to tell you the number of sparrows I have killed with a slingshot."

Flory stared up at Frieder and a laugh bubbled out of her. She took his hand, and he tucked it under his arm. They walked silently back to the house, but the smiles on their faces remained for a time. Healing both their hearts would take some time but at least it had begun.

CHAPTER 48

The Bet

FLORY MOVED BACK TO CHEYENNE AFTER MIGUEL'S funeral. Martha and Badger invited her to move in with them and she agreed. She even returned to work for Sadie in Martha's dress shop.

Life took on a rhythm of normalcy, and the routine was comforting. As the herds moved north through the summer, the number of cowboys stopping by the dress shop increased. Frieder stopped by from time to time and they visited. It was good for them both to have a friend.

Shortly before closing time on Friday, June 4, a young man fresh off a cattle drive brought in a shirt. He handed it to Sadie and asked if the new gal could sew a button on for him. Sadie stared at the shirt and slowly nodded. She turned away before the young man could see the tears in her eyes.

"Slim," she whispered, "You have been gone nearly nine years, and yet little things like this make me miss you." She wiped her eyes and laughed.

"I want to remember the happy times, and this is a happy memory." Slim had cut a button off his shirt so he had a reason to talk to Sadie. That was the beginning of their relationship and it led to their short but happy marriage. His death in 1871 had broken her heart too.

She handed the shirt to Flory with a smile.

"This belongs to a young cowboy waiting out front. He was wondering if you could sew a button on for him."

Flory stared at the shirt and then peered closer at the tuft of thread that showed where the button had been cut from the shirt. She looked up at Sadie in confusion. "This button was cut off."

Sadie laughed and nodded her head. "My first husband did the same thing. Go talk to him, Flory. You might mention it will cost him less if he still has the button."

Flory sighed and put down the dress she was working on. She swung her right leg with the heavy splint out in front of her and quickly stood. She made no attempt to disguise her limp as she hurried to the front. She gave the young cowboy a bright smile and held out the shirt.

"Sadie said that you wanted a button sewed on this shirt."

The cowboy nodded shyly.

"I can do that. However, if you have the button, it will cost you less." She smiled sweetly at him and added, "And since it was cut off, I'm sure you still have it."

The cowboy's face turned a dark red and he stuttered a couple of times. Finally, he reached into his vest pocket and took out a button. He grinned ruefully at Flory as he handed it to her.

Flory took it from him and laughed.

"How much was the bet? The bet that you would be able to meet me, I mean." Her eyes were sparkling and once again the cowboy blushed.

"Now I—I just needed my button—I mean—" He scratched his head and grinned at her.

"Dad-burn it! The fellers each bet me a beer I wouldn't have the nerve to talk to you. I said I would, but I had to have something to prove it. I figgered this might be the easiest way."

Flory laughed and nodded.

"Well, give me the button. I will sew it on right now. You may wait if you want." Her blue eyes sparkled and she added, "I will even give you a receipt so you have proof it was done here." She hurried out of the room to get a needle and thread. When she returned, she could see a group of cowboys staring in through the windows. She opened the door and called, "If you fellows don't mind, please don't block my light. I need all of it to sew this button on." As the cowboys backed up, she added, "And you all owe this gentleman a beer." The crowd of cowboys grinned, and several took out their knives. Flory paused before she commented dryly, "By the way, the price of sewing on a button just went up to $5, so think hard before you cut any more of those off." She was laughing when she closed the door.

She gave the young man a bright smile as she snipped the thread.

"I'm Flory. Please tell me your name and where you are from."

"My given name is Jack, but the fellers call me Shad." He grinned at Flory before he continued. "I don't usually talk much an' they started callin' me Shadow 'cause I was so quiet. That got shortened an' now I'm Shad." He pointed his thumb over his shoulder toward the men outside.

"We are all from Texas. We brought a herd of cattle up to Nebraska last year. We held them by Ogallala through the winter an' spring. The first part of this month, we started them on up. We thought they were all goin' to be sold here but my brother just told us that some are goin' on north. Our boss has a contract with the government. He is givin' us a little time off 'fore we head out.

"Some of us came in today an' the rest will be in tomorrow." Shad watched Flory a moment before he asked, "You don't know a feller by the name of Gabe Hawkins, do you? We heard he bought a spread around here somewhere. He brought several herds up from Texas, an' my brother was hopin' to talk to him before we head out."

Flory looked up in surprise as she nodded.

"Gabe lives south of town about twenty miles. He bought a ranch out there last year. He's married now and they have a little girl."

Shad stared at her in surprise. "Well, I'll be. I'll be sure to tell Wade that. He wanted me to ask."

Flory cut the thread and handed the shirt back to Shad. She wrote out a ticket for five cents, signed her name and handed it to him. The cowboy handed her a nickel as he smiled shyly.

She laughed as she pointed at Shad's shirt. "Remember, the next button will cost you $5 so don't be cutting any more off!"

Shad grinned at her again and nodded. He pulled his hat on, and Flory followed him to the door.

"Now enjoy your beers, Shad. It was nice talking to you."

She closed the door and was humming when she returned to the back room. Sadie looked up and smiled.

"You certainly made his day." Her smile turned to a giggle and she added, "And I'm guessing that even with the high cost of button-sewing, we are going to have more riders in here with missing buttons."

Flory sat down with a sigh. She smiled at Sadie.

"I know but he was so young. He reminded me of Nate, so sweet and so shy. Besides, it served all of them right to be out a beer. They didn't think he had the nerve." She picked up the dress she was working on and began to sew again. After a moment she paused and looked up at Sadie.

"That young man wanted to know if I knew Gabe Hawkins. I guess some of those riders know him."

Sadie looked up and nodded.

"Cowboys meet a lot of people because they move around so much. Very few of them stay with the same ranch for long. At least that is what it seems like to me. They certainly move a lot when they are young."

Flory nodded absently. "Nate is restless. He wants to test his wings. I think Sam and he are planning to go on a drive of some kind."

Sadie looked up in surprise.

"They are both quite young for that. Well, probably not as young as either Gabe or Lance when they left home, but still.

"Of course, more herds are heading north all the time so I'm sure they will have an opportunity this summer."

CHAPTER 49

A Twelve-Beer Shirt

FLORY WAS HUMMING AS SHE SLID THE BOLT TO secure the door. She was just turning away when someone knocked. She paused and called through the closed door, "We are closed but we will open tomorrow morning at eight."

The man outside twisted his hat in his hand a moment as he looked through the window. He frowned.

"I need to be several hours up the trail with a herd by that time. I was hoping you could sew on a couple of buttons for me, but now that I know the going rate is $5 a pop, maybe you can sell me a few needles and a packet of buttons instead." His blue eyes glinted with humor for a moment before his face became somber again. "Please, ma'am. I only own one shirt and I don't think it can make another drive without a few more buttons."

Flory paused a moment before she unlocked and opened the door. She stepped aside and gestured for the cowboy to come in.

"Please show me what shirt needs buttons so I know what size."

The man grinned and pointed to the shirt he was wearing. Three buttons were missing from the front of his shirt. One shirt cuff was nearly torn off and both cuffs were missing buttons. She stared at his shirt and frowned before she looked up at him.

"I think what you need is a new shirt."

The man shook his head ruefully.

"That could be, but for now, I'll just keep wearing this one."

The man's tall frame nearly filled the doorway. His hands were rough and heavy stubble covered his face. Blond hair curled from under his hat. It was his eyes that made Flory pause though. They were a brilliant blue. They seemed to peer into her soul. She quickly looked away and only looked back when she put out her hand.

"Give me your shirt. I can have those buttons sewn on in no time and I will only charge you a nickel per button.

"You sit down in that chair, and I will be right back."

The man peeled off his shirt and handed it to her. He dropped down in the chair and leaned back.

Flory hurried back to her sewing area and found a new card of buttons along with a couple of needles. When she came back out, the man was asleep. Curly hair showed above the neck of his longhandles, and exhaustion emanated from him.

Flory pulled up a small stool and carefully lifted the man's feet onto it. He barely stirred.

She sat down and began to mend his shirt.

"I declare," she muttered, "this shirt is a mess. I won't have a man leave this shop in rags though, not when my reputation as a seamstress will be going with him."

It took her nearly an hour to mend the man's shirt. She had just clipped the last thread when a door slammed down the street and a man laughed loudly. Bootsteps sounded on the walk outside and faded into the distance.

The man jerked and sat up. He looked around a moment in confusion before his eyes settled on Flory.

"Well, durn. My one chance to talk to a purty woman and I fell plumb asleep. So much for all my plans."

Flory laughed and handed him the shirt.

"That is as good as I can make it. Maybe after this next leg of your drive, you will be able to afford a new shirt."

The man chuckled. He inspected the cuffs and looked up at Flory in surprise as he pulled his shirt on.

"This shirt pertineer looks new. Why I think I can get another year or two out of it."

Flory nearly snorted. She wrote up his ticket for a card of buttons, two needles, and a spool of thread. She also charged him for sewing on five buttons.

"That will be sixty cents. And your name is?" Flory held her pencil over the ticket as she waited.

"Wade Doolan but my friends mostly call me Tex." He grinned at her as he added, "You met my little brother earlier. Shad reminded me about the buttons. I figured after he shared his free beer with me that I could afford to buy a few new buttons." He dropped some money on the table and pointed at it as he stated seriously, "That right there is enough to buy twelve beers. I reckon I own a twelve-beer shirt now."

Flory looked quickly the cowboy before she laughed.

"Thank you, Mr. Doolan. And you be sure to tell Shad to be careful. My late husband was a drover and he shared some of the things that can go wrong on drives."

Tex held his hat in his hand as he turned toward the door. He paused a moment and his eyes twinkled as he drawled, "How about me? You want me to be careful too?"

Flory slowly blushed.

"All of you be careful. I hope *all* of you make it through safely."

Tex nodded seriously. He turned his hat in his hands several times and cleared his throat.

"Thank you, Miss Flory. Thank you for taking the extra time to mend my shirt. I reckon I owe you more money than you charged me. And I'm sorry about your husband too."

Flory didn't answer. She could feel the tears forming in her eyes, and she didn't want to cry today.

Tex stepped outside and she quickly bolted the door. She grabbed her shawl and hurried to the back door. She had just locked it when a man's voice sounded behind her. Flory jumped and her hand went to her heart.

"I'd be pleased to walk you home, Miss Flory. I know I kept you later than you planned."

Flory looked quickly at Tex before she turned away.

"I thank you, Mr. Doolan, but I don't walk out with men."

Tex fell in step beside her.

"It really wouldn't be walking out, you see. You need to go home, and I am headed that same direction. It would just be two people walking together."

Flory stopped and peered up at him.

"You don't even know where I live."

Tex grinned and nodded. "That's true but Cheyenne ain't all that big. I can get to my herd from just about any direction."

Flory studied his face for just a little longer before she laughed.

"Alright, you win. But we walk. I'm not riding on that horse with you."

Tex started to answer but Flory shook her head.

"Whatever you were going to say, don't say it."

He grinned and was quiet. They walked in silence for several minutes. Flory finally cleared her throat.

Tex chuckled and said, "I knew I could stay quiet longer than you. What do you want to know? Where I am from? Am I married? Do I own a ranch? Are my parents alive? Does that about cover it?"

Flory's face turned pink as she looked up. Tex's eyes were twinkling, and she laughed despite herself.

"Actually, yes. Go ahead and answer those questions. We should be where I am staying by the time you finish."

Tex deliberately slowed his walk down and began talking.

"Well, you know my name is Wade. Folks started calling me Tex when I was just a sprout. I didn't like my name much back then, and I tried to ride anything with hair. 'Course down Texas way, we think everything we do is bigger and better. I told an old man that I'd be the best rider in Texas one day and the name stuck.

"You met Shad. He is the youngest in our family. There are two girls between him and me. Margaret is right behind me. She married last fall. Dorothea or Dot as we call her is just a little older than Shad. He's sixteen and she's twenty." Tex frowned and shook his head.

"Dot is kind of a pill. She does what she wants, and no one can tell her otherwise. She met a fellow earlier this year, and I was hoping he could tame her down some. I don't know though. I'm not sure he's enough man to rope her and hold on.

"Our folks ranch down on the Brazos in Texas. Margaret and her husband, Ned, are ranching with them. They'll take over when Pop quits. 'Course, that won't be until he dies.

"I am trailing cattle to try to get enough money ahead to buy my own place, maybe in Nebraska. I like those Sandhills.

"As for being married, I ain't married yet but I'm a lookin'. Do you know any good-lookin', single women who might want to walk out with a lonesome cowboy?" Tex's eyes were twinkling as he watched Flory.

Flory was quiet a moment. When she looked up at Tex, she had tears in her eyes.

"My late husband grew up in Texas. He lived down on the Brazos River too."

Tex stared at Flory in surprise.

"What was his name?"

"Miguel Montero. We weren't married long though. He was killed in Kansas several months ago, but he talked often of his life in Texas. His brother Angel married my sister last fall. Her name is Anna. They live just a little way out of town."

Tex stopped so suddenly that his horse nearly walked over him.

"Anna Whitman is your sister? Why, I was there when Miguel and Angel rescued her. In fact, Miguel helped me get my sister, Margaret, out of Hole-in-the-Wall."

CHAPTER 50

Miguel Was My Friend

FLORY STARED UP AT TEX AND A SINGLE TEAR SLID down her cheek.

Tex wiped it off with his thumb. He held Flory's shoulders as he spoke.

"I'm sorry, Miss Flory. I heard you had lost your husband, but I didn't know your last name." He added softly, "Miguel was my friend. We grew up together and were even pards for a time when we first left home. I heard he had died and that he had married too. I was sure the last part wasn't true, so I was hoping the first part wasn't either.

"I'm mighty sorry to bring up sad memories." His blue eyes gazed into Flory's intently. Finally, he turned her around but kept her arm tucked under his as they walked slowly down the street.

Flory's voice was soft when she spoke.

"I met Miguel at Anna's wedding. He was so wild and exciting. We had a wonderful time. I wrote him when I got back to Kansas City and invited him to come and see me. I didn't hear back from him though."

Flory took a shaky breath and Tex felt her body tense up. He squeezed her hand gently but said nothing as he listened.

"Something bad happened shortly after that and I stopped taking callers. I wrote Miguel a second time and told him not to come. He received both letters the same day. However, he pretended he didn't receive my second letter telling him to stay away. He showed up where I was staying in Kansas City shortly after that.

"I was living with a wonderful couple. Tillie knew I was—somehow, she and Ollie—they knew I—was with child." Flory took a deep breath.

"Miguel came while I was gone. I'm not sure what they talked about, but he came back later." Flory's blue eyes were full of tears when she looked up at Tex.

"I didn't know who the father was, but Miguel found out. He never told me what took place. He just said the man who hurt me would never hurt another woman. Then he asked me to marry him. It all happened so quickly.

"We were married April 3. We left Kansas City the next morning by train and stopped in Victoria, Kansas to pick up some bulls." Flory took a shaky breath and added, "Miguel was killed May 5." A shudder went through her, and Tex pulled her arm closer.

He said nothing but patted her arm as she cried softly. She finally took a deep breath and continued.

"The father of that man sent some ruffians out here to kill Miguel and me. I was injured when the buggy I was in rolled over." She held out her leg with the splint. "That is how I broke my leg. Nate Hawkins, Gabe Hawkins' little brother, was driving. He saved my life by throwing his body over mine.

"I lost the baby later that day and I nearly died. In fact, Miguel thought I was dying.

"He left. He went to Kansas City to get the man who was responsible, and he never made it back home." Flory sobbed and Tex dropped his horse's reins as he pulled her close.

"I'm sorry, Miss Flory. I'm sorry to bring all these sad memories back up," he whispered.

"Doc Williams told me to talk about it, but it is hard. I have barely spoken of it since the day he died." Flory gave Tex a shaky smile as she pulled away.

"I'm not sure why I told you all that. We barely know each other."

Flory could feel Tex's blue eyes looking intently at her and she looked away. Her voice was soft when she continued.

"I was angry with Miguel, you know. He left when he thought I was dying, and I was angry when I awoke. He should never have left. He should have stayed with me, even if I was dying. I was even more angry when he died." Flory dabbed her eyes with her handkerchief and gave Tex a quick smile. "I'm not mad at him anymore though. That was just Miguel's way of handling things.

"He tried to make it home. He lost his life saving some children in Kansas. A mother and father there have their little ones because Miguel stopped a runaway stage.

"I am trying to adjust. I like my routine here. I have a job doing what I love, and I have lots of friends. It is getting easier. Some days though, I just fall apart."

CHAPTER 51

For Love of a Sister

TEX SQUEEZED FLORY'S ARM. THEY WERE BOTH QUIET when he finally spoke.

"When Margaret ran away, our pa was furious. I wanted him to help me find her, but he refused. He said, 'She left of her own accord. She can come home when she's ready. I'll decide then if she can stay.'

"I took riding jobs all over. It seemed like I looked everywhere for her. After three years, I was ready to give up. Then one night in Dodge City, down Kansas way, a cowboy was talking about a girl he met. She had passed through there several years before. He said she was a real pretty little gal. She was traveling with a dandy-looking man who treated her poorly.

"The hostler was in that bar as well. He remembered her too. I described Margaret and he said it could have been her. He suggested that I head up north and see if I could get into Hole-in-the-Wall. He was sure that was where they were headed. After three years of looking, I finally had a lead on my sister, and it was not good news.

"I headed north to Fort Laramie. It's north of here about fifty miles or so. I met a drunk cowboy in the only bar there, and I showed him Margaret's picture. He stared at it for a time and nodded. He said her name was Nettie. She had asked him if he would take a letter to her brother. He said yes but she didn't show up the night he was supposed to meet her. He remembered that her brother's name was Tex but that was all he knew about her. When I told him I was going into that outlaw den, he became mighty scared. He made me promise I wouldn't mention him or how I knew for sure Nettie was there.

"I don't know who he was afraid of, but he was found dead in an alley the next morning. You can bet I didn't tell anyone else about our conversation.

"It was in Fort Laramie that I took up with some outlaws. One of them had bragged about hiding out at Hole-in-the-Wall so I figured I could get in there with them. They were evil though, and I was going to ditch them. Then they killed two men and took your sister.

"I tried to get her away. I got one of them, but they were bad medicine. I stuck with them to keep an eye on Miss Anna, and we all took off for Hole-in-the-Wall.

"Old Hattie ran that outlaw den with an iron fist. She had some hard rules and the man who took Miss Anna broke some of them. Hattie was furious that your sister was brought there against her will.

"Then I saw Angel and Miguel. They had ridden hard for three or four days and got there just before we did.

"Margaret was sweet on Miguel when they were younger. He wanted to take her away from the man who claimed her several years before. Hattie loved Miguel like a son though, and she wouldn't let him. She told him she didn't want him to become an outlaw. She said if he fought the man who had Nettie, he would never be able to escape that life.

"Once I showed up and could prove I was Margaret's brother, Hattie let me challenge the man who had my sister. She wanted us to leave fast if I won, and she set things up so we could.

"Miguel helped all right. We shot the men we had to and hightailed it out of there in Hattie's buggy. Margaret, me, and Ned Dawson headed for Texas. Angel, Anna, and Miguel headed back down here. That was the last time I saw Miguel until the night of Angel's wedding.

"I led that scallywag from back East out here. He was trying to hire somebody in Denver to help him kill your sister, and I figured it just as well be me. I could keep an eye on him that way.

"None of us talked much that night, and as soon as things were settled, I headed back to Denver. That was the last time I saw Miguel.

"'Course, I didn't know it would be. Miguel was always mighty wild and ornery, but he slid through danger like oil on your fingers."

Tex's voice was soft when he looked at Flory.

"Miguel was reckless, but he was a good man at heart. He risked his life to save my sister even though she would have nothing to do with him. Family was everything to Miguel. He just didn't know how to settle down.

"You brought out the good in him, Miss Flory. You helped him to stop running, to find his roots."

Flory's laugh was more of sob and the two of them were quiet as they walked the last block to Martha's house.

They stopped at the gate, and Flory pointed toward the house.

"This is where I'm staying. The woman who lives here owns the little shop where I work. She invited me to move in with them after Miguel died. Both she and her husband are wonderful, and I can walk to work from here as well." She smiled up at Tex.

"Goodnight, Mr. Doolan."

CHAPTER 52

So Many Friends!

TEX WATCHED FLORY HURRY TOWARD THE HOUSE. FOR the first time, he noticed she had a limp. He called after her, "Miss Flory, I'd sure be pleased if you would take a horseback ride with me when I get done with this drive."

Just as Flory looked back, the door to the house banged open.

"Tex Doolan! What are you doing in Cheyenne?"

Gabe strode past Flory and reached to shake Tex's hand.

"Nate and Sam asked to go on a drive up north. I told them no because I didn't know who the trail boss was. If it's you, I just might change my mind.

"Do you have time to eat supper with us? We held off since Flory was late." He grinned at his sister-in-law. "If I had known she was going to let a strange man walk her home, I would have been a little more concerned."

Flory ducked her head and blushed as she rushed toward the house. Both men were laughing behind her as she hurried inside.

Angel looked up with a smile. His smile grew larger when Flory blushed even darker. He sauntered toward the door to see who was outside.

"I'm sorry I'm late, Martha. I completely forgot you had invited family over for supper." Flory was flustered, and everyone but Angel was a little confused.

Angel called from the doorway, "Come in, my brother. Invite Flory's new man to eat with us. I wish to visit with him since he wants to spend time with my sister."

Anna looked up in surprise and hurried to the door. When she recognized Tex, she rushed out the door and hurried toward him with a smile.

"Tex! What brings you up this way? It is good to see you!" She put out her hand to the smiling man and laughed.

"I guess you met my sister. Please join us for supper. We were waiting to eat until Flory arrived home." She hurried back into the house and rushed to find another chair.

Merina said nothing but her dark eyes sparkled. She and Anna pulled the table out and added another board to make it longer. Both laughed as they looked at Flory.

Badger rushed to the door and peered out. He looked back at Martha with a grin on his face. "I know that feller." He was talking as he hurried toward the three men.

"Tex, what is you'ins a doin' up here? Ya live down Texas way an' I know ya ain't moved up here. Last time we talked any, you'ins was speakin' of takin' a wife an' settlin' down." He glanced toward the house and winked as he flicked his thumb. "Reckon you'ins is still a workin' on that," he added with a grin.

"Now ya come on in here an' eat with us. I done told ya the last time we met that I owed ya a meal an' I ain't fergot. Why, it's been close to twelve years since we last chewed the fat."

Tex was grinning as he shook Badger's hand. He followed the men toward the house. Angel stepped up beside Tex as they walked to the house. His dark eyes were dancing as he grinned.

"My friend, it is good to see you again. I did not know the man who helped me rescue my Anna would someday return and make her sister smile."

Gabe slowed as he looked at the two men in surprise.

"This is the Tex who helped you? You never told me his last name. I have known this man since I was knee-high to a grasshopper. Tex, this is my brother-in-law, Angel Montero. I married his sister last year."

Tex grabbed Angel's hand while he laughed.

"I have known the Monteros almost as long as I have known you, Gabe. In fact, Miguel and I were pards for a time." Tex's eyes moved to the grinning Badger.

"And when did you move up here, Badger? The last time we talked, you had a little ranch outside Kansas City."

CHAPTER 53

The Great Cat Drive

THE LOUD MEN CROWDED THROUGH THE DOOR OF Martha's small house and happy voices soon filled the kitchen.

Flory stared at the men in surprise and Merina laughed. She patted the seat beside her.

"Many people believe the West is large. I think it is not so big. It seems when a man moves around with the cattle, he soon knows everyone."

The meal was noisy. Angel had manipulated the seating to place Tex across from Flory. Gabe was on one side of him, and Angel was on the other. They were both plying Tex with questions.

Gabe grinned as he looked sideways at Tex.

"So tell us about that cat drive Miguel did. A bunch of the old gals around Cheyenne got all fired up after church last Sunday when someone mentioned how a bunch of cats disappeared some years ago.

"They said their best mousing cats all disappeared the same night. Word was a wagonload of cats turned up in Deadwood about three weeks later. We knew Miguel was in on that deal, but those gals said another cowboy was part of it too. They called him Tex. Was that you?"

Tex glanced quickly at Flory and slowly turned red.

"Now that was a long time ago. I don't reckon we need to talk about that tonight."

Merina laughed.

"Tell us, Tex. I heard some cowboys talking about a cat drive, and your name was all through the story I heard." Her eyes sparkled as she glanced over at the surprised Flory. "Yes, I think you should tell it tonight."

Tex grinned and leaned back in his chair. He pinched two of his fingers together as he stated, "I was maybe a small part of that deal." His eyes settled on Flory and his grin became bigger as he added, "Now, Miss Flory, you remember this happened a *long* time ago."

"Ol' Phatty Thompson was the one who organized that deal. That was back in '76. He was offering twenty-five cents for each cat that was caught. He had talked some of the local kids into helping him. Phatty didn't want lots of folks to know what he was doing though, 'cause he knew Sheriff Boswell would put the kibosh on it. 'Course, Miguel found out. He always knew what was going on.

"Well, shoot. Beer was five cents. Miguel and me figgered we'd just get us a little drinkin' money. We found us some traps and crates, and we offered to haul off the food scraps from the Rollins House that night." Tex's grin was big as he looked around the room. "The Rollins House seemed to serve the fussiest folks, and a big load of those fancy ladies had come in on the train that afternoon. Some of those gals had their noses so far up in the air, why they could have drowned if it rained. We figgered they'd leave some good scraps, and they shore did." He shook his head as he remembered. "I never seen so much wasted food in my life. Shoot, Miguel an' me even cleaned up some of that meat our own selves. Some of those steaks had barely been cut on."

Flory and Anna stared at Tex in shock, and he winked at them. Badger slapped his knee as he laughed, and the rest of the men were chuckling.

"Once we had everything we needed, we headed out. We started on the darkest streets in town. We set up our traps with those fresh table scraps an' cats come out of the woodwork. We barely had time to empty the traps before they were full again." His grin became bigger and he chuckled. "'Course, gettin' those cats in crates was a trick. Every time we tried to take the lid off, the cats on the inside would hit the top of that crate and liked to knock us over. After we lost several, we finally cut a little hole in the top an' shoved them through it that way. Then we'd slap another crate on top. We had on leather gloves, but we still got all scratched up. Those durn cats had a mean bite too.

"It took us several hours, but we caught a passel of 'em. We found us some chicken wire an' nailed a couple of layers of that over the holes. Miguel wired up the crates while I ran down to the livery to get a wagon. Ol' Rooster was so durned entertained by the whole story that he hitched up a wagon and went with us. He didn't even charge us.

"We hauled those cats outside town and Miguel went for Phatty. I tell you what—you have no idea how much noise a bunch of cats can make. Rooster was so disgusted with their caterwaulin' that he told me to just bring the wagon back when I was done—and I'd dang well better clean it out first. He walked back to town mutterin' about how he'd be deaf for a week after all that noise.

"Phatty was in the Painted Lady when Miguel found him. He told me later that Miguel sauntered in there and ordered a whiskey. He held it up and said, "Here's to cathouses. May the cats be wild and plentiful—and may they fill lots of party houses."

"Folks stared at him. Up till that time, no one had called those party houses 'cathouses.' 'Course, Miguel wasn't saying that either, but that's what folks thought. All the men at the bar joined him in a salute to the painted ladies.

"Phatty knew what he meant though. When Miguel left, Phatty followed him. He asked how many we had. Miguel said he didn't rightly know. He was right too, 'cause we lost count at fifty.

"Miguel said you never saw such an excited man. He offered us an extra $5 to help him get them in his big cage.

"'Course by that time, we were kind of cat experts. We turned that big cage upside down and dumped those cats in through the door. And you ain't never heard such a terrible racket in all yore livin' days. Those cats would hit the sides of that cage full force and then start to climb. 'Course, it was big enough they couldn't hang on upside down long enough to get to the hole.

"The only cat that didn't go crazy was this big, fluffy gray cat. She just sat down in the middle of all that noise and ate her meat. She didn't share either. Those other cats only came close to her one time. She just smacked the livin' daylights out of any who dared.

"When it was all done, we got paid for sixty-five cats plus another five bucks for loadin' them. We thought we should have extra for that gray cat, but Phatty wouldn't budge. He said a deal was a deal. We didn't think that was bad money for three hours of work though. 'Course we each had to buy a new shirt and another pair of gloves. Still, it wasn't a bad night.

"After Phatty paid us out, he asked what our plans were. I opened my mouth, but Miguel stomped on my toes so's I couldn't answer. He was always a little quicker than me.

"He said, 'We're headed south. We have us a good job waitin' down Texas way.' Now that wasn't true, but I was so busy rubbin' my durn toes that I couldn't even disagree.

"I'll be durned if Phatty didn't offer us $20 each to ride with him to Deadwood—to help haul his cats. I just stared at Miguel. That's where we were headed anyhow!

"That trip took us twelve days. Not bad for two hundred seventy-four miles. 'Course we moved right along—those cats made too much noise to waste around."

Flory's eyes were wide as she listened to Tex.

"But what if all those cats escaped from their cage? How would you ever catch them?"

Tex winked at her and laughed.

"They only got loose one time. It was crossing one of those creeks up there—Lightning Creek or Spring Creek—I don't remember which one. Phatty's wagon tipped over and they *all* got loose. We shot some rabbits and coaxed those cats back in with fresh meat.

"That big gray cat was the first one in. She sauntered back into that cage like a queen. She pulled one of those rabbits up under her paws and started to eat. She growled and snarled at any cat that tried to take a bite. She'd flat-out swing at them. I got to like that old girl though.

"Toward the end of the drive, we'd let her out at night. She'd crawl right up and sleep next to us. Her purr was so loud that it liked to keep me awake at first. Later though, it was like a lullaby." He winked at Flory and drawled, "I like a friendly gal—especially one with a little sass."

Flory blushed and everyone laughed.

"Phatty sold those cats off in Deadwood. Most of them went to the—those—Houses of Ill Repute. The madams paid $10 each for those durn cats—an' Fluffy—that gray cat fetched $25! I kind of wanted to keep her but that price was too steep for me. Besides, what would a cowboy do with a durn cat?

"And ya know, not long after that, folks did start callin' those places cathouses. No one seemed to know why, but Phatty, Miguel, and me knew!"

Anna and Flory weren't sure what to believe but everyone had a good laugh.

CHAPTER 54

Chasing Camels!

FLORY LOOKED AROUND AT THE FACES IN THE SMALL room. Everyone was smiling. *You are enjoying this, aren't you, Miguel. All your family and some of your friends laughing together and telling stories.*

She was startled out of her thinking when Angel spoke.

"Did you chase camels with Miguel one time in Texas? I have only heard parts of that story. My brother just laughed when we asked him." Angel's dark eyes were dancing as he waited for Tex to speak.

The table in unison stared from Angel to Tex.

Tex laughed. "Those camels were in several places down south. In fact, the word is they still are. The muleskinners still hate them too. There might be a few still in use, but I don't think the army uses them anymore.

"What Angel mentioned was all Miguel though. His horse, actually. Demonio is a lot like his sire, and his daddy despised camels. I'm not sure where he picked up his dislike, but by the time we ran into that military camel caravan around Fort Griffin, that big stud had a full-blown hate on. That was around '61 so Miguel and me were just sprouts.

"Most of the soldier boys who worked with camels despised them. It was those harebrained big wigs back East who came up with the idea.

They thought since camels do so well in deserts across the Big Pond, they ought to do well in deserts here.

"They could haul a lot of weight for sure—a thousand to two thousand pounds per animal. They traveled sixteen miles an hour and could live on sagebrush. They only drank every six to ten days so the brass thought they would be the perfect pack animal.

"The problem was none of the muleskinners here knew how to drive camels. Shoot, they didn't even speak the language those camels were trained with. They didn't want to learn either. They despised those lumbering water tanks. The mules and horses hated their smell too. They'd spook and try to bolt every time even one camel came around.

"The army had its orders though and those soldier boys had to keep trying to use them.

"Miguel's pa sent us out to Fort Griffin to pick up some mares. It wasn't far but we were young. It was our first real work, and we were excited to do it on our own." Tex grinned as he looked around the room. "Shoot, we didn't do a thing. Miguel's horse did all the work.

"Miguel was riding Devil Horse." He looked from Angel to Merina. "I know you remember him. He was your pa's favorite stud." Merina and Angel both smiled and nodded. Tex grinned as he continued, "Devil Horse was going crazy several miles before we reached Fort Griffin. We settled in for the night just outside the livestock pens. I think Miguel knew what would happen, but he didn't say a word.

"He never tied or hobbled any of his horses at night, so I didn't think anything about it when he turned Devil Horse loose that evening.

"Just before daylight, a heck of a ruckus broke out in the livestock pens. The next thing we knew, there were horses and mules running everywhere."

He looked around the room and asked seriously, "Have you ever seen a camel gallop? It's the durndest, most discombobulated animal I ever saw. I suppose there were twenty or so of those camels and they just bolted in all directions. I saw Devil Horse run at one from the side and try to take a bite out of it. That camel swung its—its hind end around and tried to kick. If it had connected, why I think it would have killed that horse.

"Devil Horse was too quick though. He was already chasing another camel he thought was moving too slow. By the time the camels disappeared, the noise in that soldier camp was loud. The officer in charge was yelling so loud *I* almost stood up and saluted.

"About that time, Devil Horse showed up. Miguel put hobbles on him and laid back down by the fire. I was mighty curious about what was going on, but I did the same.

"It was a smart move. Those soldier boys showed up at our camp not long after that. 'Course, Miguel and me were asleep." Tex grinned. "At least it looked like we were. They woke us up and asked us some questions. They didn't stay long though. Most of them were in a hurry to catch their livestock. One young soldier kept swearing he saw a big, black horse chasing the camels, but Devil Horse was hobbled. Besides, we were just a couple of kids. We couldn't have had any part in that ruckus." Tex winked at Flory and the men who knew him laughed out loud.

"Devil Horse did a fine job of acting old and innocent too. I swear, sometimes horses can act just like their owners.

"Those soldiers went on their way, but they never did find all those camels. 'Course, their Indian scouts refused to track them, and those muleskinners sure didn't want them back. In fact, we heard the rest of them escaped not long after that and *no one* went after them! The Apache liked their meat though. They killed them whenever they could.

"We turned Devil Horse loose the next morning and he rounded up all the mares. We sorted off the ones that weren't ours and headed for home." Tex chuckled.

"That Miguel. He was so durn ornery. I got in trouble every time I trailed with him."

Flory's face was a little pale, but she laughed with the rest of her family.

CHAPTER 55

A Fine Meal

WHEN THE CONVERSATION CAME AROUND TO THE trail drive Tex had completed, his face became serious.

"I'm glad I ran into you here, Gabe. You saved me a trip out to your ranch.

"I am taking a thousand head of cattle north to Fort Laramie. I have them contracted with the army. I've been asked to take another eight hundred head or so up to the Crow Reservation. The word is though that there is some unrest up that way. I wondered what you'd recommend."

Gabe's blue eyes became hard, and he shook his head.

"I'd stay away from that deal. They have the makings of a range war up there, and you would have to go right through the middle of the land they are all fighting over. Plus, you'll cross within thirty or forty miles of Hole-in-the-Wall. Depending on who is hiding out in there, they could give you some problems too.

"Now getting to Fort Laramie, that won't be an issue. That's where I'd stop though—unless the money is mighty good, *and* you have a tough crew."

Tex was quiet as he listened. He finally nodded. "That's pretty much what I was thinking. I believe I'll ride out to Fort Russell and talk to their commanding officer. I can see that commander at Fort Laramie telling me to either take those cattle on north into the Montana Territory or take them back south with me."

Gabe nodded and the men all agreed.

Before long, supper was over. Tex stood with his hat in his hand. He smiled at Martha.

"That was one of the finest meals I have ever had, Mrs. McCune. I can see why Badger here is so taken with you." He winked at Martha. He paused as he glanced toward Flory, but she wouldn't look at him. She grabbed some plates and hurried toward the wash area.

Tex shook hands with all the men again. He looked one more time in Flory's direction before he headed out the door. Gabe walked with him to his horse.

Martha handed a wrapped package to Flory.

"You run that out to Gabe's friend. I put together a little bear sign for those cowboys. If they all look as tired as that man did, I'd say they had a rough time of it."

Flory started to shake her head, but Martha squeezed Flory's hands as she smiled down at her.

"It is just bear sign, Flory. It never hurts to be neighborly. Now go."

Flory looked over at Anna. Her sister smiled and Flory hurried toward the door. Gabe was almost back to the house and Tex had just turned his horse down the street.

Flory ran down the sidewalk.

"Mr. Doolan! Wait!"

Tex pulled his horse around and rode back toward Flory.

She was a little breathless as she held the package up to him.

"Martha wanted you and your men to have this bear sign. She asked me to give it to you."

Tex leaned down and took the package from Flory.

"Thank you, Miss Flory. You thank Martha for me too." He sat on his horse and smiled down at her for a moment before he spoke again.

"I hope all that talk tonight didn't upset you. I was hoping you would enjoy some stories about Miguel's pranks."

"I did enjoy them. The stories made me miss him though."

Tex nodded somberly. He cleared his throat and looked down at his hands before he looked at Flory again.

"Miss Flory, would you consider taking a ride with me when I get back? I can pretty much think of a reason to go just about any direction. That way you wouldn't need to think of it as me trying to court you."

Flory knew Tex was smiling even though the evening shadows hid his face. She laughed.

"Mr. Doolan, I believe you had that on your mind all evening. Now just how did you plan to ask me before I came out here?"

Tex leaned his hands on the saddlehorn and grinned at her. He finally pushed back his hat and scratched his head.

"Well, I hadn't figured that out just yet, but I had been thinking on it all evening. And I sure never thought I would know nearly all your family.

"Speaking of family, that meal wasn't just fine eating. It was downright fun too.

"Now how about that ride? We can take it in the daylight or in the dark. Either is fine with me. And if you want to pack a picnic lunch to go along with it, that would be even better."

Flory was quiet as she looked up. Tex continued to grin at her, and she dropped her eyes. Finally, she looked up again.

"I will consider it, Mr. Doolan. But if I go, it will be only because my family likes you, not because you charmed me into it. And it certainly won't be in the dark."

Tex chuckled and tipped his hat.

"Well then, I have something to look forward to. I'll see you in a couple of weeks."

Flory could hear Tex whistling as he rode away. She listened to the trilling notes until the sound faded. As she walked slowly back to the house, she paused. Before she reached the doorway, she looked up.

"Miguel," she whispered, "Why did you have to make me fall in love with you and then leave me so soon? You broke my heart.

"Now you seem so far away, and life just keeps moving on. It is sweeping me along with it and I am afraid. I lost you and now your memory is being pushed away too." A sob caught in Flory's throat. "I only have some other woman's ring and thirty-three days of marriage to remember…and you were gone fourteen of those."

Only the sounds of the night answered Flory as she slowly walked into the house. Angel looked up with a smile on his face. He was ready to tease but stopped when he saw the tears in his sister-in-law's eyes. Instead, he hugged her as she walked by.

CHAPTER 56

A Long Wait

TWO WEEKS PASSED QUICKLY. FLORY FOUND HERSELF watching the door of the store and that irritated her. She had said nothing to Sadie about Tex coming by, and her friend seemed not to notice Flory's growing nervousness.

June 25 was one day short of three weeks. Flory was just bolting the front door when she heard a familiar voice. She jerked open the door and forced herself to be calm. Her breath caught in her throat, and she didn't know whether to laugh or cry.

Tex grinned at her.

"I waited a little longer just to see if you'd miss me. I guess you did."

Flory glared at him.

"That's not funny, Wade Doolan. I didn't know if you had gone back to Texas without saying goodbye or if something went wrong." Tears filled Flory's eyes and she whispered, "I thought something had happened to you."

The smile disappeared from Tex's face, and he stepped inside the shop.

"Here now, I didn't mean to scare you. How about you let me clean up so we can eat some supper somewhere? I'll even buy a new shirt so I don't look like such a drifter."

Flory backed up and took a deep breath. She smiled and hurried toward the back. She called over her shoulder, "I made one I thought might fit just in case you wanted one." She peeked around the door and added with a smile, "In case you came back."

She handed Tex a dark blue shirt. She had added front pockets and double yokes on the front and back of the shoulders. She hoped the double layers of fabric would provide extra protection from the sun. It might help the shirt to hold up longer as well.

Tex held it up to himself. He stared from Flory to the long sleeves as he held out one of the arms.

"Why the arms are even long enough! How did you get the size so close?" He grinned and added, "I barely gave you a hug."

Flory blushed a deep red, but she shrugged.

"You know cows, I know clothes." She cocked her head and was laughing when she spoke.

"You know, Mr. Doolan, I thought you were shy when I met you. I think I misjudged you. You are not shy at all."

Tex grinned. "Sometimes I can't find my words but most of the time, I'm not too shy. Let me pay for this shirt before I walk you home. Then I'll go clean up.

"Can I pick you up in an hour or so?" He winked at her again and added softly, "After I walk you home since you already told me you don't ride on men's laps."

Flory didn't answer. She pushed Tex out the door and bolted it shut before she rushed to the back to gather her things. She was walking down the steps by the time he led his horse around to the back. They walked side by side down the street.

Flory was quiet for a few minutes before she looked up at Tex.

"I used to ride like that with Miguel—on his lap, I mean."

Tex looked at Flory in surprise. He was quiet as he waited for her to continue.

"Not before we were married but we often rode that way afterwards." Her voice was wistful when she continued.

"Miguel was wild. He was funny and charming. He didn't worry about anything. He was quite irresponsible, but then so was I. We were like two kids playing house." She smiled up at Tex.

"I feel like I have aged ten years since he died, and that was barely two months ago."

Tex reached for Flory's hand, and she didn't pull it away.

"We had so much fun when I came out here for Anna and Angel's wedding last November. Miguel was an incredible dancer. He danced as wild as he lived, and I loved it.

"I wouldn't come downstairs when he arrived at Tillie's house in Kansas City. I didn't want him to see me. I didn't want to see anyone. My stomach had grown, and it was obvious I was with child." A small sob caught in Flory's throat. She pushed it down and laughed softly.

"Miguel threatened to come up to my room if I didn't come down. When I came down, I tried to tell him what had happened. Somehow, he already knew.

"When he asked me to marry him the next day, I said yes.

"I knew it was a silly, impetuous thing to do but I did it anyway. It seemed right to both of us." Flory had tears in her eyes when she smiled at Tex.

"And it was right for the time it lasted. We were so happy. For fourteen days, we were happy.

"Nate, Gabe's little brother, was taking me out to their ranch. Merina was in labor, and I was going to help her with her little ones.

"Those men came up behind our buggy. Nate knew they were up to no good. We tried to outrun them, but we couldn't. Nate told me to get ready to jump. The buggy started to flip and we jumped. Those men ran their horses over us. That was when I broke my leg.

"I hurt the baby when I fell. The doctor thought I was going to bleed to death. He finally was able to stop the hemorrhaging, but I was barely alive. I don't remember much about that time." Flory took a deep breath before she spoke again. Her voice was sad when she continued.

"That was when Miguel left. He thought I was dying. Miguel told Angel he couldn't stand to watch the life drain out of me. He went to Kansas City to find the man who hired the killers."

Flory's voice caught and she started crying. "Miguel was coming home when he was killed. He was killed when the stage horses he stopped were spooked and ran a second time. The horses and the stage ran over top of him. He died on a dusty street in Ellinwood, Kansas, and I never saw him again." Flory was sobbing and Tex put his arm around her. He stopped his horse and pulled her close.

"I'm sorry, Flory. I'm so sorry." He patted her back and hugged her tightly. She finally stopped sobbing and gave him a wan smile. Tex gently kissed the top of her head.

"Now we are both going to need a bath. You have almost as much trail dust on you as I do."

Flory smiled again as she looked up at Tex. She whispered, "I'm glad you came back,"

Tex wanted to kiss her right then. He really did. He held back though and hugged her instead.

CHAPTER 57

Merina's Plan

MERINA WAS WAITING FOR GABE BY THE DOOR WHEN he came in the house around four on the ninth of July.

"I think we need to talk to Uncle Chet. He mentioned to me last week that Pop was about ready to retire. We have Miguel's share of señor Cole's inheritance. I think we should buy their ranch."

"Well, that technically belongs to Flory. Maybe we should ask her what she wants to do."

Merina's dark eyes were laughing as she put her arms around her husband. "Perhaps we should ask your friend Tex."

Gabe looked down at Merina in surprise.

"Tex? What does he have to do with anything? I saw him in Cheyenne nearly two weeks ago. He had the herd delivered and was paying his men out. He should be back in Texas by now."

"He didn't go back."

Gabe stared at his wife.

"He didn't go back to Texas," Merina said with a laugh, "and he has been spending nearly every evening with Flory. The sparkle is back in her eyes, and she is smiling. Doc took the splint off her leg, and she no longer limps." When Gabe continued to stare at her, Merina punched him in the chest.

"Flory has found love again! She is in love with Wade!"

"Well, I'll be. And how do you know all this? You have only been to town once since they met."

Merina shrugged as she laughed.

"I watched them with a woman's eyes." She wrapped her arms around Gabe's neck and whispered, "I watched them with the eyes of a woman who loves her husband very much. Sí, they are much in love."

Gabe grinned down at her. "And now to ensure they stay close, you want to buy them a ranch."

Merina shrugged again. "Shad went back home. Wade told his brother to decide what he wanted to do because he was staying up here. I think Shad will sell their cattle in Texas and he will come back.

"Wade is working for several ranchers right now. He is a day worker and has made no effort to find a permanent riding job. I believe he is looking around for a ranch.

"Perhaps you should help him since he is your friend." She smiled sweetly at her husband. "Tomorrow would be a fine day to do that."

Gabe sat down and pulled Merina onto his lap. He shook his head.

"Merina, I just don't think that I will ever be able to keep up with you. That is a fine idea though. But first, how about we pack up the whole crew and go to town tonight? The Independence Dance was delayed because they were fixing the floor in the Rollins House. It was moved to July 9, and that is today. Let's get ready and just maybe Angel will do the Hat Dance with you."

Merina smiled at Gabe as she kissed his cheek.

"You think this is a surprise, my husband, but we are ready to go. I have the children bathed. Nate hitched the surrey before he left.

"We can leave as soon as I change and you clean up. And I think that Badger will announce tonight that he is having a party at his house, perhaps next week. Sí, this ride with your friend must be taken quickly."

CHAPTER 58

A Funny Thing About Love

GABE PULLED THE SURREY BEHIND THE ROLLINS House. Rigs of every kind were already parked there. Horses were everywhere as well. They could hear the music before they entered the dance area.

Rollie and Emilia bailed out of the surrey before Gabe was even stopped. As they ran off, he hollered, "You check in every hour. And I had better not have to come find you when we are ready to leave!"

The two children didn't answer and were soon in the middle of all their friends. Gabe lifted Merina down and she hurried inside.

She called back to Gabe as she rushed toward the door, "Don't forget that pan in the back. You can bring it when you come inside."

Gabe had the pan in his hands when he noticed a little boy standing by himself. He looked closer and recognized Angel's son, Zach.

Zach was the only child who wasn't playing. Gabe set the pan down and walked over to where the young boy stood. He squatted down beside him.

"What's with the long face, Zach? I know it isn't because you are hungry, and I'm just not sure what else could be a problem for a fellow your size."

Zach's face almost crumpled when he looked at Gabe. He took a deep breath before he spoke.

"Edith Smith says I don't really belong here. She says I'm adopted, and adopted means that the people who take you in aren't really your parents. She says I won't be loved as much as that little baby inside Miss Anna."

Gabe could feel the anger boil up inside him, but he pushed it down. He took Zach by the hand.

"Come with me. I want to show you something." He led the young boy through the rigs and picketed horses to a corral about a block away. A mare and a foal were inside the corral. The foal nursed briefly and then ran to play. Soon, it came back to nurse again for a little while before it ran and bucked around the corral. The mare stood quietly. From time to time, she nickered softly to the foal.

"See that, Zach? That right there is love and contentment. Now what you don't know is that foal's mother died in birth. That little foal almost died too. In fact, most of us didn't think he would live.

"The mare in that pen lived on another ranch. She lost her foal and was just bursting with milk. She nickered all the time and tried to get out of the corral. She wanted her baby, and she din't know why it wasn't with her.

"Now the ranchers who owned those horses got together. They rubbed that dead foal all over the sick one. Then they took that sick little foal and put it in with this mare.

"At first this mare wasn't sure what to do. She didn't think it was her baby but it kind of smelled right. She sniffed it all over and finally started to lick it.

"Once a mare licks a foal, her scent is on it. That's when those two men knew she was going to claim that colt. And you know what? That little foal tried to stand, and before long, he was nursing.

"You remember this little foal and his mother the next time Edith Smith says you aren't really part of your family. Angel and Anna would fight to the death for you. In fact, they both have already. And just because they will have other kids doesn't mean they will love you less.

"That's the funny thing about love, Zach. When it's divided, it just keeps growing. And another thing. If you want to call Angel Pa or Pop or Dad, you go ahead. I think that would plumb tickle him pink. You are his son, and you can call him whatever you want.

"The same is true of your ma. Just because the other kids call her Miss Anna in school doesn't mean you have to. She is *your* mother. She will always be your mother, long after you get out of school." He lifted Zach up and gave him a hug. As they turned back toward the Rollins House, Gabe continued to talk.

"And one last thing—you tell Edith Smith that you have more cousins and relatives around this town than she ever will—and they just keep coming. Why we will flat fill this part of Wyoming Territory up with all your kin one of these days.

"Edith Smith is wrong. Kids who are adopted are loved every bit as much as any other kid, and they have cousins and aunts and uncles to prove it." He grinned down at the earnest little boy who was looking up at him and listening intently.

"Just look at Granny Martha and Grandpa Badger. They aren't *related* to a single soul here. Yet they are grandparents to all of us. Nope, Edith Smith is wrong.

"You are one lucky boy, Zach. You have *two* sets of parents who love you—one set in Heaven and one set here. Most folks only get one mom and one dad to love them. God gave you two, and I'd say that makes you mighty special."

Zach listened quietly. His eyes were shining when he smiled up at Gabe.

"Thanks, Uncle Gabe. I reckon you're right. I'm going to go find my cousins."

Gabe frowned as he watched Zach run off. He muttered angrily, "And I'd better not hear Miss Edith Smith say anything in front of me about those two little kids. I might be tempted to show her just how hard an angry uncle can whack a little behind that needs it."

He was still muttering when he got back to the surrey. The casserole was gone, and Gabe grinned. *I guess Merina got tired of waiting on me. I'd better get in there and dance a little before I get asked to play my harmonica.*

CHAPTER 59

A Worried Man

GABE LOOKED AROUND THE DANCE FLOOR. HE spotted Merina on the other side and started for her. Just then, Tex and Flory walked through the door. Tex was grinning but Flory looked nervous. Gabe sauntered over to them with a grin.

"Howdy, friends. Glad you could make it this evening." He pointed across the room. "It looks like Merina saved a few spots. Come on over and sit with us." His smile became bigger as he winked at Tex.

"I thought you'd be back in Texas by now. Any particular reason you're sticking around?"

Tex chuckled and Flory blushed. Gabe tried to look surprised.

"Why, Flory. Did you mess up this fellow's plans? I sure thought he'd be gone by now."

Flory fled across the room and Gabe began to laugh. Tex smiled as he watched Flory. He turned back toward Gabe.

"Flory surely did wreck my plans. I had no idea a torn shirt would find me a woman like Flory."

Gabe nodded and pointed toward the door.

"Let's go outside. I want to talk to you about something."

The two men strolled out to where the horses were picketed. They listened to the music for a moment before Gabe turned to his friend.

"What are your plans, Tex? I know you have a ranch in Texas and family down there too. Are you planning to head back that way at some point in time?"

Tex looked down at the ground. He dug the toe of his boot in the dirt as he gazed into the starry night.

"Gabe, you and I both know that was my plan. This last drive was supposed to put a little cash in my pocket so I could expand a little. Margaret and Ned are already helping Pop. Shad wants to ranch too and our place in Texas can't support all of us. My sister Dot was engaged to be married when I left so I wasn't too concerned about supporting her.

"Things kind of blew up on Dot's engagement by the time we finished the drive up here. Her fiancé turned out to have a girlfriend on the side and Dot found out." Tex shook his head and cursed under his breath. "I honestly don't think she loved him that much so I'm glad the wedding is off. Still, Dot was mighty mad, and you know how hot-tempered she is." He frowned at Gabe and his friend chuckled.

"I do recall that. That fellow probably needs to make sure she doesn't catch him alone."

"Yeah, well he's the son of a big man in Dallas, but that won't stop Dot. She made her intentions regarding his manhood mighty clear in our area.

"I received a wire the morning before we left with the herd for Fort Laramie. It was from a friend down there telling me to get home fast.

"I couldn't leave so I sent Shad home. He's young but he's level-headed. He put Dot on a train and sent her north to stay with a friend in southern Kansas for a time.

"Shad and I own five hundred head of cattle together and he spent three weeks gathering them to start a drive. Some of our neighbors have cattle they want to send north as well. I received a wire from Shad yesterday. They are starting the herd north right away. There are over a thousand head in it now.

"I will be leaving on Sunday. I want to catch the herd before they reach the Indian Territory.

"It's late in the season to bring a herd north but we are doing it. There have been storms north of us all summer so I'm hoping we'll have enough grass." Tex's eyes moved back to the Rollins House, and he was quiet for a time before he continued.

"Meeting Flory kind of threw a kink in my plans. Before, I was willing to settle pretty much anywhere. Now…" He shook his head.

"Flory's been through too much to take her away from her family just yet, so I either need to accept some distance for a time or find a place for my family up here.

"There is land available in Nebraska and my intention was to move there. That's not where I want to land permanently though unless Flory comes with me.

"I was hoping to find a place around Cheyenne to buy, but I haven't had any luck so far. So yeah, if you have some ideas, I'm all ears."

Gabe listened quietly before he clapped Tex on the back.

"I just might have a solution to your problem, one both you and Flory will like.

"How about we take a ride tomorrow? I want to show you a place northwest of town a ways that just might work for you."

Tex frowned and shook his head.

"I was all over that area these last three days. I had heard an old fellow up that way was thinking about maybe retiring. I stopped in to see him. I talked to his son-in-law for a time, but the old man wouldn't even talk to me."

Gabe laughed and squeezed Tex's shoulder.

"You be ready to leave by seven tomorrow morning and we'll take a ride. And bring Flory if you think she would like to come.

"Now we'd better get back inside or the little gal you came with will have so many fellows piled up around her that you won't even be able to find her."

Tex laughed and the two men sauntered back into the Rollins House.

"By the way, Dot should be arriving here in just a few days." Tex sighed and frowned before he continued, "I'd appreciate it if you'd help me find her a place to stay."

Gabe couldn't see Tex's face, but he could hear the worry in his friend's voice.

"I don't think that will be a problem. Flory and Miguel bought a little house in town. Badger found it for them. Maybe Flory will be ready to move back there, especially if she has another woman staying with her."

Gabe's voice was soft when he added, "Flory was hurt bad when that buggy rolled. Nobody thought she would pull out of it. She stayed at our place for a time. Merina got her up on a horse every day. She said that would help Flory's muscles to regain some strength. That break in her leg was bad, but Merina's horse therapy seemed to help.

"Flory finally healed, and her life found a little normalcy—until you showed up." Gabe grinned at his friend. "I sure am glad you did though. Now let's go dance a little or my wife will have my hide."

CHAPTER 60

A Sassy Redhead

GABE FOUND MERINA AND PULLED HER TO HER FEET. Annie Small was seated close to them and she took Grace. Annie's stomach was so large that Gabe didn't even know how she could walk.

"Annie is going to pop any time. I don't know how she even gets around." Gabe's voice was quiet as he swung his wife into a waltz.

"She is cramping tonight. I think her baby will come soon." Merina smiled up at Gabe.

"You will take Wade to see Uncle Chet tomorrow, yes? I would love to go too but I think it will be too long of a ride for Grace."

"Yep, we are meeting at seven tomorrow morning." He pulled his wife closer. "I just don't know how you manage to find out all that you do."

He laughed and added, "Tex has a hotheaded little sister. She used to have bright red hair and I mean *red.* I haven't seen her for nearly ten years, but she was cute as a button as a kid." He grinned down at Merina.

"I thought about courting her when she got a little older, but I wanted a submissive woman. Dot had a little too much spunk for me." He grunted when Merina's elbow hit him, and they were both laughing when the dance ended.

The dance was going into its second hour when the musicians talked Gabe into playing some songs with them. Merina and Angel had just finished the Hat Dance when a young woman appeared in the doorway of the Rollins House. Several single men turned to look, and soon all the young men were staring.

The young woman's hair was bright red. Her skin was fair, and she had a sprinkling of freckles over her nose. Her blue eyes sparkled, and her smile was friendly as she looked around the room. When her eyes found her brother, she rushed toward him.

"Wade! I know I wasn't due until next week, but here I am!"

She looked around the group of women. When she spotted Flory, she grabbed her hands and pulled her up.

"So, you are the woman who messed up all of our family's plans!"

Flory's eyes opened wide, and she pulled back as she caught her breath. Tex frowned and the men who could hear began to laugh.

"I'm Dot. I'm Wade's little sister. I thought maybe I should come up and see what you were like since Wade seems to be so taken with you." She flipped one of Flory's curls and laughed.

"Wade has always had a thing for little blondes. Guess he finally found one who could put up with him."

Before she could say more, Tex took her arm.

"Folks, this is Dorothea, and yes, she is my sister." He pulled Dot toward the dance floor. "Let's dance a little while we talk."

When they were in the middle of the dancers, he swung Dot around as he frowned at her.

"You weren't supposed to come for three more days. I don't even have a place for you to stay."

"Oh, Wade, you worry too much. Besides, you know what Mother used to say about company. 'Company is like fish. After a couple of days, they both begin to stink.'

"I was at Cynthia's for nearly two weeks, and I thought I was wearing out my welcome. I was looking around for a job when Cynthia said she'd heard that the Wyoming Territory needed teachers. I figured I could find a teaching job somewhere up here without too much of a problem.

"Shortly after that, one of Cynthia's friends stopped in to see her. Somehow that girl had found a Cheyenne newspaper." She leaned closer to her brother and whispered, "Between you and me, I think she was hoping to find an advertisement for a wife." Dot grinned when her brother scowled at her.

"Anyway, there was an ad in there for a teacher this next fall. It was for a little country school south of Cheyenne.

"Well, I couldn't miss *that* opportunity. I just bought my ticket, thanked Cynthia for letting me visit, and headed up here."

Tex stared down at Dot and snorted. "You don't even like kids! I doubt you would make much of a teacher."

Dot grinned at him. "Well, I can always serve drinks in one of the saloons to make a little money. I hear sassy redheads are rare and quite popular too."

Tex glared at her and didn't answer. Dot chuckled at the look on his face.

"Come on, Wade. You know I'm joking about the saloons. I can surely find a job somewhere though. Cheyenne seems to be a hopping town. And don't worry. I'll be nice to your sweet little blonde, at least for a time. Maybe I'll even like her."

Tex stopped so suddenly that Dot tripped. His voice was hard when he spoke.

"You *will* be nice to her. You might even be living with her for a time so you can start liking her right now." He added more gently, "I love her, Dot. Give her a chance. She's as sweet as can be and genuine as well.

"Now let's get back to that table…and you'd better be on your best behavior too."

Dot laughed and shrugged.

"Fine. I'll be nice…tonight. Besides, with all the single men in this place, I doubt I'll have to sit around much." She grumbled as they walked toward the table, "You sure aren't as much fun as you used to be. You act all serious now and you never want to raise any—"

Tex gripped Dot's arm hard as he glared at her.

"No cussing either. Be a lady tonight. And stop calling me Wade. You know I hate that name."

A smiling couple was walking toward them. The man was tall and had a large smile. Tex recognized Sadie Parker, so he assumed the man was her husband.

"Mrs. Parker, meet my little sister, Dorothea Doolan." Tex put out his hand to the man beside her.

"You must be Levi. Tex Doolan. It's good to meet you."

The two couples visited a little and Levi started to lead Sadie onto the dance floor. He paused to look back at Tex and his sister. Levi turned suddenly and pulled Sadie back toward them.

"Dorothea, do you have any experience working in a law office or as a receptionist? I am going to be needing one shortly since my current receptionist is going to have her baby any time." He waved his hand toward the table where Annie and Tiny Small were seated.

Dot stared at Levi and slowly nodded.

"Not in a law office but I worked in the bank in our town as a greeter for a time. I'm not big on chitchatting though so I didn't last long."

Levi grinned at Tex's red face and laughed.

"Why don't you come by my law office tomorrow at nine? If Annie is available, I'll have her come too. I'll show you what I expect, and you can see if it is something you would be interested in."

As the Parkers walked away, Dot smiled at her brother sweetly.

"And just like that, I have a job."

Tex shook his head as he led his sister back to where his friends were sitting.

CHAPTER 61

A Roundabout Man

FRIEDER SOON APPEARED AT THEIR TABLE. HE grinned at Tex before he looked at Flory.

"How about I take a turn around the floor with Tex's best gal? Since he hasn't danced with you yet, Flory, let me be the first one."

Flory laughed and took Frieder's hand. He was a smooth dancer, and they were both quiet for a time. He finally asked casually, "So who's the redhead?"

Flory slapped his shoulder. "I knew that was why you asked me to dance!"

Frieder grinned and Flory shook her head.

"She is Wade's sister and I think she's scary."

"Scary, huh? Maybe I should ask her to dance. I enjoy a scary woman from time to time."

They visited the rest of the dance, and both were laughing when they returned. Dot was dancing with someone else, and Tex led Flory onto the dance floor.

"I guess I'd better keep you out here if I want to dance at all." He winked at Flory and she laughed.

"Oh, you don't need to worry about Frieder. He is almost like a brother. He is interested in your sister though—even though I told him she was scary."

Tex was quiet. He looked down at Flory several times and finally cleared his throat.

"I was hoping you and Dot would be friends. She is going to need a place to stay for a time and—"

Flory stopped and stared up at him.

"Are you asking me to let her live in my house? The one I shared with Miguel?"

"I was hoping both of you would live there. Like friends. Maybe you can teach her to sew. She can barely sew a button on. She can rope and shoot like a man though, and that's what she'd rather do."

"I—I don't think so. I'm not sure I want to live there at all let alone with your sister."

Tex pulled Flory closer and whispered, "She'll grow on you, I promise. Besides, I am going to be gone for several months. I think it would be good for you to move back to your own house.

"You are going to be itching for more space before long."

Tears filled Flory's blue eyes as she stared up at him. She whispered, "I don't want you to leave. I'm afraid you won't come back."

Tex spun her around and guided her to the door. As they slipped outside, he took her hand.

"Walk with me, Flory. There is something I want to talk to you about."

They walked around the back corner of the Rollins House and Tex leaned up against the wall. He held Flory in front of him as he smiled.

"What would you think of living on a ranch? Gabe told me about one I can maybe buy. I was about to give up on finding one around here until he talked to me tonight." He frowned as he added, "You wouldn't be able to work in your little shop every day though. I'm not even sure where this ranch is, but it could be over an hour away."

Flory's blue eyes sparkled and she laughed.

"Wade, are you trying to ask me to marry you? Because if you are, that was certainly the long way around a simple question."

Tex stared down at Flory and shifted his feet.

"I reckon I am, but I don't have much to offer. We might be kind of hard up for a time. If you are willing to take a chance on me, then yes, yes I am."

Flory smiled as she put her arms around Wade's neck. Tears sparkled in her eyes.

"Wade, I took a chance on you the first day I opened that shop door to a strange man after hours. You had the most amazing blue eyes, and your smile made me want to know you better.

"And I took a second chance when I prayed you would come back." She put her hands on either side of his face.

"I never planned to fall in love again and certainly not this soon, but I did. I love you, Wade Doolan. I knew I was falling for you when you were a week late in returning, and these last few weeks have been wonderful.

"So yes, I will take a chance on you."

Tex lifted Flory up and kissed her hard before he set her down.

Flory was a little unsteady as she laughed.

"I'll even take a chance on your sister—but I'm not moving everything just in case we don't get along."

"Oh, I think you will get along fine. I just hope her behavior doesn't rub off too much on you…although she could use a little softening." He stared down at Flory and cleared his throat. His voice was husky when he spoke.

"We'd better get back inside before I'm tempted to kiss you again."

They walked inside just as Frieder spun Dot by. They could both hear Dot talking. Frieder was smiling and they both seemed to be enjoying themselves.

Tex shook his head.

"That man doesn't even know the kind of wildcat he is about to tangle with."

Flory laughed as she watched them.

"Oh, I think he does. He's a tough man with big, squishy heart. Your sister just might have met her match."

Merina bumped Gabe as she pointed toward Flory and Tex.

"Look at their faces. Tex asked Flory to marry and she said yes. You should invite her to ride along tomorrow."

Gabe looked around and finally spotted Tex and Flory. They both looked happy, but they usually did when they were together.

"They look the same to me. I did tell Tex to bring her if he wanted but I doubt she will come. It's a ways up there."

Merina frowned at him.

"You let Flory decide." She looked away and muttered in Spanish. "Men. They think they know so much, but they really know so little about women."

Gabe chuckled and spun Merina around.

CHAPTER 62

A New Beginning

TEX AND FLORY WERE WAITING IN FRONT OF THE TIN House Restaurant when Gabe arrived. He grinned at them.

"I kind of wondered if you wouldn't come along, Flory." He laughed and shook his head. "Actually, Merina *told* me to invite you, but I figured that was Tex's job." His grin became bigger as he added, "She seems to think the two of you decided to tie the knot last night."

Flory blushed and Tex grinned. He took Flory's hand and nodded.

"We did. It took me a little bit of blabbin' to get my question out, but Flory said yes." His grin became bigger and he added, "Now we just have to decide whether we should marry before I head south or after I get back."

Gabe nodded. "I reckon that is up to the two of you." He pointed northwest.

"Let me tell you a little about this place we are going to look at.

"An old man owns it. He's a crusty old devil, but he's a good man. His daughter and her husband run it with him. His name is Saul Peters."

Tex pulled his horse to a stop. His face was almost angry.

"We just as well save ourselves a trip. I was out there several days ago. I'd heard that old man was ready to retire. The folks who were telling me about it seemed to think the ranch would be up for sale soon.

"The son-in-law said it wasn't his deal. We talked a little. He said I needed to talk to Peters and the old man wouldn't even see me." Tex cursed under his breath and pulled his horse around to turn back.

Gabe was smiling as he waited for his friend to look up.

"Just take it easy, Tex. The reason old Saul wouldn't talk to you is because Chet and Nancy Reith basically promised that ranch to Merina and me before we married.

"They moved in there with Nancy's pop after we bought their place.

"Reiths' ranch laid right across the fence from ours. Badger told me they were thinking of selling so Merina and I rode over shortly after we moved here.

"Rusty O'Brian is my foreman. He lives on their place with his wife, Larry, and their two little ones."

Tex growled under his breath. His horse was pointed south, and he held it still as he continued to glare at Gabe.

Gabe nodded south toward his ranch.

"Now the Monteros inherited a nice little nest egg from a man their family worked for. They used Angel's share to buy the place where he lives.

"Miguel wasn't around much so Merina held onto his money. Of course, when Miguel died, it went to Flory." Gabe nodded at Flory before he continued.

"We haven't talked about it with you, Flory. You've have had your hands full since Miguel's death. There is enough money there to buy this ranch though if the two of you want it."

Tex growled and shook his head.

"That isn't my money."

Flory frowned at him. "Wade, if you had inherited, would you refuse to share with me? Besides, it's not my money. It belonged to Miguel."

Tex slowly turned red.

"It just don't seem right is all. A man should provide for his family himself. He shouldn't be expecting his wife to support him."

Flory's frown became deeper as she looked at him. However, her voice was soft when she spoke.

"Miguel talked some about Mr. Cole. He said the man was a greenhorn and not much of a cattleman, but he loved ranching.

"I think Mr. Cole's money should be invested in a ranch. Besides, if it means we can live around Cheyenne, that will make me happy too." Flory touched Wade's shoulder and smiled.

"My family is here, Wade. Use Miguel's money to give us a start. You are a hard worker and a good cattleman. Take this money and grow our holdings." She squeezed his hand.

Tex looked from Gabe to Flory. His frown slowly faded and he chuckled. He was still grinning when he turned his horse around.

"Let's go then. We're burnin' daylight."

CHAPTER 63

LEVI'S NEW RECEPTIONIST

Dot arrived ten minutes early and Levi was pleased.

"Annie should be here soon. Tiny was going to bring her by before they headed to Doc's to have her checked this morning." Levi laughed.

"Tiny said the baby was coming last night but Annie thought he was wrong. She said she'd meet us since they would be out this morning anyway." He pointed at the receptionist desk at the front of the small room.

"That is where you would spend most of your day." He pointed toward the left. "My office is through that door, but I don't want people just walking in. Part of the job is to set appointments and keep the books. Once or twice a week, bills must be paid. I usually have Annie pick up a few payments too.

"Everything we do in here is confidential. No information from this office should ever reach the public unless I share it." Levi looked hard at Dot and she nodded.

"Would it be my responsibility to keep this room tidy? It looks like someone cleans it regularly."

"It would be. You would clean my office too. However, I don't want anything on my desk touched. Annie just pretends that it's not there."

Levi looked around the office before he turned his eyes to Dot.

"You mentioned not liking to chitchat. That is a quality I believe is necessary for this job. The people who come here come for business. Most don't want to visit while they wait.

"I expect you to be courteous and make people feel comfortable. You are not expected to carry on a conversation though.

"Your starting pay will be $15 per month, and I pay every two weeks. If you work out, your salary could increase to $20 quite quickly."

"Do you offer any kind of compensation if I send business your way?"

Levi's eyes opened wide in surprise and he laughed.

"I hadn't thought about that, but I will take it into consideration. It would certainly have to be a new client." He studied Dot and slowly nodded.

"I like that question. I will give that compensation plan some thought."

Levi cleared his throat and added, "I do expect professional conduct and dress. I'm not hiring you to *attract* customers. I'm hiring you as a businesswoman."

Dot laughed and nodded.

"Mr. Parker, I accept the job. When would you like me to start?"

"Be here Monday by a quarter till eight. I will usually be here before you. However, once you become familiar with my business and move out of your provisional period, I could possibly provide you with a key. Annie likes to do her cleaning when no one is around, and I am fine with that.

"Also, Annie uses her lunch hours to deliver meals for the saloon next door. It gives her a little more income. I will ask her if she plans to continue. I'm sure Jack would appreciate you offering to help if she is not going to return."

Dot glanced at the door and then back at Levi before she asked cautiously, "I just walk in and ask for him?"

"I'll stop over and tell him you will fill in if he needs you. He might decide to do it himself for a time, especially if Annie is planning to return. He would have to teach you the route and Jack's not what I would call a patient man." Levi's eyes twinkled and he laughed. He put out his hand.

"I will draw up a contract. You may sign it when you come in on Monday." His face colored a bit as he pointed to the room behind them.

"There is a thunder bucket in there. It is your responsibility to keep it cleaned out if you use it though." He chuckled as he added, "That was Annie's only real request when she started here."

Dot pointed to the stairs leading up to a second level.

"I am guessing that is your personal area. You don't want me to clean that, do you?"

Levi looked back at the stairs and smiled.

"No, you don't have to clean it. Sadie comes down from time to time and gives it a good scrubbing. It is barely used since I married so that is good enough."

"How about the stove?"

"If you see it needs coal, go ahead and fill it. I keep the coal outside to the left of the building. Kindling is in a wood box in the room behind you. I usually start the fire, but if you are comfortable doing that, you certainly can."

Levi pulled out his pocket watch and checked the time. He frowned and nodded toward the door.

"If you have any more questions, write them down. I'm headed down to Doc's. It looks like Tiny was right." He pulled the door open and stepped aside for Dot to exit first. He frowned as he looked around his office.

"Since Annie didn't make it today, why don't you come in at seven-thirty on Monday, and I will go over the books with you. What I require isn't difficult, but I am a stickler for neatness and accuracy."

Dot nodded and stepped out the door. She saw a gruff-looking man opening the saloon next door and she walked toward him with a smile.

"Are you Mr. Coral?" When he nodded, she continued, "I am Dot Doolan. I will be taking Annie's place until she comes back. I just wanted to let you know I would be happy to deliver your meals for you while Annie is gone. After too, if she decides not to keep your route."

Jack glared at Dot, but she continued to smile. He paused in his open door and asked, "Are you familiar with the town and the streets?"

Dot shook her head. "No, I just arrived here last night but—"

"Don't ask me again until you know your way around town." Jack slammed the door in Dot's face.

"Well, isn't he a cranky old codger. I guess I had better wander around town today and familiarize myself with the local businesses," Dot muttered to herself.

Levi had turned around to watch Dot's exchange with the saloon owner and he chuckled. He was whistling softly as he walked down the street.

CHAPTER 64

A Cantankerous Old Man

CHET AND NANCY WERE BOTH OUTSIDE WHEN GABE'S party rode up. Chet craned his neck to look behind them before he glanced back at Gabe.

"I don't see my little Merina." He scowled at Tex and jabbed his thumb at him.

"And why did you bring that transplant out here? I told him two days ago that Pop wouldn't talk to him.

Gabe grinned and climbed off his horse. He hugged Nancy and put out his hand to Chet. He pointed at the two young people on horseback.

"Chet, I want you to meet Flory Montero and Tex Doolan. Flory was married to Miguel, Merina's younger brother. I'm sure you heard he passed several months ago." Chet slowly nodded.

"Tex here, being the charming fellow he is, swept Flory off her feet. They are going to marry and are looking for a place up here so they can remain close to family." Gabe grinned again at Nancy before he added, "I thought we'd pay you a visit. Merina seems to think Pop is ready to call it quits."

An old man hobbled out of the house and shook one of his canes at Gabe.

"As long as my feet hit the floor, I won't be leavin' this here place. I done told Nancy that."

Gabe grinned and walked toward the old man with his hand out.

"Pop, you told me last year that you'd sure like to see some little ones running around this place before you died. Now here's your chance." He shook the growly old man's hand and pointed behind him.

"Flory's sister, Anna, is married to Angel. You know Angel. He is the oldest in their family.

"Tex and I grew up together down in Texas, so if you need me to vouch for him, I will. If you sell, you could probably work out something to stay here as long as you want.

"Isn't there a second house on this place? Maybe Tex and Flory could move in there after they marry."

Pop hobbled over to the horses and glared up at Tex.

"You a cowman?"

"Yes, sir, I am."

"Sir! I ain't no sir.

"How 'bout you, missy. Ya know how to rope an' ride?"

Flory shook her head. "I don't but Wade's sister does. She can shoot too."

Pop glared from one to the other. "Who's Wade? That what ya call this here feller? What kind a name is that?" He snorted before he continued.

"A woman who don't know how to rope an' ride? What good is she goin' to be to you?"

Tex pushed back his hat and grinned. He winked at Flory before he answered.

"Why I reckon I don't plan to marry her for that. I plan to marry her for all the babies we're goin' to make."

Flory's breath caught in her throat, and she blushed deeply. She reached behind her and untied a quilt from the back of the saddle. She dismounted and walked toward the old man as she held it out.

"I just finished this. I thought maybe you would like it...to keep your legs warm at night."

The old man stared at the quilt a moment before he moved his glare back to Flory.

"You a tryin' to soften me up with presents?"

Flory's chin came up as she glared back at Pop.

"Quite frankly, I don't think anyone could soften you up. I was only trying to be nice. If you don't want the quilt, I will be happy to take it back with me."

She turned around and quickly mounted her horse, holding the quilt in front of her. The two stared at each other for a time. Flory's lips were clenched together when she looked over at Tex. Fire was sparking in her eyes and her hands trembled as she held the reins.

"Let's go, Wade. You can look for a place in Nebraska."

Pop began to laugh.

"I like that little gal. She looks all soft an' purty, but she has some iron in 'er.

"Get on down here, gurl. You tell me 'bout yore family, an' that man a yores can tell Chet what he'd like to do with this here operation."

Pop hobbled toward the house with Nancy behind him.

Flory left the quilt on the saddle when she dismounted. She slowly followed Nancy toward the house.

Tex watched and asked her quietly, "You aren't going to take that quilt inside with you?"

Flory whirled around to glare at him before she answered.

"No, I'm not. That cantankerous old man can just ask for it nicely. And if he doesn't, I will take it back home. I spent a lot of time making that quilt. It can go on my bed as easily as his."

There was nothing wrong with Pop's ears, and he grinned when he heard Flory's answer. *Yes sir, I think we will just draw up those papers today. I like that sassy little gal.*

CHAPTER 65

New Owners on the Z Bar

WHEN FLORY STEPPED THROUGH THE DOOR, POP tapped a chair in the kitchen with his cane.

"Ya sit down there an' tell me why I should sell ya this place."

Nancy squeezed Pop's shoulder.

"Now, Pop, they already told you. You be nice today." She smiled at Flory.

"Why don't you tell us a little about yourself, Flory? Where are you from? I know you are new to Cheyenne."

Flory paused as she looked from Nancy to Pop. She gave Nancy a tight smile before she spoke.

"My sister and I were born in Altoona, Pennsylvania. Coal mining is the primary industry there. Our parents died in an accident when we were both quite young. Anna is five years older than me, and she managed to keep us together.

"She taught at a little country school there for about six years before we decided to make a change. We came west together as far as Kansas City, Missouri.

"I took a job there while Anna went on to work with our aunt in Kansas. She met Angel on the train from Kansas City to Council Grove, and I met Miguel at their wedding." Her face relaxed and she laughed.

"I certainly had no intentions of living on a ranch when I left Altoona. I thought my future would be in a city."

"Life out here ain't no picnic. Ya sure ya can handle life way out from town?" Pop's bright eyes drilled into Flory.

Flory returned Pop's stare.

"My sister and I grew up poor. It took both of us working to make a living.

"Kansas City was so glamorous compared to our life in Altoona. It was an incredible experience too. We made some wonderful friends there, and I learned a trade that allowed me to support myself.

"I missed Anna though. I didn't realize how much until I came out for her wedding. I would have stayed then if I'd had a job." Flory smiled wistfully.

"When Miguel and I married, I never thought for a moment that he might die young. We both assumed, or at least I did, that we would live together until we were old. We were only married a month when he died." Flory's voice caught before she continued.

"I think Miguel's death forced me to do a lot of thinking. Once I quit feeling sorry for myself, I was able to pick my life up again.

"It was hard to be a young widow, but I was learning to be happy again. I also realized I didn't need a man for happiness or security. I could support myself. That was a surprise to me but a good lesson too."

Flory shook her head and laughed softly.

"Then Wade knocked on the door of our little shop and everything changed. I had just closed for the day when he showed up. I still don't know why I let him in. Men always show up late at our shop and I never open the door for them." Flory smiled as she looked at the two people in front of her.

"Wade is nothing like Miguel. He's responsible where Miguel was impetuous. Wade studies problems before he decides while Miguel just jumped in and worried about the outcome later. It seems crazy that I could fall in love with two men who are such complete opposites, but that's what happened." She smiled at Pop and shrugged her shoulders.

"So yes, I will trade the city life for a ranch in Wyoming Territory. I'll trade it for a man who lives on the back of a horse. I'll learn to be a better cook and maybe someday, we'll have children. If we do, I'll have to learn to be a mother.

"And I'll do it all because I love Wade. I want to be with him, and I want him to be happy. He is a cattleman and that is all he has ever wanted to be.

"I have bounced all over and I am willing to try another new twist in my life."

Nancy turned away as she wiped her eyes. She hugged Flory and whispered, "You know I wasn't much of a cook either when we married."

Flory looked up in surprise and Nancy put her finger over her lips as she laughed.

"Chet didn't know the difference. He had been batching for so long that his standards were low." She smiled at her father.

"Eating was never important to Pop. He was way more interested in working and buying more cattle than anything else. In fact, he still doesn't care what he eats."

Pop snorted. "Well, I would care but ya don't stay in the house long enough to cook much. Maybe if we sell this here place, I'll be able to eat three meals a day without rushin'. Then I can sit by the window of an afternoon an' let the sunshine warm my old, cold legs."

He looked sideways at Flory, waiting for her to respond but she said nothing.

"A quilt just might feel mighty nice. A big soft one to keep the chill out of a night."

Flory cocked an eyebrow. She was almost irritated at the cantankerous old man.

"Sure wish I had one," Pop added casually as his old eyes twinkled.

Flory answered coolly, "I know where you could get a wonderful quilt. In fact, it could possibly be part of the contract for the sale of a ranch. Not just any ranch of course. A nice ranch with good grass and adequate water." Her gaze was direct as she looked at the old man.

"It wasn't accepted as a gift, but the woman who made it might possibly be willing to *trade* if the conditions were right—but you would have to ask nicely."

Pop's bright eyes glinted as he listened to Flory. When she finished, he slapped his leg and laughed.

"By gosh, gurl, ya got yoreself a deal. If you'll trade me that quilt for a chance to buy my ranch, we'll write a contract up today."

Laughter bubbled out of Flory as she shook her head.

"Good grief, Mr. Peters. Why do you have to be so difficult?"

The old man grinned at her.

"Because I don't like folks much, an' if I'm testy, they don't usually stay long. An' call me Pop."

CHAPTER 66

Happy Endings

TEX WAS TRYING TO HIDE THE EXCITEMENT ON HIS face when he walked through the door. Still, he was a little apprehensive about Flory and old Saul Peters.

He looked around in surprise. Nancy was showing Flory how to roll out pie crust and Pop was grinning.

The old man shoved a paper across the table.

"Look that over an' see what ya think. That woman of yours drives a hard bargain, but we finally come to an agreement.

"Ya kids can move in here when ya get back from yore drive. Nancy an' me decided to buy Flory's house in town. We figure we can stay in the foreman's house out here some in the summer if we feel the need, an' stay in town through the winter."

He grinned as he looked over at Chet.

"Chet there said he didn't care what we decided so Nancy an' me took 'im at his word. 'Course we talked some about this these past few months as well.

"We might even build us a house out here if we decide we don't like town life. That way I can play grandpappy to all those kids the two of ya will be makin'." His grin became bigger, and he winked at Flory.

Tex stared from Flory to Pop in surprise and the old man shrugged.

"Yore little gal ain't so helpless as she looks. Ya shoulda brung 'er along the first time ya showed up out here. Woulda saved us all a lot a time.

"An' bring in my quilt 'fore somethin' gets it dirty or tears it up. I had to work durn hard to get it."

Tex backed out the door. He returned with Pop's quilt and the men moved into the small room Pop used for his office. Pop pulled out a plat map and began to point out various parts of the ranch.

Nancy nodded toward them and laughed as she placed the top pie crust over the filling.

"Pop doesn't take to many people, mostly because he pretends to be difficult all the time. Most folks run before they really get to know him. Of course, that suits him just fine. He believes everyone who attempts to talk to him just wants to know his business, and he is determined to keep all our dealings a secret."

Flory laughed. "Anna and I met a lot of gruff old men after our parents died. Some were looking to take advantage of us, but most were gentle in their own ways. Few of them knew how to act around orphaned children let alone little girls.

"Anna was all business. She watched out for me, so I had little to worry about. I just kind of bounced around and smiled at everyone." Flory watched as Nancy crimped the top and bottom crusts of the pie together. She began to crimp the second pie herself.

"I was quite irresponsible. I thought Anna was bossy. Now I realize how lucky I was to have her as a sister." Flory's hands paused. Her voice was soft when she spoke.

"Anna almost died because of my selfishness. I answered an ad for a mail-order bride here in the Wyoming Territory. I had no intention of going, of course. The man offered to send money for fare, and I intended to use it to leave our little town."

Nancy looked up from her pie to stare at Flory in shock.

Flory's blushed. "I can't believe I was so shallow, but that was what I planned to do.

"Anna insisted on returning the money. I thought we should just mail it, but she said we owed the man an apology. She told me it was her duty as the older sister to return honor to our family name." Flory crimped the last few inches before she pushed the pie across the table.

Nancy set both pies in the oven. She sat down at the table and patted the chair next to her.

Flory laughed as she sat down. "Angel tried to talk Anna out of going when they met on the train. I think he would have gone with her, but he was headed south to sell the ranch his family inherited. Shortly after he returned to Cheyenne, Gabe and his crew left to take a herd north.

"Angel worried about Anna the entire trip. He finally decided to search for her on his way home." Flory's breath caught in her chest and her eyes were full of tears when she looked at Nancy.

"Anna would have died if it hadn't been for Angel."

Nancy put her hard hand over Flory's and squeezed.

"Now, now. You grew up and Anna found a wonderful man. And I heard they adopted some children too. Good came from your mistake and that doesn't always happen." She laughed and began to wipe off the table.

"Angel was out here earlier this summer, you know. He wanted to talk to us about selling this place then. He thought it would be a nice place for you and Miguel." Nancy's face softened and she hugged Flory.

"I'd heard that Miguel was wild and that concerned me. Chet told me not to worry though. He said, 'Miguel will grow up. I was wild too when I was young.'

"Pop told Angel we would sell." Nancy's face crumpled and she hugged Flory again as she whispered, "Miguel just adored you. We were tickled pink the two of you found love." Nancy dabbed at her eyes with the tea towel before she continued.

"Angel is the one who told us about Miguel's accident. He rode out here two days after he received the news. My heart broke for you.

"We told Angel we could keep going a few more years. We said we'd hold onto the ranch until Gabe or he was ready to buy."

She laughed as she shook her head.

"None of us ever dreamed you would be the one we sold too. We all assumed you would hurry back to Kansas City as soon as you were well enough to travel." Her smile became bigger, and she laughed again.

"And look at you. You found another good man, won Pop over, and…" Nancy pointed at the oven, "you even learned to make pie!"

CHAPTER 67

GETTING THE WORD OUT

TEX WAS PACKED AND RIDING SOUTH OF CHEYENNE before daylight on Monday, July 12. He planned to take the train south, but the station agent told him the track was torn up about twenty miles north of Denver. No trains would be running until the track was fixed.

The man's hands waved in the air as he gave Tex an animated explanation of what happened.

"Don't know when they'll get that rail fixed. It's torn up in a bad place. It will be hard to get down in there to fix it.

"Nobody seems to know what happened either. I can tell you this though—no animal did what was done. Those rails were pulled up and dragged down the track a piece. It would take several men on horseback to get that done.

"Could be Injuns but I'm guessing it was some outlaws. Who knows what they have in mind if they needed the track torn up. At least the telegraph lines aren't down."

Gabe's hands were just starting to stir when Tex rode up to the house. He tapped on the kitchen door. Gabe pulled the door open.

"Tex! What are you doing here? I thought you would be on the seven o'clock train this morning."

"I would have been, but the ticket agent said the track is torn up south of here. Telegraph line is down in several places north of you too. I thought you might want to send someone in to report those lines." He frowned as he added, "They look like they were cut about six miles back and then pulled down."

Gabe nodded. "I'll send one of the hands in. Could be somebody is planning some trouble.

"You have time to eat?"

"No, I need to keep moving if I am going to make it to Denver before that train leaves today.

"I'd appreciate it if you'd have someone look in on Flory while I'm gone though. She is moving back to her house this week. Dot is going to stay with her. We plan to sell our herd in Dodge so I should be back up here in three to four weeks." He waved as he mounted and rode out of the yard at a lope.

Gabe was frowning as he looked toward the bunkhouse. Nate was outside and Gabe hollered for him to come up to the house.

"I want you to ride into Cheyenne. Tell Elmer Tinley the telegraph lines are down about fourteen miles south of Cheyenne. Tex said they were cut and then pulled down. You might let the sheriff know too."

Nate rushed toward the barn and Gabe called after him, "Take Demonio. He could use some exercise. See how you get along."

Merina was smiling when Gabe turned around.

"I gave Nate Miguel's saddle. He was quite excited."

A few minutes later Demonio raced by the house. The conchos on the saddle gleamed in the early morning. Nate's smile was large as he waved at Merina and she laughed.

"Your Nate is nearly a man but he's still as sweet as can be." She smiled up at Gabe as she turned away from the door.

"He has been working with Demonio every day, and they have claimed each other. I'm pleased. Demonio tolerates all of us, but he is learning to love Nate."

Gabe barely nodded. He was still watching the trail where Tex disappeared between the hills.

"I don't like that the track and the lines were both destroyed at the same time. I think we need to keep an eye on things today. I am going to tell all the hands to ride careful and check the fences. If outlaws are planning to pull something, they are going to want a clean getaway." He pulled on his boots and headed down to the bunkhouse.

Before long, the hands started to drift out. They all had sidearms and each carried a rifle as well. Merina felt a chill go through her. Gabe was back inside shortly.

"I think I will ride over to Lance's and let him know. He can send a rider to tell Rowdy. We all need to be alert today."

"I will ride over to Lance's. You have a full day already," Merina offered.

"No, I want you to stay close to the house. Keep the kids in the yard too. No going to the creek to play today.

"If something is going to happen, it will probably be this morning." Gabe frowned again before he continued. "I suppose a bank robbery could take place in the afternoon, but that would cut their running time short before it gets dark—unless they are familiar with the area." He cursed softly and muttered, "I just don't know. Dark might help them get away if they know where to run."

Gabe shoveled his breakfast in and strode to the barn as he growled, "Outlaws. Why can't folks just be honest? Most of the outlaws I know of died broke. Honest living is easier on the body and for sure on the conscience." He watched as one of his riders was dumped off the horse he just mounted. He grinned.

"Well, maybe not on the body, but I'd still hate to make a living on the wrong side of the law."

Gabe saddled Buck and was riding out of the yard when he heard a single shot to the south. Most of the riders were already gone and he waited for two more shots in case it was a signal. All was silent after that, and he frowned again as he spurred Buck north.

"I can feel trouble today. It is settling all over me." Gabe's face showed his worry when he rode into the Rocking R ranch yard.

Lance walked toward him with a grin, but his smile disappeared when he saw Gabe's face.

Jonesy was racing his horse west toward Rowdy's when Gabe turned his horse for home. He paused at the end of Lance's lane and looked both directions. He finally turned Buck south.

"I'm going to ride out and see if I can find anything. That gunshot could have been one of my hands shooting a coyote, but I think I'll check anyhow."

CHAPTER 68

A Reckless Outlaw

PLUG NICKLE CROUCHED BEHIND A ROCK AND sighted in on the rider in the distance. Wes Parsons knelt beside him.

"I don't think this is a good idea. Glad said to keep an eye out for riders. He didn't say anything about shooting anyone." Wes's face was worried as he watched the rider.

"That feller is headed straight fer Denver. Who knows what news he's a carryin'."

"Yeah? What if he is just a broke cowpoke headed south? Lots of herds showing up about now and that Denver train is the fastest way to get to Texas. Besides, the lines are down so there ain't no messages coming or going.

"We done tore up the tracks south of here so a feller can't catch a train south outta Cheyenne. If we go and shoot a man that folks are expecting, that will set the law after us faster than robbing a bank—so long as no one is killed during the holdup anyhow."

Plug pulled the trigger and the man fell from his horse. He dropped heavily to the ground and didn't move. The horse ran for a time before it slowed. It came to a stop and dropped its head to grab some of the dry grass.

The outlaw looked back at the man beside him and grinned.

"Took care a that there argument, didn't I? Now we don't have to discuss it no more."

Wes looked at Plug with disgust and stood.

"I'm headed back to camp. I'm glad we are to ride in separately. Y'all are reckless and ya killed a man needlessly. I don't like it.

"If ya catch up with some cowboys headed for town, ride in with them. And keep yore mouth shut.

"That group of old men shows up at the bank to drink coffee every Monday night right after it closes. Glad and me will be there just before closing. We'll make like we're trying to do some business." Wes mounted his horse and scowled at the man on the ground. "You are a going to get us all killed." He turned his horse and growled over his shoulder, "And you'd better make dang sure you have the horses ready. Don't be showing off. You ain't s'posed to draw no attention."

"What about that old man we met in Deadwood? I thought he was in on this deal."

"He's done. He took off last week and we ain't seen him since."

Plug climbed to his feet and gave Wes a cocky grin.

"Yore jist afeared is all. Go on now. Ya play it safe now an' see how far that gets ya. 'Sides, ol' Jesse is hidin' out up to Hole-in-the-Wall. The boss should mention his name in the bank, an' folks 'ill blame this here deal on the James gang."

Plug watched as Wes rode away. The mounted outlaw was still cursing under his breath. Plug laughed. He aimed the rifle at Wes's back and held it there for a time before he shoved it back in its boot. His father had been a sharpshooter in the last war, and the first thing he taught his boys was to shoot. It was a rare thing for Plug to miss a kill shot.

"Shoot, mebbie Glad 'ill take a bad one in this deal. Never know. I could end up the boss a this here outfit." He frowned before he continued. "Naw. I don't want to argue with Wes ever' day. I'll get my own gang."

He turned and squinted his eyes at the man lying on the ground for a time. He could see the cowboy's bandana fluttering in the breeze, but the man didn't move. Plug thought about riding down to make sure the man was dead. In the end, he decided not to.

"That there were a kill shot. I hit what I'm a aimin' fer. I dropped that feller an' he ain't a movin', never again."

Plug mounted his horse, but instead of heading back to camp, he rode toward Cheyenne. He rode through the fence they had cut, and then circled around to come into Cheyenne from the southwest. He caught a group of cowboys headed into town after a drive they had completed and rode with them.

They were a friendly crowd. They had been on the trail for over four months. The one to the left of Plug jabbed his thumb to the south.

"We started this drive down in New Mexico Territory. That Big Pasture in the Indian Territory sure looked green when we finally got there. That was the easiest part of the drive.

"Well, other than the outlaws and Indians who wanted to cut our herd. The boss gave us a night on the town in Dodge an' then we headed up to Ogallala. Durn trail boss wouldn't even let us stop there an' we shore wanted to. We heard that town was even wilder than Dodge. Not sure about that though since we didn't get to see fer our own selves. It irked us some too since Ogallala brags she's too tough fer Texas cowboys.

"I might stop through there on the way back south though. My little sis married a cowboy an' he done took her north a there a piece after they married. We ain't seen her in seven years. Ma asked me to look in on her. Pop told 'er that she shouldn't marry a man she only knowed fer two weeks, but she didn't listen.

"Guess it worked out. She ain't come back home."

Plug listened as he rode. When the cowboys rode toward the mercantile to buy clean clothes, he turned into the livery.

An old man with a rooster feather in his top hat was cleaning stalls. He pointed toward some stalls in the back.

"Jist pick ya one out. I'll be done here in a jiffy. Fee is two bits if ya want grain. Half a that gits ya hay only.

"Currycomb an' brushes be a hangin' on the wall there," he added before he disappeared behind the barn.

Plug didn't answer. He pulled off the saddle and tossed the damp saddle blanket on top of the saddle. He forked a little hay into the stall before he strolled out of the livery.

"I ain't a gonna rub that hoss down an' I ain't payin' fer no grain neither. He didn't work near hard 'nough fer that kinda treatment."

The hostler dumped the manure in his wheelbarrow and was back in less than five minutes. He checked the stall and rubbed his hand across the horse's wet back. He glared and tossed his top hat up on a shelf in the little room he called his office.

"Don't think much of a man what don't care fer his mount. That there hoss is a nice one, but its feet need a trimmin' an' it could sure use a rubdown.

"I believe that there feller bears some watchin'. I'll keep an eye on him or my name ain't Rooster."

CHAPTER 69

A Visit With the Neighbors

BROKEN KNIFE LISTENED AS HIS NEPHEW TOLD HIM of the shooting.

"Is the man dead?"

"No, he was alive when I left him. I waited until the man who shot rode away. Then I rode down to him and tried to stop the bleeding. Only then did I come here. I had no way to carry a wounded man."

Broken Knife nodded.

"Prepare my horse and attach a travois to your mother's horse. We will bring the wounded man here.

"We must move him quickly. The man who shot him may go back to check." Broken Knife signaled to some of his warriors and the men were quickly mounted.

Broken Knife smiled. *Blue Feather and Gray Wolf are good parents. I am pleased they are sending their children to the white man's school. Quiet Owl is a fine young man. It is good we help the white man. He might be a friend of my brother, Angry Eyes...and Same as well.*

When they arrived, they could see where the white man had tried to drag himself. He was bleeding again, and two warriors lifted him onto the travois. One offered him some water. The wounded man's eyes opened. They were glassy and he stared at them for a moment before he spoke.

"Did you shoot me?"

Broken Knife looked at the man disdainfully.

"If I had shot you, you would be dead. Try to be still. Angry Eyes is my brother, and for this, we will help you."

The man passed out again when they lifted him onto the travois. He remained unconscious even when they arrived at camp and moved him to a tepee.

Blue Feather ran to Broken Knife when the party rode in. She peered at the wounded man and then looked at Broken Knife with concern.

"This is no good. If this man dies, some may think that we shot him."

Broken Knife's eyes gleamed. He stared at his sister a moment before he grunted, "Do you forget what Woman of the Rising Sun did for you?"

Blue Feather dropped her eyes and shook her head.

"I believe this man is a friend of my brother. You will help him, and I will ride to my brother. I will tell him of this. I think the men who cut his fence are the ones who shot this man."

Blue Feather listened to her brother and nodded. She turned to her son.

"Quiet Owl, find your sister. We must work quickly."

Broken Knife rode toward Rowdy Rankin's R4 Ranch. The land between Rowdy's ranch and Lance Rankin's Rocking R was mostly rolling hills. There were broken hills and more brush toward the northwest, and Broken Knife wanted to use them as cover when he rode. He tried to stay off the tops of the hills as much as possible. He didn't see any riders as he rode through Same's ranch yard. Same's wife was outside. She shaded her eyes to see who he was before she walked toward him with a smile.

"Broken Knife! What brings you up our way? I hope your family is well."

Broken Knife nodded somberly.

"I speak to Same."

"He is over at Lance's. He left an hour ago. I thought he would be home by now so you may meet him on the way." She smiled at him again.

"Stop in on your way back home and I will send some bear sign for your little ones."

Broken Knife smiled briefly.

"I do not think I will stop. Perhaps another time. Tell Same that Broken Knife was here."

He turned his horse and trotted toward Lance's ranch. He studied the little school as he rode by, stopping to ride around the playground equipment. He pushed on the merry-go-round and smiled as it began to spin.

Lance was just dismounting in front of the barn when Broken Knife rode into the yard. He walked toward the brave with his hand outstretched and a smile on his face.

"Hello to my good friend. Do you have time to drink a cold root beer with me?"

Broken Knife nodded somberly.

"Hello to my brother, Angry Eyes. I will drink some of your white man's drink, but I did not come to visit." As the two men walked toward the house, Broken Knife spoke.

"My nephew, Quiet Owl, found a white man who was shot. We brought him to our camp. Our women care for him. Maybe you will want to take him to your medicine man." Broken Knife shrugged. "I do not know. He is very weak and when he talks, he makes no sense."

Lance's step slowed as he listened to Broken Knife. When the brave finished talking, Lance nodded and strode quickly toward the house. Molly met them at the door with a smile on her face. She gave Broken Knife a hug, but her smile faded as she looked from one man to the other.

"Molly, grab some glasses and Badger's root beer. Broken Knife has a wounded man in his camp. A white man who was shot." He motioned for Broken Knife to sit down and poured him some root beer.

"You don't know who the wounded man is?" Lance asked with a frown.

"I do not know the man, but I have seen him with Big Talker, the tall man who lives where Badger lived. They are friends."

Lance cursed under his breath. He looked at Molly.

"That sounds like it could be Tex. Gabe said he heard a shot not long after Tex left.

"I'll send one of the men for Doc. Do you want to wait and ride out with us? Otherwise, if you tell me where your camp is, I will bring Doc out there." Lance stood and waited for Broken Knife's answer.

Broken Knife studied his friend and nodded.

"I will wait. Maybe we should go see Big Talker. You can tell him about his friend."

Lance thought a moment before he nodded.

"We probably should. Ol' Gabe's kinda sudden when he's mad though." Lance grinned at Broken Knife. His smile slowly left his face and he asked, "You think this man who shot Tex might be one of the men who cut my fence? If you know where they are camped, maybe Gabe and I should pay them a visit."

Broken Knife shrugged. "I did not see them cut the fence, but their tracks show they were the same men."

Lance and Broken Knife drained their glasses and headed for the door. Lance looked back at Molly.

"Molly, pack up some sugar and coffee for Broken Knife's family. Jonesy just got home and I'm sending him after Doc."

Rowdy was leading some horses out of a pasture. A smile filled his face. He closed the gate and walked toward Broken Knife.

"Hello, Broken Knife. It's good to see you, my friend."

Broken Knife's eyes glinted with humor. "Same. Always you look the same."

Rowdy grinned. “I reckon that’s a good thing.” He turned around when he heard Lance holler at Jonesy. His eyes were cool when he looked at his brother.

“You want me to come with you?”

“I don’t think so. You go on home and keep an eye on your place. We don’t know what these boys have in mind, so we need to be vigilant.

“I told Jonesy to tell Doc to take his doctoring buggy to Gabe’s. Gabe and I will go on horseback with Broken Knife from there to his camp. We’ll have to bring Tex back by travois to Gabe’s. That ground is too rough to drag a buggy over.” Lance frowned and shook his head as he muttered a curse under his breath.

“If Angel is at Gabe’s, he can pick up Anna and head for Cheyenne. They can be the ones to tell Flory.”

Lance looked back at Molly.

“Load the guns and keep the kids close to the house. I don’t think anyone will come this way, but we’d better be prepared. I’ll take three men with me, and the rest will stick around here.”

Molly nodded. She handed Broken Knife the bundle of food.

“There are some cookies in there for your little ones.” She smiled at him.

“Thank you for letting us know and please give my regards to Blue Feather.”

Broken Knife nodded. “It is good to help my brother.” He and Lance led the way toward Gabe’s ranch, and three riders followed them.

CHAPTER 70

An Unnecessary Shooting

GLAD PARSONS FOLLOWED WES TO THE PLACE WHERE the lone rider was shot. They studied the ground and stared at the tracks. Bent grass showed where a travois had been dragged across the prairie.

The outlaw boss cursed loudly.

"I wish I had never taken Plug on. He's reckless an' a killer to boot. This job was to be done with no killin'. Now we have a man shot an' one who is important enough to the Indians that they picked him up." He glared and turned again to look at the travois marks. He leaned down and touched the fresh manure before he cursed again.

"For all we know, he *was* an Indian! That's just what we need. A dead or dying Indian an' a bunch of angry braves out to get us when we try to make our getaway tonight." He studied the tracks again and pointed to the east.

"Let's head that way. We'll come into Cheyenne from the east side." A chill went through him and for just a moment, he thought about calling off the job. He paused and looked up at Wes.

"I don't like how this is stacking up. Maybe we should just call it off."

Wes studied his brother and shrugged his shoulders. "That would be fine with me but how will we let Brick know? I don't care much if Plug makes it or not, but Brick should already be in town. We can't leave him high and dry."

Glad nodded slowly.

"Well, let's head out. We'll ride careful. Plug may have just put the entire country on the prod."

The two outlaws rode up the main street of Cheyenne. They passed the Stock Growers Bank. Wes nodded at it.

"Why didn't we plan to rob that bank? It's s'posed to be one of the richest banks in the whole country."

Glad nodded and laughed.

"That it is. An' a security guard sits twenty feet above the cash windows. He moves his rifle back an' forth. Then he points it at folks standin' in line just for fun. It's a little eerie to look up an' see the muzzle end of a rifle pointed at ya. 'Course, he probably has to take a break now and then, but still.

"Nope, we'll stick with the First National. I wouldn't attempt that one either, but the bank president and one of the cashiers play cards on Monday nights with some of the old timers in town.

"Brick has a cousin who lives here. That's why he left us at Deadwood. He was to wander on into town an' buddy up to that ol' cousin.

"Worked out too. His cousin was so pleased to see him that he invited Brick to stay. Brick's been helping him deliver freight for Whipple and Hay. The Union Mercantile is busy these days."

Wes looked over at Glad and frowned.

"So just how do you intend to get him out of there without getting shot?"

"Not going to get him out. This is Brick's last job. He likes Cheyenne. He just might stay here."

Wes stared at Glad and almost choked.

Glad winked and laughed.

"We'll hold onto his share an' deposit it when we get to Laramie. He'll leave it there and have it wired to the Stock Growers Bank a little at a time."

Wes shook his head.

"That's brassy. Mighty brassy.

"Are you going to lock those old men in the vault?"

"I don't plan to. We sure don't want them to suffocate. We don't have time to tie a bunch of them up either. I'm hoping they'll listen to Brick and not cause any trouble."

CHAPTER 71

A Sad Day

TINY STOOD AND WALKED ACROSS THE LITTLE ROOM that served as part of Cheyenne's doctoring office and hospital. His wife's small body was curled around the still form of their son.

A single tear leaked out of Tiny's eye as he looked back at Annie. He cursed softly under his breath before he turned to look out the window.

He and Annie had been married for nearly seven years, and they had both wanted this baby. Annie's two miscarriages had been difficult but birthing a dead child had been even harder.

Doc wanted to take the baby away immediately, but Annie refused. She had held him and cried until she fell asleep.

"That little feller looks perfect too.

"Doc said this happens sometimes. He did ever'thing he could, but he couldn't fix our baby.

"I think he knowed there was a problem when we got here last night. He was too quiet when he checked Annie.

"I didn't feel it a movin' 'round fer the last day, an' I mentioned that to Annie. I was some worried but we ain't never had a baby. Annie wasn't worried though. She said it didn't have no more room to wiggle, an' I reckon that was right. She looked like she might split clean open, she was so big. I shore never thought we'd birth a dead little ol' baby though." Tiny's quiet curse was choked off as his big chest squeezed away the sob that tried to slip out.

Annie had finally fallen asleep in the early morning, and Tiny had slipped away for a few hours. He stared over at the tiny coffin sitting on the floor and shook his head. He always kept a few of the small coffins made up and stored on a shelf in his woodshop. Folks knew he gave them away for free. Some he delivered and others were picked up. He carved the flat tops on them if he was asked.

Folks usually tried to pay for them, but Tiny refused. They were simple to make, and they seemed to help folks a little. He for sure wouldn't take money from someone who was grieving over a child.

Tiny's throat tightened again. His carving on this one showed a smiling angel holding a sleeping baby.

"Jist like our little feller. He looked perfect. We kept a waitin' fer 'im to breathe, but he didn't never do it. I reckon he's with the Good Lord now." Tiny wiped his face with a big hand.

It was early morning and Cheyenne was already a busy place. A group of cowboys who looked like they were fresh off the trail were riding into town from the west. His head turned toward the east at the sound of horses. Two riders rode slowly by Doc's office. Tiny stared at them a moment and frowned.

"Those strangers are a ridin' too fancy a hosses to be cowboys. Wonder what they're a doin'? Ol' Cheyenne is a growin' more all the time, an' we ain't jist a gittin' all good folks neither." He watched as the two riders continued up the street.

Tiny turned away from the window and walked back over to sit down in the chair by Annie's bed. He didn't know how he was going to take the baby from Annie, but he had to do it. He knew his wife would wake if he tried to take the little fellow while she was asleep though, so he just sat down and watched her.

"It's a goin' to be a hard ol' day, an' that's fer shore."

CHAPTER 72

Another Little Momma

TINY FROWNED WHEN HE HEARD HORSES RACING UP the street. He strode to the window and stared out as Rooster hauled his team to a stop. The old hostler was shouting.

"Somebody git out here an' help me git this woman inside. I be too old a feller to be a carryin' a mama who's about to pop!"

Tiny jerked the door open and rushed outside. He slowed as he recognized the woman, and his face broke into a grin.

"Howdy, Rose. Here, let me carry ya. I cin git ya up that there rough walk faster than ya cin walk as much as you's a staggerin' 'round."

The woman wrapped her arms around Tiny's neck and smiled briefly.

"Just like old times, Tiny. You used to carry me around on the dance floor once you worked up the courage to ask me to dance."

"Liquid courage, Rose. It took a lotta whiskey to work up my courage." His feet moved in some fast dance steps as he carried her up the steps and she almost laughed. Tiny frowned when he felt the warm wetness on his hand that was under her.

"I think ya shoulda come sooner, Rose. Why'd ya wait so long fer?"

Rose gasped around a contraction as she squeezed back her tears.

"Juniper promised he'd stand by me. I sent for him last night, but he didn't come. One of his friends came instead. He said Juniper left town two days ago. He was headed south on a fast horse." Rose's eyes were sad as she looked up at Tiny.

"I want out of this business, Tiny. I want to take care of this baby like a mother should. I've saved a little, and once I am on my feet, I am headed back to Saint Louis. I am going to take my little girl with me, and we are leaving."

Tiny's feet slowed a moment and he frowned. "Ya have another baby, Rose? Who's been a takin' care of her?"

Rose clenched her teeth and squeezed her eyes shut. "I'm paying a family to raise her. No one knows she's mine and I want to keep it that way until I leave." She smiled up at Tiny as he laid her on a bed.

"I'm glad you married Annie. She's a sweet girl and you're a good man, Tiny. Rooster told me she was expecting. Is that why you're here?"

Tiny's face crumpled as he backed away from the bed. His voice cracked some when he answered.

"Ya take care a that little ol' baby, Rose. An' I'll stake ya some money fer yore train fare when yore ready to leave." Tiny ducked out of the room and turned back toward the room Annie was in.

Rose's eyes were wide as she watched Tiny. She looked up at Doc as he rushed through the door.

"Is Annie all right? Did they have their baby?"

Doc patted Rose's hand.

"Don't you worry about Annie. Let's just get this baby birthed."

Doc listened to Rose's heart for a moment and then placed his hand under her. His voice was urgent as he called to Josie.

"Help me get Rose on that birthing bed. This baby is coming now!"

CHAPTER 73

LETTING GO

ANNIE WAS AWAKE WHEN TINY RETURNED TO HER room. She was holding their baby and tears were running down her face again. Tiny put out his hands.

"Give 'im to me, Annie. Ya need to give 'im to me now. He's gone an' we can't bring 'im back."

Annie sobbed and shook her head as Tiny reached for their son. He nodded over his shoulder toward the little coffin.

"I brung a little box fer 'im. We cin name 'im whatever ya want, but this needs to be done. He's with the Good Lord now. We don't know why he was took, but that's the way it is. Now ya let me take 'im."

"I'm broken inside, Tiny. That's why he died. I'm broken." Annie was crying as she let Tiny take the baby. She fell back on the bed as sobs shook her body.

Tiny wrapped their little boy tighter in the blanket that was around him and laid him gently in the small coffin. He placed the lid on top and sat down on the bed beside Annie. He pulled her onto his lap and hugged her tightly.

"Doc said it weren't nothin' neither of us did. Things jist go wrong sometimes. We'll have us another baby someday, one that will live and run around like he's s'posed to."

Annie shook her head. "No, I can't bear babies, Tiny. I'll never have another baby. I just know I won't." She gripped Tiny's neck tightly as her body shook. "I'm broken," she whispered.

"Don't cry, Annie. It hurts my heart when ya cry. And ya ain't broken. The Good Lord don't make broken folks. He makes 'im jist like they's s'posed to be." His big heart beat loudly in Annie's ear and she calmed down. She finally looked up at Tiny and smiled.

"I'm so glad you found me. You are the best man in the entire world, Tiny Small. You will always be my cowboy."

They both looked toward the door when they heard a woman scream. She was crying between screams and Doc's voice was soft as he talked to her.

Annie looked up at Tiny. Her eyes were large as she looked from him to the direction of the screams.

Tiny gestured toward the sound of the screaming.

"Rose down to the Painted Lady is in there. She wants to git outta the business an' I told her we'd stake her when she's ready to leave. She's a good woman in the wrong business."

Annie smiled. "Your Cheyenne Rose. I remember when she used to talk about you dancing with her. She said that sometimes you carried her around the dance floor."

"Only till ya come along. You was the onliest woman fer me after that. An' ya still is." He patted Annie's back awkwardly and kissed her cheek.

"Yep, you is the onliest woman I ever loved, an' I reckon I always will."

Annie relaxed against Tiny's chest. She stared at the small coffin and pinched her eyes shut. *I'll always love you, little one. And I'll never forget you.* She pushed back her tears and said a prayer for Rose. It sounded like she was having a difficult birth.

"I hope Rose's baby is healthy," Annie whispered. "She's had a hard life. She deserves a little happiness. And I'm glad you offered to stake her."

Tiny didn't answer. He just squeezed his wife a little tighter.

CHAPTER 74

The Gift

THE BIRTHING ROOM BECAME QUIET. IN FACT, THERE was no sound coming from there at all. Annie and Tiny looked up when someone knocked on their door. Annie slid back under the covers and Tiny pulled the door open. Doc's face was serious as he looked from one to the other. He cleared his throat before he spoke.

"Rose's delivery was difficult and...well, things didn't go as they should have. She is gone and left a healthy little boy who is very hungry." He paused and focused his eyes on Annie as he added softly, "I was wondering if you would feed him, Annie. I know this is a difficult time but if you could help us out, it would be appreciated."

Annie's face became pale.

"Rose is gone? What happened? I—I—of course I will feed him. Please bring him in."

Doc Williams nodded. His eyes moved to Tiny.

"You come with me."

Tiny rose from the bed. He followed Doc into a room where Josie held a small bundle. Doc lifted the bundle from Josie's arms and placed a squirming little boy in Tiny's big hands. The baby's face squinted and turned red as he began to scream.

"Rose asked me to give you and Annie her little boy if something happened to her. It was a difficult delivery and I think she knew something was wrong. She called him Joey and she'd like you to keep that name." When Tiny stared at Doc, he added, "Rose asked for you and Annie to raise her son. She said there was no one to help. She knew you had just lost your little boy. She was hoping you would raise hers since she won't be around."

Tiny turned his eyes down to stare at the baby without answering and Doc added softly. "You don't have to, of course. I just thought perhaps—

"We'll raise him. We'll do that for Rose."

Tiny stumbled as he turned. He kissed the little boy's cheek, and his smile was large when he entered Annie's room.

"We have a son. Rose give her boy to us. She asked fer us to raise 'im." He handed the baby to Annie and sat down on the bed. His big chest shook silently as he tried not to cry.

Annie stared from the baby to Tiny. "He's ours? To keep?" The baby was nosing her gown and Annie put him up to her breast. The baby latched on and tried to suck. He was noisy and strong, crying loudly when the milk didn't come immediately. Annie was laughing and crying at the same time. Both she and the baby were awkward, but finally, the little boy was in a comfortable position to nurse.

Josie tapped lightly on the door. She was smiling when she poked her head in. "I can answer any questions you have about nursing, Annie." She smiled and hugged Tiny.

"Levi is waiting to see you. He wants papers drawn up so the adoption is legal. Rose either didn't know or chose not to tell us who the father was so we want to be prudent." She leaned over and kissed Annie's cheek. "I'm so happy you are going to take this little boy. He needs a mama and a daddy who will love him. Even though pregnancy made her life harder, Rose wanted him and loved him."

Tiny followed Josie out of the room. He was frowning as he asked, "What about Rose's little girl? Who is goin' to take care a her? Rose told me that she was a sendin' someone money to care fer 'er."

Josie stared at Tiny for a moment but shook her head slowly. "I don't know anything about a little girl. Rose didn't mention her."

Tiny cursed under his breath. "I won't say nothin' to Annie yet but if ya find out who it is, we'll take her too if she needs a home." He paused and then looked toward the quiet room where he had left Rose.

"What happened? What went wrong?"

Josie frowned slightly before she answered. "Doctor Williams wasn't sure. Rose hadn't been to see him since she became pregnant. He didn't know if she had any abnormal symptoms leading up to delivery." Josie had tears in her eyes as she added, "She bled heavily after the baby was born, and Doc was unable to get it stopped."

When Tiny's face paled, Josie touched his arm.

"There are many areas we don't understand yet in the medical field, Tiny. Every birth is a miracle. There are so many things that can go wrong, and yet, we have lots of healthy babies. I'm just glad you were able to take Rose's little Joey. His chances of surviving are so much higher since he will be able to have first milk."

Tiny slowly nodded.

"I'll make a coffin fer Rose. We'll bury her next to our baby." He started to turn away, cleared his throat, and added huskily.

"An' thanks to both of ya an' Rose too. We'll do our best to raise her fine boy."

Josie smiled and patted his arm. "You may take Annie home tomorrow morning. Doc wants to keep an eye on her and little Joey today."

Tiny nodded and hurried back toward Annie's room. "I reckon I'll build that coffin now. I'll line the fellers out today an' then I'll come on back." He stopped by the bed and touched the sleeping little boy's soft cheek.

"Annie, I been a thinkin'. How 'bout we bury our little boy an' Rose out behind the woodshop. We have that nice little spot out there where ya like to sit an' sew beside that lilac bush. The trees is little, but someday, they'll be big. We cin make it our own little burial plot 'stead of a puttin' our kinfolk in the town cemetery. And then ya cin talk to our little boy ever' day if ya want."

Annie's lips trembled a little, but she smiled and nodded. "That would be nice. And let's call our baby Beau. I know you hated Beauford as your name, but Beau is nice. Maybe you could add that to the top of his coffin." She paused and then asked softly, "Do you know Rose's last name?"

Tiny shook his head. "Naw. I asked her many a time. None of the women who worked there knew either. How 'bout we call her Rose Porterhouse? We jist as well give my middle name a purpose, an' I'd be honored to share it with Rose."

Annie was surprised as she looked at Tiny. Then she laughed. "That would be fine. I think Rose would like that."

Tiny grinned at his wife and then asked carefully, "I thought on buryin' 'em both today. Are ya all right with not bein' there?"

Annie nodded as tears filled her eyes.

"Yes. I've said my goodbyes. We can both visit later, but that would be fine."

Tiny kissed his wife and hurried toward the door.

"I'll get that box made an' then I'll be back. An' ya jist take it easy. Ya don't have to do nothin' but sleep an' feed that there little feller.

"I'll even bring ya some a that stew ya made yesterday when I come back."

CHAPTER 75

A Change of Plans

IT WAS JUST BEFORE FIVE ON MONDAY AFTERNOON, July 12, when the two cowboys pulled their horses to a stop in front of the First National Bank. Wes looked over at Glad.

"I sure hope we can count on Plug. I don't trust that man."

Glad nodded.

"We can trust him as long as we are carrying the money and he's not behind us. Now you go on in. I'll come in a little later. If there's only one cashier, I'll be behind you. Otherwise, I'll step in the other line."

Wes's eyes swept the room. Two cashiers had their windows open, but the second one pulled his window shut just as Wes stepped through the door. He dropped the bars down and nodded at Wes.

"This window is closed so you'll need to use the other one. And make it quick. We are already a minute past five." He walked around the end of the counter and began to close the window shades, one by one.

A group of old men pushed through the door. Each was armed to the teeth.

Brick was the last one to enter. As he walked by the two men standing in line, he laughed and commented, "I don't know. I've watched ya fellers play an' I'm jist not feelin' lucky tonight. Mebbie I'll sit this one out."

The teller looked up at Wes. His eyes were hard, and his right hand hovered below the counter.

Wes laid a $20 gold piece down.

"I just want to break that down a little. I need some beer money."

Glad was quiet as he waited on Wes. When Wes glanced back at him, he flicked a piece of lint off his vest. Wes turned away and Glad stepped up to the counter.

"I was hopin' to talk to Rupert about takin' out a loan fer a ranch. I'm a little late tonight though. Any chance he's still around?"

"He left early but if you want to give me your name, we can make an appointment for you tomorrow."

Glad paused. His eyes passed over the old timers. The group of old men seemed to be waiting for something. He smiled at the teller and shook his head.

"Naw, mebbie that was my sign. I'm not much on borrowin' money anyway. I'll jist save a little longer an' then I can pay cash. Thanks though."

He turned and walked toward the door. Wes was already outside. He had their horses untied and was waiting.

The two men looked down the street. Plug was nowhere to be seen. They calmly mounted their horses and rode west.

Wes looked over at Glad. For the first time, he noticed his brother was sweating.

"Was Brick's comment a signal? I knew the deal was off when you flicked your fingers."

"Yep. Those boys were ready. They were just hopin' we'd try somethin'. I wasn't sure how we were goin' to get away though if Plug was out here holdin' onto three horses." He frowned and shook his head. "Who knows what that fool is doin'."

Just then, a man raced out of the Stock Grower's Bank. He held a bag in each hand. He struggled with the slipknot before he jumped onto his horse. He spurred it west up the main street without looking around. Several men followed him and were shooting as he crouched over his horse's back. He swerved to the right and was soon out of sight.

Glad and Wes pulled their horses to a stop. They looked around in surprise. Just then, the First National's doors burst open, and men began to pour out. A sheriff pointed his gun at the two riders.

"You fellows see a man run out of the Stock Grower's Bank?"

Glad nodded. "Sure did. He seemed to be in a mighty big hurry."

The two men who had been shooting were running for their horses and the entire street was in chaos.

The sheriff watched the commotion and then asked, "Did you see where he went?"

Glad pointed west. Nearly twenty men were soon mounted and ready to ride. The sheriff frowned and paused. He slowly walked back to where the two strangers were waiting.

"Where are you boys from? I haven't seen you around before."

Wes chuckled and rubbed his bristly chin. The sheriff looked at him with hard eyes.

"We were headed to Laramie but now that all you boys are headed that way, we might go north. I'd hate to get shot on accident."

The sheriff took a step closer, and his gun moved up.

"How did you happen to be right here just now?"

Glad pointed behind him. "We were in the First National just before closing. There were a bunch of old timers in there. They can tell you we were there." He paused and pointed behind him as he added quietly, "Be a foolish thing to do to stop in one bank when you plan to rob the other." He nodded his head toward the Stock Grower's Bank.

"Anybody hurt in there?"

"Not in there but a man was shot south of town this morning. Doc just brought him in. Some Indians found him." He pointed with his thumb behind him. "I'm guessing that thief had something to do with the shooting too."

Sheriff Boswell looked hard at the two men again before he jerked his head.

"Get on out of here. But if you show up in Cheyenne again, you had better have a reason to be here."

Glad nodded and the two men turned their horses north.

"Deadwood is soundin' better all the time," Wes muttered and Glad chuckled.

As the two men rode slowly north, Wes looked over at his brother.

"I think I'm done with this life. We could have died in there and for what? For taking something that ain't ours? I'm through."

Glad nodded and chuckled. "I'll agree with that, but let's head south. I think Texas is calling my name."

They were both smiling when they turned their horses around. They wouldn't make it to Denver that night, but they'd be there by the next evening. And just maybe, they'd get lucky and find a job.

"I heard the stages around Denver are hiring drivers and guards. Besides, with a growing city like that, delivery drivers should be needed too." Wes looked over at his brother.

"We should get in the freighting business, Glad. We know all the trails and the outlaws too. We'd know where to go *and* who to keep an eye on. I think that would be a fine business for us."

Glad nodded. "Parson Brothers' Freight and Delivery. It has a nice ring. Sounds almost honest, don't it?"

CHAPTER 76

Risky Behavior

PLUG RACED DOWN THE STREET, STUFFING THE money in his saddle bags as he rode. He made a quick turn to the right and slowed down as he rode into the residential section.

A small, blonde woman was hurrying down the street and he rode up beside her. He pulled his gun and pointed it at her.

"Drop that basket and climb up here. An' don't try nothin' funny. I'll shoot ya same as I would a favorite dog if he tripped me."

Flory stared up at the man and stepped back in surprise.

"I most certainly will not sit on your lap. I am engaged to be married."

Plug pulled back the hammer on his pistol.

"I don't have time to argue, lady. Take my hand an' climb up here or I'll shoot ya dead. I'm a desperate man an' I have little to look forward to but a noose if I'm caught."

Flory looked around in fear. She was almost home but Dot was nowhere to be seen. The street was quiet. Her hands were shaking when she looked up at the man, but her voice was angry.

"My family will track you down if you force me to go with you. Ride away. I will be of no help to you."

"That might be true but with you on this horse, they won't be so eager to shoot at me. Now climb on up here."

"I will not sit on your lap."

"Lady, git up here before I drop ya where ya stand!"

Flory took the man's hand and swung up. He tried to push her in front of him, but she fought him until he let her slide behind the saddle.

"That jist might be better anyhow. Now if they do shoot, they'll shoot you."

He jabbed his horse with his spurs and Flory almost went off the horse backwards. She grabbed for the saddle strings. She pulled herself back up and over the rump of the horse.

Dot stepped out of Flory's house as the horse went racing by. She caught a glimpse of Flory's frightened face and ran for her mount. Frieder was taking her riding that evening and she had picked her horse up early to save him some time.

Plug looked around in surprise when he saw Dot. She was gaining on him. When she was nearly beside him, he fired once at her and then pointed the gun at Flory.

"Ease off or I'll shoot 'er!"

Dot pulled her horse to a stop. She wheeled it around as she raced for the sheriff's office. When she turned her horse onto the main street, she charged right into the sheriff's posse.

"He's headed south, and he has a woman behind him." Dot began screaming when some of the men raised their guns to fire at the fleeing rider. "If you shoot at him, you'll kill her!"

Flory was terrified. She wanted to let go and fall but memories of the buggy wreck froze her with fear. She gasped, "You need to—slow down. You are—going—to—kill your horse."

Plug's horse was breathing heavily. It had run for over a mile and with the weight of a second person, it was nearly done. It slowed of its own accord and Flory slid off. She rolled when she landed and crawled into the brush.

The angry outlaw charged the horse in after her, but Flory was able to crawl through tighter spaces than a man on a horse could ride. Plug finally turned his horse back to the path. His voice was soft and deadly when he spoke.

"I'll find ya. I'll lose this posse an' I'll come an' git ya. I know where ya live."

Flory put her hands over her mouth to muffle her breathing. She was shaking as she sank down in the brush. She held her breath to keep from crying.

She watched as the posse rushed by and then began to crawl back out to the path. The leg she had broken hurt, and she was afraid she had broken it again.

Dot and Frieder were racing toward her, and she sank down on the trail. The sobs would no longer stay inside, and Flory began to cry.

Frieder grabbed her and lifted her up. When he saw she was all right, he grinned.

"I was hopin' you would take a dive off that horse. You hurt anywhere?"

Flory pointed at her leg. "I think I broke it again," she said as Frieder lifted her up behind Dot.

Dot lifted Flory's skirt and shook her head.

"No, but you have a nasty cut. Still, a cut is better than a break.

"Hang on and we'll take you back to town. Doc ought to look at that leg." She started to say something else, but Frieder shook his head slightly.

When Flory was settled behind her, Dot whispered, "Or I could just let you ride this horse while I sit on Frieder's lap. Just look at those big shoulders!"

Flory stared at her friend. She gasped as she laughed softly.

"Dot, you are terrible. That is such an unladylike thing to say!"

"I never claimed to be a lady, did I?" She grinned back at Flory and added softly, "Besides, Frieder likes me just the way I am."

Flory looked quickly at Frieder to see if he had heard. The cowboy's neck and ears turned red, and he grinned at Dot.

"Sure do," was all he said.

CHAPTER 77

A Lost Outlaw

PLUG'S HORSE WAS ALMOST STAGGERING WHEN IT finally stopped. He cursed the tired animal and tried to whip it with his rope. When it refused to move, he made camp in a shallow draw. Even though it was dark, he didn't light a fire, and that made him even angrier. The horse's sides were heaving, and its head was hanging low when Plug finally pulled the saddle and blanket off. The bridle he left on.

"I didn't bring a halter an' I cain't take a chance on ya wanderin' off," he growled at the exhausted horse. He pulled his bedroll off the back of the saddle and jerked the blankets over himself.

Plug didn't hear the Indians come close to his camp, nor did he see Broken Knife stand over him.

The Indians took his horse, his rifle, his saddle, and his saddle bags. They even managed to lift his six-gun out of his holster.

When Plug awoke, he could sense something was wrong. His brain was too foggy for anything to register though. He reached his hand for his gun. His fingers fumbled at the empty holster, and he stared in shock at the space where his gun should have been.

He whirled around and grabbed for the rifle, but it was also gone. *My money!* He rushed to where he had dropped his saddle, but the saddle and saddlebags were gone as well.

Plug's mind was blank as he looked around. His eyes told him his horse was missing but his mind couldn't accept it. A chill came over him as he remembered the story an old Indian had told him one time.

It was about the little people who lived inside the earth. They were vengeful little things and if one camped or slept too close to their homes, they came out at night and robbed you. They stole your horses too and they followed you when you tried to get away. Night after night they followed you, sticking thorns in your back and your feet while you slept. When you finally lost your mind or could go no farther, they dragged you away and you were never seen again.

Plug frowned and shook his head. "Jist an Injun story. Ain't nothin' true 'bout that a'tall."

Still, for the first time in a long time, Plug felt true fear.

Not only was he lost but he was also on foot. Plug looked around but he didn't recognize anything. The morning was hazy, and he couldn't see the sun. He finally chose the route that looked the easiest and began to walk in that direction. He hadn't filled his canteen before he robbed the bank the night before because he assumed he would be in Denver by dark. "I'll be there by midnight at the latest," he muttered to himself. He took a long drink and then threw the empty canteen on the ground.

What Plug didn't realize was that Denver was not twenty miles south as he thought. Instead, it was over one hundred miles southeast…and Plug was walking southwest.

The posse lost Plug's tracks and returned to town the next morning. They thought he might have lost his horse because its tracks led away from where he camped for the night. However, they never found the horse, so they weren't sure. The outlaw's tracks on foot were harder to see and his erratic route made it even more difficult. They decided to restock their supplies and begin their search again the next afternoon.

It was after dark when Gabe finally made it home, and he only left Cheyenne because he knew Tex would live. It had taken them nearly five hours to get the man to town, first across the prairie by travois and the rest of the way in Doc's buggy. Tex had lost a lot of blood and Doc was worried about him.

No one seemed to know where Flory was, and Gabe frowned. "Maybe I should ride back to town and make sure she's all right. 'Course, she could have been working late. Dot wasn't around either so the two of them are probably together.

"Merina told me Frieder headed in town last night. I didn't meet him on the way home so he must have gotten there before I left Doc's."

He grinned when he thought of how often Frieder was riding to Cheyenne. "That cowboy is hardly getting any sleep at all, but he has a smile on his face every morning. He is never late for work either."

Gabe saddled Buck the next morning. He was going out to search for the outlaw himself. He was just mounting his horse when one of the riders called to him.

"I don't think you need to look for that feller, boss. I don't think he's a gonna make it back." The cowboy pointed toward a small pasture close to the corrals.

A strange horse was in the pasture and full saddle bags were hanging on the fence.

Gabe looked around in surprise. He saw unshod hoof prints around the corral, but other than that, there was no indication of who left the horse. He led the animal into the barn and scowled when he saw the saddle sores on its back.

He stepped out of the barn and called for Merina.

"Why don't you come down here and fix this horse up. I'm going to pull his shoes off and trim his feet. That should have been done weeks ago. Maybe you can give him some of that mixture you make up for sick horses." He turned back to the horse. He patted its neck and talked softly.

"With a little rest, you just might recover—if that outlaw didn't break your wind. Sorry he used you so hard, old fellow. If your lungs are shot, we won't be able to help. We'll sure give it try though.

"I'll turn you over to Merina and you will be in the best hands around. You are too fine of a horse to not try to save."

Merina talked to the horse as she worked with it. It tried to pull away when she rubbed cream into its sores, but it responded to her gentleness.

Gabe grinned as he watched her.

"It looks like you have a new friend. What are you going to call him?"

Merina smiled as she brushed the horse. "He is un caballo afortunado. I think I will call him Lucky."

Gabe chuckled. "I'd better get those money bags to the sheriff. I'm guessing the posse didn't find anything of that outlaw last night. Since we have the money back and Tex is going to live, they probably won't go out again."

He looked toward the southwest and shook his head. "That's not a good place to be without a horse. There's not much water out there and wolves are plentiful. I almost hope he has enough bullets. If he doesn't…well, I guess I won't feel too sorry for him. He brought this all on himself."

Gabe tied the saddlebags onto his horse and rode north toward Cheyenne.

CHAPTER 78

A Frightened Sweetheart

IT WAS NEARLY SEVEN IN THE EVENING WHEN FLORY, Frieder, and Dot arrived at Doc's office. Frieder held Flory's arm as she limped up the steps. She had just stepped through the door when she heard a man shouting.

"You tell me where she is right now! Tell me or I'm getting out of this bed!" Flory stopped to listen and then limped toward the room where the man was still shouting.

"If that outlaw hurt her, I'll kill him with my bare hands."

Flory rushed into the room. Her eyes were wide as she stared at Wade. She hurried toward him. He wrapped his arms around her and then groaned.

His voice was soft as he looked up at her. "No one would tell me where you were." He frowned as he touched her face.

"You look like you have been rolling in dirt. Are you all right?"

"I fell off a horse but I'm fine. I cut my leg, so Frieder and Dot brought me up here." She touched the bandage on Wade's chest.

"You were shot? What happened?"

Doc took Flory's arm and led her away from the bed.

"You come with me and let me look at that cut. Frieder says it's deep and I need to get those stitches in now. Once I finish, you may come back and sit with this unruly patient. Maybe then, we will have some peace around here.

"That man of yours has made so much noise that no one here has gotten any rest.

He pointed at Tex. "And you need to lie still. That bullet went all the way through your back without hitting anything important. You are a mighty lucky man.

"You stay calm and you can leave here in a few days. You keep moving around though and you'll be in here longer."

Tex stared at the doctor and grinned.

"I'll be good now, Doc. You take care of that little gal though. We have a wedding to talk about."

Dot followed Flory into Doc's office. He shook his head and pointed at the door.

"You wait outside. I don't need a woman in here passing out while I'm trying to stitch."

Dot snorted and shook her head.

"Doc, I'm staying right here. You can give me a job or hand me a chair. Either is fine, but I'm not leaving." She pointed at the room where Tex lay.

"That man in there is my brother. Flory here is my friend and she will soon be Wade's wife. That means I have double reason to stay with her."

Dot's blue eyes were sparking, and her chin was set.

Doc studied her face and slowly sighed.

"Wash your hands then. We need to clean this cut before we stitch it. And I need some hot water."

Dot was quiet as she helped Doc. He was quick and efficient. He smiled at her when he was done.

"You are fine help, Miss Doolan." He spoke cautiously as he added, "We have been asked to stay open on Saturdays. I haven't agreed because

Josie refuses to help me. Our family is growing, and five days is almost more than she can handle some weeks." He watched Dot closely as he said, "If you'd be interested in helping on Saturdays, I would sure hire you."

Dot squinted her eyes as she evaluated Doc carefully.

"To be a receptionist or to help you with the sick? I don't like chitchatting with people, but medicine does interest me."

Doc chuckled and shook his head.

"It would be to help me with my doctoring." He colored slightly and added, "However, a pleasant bedside manner is important too."

He smiled at Flory and gave her his hand.

"Miss Flory, try to keep weight off that leg. I'm not going to put you on crutches, but I do want you to take it easy.

"Now please. Go in that other room and sit with that lovesick cowboy. I would like for all of us to get some sleep tonight."

Doc smiled as he watched Flory hurry out of the examination room.

"Would you like me to start on Saturday? I can be here as early as you want." Dot lowered her voice and glanced out toward the waiting room where Frieder sat. "At least until Frieder asks me to marry." She grinned at Doc and whispered, "I just might ask *him* if he takes too long."

Doc laughed and shook his head as he walked back to his living quarters.

Frieder's neck was red. He grinned at Dot as he stood and walked toward her.

"Marry you, huh? I reckon that would be fine. I don't have much to offer just yet though."

Dot took his arm and smiled at him.

"My brother is going to need a foreman, and I think I know just the man. Besides, you can sell your little homestead in Kansas. We can use that money to buy a place of our own, one with a few chickens and a milk cow. We'll need cattle and some horses too because I don't intend to sit inside and play housewife."

Frieder laughed and his blue eyes twinkled as he wrapped his big arms around Dot.

"Dot Doolan, I knew the first time I laid eyes on you that I wanted to know you better. I sure never figgered you'd ask me to marry though.

"Well, I'm sayin' yes. Yes to the purtiest an' sassiest woman I have ever roped an' raced horses with. An' I will be proud to work beside you ever' day, for the rest of my life.

"Now I'm a gonna walk you home an' then I'm leavin.' We'd better make this weddin' soon though or your brother will be whuppin' up on me for not behavin' proper with his sister."

Dot laughed and the two of them strolled out of Doc's office.

Flory listened to them talk. She whispered, "How about a double wedding, Wade? You and me with Dot and Frieder?"

He murmured something and Flory laughed. She pulled his blanket higher and snuggled down in the quilt Doc had set out for her. Soon the little clinic was quiet—just the way Doc liked it to be.

CHAPTER 79

THE NEW TRAIL BOSS

DOC WILLIAMS' VOICE WAS ANGRY AS HE ADDRESSED the man in front of him. "You are not going on a trail drive, Tex. You can't ride for at least ten days. That bullet was deep, and you are still in danger of infection."

Tex glared at Doc Williams and shook his head.

"I don't have a choice. Men are counting on me. I can't leave them without a trail boss."

Gabe frowned as he listened to the two men.

"Let me see what I can do. Tall Eagle is delivering horses here in the next few days. Maybe he will cover for you. He wouldn't trail for just anybody, but since you are friends, he might. I can even go.

"I agree with Doc though. You shouldn't be riding, and you certainly shouldn't be doing anything as hard and dirty as a trail drive.

"Who is volunteering me for a trail job?" Tall Eagle's face appeared in the doorway as everyone turned around in surprise.

Gabe laughed. "I did. I thought maybe you would take Tex's place. He went and got himself shot, probably so he could stay closer to Flory here. It worked too. He almost died and Doc doesn't want him on a horse."

Tall Eagle's eyes moved from the cowboy in bed to Flory. He studied her face before he looked back at Gabe. He watched his friend a moment before he nodded at Tex.

"You will marry this woman?"

Tex tried to pull himself up in bed but eased back down with a grunt. He nodded and grinned at the tall Indian.

"I sure am. You want to be my best man?"

Humor gleamed in Tall Eagle's eyes as he chuckled.

"I have never been in a White man's church. I wouldn't know what to do. Perhaps I should meet your herd and lead it north. I think I would rather do that.

"I have some horses that need to be delivered to Fort Sill." He grinned at the man lying on the bed. "If I lead your herd, I will get paid twice—once to deliver the horses and once for the trip back home. But I will take them no farther than Dodge City. A month is all I can spare, even for a broken up old friend like you."

Tex stretched out his hand and grimaced as it pulled on his stitches.

"Thank you, Tall Eagle. I think I will let Gabe line you out." He sank back on the bed, his face pale. Flory pushed the group of men out of the room.

"Make your plans outside. Wade needs to rest now." She followed them out the door and touched Tall Eagle's hand.

"Thank you, Tall Eagle. Wade has been worrying about that herd. His little brother is in charge right now, but he is very young."

Tall Eagle slowly nodded. He followed Gabe outside. As they walked down the steps, Tall Eagle pointed over his shoulder.

"Where is Miguel? He did not marry Miss Flory?"

Gabe shook his head. "They married but Miguel was killed a month later. I'm sure Angel will fill you in on the details of how Miguel died. He said you had some horses for him."

"I do, and for Miguel as well. He ordered a matching set of Appaloosas as a wedding gift for Miss Flory. He was specific about the color. I brought them with me. What do you think I should do with them?"

Gabe's face tightened for a moment before he looked away.

"I'll buy them. Merina and I will give them to Tex and Flory as a wedding gift. I think she would like that. Angel too.

"Why don't you come on out to the house? Nate is frothing at the mouth to go on another drive, and with you as trail boss, I can't say no. Sam Rankin too. They will probably want to drag young Tuff along as well so you will have three hands joining you. Tex said they were short on riders since it was so late in the season. I think his men will welcome some extra cowhands." He continued to talk as they walked to their horses. "I forgot you knew Tex. It plumb slipped my mind.

"I'm guessing you will want to head out in the morning?"

Tall Eagle nodded. "Yes, I want to leave as early as possible. Do you have pens for my horses? We will head south at first light, maybe sooner if things work out."

Gabe nodded. "I have some open pens. I'll send Nate north to find Tuff. He can bring him back to spend the night with us. That way, they will be there in the morning and won't slow you down." He slapped Tall Eagle on the back.

"It's good to see you, my friend. And once again, you were right where you needed to be.

"Angel will likely trail with you as well. He added some cattle to the drive, and he mentioned going down to help since Tex is laid up."

The two men walked down to the street. They rode out of town to where two young men watched Tall Eagle's horses. He tossed each of them two bits, and they grinned as they turned their horses back toward Cheyenne.

CHAPTER 80

TALL EAGLE'S WISDOM

THE HORSES MOVED EASILY, AND THE TWO MEN followed them. As they drove them into the yard, they met Nate and Sam. Both were grinning. Gabe shook his head and laughed.

"So who said you two could help on this drive?"

"Angel did. He said he was going too. We are headed north to get Tuff. We'll be back before dark." Nate was talking hurriedly as he urged Demonio to catch Sam.

Tall Eagle laughed.

"Ah, to be young and excited about a trail drive. How do you want me to send them home?"

"I'll leave that up to Angel. He had some Angus and Hereford cattle down there on the Hashknife Ranch—he held onto the best livestock out of Cole's herd, those that weren't stolen after Cole passed. He and Miguel sold most of the cattle when they went down there to finalize the sale of Cole's assets, but they kept Cole's purebreds. Those cattle are going to be part of this drive. That's part of the reason Angel offered to go along.

"Of course, it will be a short drive too. He can put those cattle on the train in Dodge City and ride up here with them." Gabe frowned slightly. "That herd could be in Indian Territory by the time you meet them."

Tall Eagle nodded.

"Yes. That is one of the reasons I want to get down there quickly. Shad is young and I'm not sure how tough their riders are…plus they are short-handed. I would like to catch them before they cross the Red River if possible."

Gabe looked to the south and slowly nodded. "Maybe I should go with you."

Tall Eagle shook his head.

"No, my friend. You are needed here. I will have Angel and the three young men. We will have enough men when we reach the herd. We will move quickly. Angel can be in charge while I sell some of my horses. I will wait to go to Fort Sill until we meet the herd." He looked over at his friend and his eyes sparkled.

"Perhaps your wife will send some food supplies with us tonight. Then we won't have to take the time to cook when we camp. I can live on hardtack and pemmican but the young men—I think they will want to eat something more than hard biscuits, tallow, dried meat, and berries."

Gabe laughed and nodded.

"Knowing Merina, she has food prepared and a pack for each of them already. I have a hard time keeping up with that woman. She is always thinking, and she doesn't mess around once she has decided something." He grinned and added, "She bought a ranch while we were gone on that drive north. She and I had talked about it briefly, but the place we were interested in wasn't for sale yet.

"She went to see Margaret Endicott the day after we left. By the time we made it back, she had the deal closed and cattle moved over there!

"Charles Cole left some of his holdings to the Monteros, and Merina used Angel's share to buy that ranch." He frowned and shook his head.

"We all thought Miguel was going back to Texas. We had no idea he would bring a wife home when he returned with those Angus bulls from Kansas.

"When he did, Angel talked to Reiths about buying Pop's ranch. They were ready to sell too. Then Miguel died." Gabe shook his head. "If he had stayed with Flory until she awoke, he might have lived. Of course, those kids he saved might not have made it either. You just never know.

"Now Reiths are going to sell their ranch to Tex and Flory." Gabe was quiet a moment. His voice was soft when he spoke again. "It's a strange old world. Miguel was always reckless, but I sure didn't think he would ever be trampled by horses. I guess we just never know how we will go."

Tall Eagle said nothing as he listened. Finally, he looked over at Gabe.

"I think when the Great Spirit wants us to come, it is our time. Nothing can be done to change that. It was Miguel's time to go. Perhaps he should have stayed with his wife while she was in danger of dying. Perhaps the Great Spirit was angry with him, and he was punished. Or maybe it was so Miss Flory would marry Tex. We do not know. Men can only guess when things like this happen. One day, when we pass from this earth, all our questions will be answered. Until that time?" Tall Eagle shrugged his shoulders. "Until that time, we only guess. I think we should not spend so much time wondering why. Maybe we should spend more time thinking on our lives and what changes we need to make."

Gabe listened quietly. He chuckled softly when Tall Eagle finished.

"You are a wise one, Tall Eagle. I'm glad we are friends. And maybe someday, some woman will latch onto you. Then we will see if you stay as wise as you are now!"

Tall Eagle laughed out loud and shook his head.

"I am not looking for a woman. I am contented to spend my time with horses."

Gabe laughed ruefully. "You will get tripped up one of these days, and I hope I am around to meet her. It will take quite a woman to turn your hard head though."

Tall Eagle's eyes glinted with humor.

"Perhaps, but right now, I want to pen these horses. Then I will eat dinner with you and your woman. If the young men return early, we will leave tonight since there will be a full moon. I think maybe my brother doesn't rise as early as he used to. Maybe marriage makes him want to lie about in the house longer now."

Gabe could hear the humor in Tall Eagle's voice, and they laughed together as they herded the horses into the pens by the barn.

Merina came out of the house and called to them.

"I have dinner ready. I packed some food and supplies for you to take with you, Tall Eagle. I doubt you will want to take much time to cook anything, and those boys will be hungry."

Gabe grinned at his friend and then waved at Merina.

"We'll be in right away."

He handed his reins to one of the hands and pointed to Tall Eagle's horse, Wind Dancer.

"Rub these two horses down and give them some grain. We are going to eat a quick bite. Tall Eagle is going to leave later today."

CHAPTER 81

The Ponderings of Young Men

NATE AND SAM RODE QUIETLY FOR A TIME BEFORE SAM spoke.

"You reckon we'll meet any women on this drive? We sure ain't met many in all the ridin' around we do, and for sure not many I ain't related to. Oh, a few at the dances but I don't think there are many women in this territory."

Nate was quiet for a time before he answered. They were just passing the turnoff to the Rankin ranches, and he stared down the road before he looked back at his friend.

"There were a lot of women in Dodge. I didn't talk to any, but they all really liked Miguel. If he didn't know them before he got there, he sure knew them when he left. It was the same way in Cheyenne before he married Flory. He knew all the gals in the saloons. The boarding houses too and they liked him.

"They liked Spur too. I think maybe women just like wild men. I don't reckon I will ever be that wild."

The two young men were a contrast to each other. While both were tall with wide shoulders and rode easily in the saddle, Nate had dark, curly hair. Merina cut both his and Gabe's hair. It was long enough to curl but not long enough to curl up around his hat. His eyes were a deep blue, and his face held a smile most of the time. He tended to be quieter around people he didn't know and thought before he acted or spoke. His face still held a boyish look even at fifteen, but he would soon have the rugged good looks of his older brother. When the two young men were together, Nate was usually the one to hold back. He was also the one most likely to avoid serious trouble.

Sam's blond hair was curly and longer than Nate's. His blond curls poked out wildly from under his hat. His blue eyes were a lighter blue than Nate's and sparkled with a zest for life.

His father often told him that he needed to stop "chawin' at the bit" and focus on things that were important. Sam couldn't wait to test his wings, and his mother was worried his good looks were going to get him into trouble.

Molly was not in favor of Sam going on this drive. Lance just shook his head.

"He's nearly sixteen, Molly, and that's older than I was when I left home. If we don't let him go now, he will leave before long anyway… and likely take a riding job farther away.

"He's a heck of a hand too. He won't have any trouble finding a job as a rider.

"Let him test his wings. He's a good boy. He'll be back when he's ready to settle down. Besides, Tall Eagle and Angel are both going, and the drive will be less than a month long. Maybe those rivers down south will be enough to discourage him from doing more drives. Besides, Nate will whoa him down if he tries to get too crazy."

Molly wasn't convinced but she agreed. In her heart, she believed their oldest son was leaving home for good. She cried that night.

"I know it's silly," she whispered to herself, "but he will always be my little Sammy. When I look at him, I see the little boy we picked up on the trail on our way up here, and it breaks my heart to let him go."

Sam had hugged his mother before he left to find Nate. "I'll stop back by to pick up my bedroll. We are going north of Cheyenne to find Tuff. We should be back after dinner sometime." He had kissed Molly on the cheek and grinned at her. As he'd raced out the door, he had grinned at her again over his shoulder.

"Love ya, Ma!" he hollered and then he was gone.

The two young men rode quietly for a time before Sam spoke again.

"I've been thinkin' on those saloon gals. I think I'm gonna find one of those dance places in Dodge and dance with some of those purty gals." Sam leaned forward to rub his horse's neck while he spoke. When Nate didn't answer, he looked over at his friend.

"Did ya hear me?"

Nate nodded his head toward the lane they all called the Rankin Ranch Road.

"You have any reason to go over to Rowdy's before we leave? I've been thinking on tellin' Mari goodbye."

Sam sat straight up in the saddle and stared at his friend.

"Mari! She's my cousin an' she ain't nothin' but a kid girl. No, I don't have no reason to go over there, and I ain't wastin' the time."

Nate turned his blue eyes on his friend and his face blushed a little under his tan.

"Well, she ain't *my* cousin. And she ain't no kid girl neither. She's fourteen. She told me her birthday is in January, so she'll be fifteen before long."

Sam snorted again. "I can't believe you're sweet on Mari."

"I didn't say I was sweet on her. I said I'd like to tell her goodbye. She's a sweet gal and good lookin' too.

"Jack Presley from town has been tryin' to work up the courage to stop in and see her." Nate grinned and laughed. "He ain't brave enough though. Besides, Rowdy don't like him. I heard Rowdy tell your pa that he'd run Jack off if he came around. He said Jack's too old, and he don't want any feller out there who brags about all the gals he's taken behind the barn."

Sam frowned as he listened to Nate. His blue eyes were cold when he looked over at his friend.

"Maybe I should have a talk with Jack Presley before we leave. I could thump him good. I sure don't want him hangin' around any of my girl cousins—or my sisters neither—an' I have a passel of 'em." He finally grinned at Nate.

"I reckon if Mari is growin' up like ya say, I cain't think of anyone else I'd rather have hang around her than my best saddle pal. I still say she's a kid girl though. You must be seein' something I ain't.

"Ma mentioned she had Rowdy's coat at our house. He had torn the sleeve completely out of it and Beth couldn't get her needles to go through all the layers. Ol' Rowdy's tough but he sure gets cold easy.

"Anyway, she left it with Sadie, and Ma picked it up several days ago. I could offer to take it over before we leave if you really want to go by there.

"We ain't stayin' long though. We need to get back to your place. I think Tall Eagle will leave yet today if he thinks his horses are ready—and I don't want him to leave us behind."

CHAPTER 82

MAYBE WE SHOULD WORK OUR WAY HOME

THE TWO YOUNG MEN WERE NEARLY TO CHEYENNE when they saw a smiling Tuff riding toward them. As they met on the road, Tuff nodded his head toward town.

"We were in town early this morning, and Rooster down to the livery told us about the trail drive. He said Tall Eagle would be trail boss. Said he was most likely going to need a few more riders." Tuff's smile became larger and he added, "Stub said since he knew Tall Eagle it would be all right for me to go along and help you fellows."

At fourteen, Tuff was a little younger than Nate and Sam. Still, he had been following his older brother from job to job since he was nine years old. He was every bit as good as the other two young men when it came to cowboying.

Tuff wasn't as tall as either Nate or Sam, but he was close. Besides, his lanky body had more growing to do. He ate enough for three men and was still always hungry. He pointed behind his saddle.

"I'm already packed, and my bed roll is right here. Unless you have business in Cheyenne, let's head out. Rooster thought Tall Eagle might want to leave today yet. He said Tall Eagle was a little worried about that herd making it through the Territory short-handed."

Sam looked over at Nate and grinned.

"Well, I reckon we have time to go by Rowdy's now. We'll grab his coat from Ma and head on over there."

Tuff looked at his two friends in surprise.

"Rowdy? Isn't he Mari's pa? Say, I wouldn't mind seeing her before we leave."

Sam glared at Tuff and snorted.

"Not you too! She's just a kid!"

Tuff laughed and Nate blushed again. Then the three began to talk excitedly about their trip.

Molly was hanging clothes on the line when the young men rode into the yard.

"Ma, we are runnin' a little early since we met Tuff on the road. If you want us to take Rowdy's coat over to him before we leave, we can do it."

Molly smiled at the three friends.

"That would be just fine. Beth was going to send Mari over for it this afternoon, and that would save her a trip.

"In fact, you taking it will be even better because Beth wants to tell all of you goodbye. And I'm guessing she will invite you to stay for dinner." She laughed as she hurried to the house, calling over her shoulder, "If you don't eat with Beth, you plan to eat here. I'll have enough for the three of you. I certainly don't want three starving young men to show up at Merina's table. You would eat her out of house and home."

Molly returned quickly and handed the coat to Sam. She pointed from one to the other as she said, "And you be sure to give me a hug when you come back by. Don't you be trying to run off without a proper goodbye now."

Sam rolled his eyes and the other two young men grinned.

Nate laughed and nodded, "Yes, ma'am. I don't think we'll be too long. We need to get back to my place in case Tall Eagle wants to leave today." He tipped his hat, and the three friends were soon on their way to Rowdy's.

"How long do you reckon we'll be gone? Stub said it would be a short drive." Tuff's face was excited as he questioned his friends.

"Gabe said probably three to four weeks depending on how far north they are when we meet them. Tall Eagle will cut out once we reach Dodge City, and Angel will take the train up here." Nate looked sideways at his friends and commented softly, "Maybe we should just work our way back up here. Old John Kirkham in Nebraska might have a herd heading north. It is late in the season, but you never know.

"That route north of Dodge isn't too bad either. It's dry but if the trail boss is any good, he will know where to find water. I think I would rather work with Kirkham though. Gabe says a trail boss can make or break a drive.

"Branding and fall gather won't be for another month or longer so there isn't as much work around here right now. We could always send word with Angel if we decide to do something. And even if Kirkham doesn't have a herd now, he might next spring. We could always take the train as far as Ogallala, hop off, and go see him.

"I don't know what trains cost, but we might not make enough to get all the way home by rail anyway."

The other two friends stared at Nate as they thought about what he was suggesting. Tuff shook his head.

"Not me. Stub gave me strict orders about coming home. He even gave me a little money for expenses in case I don't get paid as much as the older cowboys. He said I'll have more freedom in a year or so but not till I'm fifteen."

Sam stared from Nate to Tuff. He finally grinned and nodded.

"I'm in. Let's don't say anything before we leave though. Maybe our folks won't think of it. Then they can't give us any orders like that." He frowned at Tuff.

"Why would Stub even think you might take a job? He seems like a buttoned-down, straight-shootin' kind of feller. Kind of a funny thing for him to think ahead like that, ain't it?"

Tuff grinned at them and shook his head.

"Stub wasn't always like he is now. He left home when I was just a little tyke. He always had a big, black beard and his friends started calling him Black. When the folks died, he came back for me.

"I tagged around with him from about nine on. Part of that time, he was an outlaw. That's how he came to know Curly Joe Sturgis.

"Curly's pop remembered him as Black. He remembered how Black tried to whoa Curly down some when he started to lose control. Black—Stub, I mean—he didn't like killing. Shoot, he didn't even like stealing, but we did it for a time.

"That's how we came to know Clare up in Montana Territory. She is the one who made him straighten out. I got shot on the last job and almost died. Clare took me in and cared for me. Her and little Nora."

Sam stared at his friend. "Ya almost died? Ya never said anything 'bout that before."

Tuff grinned and shrugged. "It never come up. Besides, Stub doesn't like to talk about his past. He says what happened in the past is dead and gone. No point in digging up old trash."

His face became more serious when he added,

"Stub and Rock were pards for a time, but they parted ways over some kind of argument. That's when Stub became an outlaw.

"Rock wasn't happy to see either of us at his house, but Clare stepped in. She got Rock calmed down. He could see I was in bad shape, so he sent for the doc. That priest doctor pulled me through. That's when Stub left the outlaw trail and started over."

Nate and Sam both stared at their friend in surprise. They knew Stub had been called Black for a time, but they had certainly not heard all this. No mention of Stub's past life had been discussed on the drive they had followed north.

"I never saw Stub happier than the day Rock and him put things in the past. We went to work for the Becklers then." Tuff grinned. "That's when I had to start calling my brother by his original nickname—Stub. It was hard to remember at first but it's easy now." Once again, Tuff's grin faded. He was quiet as he looked over the rough road in front of them. His voice was soft when he spoke.

"I think we would have stayed up there if Rock had lived. Stub liked Spur but he was just a little sad. Kit was ready for a change too. I don't really know why. She had lived in that area for quite a few years. Clare and her were close too, so I couldn't figure it out.

"I guess maybe she was just a little tired of the long winters." Tuff shrugged. "Don't know. They don't talk over private things with me.

"Then Curly Joe's pop contacted us. Mr. Sturgis wanted Stub to come and work for him. I wanted to come south to be closer to you fellows anyhow, so I was all for it. That's how we ended up down here.

"I like it too. Stub enjoys Sturgis and Kit is happy." He blushed a little as he added, "They are going to have a baby. I think it will come around Christmas, but I don't know how long all that takes. Stub doesn't like to talk about personal things, and I'm sure not going to ask Kit.

"Anyway, I gave Stub my word that I would come right home. That's the only way he would let me go with you fellows. He said a man's word is the most important thing he owns, and I reckon it is. Another year or two though and I'll be ready to head out."

The three friends rode quietly for a time. Sam looked over at Tuff curiously.

"So where were you shot? Let me see."

Tuff jerked his shirt out of his britches and pointed at his stomach.

"You can't see the scar through my longhandles, but I can show you tonight. The bullet went in through the front. That priest had to take it out. His name was Father Ravalli. He's the one who married Kit and Stub. I like him.

"I like Clare a lot too. She was some worried about me when I was shot. She is just about the nicest lady I have ever met.

"I miss their kids too. Nora is a real sweet girl, but that Annie is a stinker. She is in trouble all the time and she just doesn't care. Zeke is a good kid. He's a real serious little fellow. Clare had another little boy around Thanksgiving. He was a round, little feller when we left. I don't know much about babies, but I like them.

"'Course, everybody likes Spur. He's a good pop too. I wouldn't even mind having him for my pop. I don't think Clare liked him much at first, but she was smiling a lot by the time we left. He always teases her and that makes her laugh." Tuff laughed and shook his head.

"One night, Spur was washing dishes. He put on one of Clare's little pink aprons and wore it. He even wore it outside in front of the men. They were all teasing him, but he didn't care. He's plumb happy. He told me once that love is a wonderful thing if you find the right woman. I guess Clare is just the right woman for him."

The three were quiet for a time as they thought about all Tuff had shared. Sam looked at his friend sideways a couple of times, but he didn't ask any more questions. *I sure wouldn't have guessed that about Stub. He's mighty quiet for an outlaw. 'Course, I don't really know any outlaws. I'll have to keep my eyes open on this trip.*

CHAPTER 83

A Cowboy's Bandana

ROWDY CLIMBED OUT OF THE CORRAL AS THE THREE young men rode into the yard. He pushed his hat back and grinned at them.

"Well, there's trouble, all packed up and ready to ride! When do you fellows leave?"

Sam grinned and held out the coat. "Today most likely. Gabe originally said tomorrow morning, but everyone seems to think it will be earlier.

"Tuff here met us before we had to ride all the way north to find him, so we figured we had time to bring your coat by before we left."

Beth rushed out the door followed by Mari.

"You boys get down and come in this house. We are just getting ready to eat." She turned to the young girl behind her.

"Mari, you put on three more plates. These young men need to have a good meal before they go riding south. Who knows when they will be able to sit down to a decent meal again!"

Rowdy laughed and waved toward the house. "Just tie your horses up there at the hitching rail. Beth has things ready, and she always makes plenty. It seems like we have extras for meals on a regular basis." He grinned and put his arm around Beth as they walked toward the house. "Probably because she is such a good cook."

The three friends followed Rowdy and Beth into the house. Mari had taken off her apron and washed the flour off her arms. She smiled at the guests.

"Please sit down. Mother and I have been baking this morning so you will have fresh bread to eat with your meal."

Mari blushed when she looked up and saw Sam staring at her. She sat down beside him and asked, "So when do you leave? How exciting to be able to just take off like that. Mother says I can go to college in Kansas when I finish high school. I'm ahead for my age but that is still nearly two years away. How I would love to go on a trail drive."

Nate nodded as he answered seriously, "Sometimes women do go. We had gals on our drive all the way from Texas to Ogallala. Larry worked as a cook's helper and Merina was wrangler. Maybe—" When he caught Rowdy's hard glare, Nate ducked his head.

Beth put her hand over Mari's and patted it.

"Please lead us in prayer, Rowdy. These young men need to eat quickly so they can be on their way."

Mari was quiet during the meal, but she listened closely as Nate, Sam, and Tuff answered Rowdy's questions.

Finally, she asked, "When do you think you will be back?"

Nate paused and ducked his head. Sam waved his hand toward the south and tipped his head that way.

"The drive should only take three or four weeks. We don't know if we are going to take the train back up here or ride back. It's not a very long drive so we might not be able to afford the tickets.

"That's all right though. We don't mind riding. If we ride back, it will take a little longer." He reached for another slice of bread and slathered butter all over it.

"You sure make good bread, Aunt Beth. It just falls apart in my mouth."

Beth smiled and looked proudly at Mari.

"This young lady is the bread baker in this house, and yes, it is delicious. She helped me for a few years but now I just leave the bread baking to her. Mari makes better bread than I do."

Mari blushed when everyone looked at her. She met Nate's eyes for just a moment before she looked away. She quickly stood.

"Chocolate cake, anyone? Mother had some sour cream we needed to use, and Pa's favorite cake is chocolate."

Mari handed each person a slice of cake before she dropped back into her chair. She leaned forward excitedly as she talked to Sam.

"Rudy and Leo are coming home!" She looked over at Nate. "You remember Leo, don't you? Levi and Sadie adopted him when he was nine. That was in '70. They both finished their second year of college in May. Rudy is three years older than Leo. They are the oldest of all the cousins, and they became fast friends.

"Rudy worked for Pa for a year after he graduated. He went to work for the Stockgrowers's Bank in town the next two more years just so Leo and he could go to college together. They both worked some for Levi too. They decided since they both wanted to be lawyers, they would study law together.

"They have been working this summer in Manhattan, Kansas, for some friend of Levi's. They are coming home for a month before they begin classes in Saint Louis in the fall. I am so excited! We haven't seen Rudy since last Christmas. I can't wait to see my brother." The conversation moved on to other things and before long, the twins began arguing.

In their bumping around and pushing on each other, they spilled a glass of milk. It almost ran onto Nate's lap. He pushed his chair back quickly to get out of the way and bumped the table, rocking the pans and dishes sitting on it and nearly spilling more milk. His face turned a deep red as he backed away.

"I'm sorry, Mrs. Rankin. We have so many messes at our house that I'm always ready to jump."

Beth giggled and Rowdy laughed out loud.

"Sit down, Nate. And you kids—one more fight and you will eat with the baby when we are all done. Emma is sleeping and she would love to spill food all over the two of you when she wakes."

Pauline was four. She climbed up on Rowdy's lap with a smile. Her blonde curls and green eyes melted his heart.

"I didn't make a mess, Papa. I want to sit on your lap and eat my cake."

Rowdy slid her onto his other knee. "I reckon you can because then I will be able to help you eat your cake and mine too."

He winked at Nate and the meal was soon finished. Beth shooed the young men out of the house.

"Don't even offer to help. I know you must be on your way. I do get a hug from each of you though."

Rowdy shook their hands and Beth almost cried as she hugged each one. Then all the kids wanted hugs too.

Mari stood back shyly. While Rowdy was talking to Sam and Tuff, Nate walked over to where she stood.

"That was a mighty fine meal, Mari, and the best bread I have ever eaten." He pulled off his bandana and handed it to her as he blushed.

"I'm not sure when I'll be back. We might work our way back up here instead of taking the train. Maybe you can hang onto this for me until I see you again."

Mari smiled up at him. "Thank you, Nate. I might even wear it while I'm baking. It will help keep my hair out of my eyes."

Nate glanced around and saw Rowdy glaring at them. He backed up quickly and tipped his hat to Mari.

"I'll see you when I get back."

His smile was big when he mounted his horse even though he was blushing again.

Sam looked from Nate to his cousin and started laughing. Rowdy glared at Nate again and Mari fled into the house.

They were nearly a mile away before anyone spoke. Sam was grinning and he finally laughed.

"You might miss that bandana on the drive."

Nate looked at him coolly and shrugged. "I have an old one at home. I'll take it." He was whistling as he rode and said nothing more.

Tuff looked back once at the house.

"Yessir, that Mari sure is a pretty gal. All that dark hair wound around her head. And those big, brown eyes just kind of pull a feller in."

Nate missed a note and Sam laughed again.

Before long, the three of them were banging on each other as they rode.

Molly was waiting for them when they rode up. She smiled as she looked from one to the other.

"I see Beth fed you. Well, that's good. Lance had a couple of cattle buyers come by at dinnertime, so we don't have many leftovers today."

She placed a package of oatmeal raisin cookies in Sam's hands and pulled him in for a hug. There were tears in her eyes when she let him go.

"Don't be reckless, Sam. And you boys stick together. We want all of you to come safely home."

Sam blushed and muttered under his breath about mushy women. He grabbed his bedroll and pecked his mother's face as he ran by. Paul seriously shook his hand while Abigail, Henry, and Livvy rushed to hug him.

Livvy called loudly to him as they rode away, "Don't forget to come home, Sam. Otherwise, Henry gets your bed!"

Sam grinned and waved at his little sister.

The three friends were quiet for a time as they rode. Then they began to bang on each other again, teasing about anything they could think of. They finally raced the last half mile to Nate's house.

CHAPTER 84

Rusty's Creation

THE THREE YOUNG MEN PULLED THEIR HORSES TO A stop and stared. Rusty, Gabe's partner, was breaking the tops off bottles of all sizes and carefully laying them in a pile beside him. Smitty, one of Rowdy's hands, was whittling small pieces of wood. Jonesy, who rode for Lance, was drilling holes in the center of the wood. He carefully pushed the wooden plugs into the necks of the bottles. Another cowhand was cutting small strips of leather from a broken harness and threading them through the hole in the wooden plug.

The three young men walked their horses forward slowly and stared down at the pile of broken glass.

Sam was the first to speak.

"Ya fellers jist a playin' or are ya tryin' to build somethin' important?"

Rusty looked up with a grin.

"Ever hear of a telyphone, Sam?" Rusty held the bottom to one of the broken bottles up to his ear. "We cin put one of those new-fangled telyphones they are sellin' in town in each house or barn. We hook one of these here insulators to the top wire on each post of that bobbed wire fence between mine, yores, Lance's, an' Rowdy's ranches. We run another wire to hook 'em up to the telyphones, an' jist like that, we cin all talk to each other any time we want—or at the same time if we please.

"Shoot, ol' Gabe cin pull out his harmonica an' we cin all enjoy his music while he serenades Merina of an evenin'!"

Nate stared at the ornery cowhand for a moment and shook his head.

"I don't think so. I think you are runnin' a joke on folks, Rusty. No way will that work. I know some folks in Cheyenne who have those phones, and they don't use barbwire to make them work."

Rusty's blue eyes sparkled and he laughed.

"Say what ya want but whilst y'all are gone, we are a goin' to make our own lives easier. We'll keep track of y'all's whereabouts too. Then we'll have us a little confab with yore folks about yore goin's on. We might even string it to the schoolhouse up yonder by Lance's house. Shoot, by the time y'all get back, we might be hooked up with Angel too!"

Tuff stared at the men's creations for a moment and asked excitedly, "Can you talk to Stub from here?"

"Not yet but that day 'ill come. There ain't no continuous fence strung all the way from here on west past Cheyenne. When that happens, we'll be able to talk to even more folks."

Nate rode around the piles of scraps and studied what each man was doing.

"Where did you get such a crazy idea, Rusty? I sure never heard of such a thing."

"I heard some of the folks in Dodge City talkin' about it. Then I run into a talkative Texan last week in town an' he done told me how they did it down south on the XIT Ranch in Texas.

"Each phone has its own ring sounds of longs an' shorts. He said y'all cin answer on yore own ring, but ya cin listen in on all the others talkin' too. He said it was right interestin' what some folks said on their telyphones.

"We're a goin' to make ours have a sudden ring too. Five short rings 'ill mean ever'body needs to pick up 'cause there's news that needs to git 'round quick."

Gabe strolled up and shook his head as he laughed.

"It's true all right. I was there when Rusty was quizzing that fellow. Probably made that cowboy late getting back to work as many questions as he asked.

"Then Rusty went around to all the saloons and offered to take their old bottles off their hands. Most of them even paid him for hauling them off.

"Jack Coral didn't though. He knew if Rusty was offering to take old bottles, there was something of value in it for him.

"Those other saloons got all excited though when Rusty said he'd be back in a week for some more bottles." Gabe laughed and pointed at the pile of broken glass.

"Now it is our problem to get rid of what's left. Rusty suggested tossing them in the hole the outhouse sits on, and I guess we will do that. That hole will be filled in anyway when we move it in the next week or two. Between our four ranches, we have four outhouses—five if you count the one at the school. We for sure aren't going to let them lay around here. I won't trash up my ranch for one of Rusty's hairbrained ideas—even if it does work."

Gabe looked back at the three young men.

"You three need to get down to the barn. Tall Eagle is leaving today yet. He'll line you out. Come up to the house when you're done, and Merina will give each of you some food to pack in your saddlebags. Tall Eagle intends to make this a fast trip with as little stopping as possible.

"You each need to take an extra horse with you too. Tex wasn't sure how big the remuda down there would be. Sam, you and Tuff each take one of those horses in the corral there. You won't be gone too long so we can get along without them."

He looked closely at Nate and frowned as he commented, "I'm not sure where you lost your bandana, Nate, but you had better grab a couple of mine. The dust is going to be bad on this trip."

When Nate's neck turned red, Gabe's eyebrows went up. He turned around without saying anything else and walked toward the house, muttering to himself. When he was almost there, he pulled off his hat and slapped it against his leg.

He looked back at Nate one more time as he growled, "And take your old saddle. Save that flashy one for all your girlin'." He was still frowning when he strode into the house.

CHAPTER 85

A Big Brother's Problem

MERINA WAS LAUGHING WHEN GABE STOMPED through the door.

"And who has your first bandana, my husband? I would never have guessed that so you must have given one away at his age too."

Gabe glared at Merina. He growled again but his frown slowly changed to a grin. He chuckled softly before he dropped down in a chair.

"Her name was Sylvie and she lived on a neighboring ranch down south of us in Texas. I thought she was the most beautiful girl in the world—at least in my small world. That was right before I left home. I was barely fourteen and green as the grass.

"She batted her eyes at me and then took bandanas from four or five more fellas. She even took one right in front of me. She was married by sixteen and when I saw her at eighteen, I just couldn't figure out what I had seen in her. She was angry and grumpy. The cowboy she married was a nice fellow, but he didn't have much. She complained about him all the time." Gabe reached for Merina. He whispered, "And that was the last bandana I ever gave away."

Merina smiled as slipped onto Gabe's lap.

"I do not think Nate gave his bandana to an angry woman. I believe he gave it to a very sweet girl who loves to bake.

"Your little brother will be a fine man someday, perhaps sooner than you want him to be…but I do not think he is planning to come home on the train with Angel. He has said nothing about money or train fare, and I doubt they will make enough to afford a train ride home. I think he and his compadres plan to work their way back up here."

Gabe stared at Merina in surprise. "He didn't say anything to me. Why do you think that?"

"Because both he and Sam are anxious to leave, to 'sow their oats' as some of your friends say. And, because he has said very little about the drive. He is trying to stay quiet so you don't ask him any questions.

"Nate does not lie, but perhaps he doesn't tell all that he knows either.

"I, for one, am pleased he gave his bandana to Mari. At least we know he intends to come back."

Gabe stared down at his wife for a moment and shook his head.

"Who? Not little Mari Rankin? Why she is just a kid." He grinned at Merina and added softly, "How did I ever marry such a wise woman?" His grin became bigger, and he winked at his wife.

"I think if I had met you sooner, I would have given away another bandana."

"And I would not have taken it. I trusted no man who was all the time on cattle drives." She laughed as she looked up at him. "No, I would have made you wait to be sure I could trust you—and then every night, I would have dreamed of you."

They were both laughing when Nate rushed into the house.

"Tall Eagle wants to leave in an hour. I am going to take Demonio. What horse do you think I should take as a second one?

"And can I stash Miguel's saddle and bridle in the house. I don't want the mice to get at it while I'm gone."

Gabe studied his brother's face.

"I reckon that would be all right. And take that Appaloosa gelding you have been working with." He frowned at his younger brother. "Just how long do you plan to be gone anyway? Not likely to have a mouse problem in three weeks. Besides, Lance gave us some of his cats."

Nate stopped and stared from Gabe to Merina.

His neck turned red, and he turned to face Gabe before he replied. His gaze was direct as he spoke.

"Sam and me are going to work our way back up here. I thought we might stop in and see John Kirkham in Ogallala or maybe try to catch a cattle drive headed north out of Dodge."

Gabe was quiet for a moment before he answered.

"Before you join a drive, Nate, look hard at the men who are already hired on. Ask yourself if we would hire them here or if we would send them down the road. And compare the trail boss to Angel or Tall Eagle." He smiled slightly.

"If you do stop in Ogallala, tell John hello for us. And, Nate, next time—just be honest with us."

Nate dropped his eyes and nodded. When he looked up, he was smiling again.

"Thanks, Gabe. You are about the best brother a fellow could have." He gave Gabe a quick hug.

Merina handed him a large pack of food. Nate stared at it before he grinned at her.

"Thanks, Merina. I reckon I'll be home before it gets too cold. I'll sure miss your cooking."

Merina hugged Nate and kissed his cheek.

"Be sure to tell Rollie and Emilia goodbye before you leave, or we will never hear the end of their questions. They should be playing down by the creek.

"And you write us, Nate. Let us know what you are doing."

Nate nodded excitedly. He grabbed his bed roll and rushed to the barn. He dipped a can into the oat bin and headed for the pasture. He was back quickly with a leopard appaloosa. When he rushed out of the barn, Demonio had an old saddle on his back, his bedroll was tied behind his saddle, and a halter with a rope was on the gelding. He looped the reins and rope over the hitching rail in front of the barn and ran toward the creek, hollering for his little brother and sister.

Merina smiled as she watched him.

"He is a good boy. You did a fine job, Gabe. And don't worry. He will be back. He loves his family. Now come. Let us tell those other young men goodbye. I have a pack of food for each of them too."

CHAPTER 86

A New Grandpa

JACK CORAL WAS WAITING OUTSIDE LEVI'S DOOR when Dot arrived on Monday morning, July 19. It was her second week of work, and she wasn't quite as nervous as the first day.

"Good morning, Mr. Coral. I didn't know you had an appointment this morning," Dot commented with a smile as she sat down beside him.

"I don't have one. I come early hopin' Levi could visit with me a little 'fore any other folks come in. An' I ain't plannin' to share no information with ya neither." He glared at Dot and looked away as he muttered, "Durn women. Always a stickin' their noses into business that ain't theirs."

Dot's smile turned to a glare. "Well, just so you know, I *am* Mr. Parker's receptionist now. That means if you want to make an appointment or see him at all, you *must* go through me."

The two of them were glaring at each other when Levi arrived a few minutes later. He looked from one to the other and grinned.

"Morning, Jack. I see you met Dot Doolan. She is my new receptionist. She can tell you what I have open if you want to make an appointment."

"I done told 'er I don't want to talk to 'er. I want to talk to *you*. An' since yore bein' so smart this mornin', I'll jist say it plain. I want to sell my buildin', an' I want to offer it to ya first.

"Annie an' Tiny done had their baby an' I'm the closest thing to a grandpappy that little boy 'ill ever have. I bought a house 'bout a block from 'em an' I'm a gonin' to retire so's I cin be around. Annie don't like the smell a smoke or whiskey so I'm a sellin' out. The Gold Room is gonna buy my whiskey supply an' I reckon I'll sell outta beer 'fore the week is out.

"I want ya to buy my buildin'. You'll probably have those two youngsters comin' back 'fore long an' yore a gonna need more room." He glared at Dot and added, "An' I didn't need no appointment to say that now, did I?"

Dot glared back, but before she could respond, Levi grinned and put out his hand.

"Why, Jack, that is right neighborly of you. I'd be pleased to buy your building. How soon do you want this to take place?"

"You cin draw up the papers today. I intend to be closed after the weekend, but it'll take some time to get 'er all cleaned out.

"I'm a gonna leave the big bar. Ya cin sell it or tear it down, whichever ya want. It's too big to move an' my house ain't that big nohow."

Levi looked at Jack in surprise.

"Didn't you have that bar built especially for the Painted Lady when you bought the saloon?"

"Shore did but that was twelve years ago when Cheyenne was a new town. That bar an' saloon served me well. I made me enough money to take it easy in my old age. Now it's time to move on.

"'Course a big-talkin' lawyer like yoreself might like a bar in his office to schmooze with all the fancy fellers he intends to take money from."

Levi stared at Jack in surprise and the ornery old man grinned.

"I knowed that would get a rise from ya, Judge. Like I said, I don't care what ya do with it. I'm movin' out an' movin' on."

Levi studied Jack's face for a moment and slowly nodded.

"Well, come into my office and let's settle on a price. You are right. Sadie and I were just talking about this building. It is going to be too small if Leo and Rudy both come back. They'll both be done studying law in three years. That's the plan anyway unless something changes." He paused as he unlocked the door. He looked over at Dot.

"I believe the Doughertys have an appointment at nine this morning. Jack and I should have enough time to get a contract drawn up before then. Come on in, Jack."

Dot followed the two men into Levi's law office. She opened Levi's appointment book. He was correct. Mr. and Mrs. Dougherty were Levi's first appointment. *I don't know how he remembers his appointments. He barely looks at his book at all when he comes or when he leaves.*

She was busy placing bills in envelopes when the door opened. An old man held a sleeping little girl around five or six years of age. He was straining to carry her, and Dot hurried toward them.

"May I take her? I can lay her down in the room behind me. Mr. Parker's wife keeps a little bed in there. I think it would be large enough."

The old man slowly nodded. When Dot returned to her desk, he turned to face her. "Are you the receptionist?" he asked.

Dot smiled and nodded.

"Yes, I am. I'm not sure for how long though. I am getting married in two weeks. If we move to my brother's ranch, I will be leaving."

The old man nodded and smiled. "Family is important. You should always try to stay close to those you love."

Dot studied the old man. He almost looked sad. She looked down at her appointment book. She knew all the people who had appointments and this old man was not one of them.

"Do you have an appointment with Mr. Parker? He is with another client right now, but they should be finished soon."

The old man shook his head.

"No, I don't. I lost my wife two days ago. I came to town today and just found out that our sweet little girl's mother passed. I can't see to cook let alone care for little Lizzie by myself. I need to talk to Mr. Parker today." The old man's last words almost ended in a sob. "I'll just wait until he's free."

Dot walked around the desk and took the old man's shaking hands. "Tell me your name and I will ask Mr. Parker if he can see you right away. I don't usually interrupt him, but today I will make an exception."

"Mullen. Elmore Mullen. He won't know who I am though. I have never been here before."

Dot and Elmore looked around as Levi's office door opened. Jack and Levi were both smiling as they walked to the door. They said a few more words before Levi turned to hurry back to his office.

"Mr. Parker—"

"You know I can't take walk-ins unless I have a light schedule, Miss Doolan. I am already behind today."

"Mr. Parker, I think you should see Mr. Mullen now. It was difficult for him to come today."

Levi turned around to look at Dot in surprise. A scowl filled his face, but Dot wasn't deterred. She put out her hand to Elmore.

"Come, Mr. Mullen. I will help you to Mr. Parker's office." She smiled sweetly at Levi as she helped the old man to the chair in front of Levi's desk.

Levi was angry as he followed Dot into his office. He took a deep breath and forced a smile as he walked around the desk to his chair.

Levi moved Jack Coral's saloon contract to the side of his desk. *Dot and I are going to have a conversation about protocol and her inability to follow orders.* However, when he looked closer at the old man in front of him, some of his anger faded away.

Dot pulled the door shut and smiled as she sat down. She knew she shouldn't listen but today was different. She moved her papers as quietly as possible and tried to hear their conversation.

CHAPTER 87

A Sad Old Man

THE OLD MAN PLACED HIS GNARLED AND TWISTED hands on Levi's desk. He tried to grip them together to keep them from shaking. When they shook even more, he dropped them to his lap.

"Mr. Parker, you don't know me. I am Elmore Mullen. I live northwest of town about ten miles. I have a little ranch there. It doesn't amount to much, but it gave my wife and me a good life." He smiled softly and looked away before he continued.

"About five years ago, a young woman drove out to our ranch. She asked us to take in her precious little girl. Lizzie was about two months old at the time and her mother—well, her mother lived a lifestyle that wasn't proper for raising a child.

"That little mama was crying. It was hard for her to give up her baby. She didn't want anyone to know she was the mother though. We were to pretend Lizzie was our granddaughter. She caught us off guard, but we said yes.

"The mama's name was Roseann Linder. She told us when she had enough money saved, she would be back for Lizzie. If we needed to reach her, we were supposed to slip a letter under the door at the stage office. We were to address it to Cheyenne Rose at the Painted Lady.

"She wanted to send us money once a month to help with Lizzie's expenses. We told her she didn't have to, but she insisted.

"Rose didn't stay long. She handed us her baby and a bag of diaper rags. She turned her buggy around and drove away. We could hear her crying as she left.

"She sent a little money each month like clockwork. Sometimes it was $10 and other months it was $20.

"We didn't use the money though. We put it back for Lizzie. We figured someday Lizzie's mother would come to get her. They could use that money as a little nest egg to get a fresh start.

"Rose said she was originally from Saint Louis, and she wanted to go back there someday. I don't know if she had any relatives there though. She never mentioned anyone to us." Elmore rubbed a shaky hand across his cheek to wipe away the tear that was leaking from his eye.

"That little girl is the best thing that God ever gave us. We never had children of our own and we just poured all that saved-up love on Lizzie." The old man wiped his eyes again before he continued.

"My wife, she was younger than me. I can't see much, and my Aileen, well, she has been my eyes for nearly four years now.

"Years make a difference as you age though, and me, I went and got old." He held up his shaking hands. "And with these hands, I can barely hold a pot let alone see to cook." Tears ran from the old man's eyes as he struggled not to cry.

"My Aileen took ill this past spring, and she never did come out of it. She passed away two days ago.

"I can't care for little Lizzie, so I brought her to town today. I was going to give her back to her mother, but I heard on the street this morning that our Rose had died." The old man put his head in his hands and cried.

"I can't care for little Lizzie and her mother is gone. I'm asking you to help me find a home for her."

Dot laid down her papers and covered her mouth. She could feel her eyes fill with tears, and it had been a long time since she had cried.

Just then the door opened and the Doughterys walked in. Dot wiped her eyes and smiled at the couple in front of her.

"Good morning, Mr. and Mrs. Dougherty. Mr. Parker is with a client, but he should be done shortly."

Dot could hear Levi talking to Elmore and she rattled the papers on her desk to hide what he was saying. She continued to noisily stuff envelopes until Levi's office door opened. The tall lawyer held Elmore's arm as he led him toward the door.

"Miss Doolan, I have an emergency that needs to be handled right away, and I need to leave this morning. Please reschedule all my morning appointments. Book whomever you need to before nine and after five this week to fit them all in." He smiled at the Doughertys.

"Betty and Hal, why don't you come out to the house for supper tonight? We can talk over Sadie's roast beef. I'm sorry you had to make an extra trip, but hopefully, that will work for you."

The Doughertys looked confused, but they nodded. "That will be fine. Around six?" When Levi agreed, they quickly left.

"Miss Doolan, if you will help Mr. Mullen to his wagon, I will grab my coat."

CHAPTER 88

Rose's Children

LEVI WAITED UNTIL THE DOUGHERTYS HAD DRIVEN away before he appeared with the little girl on his hip. He had little ones close to her age and was talking to her as he walked out the door.

"My, aren't you a pretty young lady. Did your grandpappy bring you to town today?"

Lizzie nodded somberly.

"Granny went to meet Jesus, and Pappy is sad. I think he wants to go meet Jesus too." She stared at Levi with big, blue eyes as she asked, "Have you ever met Jesus?"

Levi shook his head. "No, but I almost did once. Now you hold on tight to me while I climb up in this wagon. We are going for a ride." He jumped into the wagon before he handed Lizzie to Elmore. He turned the wagon toward the north and urged the horses to a trot. When he pulled them to a stop in front of Tiny's woodshop, one of the men hollered for Tiny with a grin on his face.

"Judge is here to see you, Tiny! I reckon you're in trouble now."

Tiny stuck his head out of his woodshop. He stared from Levi to the little girl and then at the old man. He dropped the piece of wood he was holding and strode toward the wagon.

"Annie! We have company!"

Tiny put his hand out to Levi.

"Judge. Good to see you. I guess ya ain't workin' much today."

Levi grinned and pointed to Elmore.

"Tiny, this is Elmore Mullen, and this sweet little girl is Lizzie. Lizzie Linder. Her mama was a friend of yours."

Tiny scratched his head and cocked an eyebrow as he looked from Levi to the old man. His eyes finally settled on Lizzie and realization washed over his face.

"Well, git on down an' come in. I was ready to take a break anyhow." He turned and hollered toward the house again, "Annie! Bring our boy out to meet his big sis!"

Annie hurried from the house holding Joey. Her eyes were wide as she looked from Tiny to Lizzie.

"Please. Get down, all of you, and come in. The coffee is hot, and Martha McCune sent over cinnamon rolls this morning."

Tiny reached for Lizzie and Levi helped Elmore down. The old man was even more wobbly than he had been in Levi's office. Tiny held out a big arm.

"Here, Elmore. Take a hold a my arm. I ain't built much of a walk yet an' she's a little rough."

Lizzie wiggled out of Tiny's arms and ran up to Annie.

"Is that your baby?"

Annie smiled and leaned down to show the baby to Lizzie.

"Yes, he is. His name is Joey."

Lizzie touched Joey's face. "I like babies. Can I play with him?"

"No, he is too little to play with just yet, but I have a dolly you can play with. Would you like that?"

Lizzie nodded excitedly and Annie led her into the house.

"See, she has a bed and lots of clothes. You can even put her in her own chair and play with her at this little table."

Lizzie was soon engrossed with her doll and Annie hurried over to the kitchen table. Tiny poured coffee while Annie tried to serve the cinnamon rolls with one hand.

Levi reached out his hands for Joey. "Here, let me hold Joey. What do you think, buddy? Life pretty good here? I'd say so. Look at those little round cheeks." He grinned at Annie. "He's filled out even more since I first saw him. I'd say he's eating well." He whispered softly to the little boy as he kissed him, "Your mama loved you, Joey. She made sure you had a good home before she left this world and now your big sister is going to live with you too. Yep, I'd say the Good Lord knew what he was doing when he arranged for a new family for both of you."

CHAPTER 89

One Big, Happy Family

ELMORE TOOK HIS COFFEE WITH SHAKING HANDS. HE blew on it and smiled at the sleeping baby.

"He looks a lot like Lizzie did when she came to live with us." He set the hot coffee down. His hands trembled even more as he asked, "You will take Lizzie in?"

Annie sat down at the table and put her hand over Elmore's. Her voice cracked as she spoke, but she was smiling.

"Elmore, we will take both of you in. You stay here as long as you want. Children need their grandparents." She smiled at Tiny and he grinned.

"I don't argue none with Annie. When she takes a notion to make things happen, I jist agree." Tiny's grin became larger and he added, "It's safer that way."

Elmore started to protest but Annie shook her head.

"It will be easier for Lizzie if you are here. We have an extra room, and we want you to stay. Besides, I could use another set of arms to hold Joey and rock him from time to time.

"Tiny added onto the house last summer. You may share a room with Lizzy or have one all to yourself."

The old man's eyes filled with tears and he looked down. Annie squeezed his hand before she let it go. Everyone looked toward the door when they heard a man talking loudly outside.

Tiny jerked the door open and hollered, "Git in here, Jack. I reckon ya heared we was eatin' cinneymon rolls first thing today an' ya thought ya ought to have one!"

Jack Coral stomped through the door. His hard face softened when Annie smiled at him.

"I thought I ought to check on my grandson this mornin'," he growled. He spotted Elmore and his eyes opened wide.

"Elmore Mullen, ya ol' sidewinder. I ain't seen ya in a coon's age. What ya doin' in town so early?"

Elmore smiled for the first time that morning.

"I brought my little granddaughter in to meet her parents. I guess we can be grandpappies together."

Jack's eyes opened wide as he stared around the room. He watched Lizzie talk to her doll and glanced back at Elmore with a grin.

"Well, I'll be. So that's Rose's little one. I always wondered where she went. I thought mebbie Rose sent 'er back East somewhere to be raised by an ol' aunt she used to talk about. I shore never knowed little Lizzie was right here in Cheyenne." He looked around the room before he asked, "Where's Aileen?"

When Elmore rubbed his face with shaky hands, Jack frowned. "Durn it, Elmore. I'm mighty sorry. I didn't know. Aileen was a fine woman."

Lizzie ran up to Elmore and held out the doll.

"Look, Pappy. It's a pretty dolly and she has so many clothes! Do you think we can stay here for a while so I can play with her longer?"

Elmore leaned over and kissed the little girl.

"I reckon we can stay here as long as you want.

"Do you remember how you told Granny and me that you would like to have a Mama—how you prayed every night for one? Well, how would you like to have a *mama* and a *papa* and a *baby brother*?"

Lizzie stared from Annie to Tiny. She pulled Elmore's head down and whispered loudly in his ear.

"Granny said if I prayed really hard, Jesus would send me a mama. I think after Granny met Jesus, she asked Him to send me a papa and a brother too."

Tiny picked up the little girl and gave her a hug.

"She shore did!" He handed her to Annie who was trying hard not to cry. Annie squeezed the little girl and kissed her cheek.

"You sit up here, Lizzie, and you can eat part of my cinnamon roll. Do you like cinnamon rolls?"

Lizzie nodded somberly. "I do but Granny doesn't make them very often. She says her back hurts if she stands for too long. Do you like to make cinnamon rolls?"

"I do, Lizzie, and I would like it even better if you helped me."

Lizzie smiled at Annie and scooted closer to the table. She was quiet as she ate the cinnamon roll. She finally looked up at Jack.

"Are you a grandpappy too?"

Jack dropped down in front of the little girl. His old eyes twinkled as he talked to her.

"I shore am an' now I'll be yore grandpappy!"

"I didn't know I could have two grandpappies. Are you Baby Joey's grandpappy?"

"Yep, him an' yores too. Ya never know—ya might even want to git ya more grandpappies. A little girl cin never have too many grandpappies—or grandmammies neither fer that matter.

Jack grinned at Elmore as he stood up.

"Ya still like to play cards? If ya are goin' to be stayin' 'round here, there'll be 'nough of us old timers to play cards ever' day. I like to make beer and old Smitty, he makes a mean bottle of moonshine from time to time. This gettin' old business is lookin' better all the time."

Annie frowned slightly and Jack winked at her. "Mebbie I'll make *root* beer. That'll make little Annie here happy." He pulled out a chair and helped himself to a cinnamon roll. He grinned at Annie as he added, "An' if we cin have us a home-cooked meal from time to time, that'd be even better."

Everyone looked up when someone banged on the door. Tiny hollered and Badger poked his head in.

"Martha done told me she sent my cinneymon rolls over here. I thought I'd better see what was goin' on. I shore didn't know you'ins was havin' a party so early in the durn mornin'!"

He strolled into the room and stopped as he looked from child to child.

"Well, I'll be. Little Rose found 'er young'uns a family an' a fine one too." His ornery eyes sparkled as he pulled up a chair.

"How 'bout you'ins all come over on Friday night? We'll have all the kids in an' have us a first-class family shindig to celebrate more youngins." He grinned at Annie and Tiny.

"You'ins don't have to bring nothin'. We'll innerduce these little ones ta all their cousins, an' we'll have us a loud ol' time." Badger took a big bite of cinnamon roll and closed his eyes.

"Yessir, my Martha is shore a good cooker." He grinned at Tiny and added, "Tiny, put me on yur list a jobs. My Martha needs more room fer havin' parties. Our family jist keeps a growin' an' we's a runnin' outta room in our little house. We'll jist knock out a wall or two an' make us a big ol' kitchen—big 'nough ta hold all our kin."

Levi leaned back and smiled as he looked around the noisy room. *I guess Dot knew what she was doing when she messed up my schedule this morning. Yep, this turned out to be just a fine day.*

Made in United States
Troutdale, OR
04/06/2024